WHAT
THE
ENEMY
THINKS

WHAT THE ENEMY THINKS

A Beck Carnell Novel

Very best wishes,

GAIL PICCO

iUniverse®

WHAT THE ENEMY THINKS
A BECK CARNELL NOVEL

iUniverse books may be ordered through booksellers or by contacting:

iUniverse
1663 Liberty Drive
Bloomington, IN 47403
www.iuniverse.com
1-800-Authors (1-800-288-4677)

Because of the dynamic nature of the Internet, any web addresses or links contained in this book may have changed since publication and may no longer be valid. The views expressed in this work are solely those of the author and do not necessarily reflect the views of the publisher, and the publisher hereby disclaims any responsibility for them.

Cover illustration by Wallace Ryan
Author photo by Sandy Tam Photography

ISBN: 978-1-4917-7003-0 (sc)
ISBN: 978-1-4917-7005-4 (e)

Library of Congress Control Number: 2015909250

Print information available on the last page.

iUniverse rev. date: 07/28/2015

For Katie and Evan
and
in loving memory of Bob and Lilly Picco

CONTENTS

PART
THREE

PART
FOUR

PART
FIVE

PART
SIX

PART
SEVEN

PART
EIGHT

Always remember the first rule of power tactics; power is not only what you have but what the enemy thinks you have.

—Saul Alinsky

PROLOGUE

Herring Neck, Newfoundland, 1975

B*eck was sitting next to her poppy in a trap skiff that had been pulled up onto the beach rocks next to the wharf. They had mugs of tea in their hands, and Nanny had just brought them down a few raisin biscuits wrapped up in a tea towel, still warm from the oven. Beck's tea was mostly water, Carnation milk, and sugar. Poppy's was almost black.*

Poppy was teaching her a song. "Okay, my duck. You sing it now," he said. "I'll start, and then you finish it off, all right?"

Beck nodded.

Clearing his throat, Poppy began, "We are coming, Mr. Coaker, from the east, west, north, and south …"

Eyes straight and chin in the air, Beck picked up the verse without missing a beat.

"You have called us, and we're coming, for to put our foes to rout.

"By merchants and by governments, too long we've been misruled;

"We're determined now in future, and no longer we'll be fooled."

"Heh heh heh." Poppy laughed as he clapped Beck on the back. "Listen to you, sure, saying that rhyme as strong and true as any fisherman who ever fished off these shores. Yes, my darling! That's the anthem of the Newfoundland Fishermen's Protective Union you're after reciting that time. You're Poppy's little fisherman girl, you are," he said, putting his arm around her as they turned to look out at the longliners making their way toward the wharf. Beck rested her head against his wool sweater, the one Nanny had knit for him last winter.

PART
ONE

Well, I wish I had some whiskey
And I wish I had some weed
On nights when I feel so alone
Baby, that's just what I need.

—"Demons Don't Get Me Down"
Words and music by Lindi Ortega and Bruce Wallace

CHAPTER 1

Beck leaned over the side of her bed and threw up into the wastebasket she had remembered to put there the night before. When she figured she was done, she blew her nose, wiped her mouth and gave herself a pat on the back for being organized. After a couple of sips of water, she lay back on her pillows, the endorphin rush from vomiting making her feel better.

She remembered leaving the office at six o'clock the previous evening and meeting Henry at the Blue Door. They had been watching the news and imploring the bartender to switch the channel to MSNBC. He always made a big deal of it, but had given in, since they were the only ones there. She had drunk about four glasses of their house white, which was so bitter she'd added ice. They'd left the bar at some point and walked the three blocks over to Henry's house because she had needed a cigarette. He'd had a bottle of Fevre Chablis in his fridge, which she remembered drinking most of, as well as smoking two or three of the joints he'd rolled with tobacco from her package of duMauriers. They might have danced around his massive kitchen to the Black Keys' "Lonely Boy." Or maybe that was just a dream—she couldn't be sure.

When she'd called a cab to come home, she'd thought the clock on Henry's kitchen stove had said twelve-thirty, but it could have been two-thirty. The time would be on her Visa slip. Today was Friday; the kids were away at school. Anthony was long gone.

She did a quick calculation of her company's billings for the month. On retainer, they were invoicing one client $50,000 and one client $30,000; that was $80,000. Then, four clients were being billed $20,000 each; that was another $80,000. There were another three clients at $10,000 each; that was $30,000. Altogether that came to $190,000. Then she had about $100,000 in project billings and another $80,000 or so in production markup. That was $370,000 in all. Expenses were $300,000. All this added up to $70,000 in profit for October if all the non-retainer work was completed and billed on time. It seemed like a safe enough margin for one month.

She pulled back the covers and put her feet on the carpeted floor.

Kneeling down, she tied up the four corners of the white bag she'd just thrown up in and headed downstairs to the kitchen. After putting the bag into the organics bin under the sink, she washed her hands. Her purse was on the kitchen table. She took out her wallet and found the Visa slip. She had arrived home at 12:43 a.m. Rummaging in the outer compartment of the purse, she found her cigarettes and lit one with a lighter from the kitchen counter. She took a puff and then turned on the kettle to make tea.

"Make sure the kettle is filled up before you go to bed, my darling," her mother used to say as she stood in the old kitchen in Herring Neck wearing her nightie and holding the kettle in her hand. "You never know if the water is going to come out of the tap in the morning."

Beck doubted she'd be her mommy's darling girl now, seeing as how she was as hungover as a pissed cat and not for the first time this week, either. "Thanks be to Jesus it's Friday," was all Beck could say, and she did say exactly that, standing there alone in the kitchen where no one could hear her.

She laid her cigarette in the ashtray and checked her iPhone. It was 7:40 a.m. Her first meeting outside the office was at one o'clock, a regular lunch with her friend Samantha Reed. But the possibility of an illegal strike by their biggest client, the province's 100,000-member teachers' union, would be the day's award-winning shit show. Figuring out how to keep parents lining up to give their favourite teacher an apple while one million of their kids were out of school and the union leadership potentially in jail would be job one today. Beck shook her head and muttered, "Oh, for frigging, fucking fuck's sake," as a rejoinder to the whole mess. She walked out to the front door to pick up her *Globe and Mail*. When she stood up and looked down her tree-lined street, the cool breeze found her cheek. The sun was shining, and the leaves were beginning to fall. All she wanted to do was vomit.

CHAPTER 2

Although she had managed to choke down a slice of white bread toasted and a cup of tea, Beck's stomach still felt queasy as she rode across Harbord Street and through the University of Toronto campus in the back of a cab. Beck felt soothed riding in a taxi. She didn't have to worry about parking or her blood-alcohol level.

The campus was ablaze with colour. The red, orange, and yellow maple, beech, and elm trees flamed against the sky, their branches moving like merry old burlesque dancers, as they tossed their gloves over the heads of the groundskeepers rolling out spools of plastic orange snow fencing below. Pale apparitions of the school's celebrity alumni gazed from taut canvas flags hanging on the utility poles lining the street—an unearthly honour guard performing a haunting benediction for the school's $2-billion fundraising campaign.

When she'd stepped out of the shower, Beck had thrown open the door of her closet and stared. Given the monumental size of her hangover, she'd wanted an outfit that looked dressy enough for work but felt like a housecoat. In her cupboard, suits hung next to suits, tops with tops, dresses with dresses, jackets with jackets. Everything was size 8. Beck had worn size 8 ever since she could remember—size 8L, actually, as in 8 Long. "See if they've got that in an 8L, my love," her mother would say as they'd flicked through the Sears catalogue. "The L is better for you because you're tall. You've got long legs, like your father." So size 8 it was, and Beck never deviated from that. Some months her clothes felt loose. At other times they felt tight, but she always kept a steady course concerning the size of her outfits.

Beck held high expectations of her clothes. For her part, she treated them well—paid good money for them, hung them on wooden hangers, sent them to the dry cleaners if instructed, washed them on the delicate cycle if they needed it, and never threw them on the floor. In return, she required them to pick up the slack when necessary. And, Christ knows, today was a day she needed them to work hard—very hard—for her, because she totally felt like shit.

After pulling a long-sleeve cashmere tunic off the rack, she'd chosen black velvet leggings and a grey calf-length raw silk vest that swished when she walked. She'd gotten down on her hands and knees to recruit a pair of low-heeled black suede boots that had taken up residence at the back of her cupboard. They were stuffed with newsprint to keep their shape. It was the first time she'd worn boots since March.

When Sarah Palin was preparing for her television debate, the vice-presidential candidate had asked the McCain strategists whether her brand was "hair up or hair down." Beck considered her own brand and pulled the top half of her long mane of red hair away from her face into a large clip, resulting in a diplomatic do that was half-up, half-down. She'd drawn dark brown eyeliner around her green eyes and brushed powder on her face to even out the palest of freckles that someone would only ever notice if they leaned in close enough to kiss her. To finish it off, she'd clamped on her Tag Heuer watch and added a dangly pair of earrings that might, subliminally at least, reinforce the sashay of her silk vest.

The cab dropped Beck off at the Starbucks around the corner from her office. She picked up a grande Earl Grey tea and walked the rest of the way to her work in a renovated warehouse on Adelaide Street. Standing in front of the elevator, she pushed the Up button with the middle finger of the hand that was holding the tea. The door lurched open. She got in and pressed 3.

Leaning against the elevator wall, she closed her eyes and listened for the familiar groaning of cables, which to her sounded as though a sailor were hoisting her up in the elevator car, hand over hand, in the same way he'd raise a sail. Rumble-rumble-creak, rumble-rumble-creak, rumble-rumble-creak. The elevator stopped with a lurch, and the doors opened. Her sailor was shooing her out, and if his grunting was any indication, she should think twice before getting in his way again that day. Beck opened her eyes and stepped into the hallway. The elevator door closed behind her.

When they had moved into this building, her company had had a two-room office and four staff. Now they had 35 employees and took up 10,000 square feet of space on the third floor. She was the CEO of what the marketing press called "an edgy, dynamic shop" catering to charities and interest groups, an agency that "simply spilled over with raw talent." The third-floor hallway was wide and bright, its walls painted white, or more precisely, orchid. The glowing floor was so thick with varnish it looked as if clear molasses had been poured over it.

The two doors to the firm were made from translucent glass, tall and heavy, with the words *SOCIAL* and *GOOD*, the firm's name, etched one to each door. With the letter *C* at eye level on her left and the letter *O* on her right, she took a deep breath and opened the door on the right.

CHAPTER 3

Yvonne Precipa stared at the three screens on her desk, her eyes wide as if what she was seeing surprised her. One monitor was streaming Canadian cable news, one was on CNN, and the third screen was her laptop. Yvonne's dark hair was parted in the middle and hung on the sides of her round face like quotation marks ready to frame the words that came out of her mouth. She was waiting for Beck to arrive and was starving—starving and freezing. She had taken her two suit jackets to the dry cleaners yesterday after work and paid extra for a one-hour cleaning, but with all this teachers' shit going on, she had forgotten to pick them up.

She tugged at her clothes and squirmed to get comfortable in her chair. Her leggings had shrunk in the wash, and she pulled her top down to cover her belly and the tops of her thighs. Yvonne felt nervous, and she knew she *was* nervous. She was going to be responsible for the media relations on the teachers' illegal strike—if they actually went on strike, that is—and it would be her biggest assignment yet. On the one hand, she couldn't wait; on the other hand, she didn't want to go near it with a 10-foot pole, because she didn't want to fuck it up. Contrary to the image of a free-thinking, plain-speaking person Yvonne thought people had of her, Yvonne felt she was in reality an unedited mess, blurting out all the wrong things at all the wrong times. She got especially nervous around Beck and then fell into the trap of what she categorized as the archetypal girl who tries too hard. She knew she had mother issues, but what a cliché. It was essential that she try to smooth out her rough edges, Yvonne thought, and so she lately had been investing in a library of self-help books to improve her workplace communications.

A talent for small talk would help her cause, Yvonne knew, and she had been trying to cultivate that in herself. But most of her work experience had been with political campaigns, and in politics she found that even the best professionals had very little in the way of interpersonal communications skills. Yet she was prepared to work hard at improving herself. Social Good had hired her when she hadn't had anywhere else to go. In addition to making use of her skills, this job was basically keeping her out of hell.

CHAPTER 4

It was six in the morning, and Asmi shook her husband's shoulder with a little more vigour than usual.

"Jaisalminder Awashti, it's time to get up. I have your chai here. You must get up now," she said, continuing to shake his arm.

Jaisalminder groaned. "Why so early, Asmi? I haven't to be at work for three hours. Where are you off to?" he asked, rubbing the sleep from his eyes.

Asmi sat down on the edge of the bed, dressed in a black skirt and matching jacket, fuchsia top, black tights, and black high heels. Her long, dark hair was draped in a ponytail over her left shoulder. Her legs were crossed at the ankle, and her back was ramrod straight.

"I have to go to work early, Jai," she said with flinty impatience, her dark eyes sparking and her generous lips pressed together in a frown. "We have a matter of urgent importance to deal with at work today, and there is other business to which you must attend. And I mean for you to have it dealt with this day."

"Ah, Asmi. Do we have to go through this again? I tell you, my mother is not yet ready for the news," he said, throwing his hands up in the air as if they had to let fate decide.

Asmi set the chai on the nightstand. "Am I your wife, or am I not your wife, Jaisalminder?" she asked, crossing her arms over her chest.

"Of course you are my wife," he said as he put an arm around her shoulder and gave her an affectionate squeeze. "Come and show me how much of a wonderful wife you are."

"Oh no, you don't. If you do not do something about our wedding, I will do nothing about being your wife, Jai. On that matter I am quite serious."

Asmi thought Jaisalminder Awashti a fine-looking man. At almost six feet tall, he towered over her. When Jai wore a *kurta* and Asmi dressed in one of her *sarees,* they looked as if they could have walked off the set of a Bollywood movie. He wore his dark, wavy hair brushed back, showing off his medium brown face and a high forehead; he had a gentle mouth and defined cheekbones. But at that moment, Asmi, in her impatience with him, noticed that underneath his T-shirt, he was beginning to get a bit soft around the middle.

Jaisalminder flopped back down on the bed.

A justice of the peace at Toronto City Hall had overseen their wedding vows one year ago today. Asmi's two cousins from Brampton had been witnesses, and the man who owned the pizza shop where Jai worked on the weekends had hosted a small reception at his house. It had cost a total of $250, and all 15 guests had been sent home with enough food to eat for the next day. Both Jai and Asmi had been very pleased with how well it had all worked out.

But Jai had not told his parents. "I just can't do it to them. Not yet, Asmi," he'd been saying for months. "You know what they are like. They are my parents. I must have respect for that."

Putting his hands together as if in prayer, he'd added, "We have to do this at the right time. This is not the right time. I have to break it to them in a *gentle* way."

Asmi had been impatient when Jai said this. Now she was growing alarmed. Jaisalminder Awashti had been born into a different caste from Asmi. In the order of things, he was a direct descendent of Krishna; he would laugh and tell her he was someone "the goats once bowed down to."

Suffice it to say, Asmi was not. Although her caste was respectable enough—her father had a shop in the village and her mother owned a small import-export business—to Jai's mother she would always be the little girl from the Punjab. Jai had been to Asmi's house many times to visit. He told her he was proud of the fact that he would be the first in his family to break out of caste. He felt it showed courage and was in keeping with the times. But telling his mother was another matter. Now a year had gone by, and still Jai could not find the right time.

Asmi was stuck. If Jai wouldn't tell his mother, then what kind of progress were they going to make? She and Jai had every intention of starting a family and being together for life. Having the respect of marriage in the eyes of his family, her family, and their town was not negotiable. And what of the children they would have?

But Jai would not budge, and the longer he *wouldn't* tell his mother, the more he *couldn't* tell her, thought Asmi.

"Jaisalminder, if you do not speak up to your mother on behalf of our family today, tonight I am calling my mother to tell her what you will not do," Asmi said with finality.

Jai sat up with concern. "You will call your mother about this?"

"Yes, I will, Jaisalminder," Asmi answered. "You may not possess the state of mind for this. But I most certainly do." She turned and walked out of the room.

CHAPTER 5

Just as Beck stepped into the reception area, Yvonne Precipa burst out of the office kitchen, juggling her coffee and cellphone in one hand and her breakfast in the other.

"Hiya, Beck," she called out. "Did you see Jon Stewart *eviscerate* Rob Ford on *The Daily Show* last night?" she said, walking over to greet her. She was pleased to be offering up the newsworthy nugget made possible by her late-night vigilance.

"Didn't get to it. Do you want to send me the link?" Beck asked.

"Nah, you don't *need* to see it," said Yvonne, shrugging her shoulders, "unless you *want* to see something hilarious. Do you want to see it? I'll send it. It's funny as hell—but also tragic too, of course." She hoisted herself up on the reception desk, set her eggs and her cellphone down, crossed her arms, and looked at Beck with expectation. Her cellphone vibrated on the desk. Yvonne picked it up, looked at the caller ID, and put it down again. "Can we talk?" she asked.

"Okay," said Beck, pulling an armchair from the reception area and sitting down at eye level with Yvonne's knees. She could see thin white check marks on the sides of her calves, dozens of them. Beck had seen that kind of mark before. There was a family of children who had lived around the back of the bay in Herring Neck and had them all over their legs too. Her mother had told her they were scars made with the buckle of a belt.

"You warm enough in those capris, Yvonne?" asked Beck.

"Jesus, Beck, I know," Yvonne said as she pulled at her top. "My jackets are at the cleaners. I forgot to pick them up this morning."

The smell of Yvonne's microwaved eggs was turning Beck's stomach, and she took a sip of her tea to quiet it down. "Where are things at with the teachers?"

"They're pissed, of course—no news there," said Yvonne. "This morning they are calling on all public-sector unions to join them in general strike to oppose to the legislation."

"Highly unlikely," responded Beck.

"Well, yeah. Teachers are not known for walking other people's picket lines, so there are not many favours to call in on that front. The executive is meeting right now. Bain is over there. He should be back in about an hour." Jack Bain was Social Good's director of campaigns.

Beck's stomach was starting to pain now, and she bent over a little in her chair. "Can you summarize the media for me?" she asked Yvonne.

"Predictable. They're focused on the wage freeze, which makes the teachers look greedy. Reporters are hanging around in school parking lots, asking parents what they think. The teachers are sending out spokespeople today to change the channel to the right to strike, and we'll see how that plays out over the next 24 hours."

"We're going to have to build an alternative narrative here," said Beck, "and we've only got between now and Christmas to get it firmly entrenched. Any thoughts on that?"

"I don't know about that. I'm not the one to tell you what to say, Beck," said Yvonne. "I just spread the word. You're going to have to figure that other part out—" Yvonne stopped in mid-sentence with an expression of alarm on her face, as if she'd just thought of something.

"But … but," she stammered, "whatever strategy you and Nick come up with, I will do my very best work to make sure it's entrenched—that's an excellent description, by the way, Beck—*entrenched*. Our goal is *entrenchment* before Christmas. Your media-relations department will make that happen for you and will be behind your strategy 110 percent.

"Now, if it's okay, I just think I'll get back to work." She hopped down from the desk and headed into the production room to where her office was, disappearing around the corner and leaving Beck somewhat surprised at the suddenness of the adjournment. The production room was a large rectangular space with cubicles for about 15 people and little meeting areas with comfortable chairs and coffee tables. People came and went all day, having little tête-à-têtes about the work, or whatever tête-à-têtes they felt like having. Five smaller offices branched off the production area, for the managers responsible for the work in the big room. Asmi had her office in here, right next to Yvonne. A couple of dozen people were on the phone or hunched over their desks, most of them eating. The smell of eggs was nauseating to Beck. She wished people would eat their breakfasts at home.

Beck could see Tilda Grubbs, the bookkeeper who worked three days a week, going through some files in a cabinet that she kept locked. *She'll come after me at some point today*, thought Beck. *I know it.*

Beck's office ran almost the width of the firm and was roughly half the size of the production area. Her desk was to the left of the door, with an Aeron chair behind it. On the right was a living-room type space furnished with a flat-screen TV, sound system, two couches, three armchairs, and a circular glass-top coffee table in the middle. Floor-to-ceiling bookcases stood on the far wall and contained an array of reference books, biographies, books on popular culture, and selected campaign manuals such as *How to Knife Your Opponent in the Back, What Your Consultant Hates about You* and *Ready to Brawl on Twitter? Here's How!* Beck had been going back and forth on carving out an office space for Asmi at this end of the firm, closer to her own office—and Nick's—since she worked with them closely and was a part of everything Beck did at work; she was pretty close to indispensable as far as Beck was concerned.

Nick Taylor, Director of Strategy, stuck his head around the corner. His brown hair was pulled back in a loose ponytail. His light green shirt was baggy, the top button undone. He wore a narrow blue tie. Nick was built like a baseball player: specifically, like an elegant version of San Francisco Giants' pitcher Tim Lincecum, before Lincecum cut his hair. He had the same long face, same big smile, and same long-limbed elegance. He had played in the bullpen at the University of Michigan with former Toronto Blue Jays pitcher Tim Crabtree. Who knew that inside his jersey beat the heart of a political operator?

"Hey, buddy," said Beck. "Come in. Sit down. Can we pull together some kind of meeting when Bain gets back? I'm thinking me, you, Bain, Yvonne, Kumail, and Asmi. Do we need Todd, you think?"

"No, Todd's got some other stuff on the go today. I'll brief him afterward. He'll be good not to be there. I'll call Asmi. She'll pull everyone together."

"Can we start putting some estimates on how much this teachers' campaign will cost?" Beck asked. "I don't want any of the work we're doing with this strike shit to be covered under the retainer. We're going to have to put four or five people on it, including you and me, and I don't want us to be eating anything on the billings. We bill extra for tub-thumping." Nick owned 10 percent of the company, and Beck was happy to have at least one other person whose eye was on making payroll.

"Sure, sure, Beck. But it's a bit early, don't you think? A lot depends on what they decide at their meeting and then what we decide at ours."

"I know Nick," said Beck, dismissing her words with a wave of her hand. "I don't know what's wrong with me. I'm fucking fixated on the money these days. It *haunts* me, I'm telling you."

"Nothing wrong with you, Beck," said Nick, smiling. "That's what you're supposed to be fixated on. I'll start thinking about it. Now, let's get to work. The day's half gone, and we have to figure out something to avoid the teachers being tarred and feathered."

✳ ✳ ✳

When they'd finished talking about a strategy for the teachers and Nick had left her office, Beck stepped out onto a small terrace, which was big enough for a café table, two chairs, and an ashtray. Her stomach still felt uneasy, her head was pounding, and her eyelids felt as though they were made of sandpaper; every blink was coarse and painful. She sat down on the folding chair and lit a cigarette.

When Beck had worked as a journalist, she had done a piece on teachers, "Seven Days of a Teacher's Life Makes One Week," which had won a National Magazine Award. She had shadowed a high-school teacher; sat in on all of his classes; eaten lunch in the lunch room; and interviewed some of his students, his ex-wife, and principal; as well as accompanying him on his weekend errands, including a chess tournament in Brampton. The Ontario Teachers' Union (OTU) had helped with the access for that story.

When Beck had traded in journalism for consulting and her firm gotten big enough to handle some of their communications work, the teachers' union had been happy to hire her, and they'd been an anchor client ever since. The guys on the executive loved Social Good's campaign director, Jack Bain, who was a veteran political strategist with a long history in the labour movement. And Beck had a close connection with Joy Kobayashi, the general secretary of the union.

The union never asked Beck what she thought they should do. They told her what they wanted to do. And that was the golden rule in dealing with the teachers' union: You were never going to tell teachers what to do. Ever. And that's what the Government had seemed to forget all of a sudden, as it tried to freeze their wages and strip them of the right to strike as part of its "dealing decisively with the worst recession in modern history." What in fuck's name had they been thinking?

Why shouldn't the teachers kick up shit? thought Beck. What was it that American labour leader, Sam Gompers, had said? "We do want more, and when it becomes more, we shall still want more. And we shall never cease to demand more, until we have received the results of our labour." Those were words to live by if your client was a teachers' union. She texted Joy Kobayashi.

> *My heart goes out … We're meeting as soon as Bain gets back and, according to what he says, will have the outline of a plan to you this aft.*

Beck gulped the last of her tea. It was cold, and her stomach knotted up like a clove hitch.

CHAPTER 6

"Fix my clips, Poppy, fix my clips," Beck said to her grandfather as she crawled up on his lap. She held her head still, and he looked down at the top of it. With hands cracked as tree bark and bent by thousands of miles of fishing line, he gently took out the loose barrettes, picked up a few strands of thick red hair, and refastened them so they wouldn't budge.

"Is they held fast enough fer ya, my duck?" he asked her.

She shook her head to make sure they didn't move and then nodded her head to say they were.

"You're best at fixing my clips, Poppy," she said, kissing him on the cheek and hopping down again.

Nanny looked on. "Sure, if I gives you my apron, me son, ye'll soon be a hairdresser," she said.

Beck laughed as she pictured Poppy in Nanny's apron. He cocked his head and winked at her. Poppy spoiled Beck; everybody said that. He'd stop whatever he was doing to tell her a story, show her how to fix a piece of a net, or put the bait in a lobster pot.

"Did you ever hear about the fishing admirals, girlie?" he said one night after they'd finished supper. Beck ate supper at her grandparents' house as many nights a week as she ate at home. Nanny had just cleared the dishes off the table, and Poppy sipped the last drop of his tea from the saucer.

Beck was about to open her mouth, but he wasn't waiting for a response.

"They were called fishing admirals," said her grandfather in a low voice, "but they weren't real admirals, not like the admirals in the navy. No, these men were called fishing admirals because they were the first ship's captains to get into the harbour at the beginning of the fishing season in the spring— after they had sailed all the way over the Atlantic Ocean to get there. Those were the days when no one was allowed to live on the island when it wasn't fishing season. The merchants wanted it all to themselves.

"Can you imagine that, girlie?" said Poppy, shaking his head. "No one could live on the island through the year. Not that the winter is very good, all the same." He chuckled.

"In the spring of the year, hundreds of ships came here to the island to fish, from England and France—you name it. They fished and fished and fished, and salted it all right here on fish flakes, big wooden stages they made out of trees they cut down right here, just over in the meadow there. When they'd caught and salted as much as they could carry, they sailed right back across the ocean, the ship's holds laden down with salt cod. People ate Newfoundland salt fish the world over."

Beck gazed transfixed at her grandfather, the plate of Nanny's molasses cookies forgotten in her lap.

"The captain of the first ship in a cove was the boss of everyone in that cove for the season. He was the fishing admiral, and he ruled the roost. If the men did anything wrong—if they stole, got into a fight, or were saucy—the fishing admiral would set the punishment and be the one that carried it out. He would whip them. Das right, girlie—he'd whip them, right out in the open for everyone to see. Because that would make the other fellas take heed, you see. But he didn't use any old stick or a whip. He'd use what they called a cat-o'-nine-tails. Did you ever hear of the cat-o'-nine-tails, my duck?"

She shook her head, her jaw slack. She was mesmerized.

"Let me draw you a little picture," he said. He took a thick stub of a pencil from his shirt pocket and tore off a piece of paper from a little notebook lying on the kitchen table.

"That's the base of her right there, see," he said, drawing a heavy stick. "Das the handle, the part the fishing admiral held in his hand." Then he drew nine curved lines attached to the stick. "See," he said, pushing the paper toward Beck so she could take a closer look, "they look like cattails, right? Tha's where the name comes from, the tail of a cat, all curvy. The tails could be made up of braided rope or maybe leather, depending on how strong the fishing admiral wanted them to be."

He drew a little knot at the end of each tail. "See those little knots at the end of the tail? That would make it hurt more," he said, "when it struck the skin—usually a man's back."

Pleased with his work, he nodded and looked at Beck with a satisfied expression, saying, "Dere you go, my duck, das it right dere. Dere's yer cat-o'-nine-tails.

"But let me tell you something else, girlie," he said, leaning forward in his chair. "Just because people weren't allowed to live in Newfoundland the whole year round in those days didn't mean that nobody lived here. How else would we be here today if nobody lived here year-round?" he laughed, holding his palms up and shrugging. "But if the fishing admirals found them, then they might get the cat-o'-nine-tails. That was the danger, see."

"Did you ever get the cat-o'-nine-tails, Poppy?" Beck asked, finally taking a bite of her cookie.

"No, no, not me, my duckie," he chortled. "Dat was a good long time ago, a hundred years ago now, well afore I came into de world. You don't have to worry about your old Poppy. Does she, Nan?" he asked, looking across the kitchen at Nanny, who was drying the last of the supper dishes.

"You stop talking your foolishness to that youngster," she said. "She's a girl, not a b'y. Ye'll have her scared of the night."

CHAPTER 7

After she finished briefing Beck about the teachers' campaign, Yvonne walked back to her office, taking bites out of her now-cold eggs and toast along the way. She nodded at the bookkeeper, Tilda Grubbs, who looked to be poring over some bills.

She thought her attempt at small talk with Beck had gone pretty well, overall. Rob Ford was always good for that. But what the fuck was that thing she'd blurted out? "I'm *not* the one to tell you what to say—I'm *not* the one"? Yvonne was committed to self-improvement, and she knew that you were never *not* the one. The books were very clear on that. You had to be positive. It was about what you *could* do, not what you *couldn't* do. Let there be no doubt about Yvonne Precipa and her goal to get better at communicating with people. She'd have to, or it would be her Waterloo. Whatever she did, it had to be good. She had to succeed. Hell had to be avoided at all costs.

For Yvonne, hell was a house on Brunswick Avenue. She had lived there with her parents until she'd left for Ottawa to work on the last federal election. If it hadn't been for her grandparents, she figured she'd be, right this minute, managing media relations from the grave. Her father was a loving role model, she thought with ironic detachment. One time, when she was about eight, he'd tied a skipping rope around the neck of the neighbour's cat and swung the rope around his head like a lasso. The animal had hung from the rope, limp as a wet rag, as her father had whirled it around in the air, the knot in the lasso, choking the life out of it with each spin. His brothers—her uncles—had stood around laughing while he did it. Those were some pretty crazy genes right there, Yvonne reckoned.

To this day, Yvonne felt sure that her mother, full of misery, dwelled in an alternate universe altogether. They had been washing the dinner dishes when Yvonne had told her she had gotten the job in Ottawa. The kitchen had looked like a turn-of-the-century insane asylum that night. One of the bulbs in the kitchen was burned out, so the light was dim and the room full of shadows. The cutlery shone like rough medical instruments. A crucifix of the bleeding heart hung on the wall over the doorway.

Her mother's response to the news was to raise the metal spoon she held in her hand and whip it across Yvonne's face, smacking it hard down on her cheek. "Ottawa? Ottawa?" she mocked, her lips set like a piece of grey string frozen into the ground. "You, Miss High and Mighty, marching off to *Ottawa* by yourself like a whore? I don't *think* so."

When she raised her hand to hit Yvonne again, Yvonne caught the spoon, wrenched it from her mother's grasp, told her she was leaving in the morning, and threw the spoon into the kitchen sink. As soon as it had gotten light out, Yvonne had packed up the black Toyota Tercel her grandfather had signed over to her before he'd died, and she' d started driving east, reciting the Lord's Prayer as she drove up the Don Valley Parkway.

When Yvonne got back to her office, she plunked down in her chair and put her feet up on the desk. Staring at her plastic orange shoes, she blinked a couple of times to shut down the family-file section of her memory bank and turned her attention to the 50 or so wind-up toys she had on her desk. There were wind-up post boxes that flipped over, umbrellas that opened and closed, rabbits that hopped, and woodpeckers that pecked their wind-up toy beaks against a tree.

She picked up one of the toys and rolled the wind-up mechanism between her thumb and forefinger. It was a pair of sumo wrestlers whose arms, in a semblance of a wrestling move, went up and down until they tipped over. She set them down on her desk to start a match while she checked her email, texts, and Google alerts—lots of blah, blah blah but no new developments, and nothing from Bain.

The mainstream media needed to get knocked off their well-kindled groove, she thought. The question was how. What kind of narrative would interest them? Lord knows they were tired of reporting the same old shit. Maybe the campaign could just write mainstream off and go for social media? Nah, you couldn't. The union leadership would never stand for it.

Yvonne looked at her sumo wrestlers. They had wound down without tipping over. A good omen, maybe?

CHAPTER 8

Todd Purcell backed into the parking spot in the underground garage of First Canadian Place. It was expensive to park there, but he didn't want the Lexus to get dinged by someone who didn't know how to parallel-park. And besides, Social Good would pay for it. He was meeting with a potential client. If the rumours were right, the National Breast Cancer Society, the country's largest cancer charity, was about to tender their whole account. Sylvia Bumley, their director of development and the woman he was meeting with, would know what was going on.

If Todd played this right, he could be responsible for bringing in Social Good's biggest account, even bigger than the teachers. His last big accomplishment—what he considered his last big accomplishment, at any rate—had been getting Beck to hire Yvonne Precipa. She was eccentric and couldn't go in front of a client unaccompanied, but her skill had turned the media-relations department into a brand-new revenue centre. And it had been Todd who had spotted that talent. If they did land this breast cancer society account, Todd was planning to make a case to Beck and Nick for an equity stake in the company. He knew Nick had a percentage, but he didn't know how much. If Nick, why not Todd? He just had to prove he was worth it.

Todd was 30 minutes early for the meeting, so he flipped down the visor mirror to check his look. The remnants of his seven-year-old self looked back at him. The crisply ironed shirt he had on was the same as the one he'd worn back then, only in a bigger size. Its snowy whiteness gleamed against his dark skin.

His brown eyes with the long lashes—*sweepers*, his mother called them—were still there. His smile, which he'd just then tried out in the mirror, looked the same—a broad, easygoing grin he'd heard his aunties call nice. His skin was the same chocolaty colour, but his face looked more sculpted. The hair was gone. After he'd noticed it getting thin in spots, he'd decided to shave it all off.

It had been five years since Todd had graduated with his MBA. He'd done a stint in the corporate world, but when he'd seen the posting for Social Good's business development director, he'd jumped at the chance. More fun being a big fish in a small pond, he'd thought, plus he liked the idea of working for charities—making the world a better place and all. It made his mother happy. She liked the idea he was helping people.

Alma Purcell had come to Canada from Grenada with Todd when he was 2 years old. She said she loved Todd, God, and music—in that order. When Todd had opened his mouth to sing at age 3, his mother had fallen to her knees and declared that the three loves of her life had fused together into one little boy, *her* little boy.

At the age of 7 he'd been accepted to go St. Michael's Choir School on a scholarship, and he stayed there until he graduated Grade 12. He'd travelled all over the world with the school choir, singing at the Vatican, in Paris, in Vienna, and many other places.

Todd looked at his reflection and began to sing and sway to the rhythm of the gospel song he'd sung at his audition.

Not my father, not my mother,
But it's me, oh Lord,
Standing in the need of prayer.

Not my sister, not my brother,
But it's me, oh Lord,
Standing in the need of prayer.

Not the people that are shoutin',
But it's me, oh Lord,
Standing in the need of prayer.

CHAPTER 9

It was eleven o'clock by the time Bain got back from the Ontario Teachers' Union meeting, and the account team filed into Beck's office. Beck got up from behind her desk as they walked into the room. Asmi came in first, carrying a tray of tea and biscuits. She put the tray on the coffee table, left the room, and came back with her MacBook under her arm. Yvonne arrived in her leggings and stretch top, with her phone and a cup of coffee in her hand; she was still trying to warm up.

"I can see goosebumps on your arms," Beck exclaimed as Yvonne walked by her. "You're freezing!" Yvonne shrugged.

"Here," Beck said, reaching for a shawl that hung from her coatrack, "put this on."

"You sure?" asked Yvonne, eyeing the shawl as Beck held it out to her.

"Yeah, sure—here, take it," said Beck as she threw it over Yvonne's shoulders. Yvonne sat down on the couch and pulled the shawl around her, trembling at the softness of it and feeling the warmth of it right away. What the hell was it made of? She saw the label on the bottom hem—100 percent cashmere. She was comfortable for the first time today, maybe for the first time ever.

Kumail Kapoor trailed in after Yvonne. With his short, dark brown hair and big brown eyes opened wide, he looked like a boy who had just walked into his own birthday party. His eyes darted around the room, out the window, at the bookcases, at Beck's desk, and around the corner to the café table on the terrace. Yvonne called him the boy genius, and she had urged Beck and Nick to bring him on as their social media specialist. "He's not as young as he looks," she had said. "Don't let that fool you."

"All set?" Nick asked Beck as he strode through the door, tall and graceful. Beck nodded.

Jack Bain, or Bain, as he was known—most people didn't know his first name was Jack—came in last, cellphone in his hand, arms swinging at his sides. He was wearing a pair of navy Chino pants and tan suede shoes with thick rubber soles that squeaked when he walked. He ran his hand through his blond-grey hair and then stood with his hands on his hips, showing off his royal flush belt buckle to good effect. He had won the buckle 20 years ago from a candidate in northern Ontario, on a bet related to the point spread of his nearest challenger. Bain had come to Canada from Scotland when he was a boy and never lost his Scottish accent, maintaining it was the most trusted accent in the world.

For years, he had bounced from federal to provincial to municipal elections, collecting unemployment insurance when there was a dry spell. He came to work with Beck after he met Lesley, a woman he soon wanted to marry and, much to his everlasting surprise, who wanted to marry him. It was time to settle down, he thought, to sleep in the same bed every night, drink Scotch and do crosswords, and have the companionship of someone who loved him. Loved *him*. Bain couldn't let the opportunity go by. He wasn't sure he would ever get the chance again, but he needed a steady job and steady income. Lesley deserved that. He called up Beck Carnell. She had something going on with Social Good, clients who could pay the bills, and had a few good people working for her. He figured someone like him could be useful to her. They had lunch and agreed to a working relationship right then and there. He liked that about Beck—she was quick off the mark. It would be eight years this month. And now, he was the father of two 6-year-old boys. It was all a bit bewildering to him.

Bain sat down in an armchair and started talking without being prompted.

"The Government has said the first reading of the bill will be Monday. The union says they were blindsided by it. It imposes a pay freeze and takes away their right to strike for three years; it has to go through two more readings before it's passed. That will take about eight weeks. They can't let it go.

"They want to fully ramp up. Rotating strikes, legal or illegal, rallies, an ad campaign, and teachers bused in from all over Ontario. They want a schedule of actions that will take us right up to before Christmas. The first thing in the New Year, they'll start on the work stoppages. They'll be challenged legally on that front, because the new bill will be law by that time. It'll go to court. When the court rules it illegal, which it almost certainly will do, they'll work to rule. That's the next 12 weeks, roughly."

"Do they have any ideas about keeping their members happy during all that?" Beck asked.

"They're open," said Bain, turning his palms up.

"They're open?" asked Nick, raising his eyebrows.

"Yep, totally open," responded Bain. "They're open to any idea we can bring them, especially new ideas. They especially like the idea of social media."

Yvonne and Kumail burst out laughing. Yvonne was holding her sides for effect.

"Lots of people like the *idea* of social media. It's a real keen thing these days, I hear," said Kumail with a laugh. "*Using* social media, now, that's a different ball game—that takes brains."

Bain scowled. "Okay, I know you guys are smart and all that, but let's spell out our basics here before we get to media, social or otherwise. These OTU politicians have decided to wage a war, with the teachers as the soldiers. Not only will they have to keep discipline, they'll need allies," said Bain, "and who do you brainiacs think that might be?"

"The natural allies are parents and students," Yvonne said.

"And what do *they* need to convince them to join a war that will, in fact, cause them major inconvenience?" asked Bain.

"They need to share a goal, a common purpose," said Yvonne. "They want to feel like they are doing the right thing."

"What's the right thing going to be in this case?" asked Kumail, poised over his notebook, ready to type the answer into it.

"Well now, I would have figured you, being a media genius and all, might have that figured out already," Bain said, leaning back in his chair, having seen the end of that skirmish coming before it ever began.

"They need to be seen as preserving workers' rights," interjected Nick, "not for themselves, but for the students they teach, their children, and grandchildren. Beck and I figure they need to show that teachers *care about the future*; in particular, they care about kids graduating today being able to earn a decent living tomorrow. What do a couple of months of inconvenience mean when you hold it up to that?"

"Speaking of the future," Bain interjected, "what else do politicians often rely on when they are trying to justify a war? They rely on history. And there are a few history lessons these teachers could teach, lessons not in the history books, that's for sure."

"Exactly," said Beck. "That's the concept Nick and I have been discussing—'Teachers care about the future because they remember the past' can be the one freestanding factoid that will bind the campaign. The idea would be most fully realized on a virtual headquarters, a campaign website where the history of the teaching profession could encompass the fight for women's rights, public education, child nutrition, public health, and so on, but it would be boiled down for TV and all the other media.

"We want the job action to be inconvenient, because no one will notice it if it's not," she continued. "But we want parents to feel as if the teachers are on *their* side and to blame any inconvenience on the Government's bully tactics. Parents wouldn't have to listen to the news to find out whether their child's school was going to be closed as a part of rotating strikes, for example. All the closure information would be on the OTU website, and parents could sign up for social media alerts. The teachers would control how that information was disseminated, so while parents were getting the most up-to-date information about the job action, they'd also be reading about the reasons for it."

"To push traffic to the website and have people sign up for Twitter alerts, we'd produce a traditional media campaign with bus shelter ads, television, and radio," added Nick. "But no Facebook. We don't want to give a fucking forum for the haters to be able to speak in full sentences. This is about information getting out, not coming in."

"And, of course, a media-relations strategy," said Beck, nodding toward Yvonne, "that drives media to the website where they'll find a ton of colour, B-roll they can just download, pictures, whatever they need. We need to keep them there as much as possible, so they're exposed to the *context* of the job action—the context being a historical fight for collective bargaining. Yvonne, you set up some interviews for the union president, but make sure he's got the talking points internalized first. Make him practice with you in the room."

Yvonne nodded as she made notes.

"It's good—it's very good," said Bain. "I like it, but—and I hate to say it—we might have a problem with it. I can tell you, there are some guys in that room over at OTU who just can't wait to rattle their sabres and get all up in the face of the Government. They see the protest signs and marches as the ultimate in campaign technique and might view the 'Teachers care about the future' thing as a bit soft," he said, making the gesture for air quotes around the word *care*.

"Yeah, I think that's a fair point, Bain," said Beck, "but I'm thinking that we can lead with TV in the pitch. We'll buy some advertising time during a prime-time newscast, including a few national spots, so the membership, the union politicians, and their friends can watch. It'll give the perception of heft."

"Spots buying on *The National*," said Yvonne. "Excellent play. Nicely done, Beck. We'll make sure all members know the *exact* time their ad will be televised. *He he*. And won't that help them feel tall and mighty? In my estimation, worth, I dunno, four inches of a penis for those guys."

She laughed and snorted as she high-fived Kumail. The rest of the room fell silent.

"Aye, Yvonne," said Bain slowly, "you are a very bright young woman to be sure, and there's no denying it, but there are clearly a few things you don't know. And I hate to be the one to tell you, dearie, but no man wants a *four*-inch penis. Yvonne ... *four inches?*" he said, looking at Yvonne with sympathy. "Nay, lassie, not four."

"For Chrissakes, Bain. What do you take me for, for crying out loud? An idiot?" she blurted. "I mean four inches on *top* of what they already have!"

"Oh, right. Well then, that's obviously different," Nick cut in. "Now it all makes sense. Right, Bain?"

Bain shook his head.

"All right, all right," said Beck, "To wrap up—the main message is that *teachers care. Teachers care about the future because they remember the past.* The channels roughly break down into social media for parents and students, the website for media, and television is for the teachers themselves. Asmi, do you have enough to do the write it up?"

"Yes, I do, Beck. I'll get on it right away," she said as she snapped her laptop shut.

"Time for lunch," said Bain, standing up and patting his belly. "I must be fed."

Yvonne took off the shawl to hand it back to Beck.

"It's okay, Yvonne. Hang on to it."

"Oh, Beck, I couldn't," Yvonne said even as she pulled the shawl closer to her body. She had never worn a piece of clothing like this. It didn't make marks on her belly or arms. It *caressed* her.

"Of course you can," said Beck, "keep it until your jackets get sprung from the cleaners."

"Thank you, Beck. I don't know what to say," she said in a soft voice as she lowered her head for a second but then snapped it up. "I owe you one, boss," she said with a wink. She cocked her trigger finger at Beck and strode out the door.

"That was a real blast," Kumail said as he caught up with Yvonne. His gaze was intent and his arms were swinging with the zeal of an evangelist. "Now we go to work!"

Beck turned to Asmi, who was still standing by Beck's desk. "Can you go over the draft with Nick and Bain before bringing it back to me?"

"Yes, Beck, of course," she said with a sigh.

"Everything okay, Asmi?" Beck asked as she propped herself up on her desk, the meeting adrenaline beginning to wear off. "How is everything with Jai? Has he figured out how to break the news to his mother?"

"No, Beck, and I'm getting impatient with him—and a little scared, to be honest with you. Maybe he is not serious about our marriage. It is keeping me awake at night, I'm afraid," said Asmi. "I am coming close to my wits' end."

"He is going to have to make up his mind soon, don't you think? Do you have a plan?"

"My plan is to call my mother this evening, to tell her the whole sorry tale. You are a mother, Beck. What do you think?"

"It's time to call in the heavy artillery," said Beck.

"Good," Asmi agreed with a nod, and she walked out of the office.

Beck sat behind her desk and looked over at Nick, who was still sitting on the couch with his arm draped over the back, his long legs crossed, and a smile on his face. "You know, Beck, this is pretty good. It could be good."

"It might have something to it, Nick," she said leaning back in her chair and smiling at him.

""In terms of budget," Nick said, "I think we're talking about a million to them to get us up to Christmas—more if they want to go heavier on TV— and about a quarter of that to us over 12 weeks. We'll set up a videoconference for this afternoon. I'll let you know the exact time as soon as I know."

Beck went through the revised potential billings in her head. *On retainer, we are invoicing one client $50,000 and one client $30,000; that's $80,000. Then, four clients are being billed $20,000 each; that's another $80,000. Plus we have three clients at $10,000 each; that's $30,000. Altogether, that is $190,000. Add in the teachers' work and we have about $150,000 in project billings and another $120,000 or so in production markup. That is $460,000 in all—roughly. Expenses are $300,000. That means $160,000 in profit for the month—theoretically—if all the non-retainer work is completed and billed on time—a big if.*

CHAPTER 10

Henry Hill stirred in his bed and licked his lips. He could feel the warm sun streaming through the window, and he adjusted himself on the mattress, stretching his aching back and moving toward the heat. He'd hung out with Beck last night, first at the Blue Door and then at his place. That had been nice, but she'd had to work today, so she'd left around midnight.

He thought about opening his eyes and then did, blinking at the bright light. He closed them again. It felt as if a nail were being driven up his spine from his tailbone to his lower back. He reached over his body with his left hand to open one of the prescription bottles on the night table to his right. With a gulp of water from the dusty glass beside him, he took two of the Percocet and looked at the clock; it was a quarter after noon. *I'll just wait here for these to kick in before I get up.*

He had dreamt again last night. The flames, the screaming, his father carrying the burning mattress out of the trailer, the smell of melting plastic. He'd smelled the acrid smoke that makes boils break open on your lungs, hard and hot, the devil's bad breath, and seen his mother barely there as she hopped away from the flames like a lame fox.

They'd stood outside, all five of them—his brother, his sister, his mother, his father, and him—and watched the trailer burn to the ground. His homework, his clothes, his winter coat, and his school bag were all gone. His textbooks, the ones the school had lent him, had burned. All he had left were the pyjamas he was wearing. His sister screeched. His brother stared ahead, mouth open, hypnotized by the flames.

His mother had done it again. She'd been stoned and smoking, he knew it—stoned and smoking in bed. And she'd fallen asleep. Those trailers were like kindling: one match and it was up in smoke. His father said that all the time. "Watch your cigarettes, Diane, or you'll burn the place down."

Henry looked at his mother. Her eyes were round and wild. She was whooping "Oh, oh, oh, oh, oh, oh," and dancing as if she were standing on hot coals. "Oh, oh, oh, oh, oh, oh!" She just kept on like that. She wouldn't shut up. It was all Henry could hear. "Oh, oh, oh, oh, oh, oh!"

He put his hands over his ears and looked down at his bare feet. He couldn't look up. His head wouldn't move. His hands wouldn't move. He stared down at his feet and at the ground. He was paralyzed.

Now Henry raised his head off the pillow and looked down to the end of the bed. There they were, the same feet, sticking out from under the sheets, the same ten toes he'd had the night the trailer burnt down. A couple had gotten bent because he'd broken them, but they were all still there. The elastic cuffs on his flannel pyjamas, the ones that had hugged his ankles, were gone, and dark hair had sprouted out on his legs, but the feet, they were the same.

"I gotta piss," he said out loud. He threw back the covers, swung his feet to the floor, and made his way to the bathroom.

CHAPTER 11

Beck put down the phone. Joy Kobayashi liked the overall plan, especially the TV. The preliminary budget number sounded reasonable to her.

Beck had to go meet her friend Samantha Reed for lunch in half an hour. She'd met Sam when she—and the community centre she ran—had been a client. They'd had lots of fun on the project, and when it was done they'd started having lunch together every couple of weeks. They joked that it was like having a psychiatrist. They never cancelled on each other and had never met each other's families but knew all about them. They met during work hours, and each only knew what the other chose to reveal.

But before lunch with Sam, Beck had time to check her emails. There were 51. She was cc'd on about 20 from people inside the company. She stuffed those in a folder to look at later with a drink in her hand. There was one from Tilda Grubbs, the bookkeeper, asking to meet before the end of the day. Beck responded:

Hi, Tilda. Okay 4:00. Cheers, Beck.

Todd wanted to talk to her about something.

Hi, Todd. Okay 4:15. Talk soon, Beck.

That would be one way to keep Tilda short. If she made an appointment with Todd for 4:15 p.m., he was going to be standing by her door at precisely 4:15 p.m. She looked for anything from the teachers' union in case someone had decided to email instead of texting or calling. Nothing.

She saw a friendly email from the rumpled and eternally optimistic

Donald Pearson at the Canadian Peace Agency; he wanted to set up their regular quarterly get-together. She responded:

> *Hi, Donald!*
> *Looking forward to seeing you. Asmi will email you by end of day with a couple of times for next week or the week after—whatever is good for you. Lots to talk about.*
> *Cheers, Beck.*

She cc'd Asmi so she could set up the meeting.

There was an email from Dimitri Wattage, executive vice president of the Seniors' Organization of Canada, or SOC, as they were commonly known. SOC had 350,000 members over the age of 55 and was Canada's largest organization for seniors. They offered discounted insurance, deals on travel, and a whole array of benefits. They communicated with their members mostly by mail, and Social Good handled all of it: writing, designing, packaging, and posting more than 10 million pieces of mail a year on their behalf. It was Social Good's second-largest client, after the teachers. And Dimitri Wattage couldn't lord it over Beck often enough. One week he would want to meet to get her "expert opinion" about their marketing. The next week, he'd be considering tendering the whole contract. He didn't want his vendors getting too comfortable, he said. "You're not too comfortable, are you, Beck? … *Heh heh heh…*"

Dmitri could get creepily personal. At a lunch last year, Beck had dragged the cuff of her lemon-yellow silk suit jacket into a plate of olive oil and balsamic vinegar while she was dipping her bread. Dmitri hadn't seemed to notice, and the lunch had continued without a mention of it. Then, when they were getting up to leave, Dmitri had said, "Hey, Beck, you've got a stain there on the arm of your jacket. Lookit. It's right there. You've got to watch that sort of thing, you know—check out your clothes before you put them on. It kind of looks unprofessional."

Beck looked at her suit cuff. She'd forgotten about the stain until that moment and blurted out, "Oh, for Chrissakes, Dmitri, that just happened half an hour ago." But she'd still felt weirded out by it.

"He is a smarmy one, do you think, Beck?" Asmi said after meeting him the first time. "This one I wouldn't have tremendous trust for ... others, yes ... but this one ... no. I could be wrong, of course," she'd added in a tone indicating she didn't believe herself to be wrong for one second.

Dmitri was emailing because another vendor had offered to do a "test" mail campaign for free. This vendor wanted to have a contest with Social Good. They would post 100,000 pieces to prospective members, Social Good would do the same, and they'd see who got the best results. If this new vendor "beat" Social Good by getting more responses to the mailing, then maybe SOC might like to parcel out more of their work, Dmitri suggested.

It was a farce, of course. Beck knew you could send out 100,000 pieces of mail promising the recipients a chance of winning a flat screen TV or whatever you wanted to and they'd respond. But would that make them renewable members, or bits of stagnant data, clogging up the analysis? Beck thought the whole idea was stupid, but in the short term she thought a distraction might work. Maybe lunch at a fancy restaurant?

> *Hi, Dimitri,*
>   *Not a huge fan of contests. Will think about it. How about lunch at Canoe in the next couple of weeks?*
> *Beck*

There were two requests for Social Good to pitch projects, one from the national breast cancer organization and the other from a small charity that served people with mental health problems, someone that Sam had recommended. She wrote a quick note to both.

> *Hi there,*
>   *I've just read your email. Thanks so much for your interest in our work. We're honoured you would think of us. I'm cc'ing this email to Todd Purcell, our Director of Client Services and Business Development. He will be in touch to get more details. Please give me a ring if you'd like to chat.*
> *Regards, Beck Carnell*

She scanned her Google Alerts and saw almost all of them were about the teachers' union—no surprise there.

She was left with 10 emails—one from someone asking her to speak at a conference and two from Maggie Blackwood, her friend from Herring Neck who now worked in St. John's. The power was out in St. John's because of a sleet storm. Mick, Beck's son, who was at Memorial University in St. John's studying naval architecture, was coming over for dinner. Answer later.

There was an email from Sam confirming lunch at one o'clock—no response needed. Two people sent Beck their resumes. She forwarded them to Nick.

Four emails were from other clients asking her opinion about strategy. She'd need to talk to the account people before she replied with something contradictory to what the account team were trying to do. She wrote them each an email.

> *Hi there,*
> *Great to hear from you. I want to give your questions a bit of*
> *a think. I'll call or email on Monday. Does that work for you?*
> *Cheers, Beck*

Beck looked at her watch—12:38 p.m. She grabbed her bag to go meet Sam.

CHAPTER 12

Beck arrived at the restaurant ahead of Sam. She ordered a Diet Coke and sat back in her chair to scan the newspapers she had taken from the office. Like most of Toronto, she was unable to turn her head from the train wreck that was Rob Ford. Now, his friend and "occasional driver," the same guy who was linked to attempts to retrieve the crack video, had been arrested for trafficking pot.

"I'm surprised; I'm really surprised," Ford was quoted as saying. "He's a friend, he's a good guy. I don't throw my friends under the bus. He's straight and narrow, never once seen the guy drink, never seen him once do drugs, so … I'm surprised; I'm actually shocked."

A waitress brought bread. Beck folded up her newspaper and set it down to her left where she could read and eat at the same time. The bread looked like that from Ace Bakery. She buttered it and pulled at the chewy crust. She loved Ace bread—almost as much as her own.

Beck could honestly say that Sam was her only female friend in Toronto since Anthony had left. When Anthony had been around, they'd seemed to have lots of friends. Every weekend they'd go somewhere or have people over. The kids were part of it too. The people were those they'd met in the neighbourhood, at skating lessons or in the kids' schools. They'd talked about how busy they were, how many things they were trying to juggle, and how it was all so *hard*. Then someone would say, "Would you mind pouring me another glass of the red there, darling?"

"Not at all, sweetie. You deserve it," would come the answer, and everyone would get pissed.

Beck had liked having people over for dinner. She'd always cooked— first, standing on a kitchen chair next to her mother. When she'd gotten a bit taller, her grandfather had made her a little wooden stool. She'd called it Poppy's Stool and she'd dragged it back and forth between the kitchen and the bathroom, where she needed it to brush her teeth and wash her hands. Eventually she had stood next to her mother with her feet on the floor. Then, one day, she had been tall enough to do her own mixing, sifting, rolling, buttering, baking, boiling, and basting.

Without Anthony, she wasn't sure what to do with the dinner-party friends, so she didn't do anything, and they didn't call. Samantha Reed had been around for all of that. She was the one who said it was normal to lose your married friends. Not that she knew from experience, said Sam. She had read it in a magazine.

Sam's community centre was located in one of toughest parts of the city. The homeless, the marginalized, and the addicted orbited the building night and day like giddy electrons barely holding their trajectory. On Saturdays and Sundays, police came to clear a path to the doors of the skating rink next door, so skaters and hockey players wouldn't have to run the jittery gauntlet.

Across the street, the 600-bed shelter for homeless men dumped its ambulatory contents onto the sidewalk every morning. Mingled with what looked like sacks of rattling bones shuffling down the street to rest at the nearby park were the grimacing, drug-addled teeth grinders scurrying off to find Vaseline for their nerve endings.

Meals on Wheels vans parked on the street with awnings propped open—snack trucks for the homeless. Volunteers handed out cartons of rice, beans, and chicken. Other helpers came by later, distributing toothbrushes, toothpaste, and clean pairs of socks.

Napkins and Styrofoam containers hovered just above the ground on gusts of wind, darting in every direction. Plastic forks and spoons tinkled alongside. Pigeons swooped low to grab spilled food. Some walked toward the scraps, too fat to fly.

During the city strike in the summer of 2009, the park had been used as a garbage dump. Industrial-sized garbage bags had been heaped three stories high and had covered the baseball field next to the swings. For six weeks in June and July, the stench of garbage and pesticide had been unbearable.

Rats had had a field day. The pool couldn't be used. Stink was everywhere. Samantha had been apoplectic. And what had it all been for? The city had signed for what the workers had walked out for at the beginning. Sam swore that it was during the strike that Rob Ford had started to get traction. It began the rise of what had been described by a pollster as "the urban stupid."

Walking around the neighbourhood with Sam was a slow process, because so many people stopped to say hello. Teenagers would do the *whassup* thing. "Whassup, Sammie?" they'd say. Homeless men would hang back and look at her, slowly approaching to say thank you. Sometimes they called her Lady Merciful. She was tall, with long, wavy hair to her waist that looked sun-bleached but which Beck realized had to be highlighted. She wore bangles and chunky jewellery, jeans and boots, and she loped rather than walked. Her smile lit up her face, and she had laugh lines at the side of her eyes. Sam was cool—and she was smart. When reporters did a story on the neighbourhood, it would be Sam they interviewed, and more often than not the story would include a photo of her in her jeans and cowboy boots with a gritty streetscape in the background.

Beck looked up to see Sam walking toward her.

"*Buenos días, mi amiga*," she said, gathering Beck up into a hug. With their arms wrapped around each other and their long heads of hair hiding their faces, they looked like an Irish setter and a border collie cuddled together.

"*Lo siento*," said Sam. "I'm so sorry I'm late."

Sam had worked in Mexico for more than 10 years and loved everything Spanish—the language, the music, the art, and the men. She sprinkled her conversations with Spanish phrases. Instead of "Let's go," she'd say *vamos*. If she liked something, she'd say *Me gusta*. If she didn't like it, it would be *No me gusta*. She signed her emails NV for *nosotros venceremos*—we shall overcome. She had a daughter named Constanza, whom she called Stanzie, but she would say nothing in any language about the child's provenance—except that her father was honourably Spanish.

"You're not late," said Beck, "I'm just sitting here catching up on what's going on at City Hall."

"How long do you have?" Sam asked her.

Beck looked at her watch, "About 45 minutes, maybe 50. We've got the teacher thing."

"Right, yeah. Well, let's order something. You want soup? You want to have soup, and we can split one of those paninis?"

"Yeah, yeah, that's great," agreed Beck.

They ordered their food and asked for water. "Still or sparkling?" asked the waitress.

"Still," they both said at the same time and laughed.

"And can you bring me the bill when you bring the order, just so we don't have to wait at the end? One bill," Beck said to her, holding up her index finger.

"Come on, Beck, let me pay half," said Sam with a frown.

"Let me do it today, Sam," said Beck. "It's quicker. How you doing? How's Stanzie?"

"She's a smart one, *mi pequeño,* that's for sure—top of her class in math. She has a piano exam on Saturday, so it's practise, practise, practise. But she wouldn't have it any other way. She's pretty driven. How about Annie and that handsome young *hombre* of yours? How are they doing?"

"Christ, I think they're okay, Sam. They say they are. Mick is out there at Memorial, with Anthony not living a mile away. But he won't speak to him, Sam, not a word. He's refusing to speak to his father. He's over at my friend, Maggie's, once or twice a week, which is how I know he's doing all right, apart from what he tells me. But his father, forget it. And not only that, he's stopped using his father's last name. He's calling himself Michael Carnell now. Carnell is his middle name. He's dropped the Murray completely. He wants no association with his father's family whatsoever, he says. Nor will he go see his grandmother. He calls her 'complicit.' If he wasn't committed to doing naval architecture, which is not offered in many other places, he wouldn't be there, I don't think."

Sam covered Beck's hand with hers. "It takes time, *querida*. Mick's got to work through this in his own time."

"It's been almost two years, Sam. That seems long to me. I mean, I'm done with Anthony, but I also believe a young man needs his father, don't you think?"

"Yeah, it's long time, but it's also short," said Sam. "You know, it might take a long time … and it might never get resolved. Behaviour has consequences. What about Annie? How's she liking the University of Waterloo?"

"Annie's good, she says. I went out there for Thanksgiving weekend, and we had a great time. She misses being home. But I think she likes being away, too. It's good for her confidence, knowing she can do things for herself. I miss her a lot—both of them a lot—but I think they're better off not being around me right now."

"Why's that?" said Sam.

"Oh, I don't know," said Beck with a laugh. "Lots of reasons, I suppose."

"Does Annie speak to Anthony?" asked Sam.

"Well, she says they email every now and then—not exactly sure what that means."

"Hmm … those kids love their mama," said Sam, "that's for sure. Knowing you have the love of your children—that must mean something, hey?" As the waitress arrived with the soup, the water at the back of Beck's eyes started to move toward the front. She loved her children so much, and her heart ached at what had become of them.

Sam switched the subject then. "You know what they said last night? Do you want to hear what kick my board is on now?" Sam was jabbing her soup spoon in Beck's direction.

"Give it to me, Sam. What are they up to?" Beck said, grateful for the change in topic.

"They're saying we have to clarify our fucking brand—that we need to do a marketing scan to understand what our brand is. Then they all sat around agreeing with each other, nodding, 'Oh yes, a marketing scan, yes; that sounds smart.'

"I suggested that perhaps waging a war on poverty could be part of our so-called brand," Sam continued, her voice rising. "Lobbying for permanent housing for the homeless, drug programs, and after-school programs for young people could be part of the brand values. Help me here, Beck."

Beck opened her mouth to respond. The Centre had programs for children, youth, people in poverty, the homeless, and the unemployed, but what Sam wanted in the Centre was expensive, and she spent a lot of time fundraising. The board of directors was made up of people who were supposed to help her do that.

"And wait, here's the kicker," added Sam, still holding out her soup spoon. "They've gone to a multinational consulting firm, one that provides advice to *mining* companies, for Chrissakes, among other fine corporate citizens of the world, to get *them* to do an anti-poverty strategy planning session—for free. Are they joking? Are they idiots!"

Sam had her elbows on the table and raised her hands upward as if seeking an answer from the heavens. "And then they say, 'Oh Sam, we know you're *passionate*,'" she continued. "'You're *passionate* about the work. We get that—and we're *passionate* too. Or else we wouldn't be here on our own time. But we need a good anti-poverty brand that corporate sponsors will buy into.'"

"Well, my dear," offered Beck, "I've never found it a good sign when they start calling you passionate."

"I'm probably fucked," said Sam, reaching down to pick up her purse from the floor. As she leaned sideways, she winced and put a hand to her shoulder. "Ah, shit," she said.

"You okay?" asked Beck.

"My shoulder is killing me," said Sam. "I was cleaning like a mad woman on the weekend, and I think I strained it. I went to the doctor. She said I should relax and get my husband to give me a massage."

"Husband?"

"Yeah—I know, right?" said Sam, rolling her eyes.

"What did you say to her?" asked Beck.

"I told her that in my case I was going to have to pay for it."

Beck laughed. "Did you book a massage?"

"Yep. I'm going today at five o'clock," said Sam.

"That's good," said Beck. "But before I have to go, let me just say a couple of things about your board, Sammie. For one, if they want to talk about brand, they have to realize that *you* are actually a huge part of the brand. You are synonymous with the Centre. For two, you can't keep having your meetings at a corporate boardroom downtown. You've got to start having board meetings at the Centre. Let *them* run the gauntlet.

"Now, Sam, I'm sorry; I'd love to stay longer, but I have to go," said Beck, signing the bill and putting away her Visa card. "If it gets too horrible, maybe we can get together next week. Just let me know."

"Thanks, Beck. And don't worry about Annie and Mick. They'll be okay," said Sam, holding her arms open. Beck bent down to hug her before she turned around to leave. As Beck walked through the door, Sam sat back in her chair and ordered a cup of coffee.

Beck lit a cigarette as soon as she stepped out of the restaurant, and strode toward the office. Her meeting with the teachers' union was at three o'clock. It was now quarter after two. She slowed down. Once three o'clock hit, she'd be ramped up until the end of the day, so she might as well take her time getting back there. She felt slightly better after having had something to eat, but her head and her neck were still stiff, and her stomach was starting to rumble.

CHAPTER 13

Beck's father and Uncle Sceevie were sitting at the kitchen table with a bottle of Old Sam open between them. Uncle Sceevie had a couple of spoons in his hand. Her father was playing an old fiddle that Beck's mother said he'd had since well before they'd gotten married. They were giving "Lukey's Boat" a go, with Uncle Sceevie providing accompaniment on the spoons.

> Well, I says, "Lukey, the blinds are drawn,"
> A-ha, me boys!
> I says, "Lukey, the blinds are down;"
> My wife is dead, and she's in the ground.
> A-ha, me riddle-i-day
> A-ha, me riddle-i-day!

Beck's father put the fiddle down. "Poor old Lukey," he said with a sigh. "Those times are all over now. We've had the lot of her sold right out from underneath us, Sceevie, me son. The king *sold* Newfoundland to Canada!"

He balled his hands up into fists, and his eyes flashed, the blond lashes barely visible as he blinked. His red hair, the amount of red hair he had left, stuck out all over his head. His face became redder as he spoke, and his tall, muscular frame and broad shoulders were hunched over the chrome kitchen table, making the table and chairs look as if they had been made for a child.

Sceevie Batt wasn't Beck's actual uncle. They were of no relation at all. Her mother said his real name was Ernest, and she didn't know where he got the name Sceevie. It was a Saturday night, and 15-year-old Beck was sitting on the daybed in the kitchen with her mother, watching the two men.

"He *sold* Newfoundland—after we give him the lives of 2,000 men in two world wars," her father said, thumping the table and making it shake. "We were *sold!* And our country, our *heart* was gone," he said, choking back a sob.

Beck's father had voted against confederation with Canada. Beck's mother had voted for it.

"The men were big talkers," her mother said to Beck, keeping an eye on the kitchen table, where the men were now talking intently about something else. "Some of them raged against confederation with Canada. Some wanted union with the United States. I suppose you can't blame them with the losses suffered in the war. The confederation vote was in 1948 and the war had just ended in 1945, so it was still very fresh in people's minds. But people were very poor then, my love; you just can't imagine it. Life was hard, and the children grew up hardened because of it."

In the low light of the kitchen at Herring Neck, Beck's mother picked up Beck's hand to hold it in hers. "Youngsters came to school with their heads shaved," she continued, "and doused in kerosene, because they had head lice. Women died trying to have their babies. That was common too."

There was a scraping of chairs as Uncle Sceevie and Beck's father got up from the table. Sceevie had the bottle in his hand, and Beck's father was reaching into the cupboard for more glasses.

"Now, don't you leave those juice glasses down on the wharf, Baxter Carnell," her mother called out as they were walking out the door.

"Don't worry, girl, I'll bring 'em back safe and sound," he said, smiling at the two of them as he headed out the kitchen door. "Look after your mother now, my love," he said to Beck with a wink. Beck gave her father a little wave.

"They used to bury those little stillborn babies in wooden crates," her mother went on to say, as they were left alone in the kitchen. "That was common too. Honest to God, they looked like pieces of marble ... they were white and blue as marble. Someone would knit a blanket and someone else would crochet a doily for a pillow. They dressed up the baby just like it was a little doll."

Beck patted her mother's hand and laid it back down on the daybed.

"I'm going to put the kettle on for our tea, Mom, and I'll make some toast," she said.

"That'll be nice," said her mother. "There's a few of those lemon squares left too. You can take those out. They're in the red tin over the breadbox."

Beck cleared up the little bit of mess her father had made, put on a small tablecloth, laid out teacups and plates, and took the sugar bowl down from the cupboard and the Carnation milk out of the fridge. She left the milk in the tin. It was only the two of them.

"My mother was a midwife; I told you that before, I know," Beck's mother said, smiling at Beck as she laid the table.

"Come sit now, Mom," said Beck, waving her mother over. "The toast is just about done."

"Doesn't this look lovely," Beck's mother said, smoothing out the tablecloth as she sat down. "A nice cup of tea before going to bed." She picked up the tin of milk and made a tinkling sound on the side of the bone china cup as she stirred it in. "As a midwife, my mother could be called anytime of the day or night, whenever a baby needed to be born—winter or summer.

"One time she was gone from the house for almost a week," Beck's mother said. "I think it was February. One evening somebody came to the door to say she was needed, but she'd have to be picked up off the ice. That meant she had to walk out to the edge of the sea ice to wait for a fisherman to row his trap skiff up between the broken ice to take her through a narrow stream of open water across the bay.

"She stood there on the ice for a good long time, she told me, stiff as a poker, clutching the collar of her coat and her bag, rising up and down with the swell, afraid to budge because she didn't want to end up in the water. She lost her nerve that night, she said, and she never set foot in a boat again. They had to find a horse and sled to take her home the long way."

Beck put her teacup down in the saucer and gazed at her mother, who was tracing the pattern of the tablecloth's embroidery with her finger.

"You can say what you like about it now," her mother said, boldness creeping into her voice, "but a mother's vote for Confederation was a vote to feed her youngsters. Joey Smallwood, the father of Confederation, promised the baby bonus for every child. And the promise was kept. After Confederation, the cheque came in the mail every month."

Beck's mother gently brought her two hands together on the table, one on top of the other, as if to hold onto something. "The men couldn't cash that cheque," she said. "For some women, it was the only thing they ever saw with their own name in it, and that's why women all up and down this coast voted for Confederation with Canada. They wanted their children to be fed. Some of them, including your own grandmother, my mother, are buried with pictures of Joey Smallwood clasped in their hands."

Beck reached for her mother's hand and held it to her face so she could feel its coolness on her cheek.

CHAPTER 14

Ed Scrimshaw was incoming president of the Ontario Teachers' Union, having been elected the previous August. Prior to becoming involved with OTU, he'd spent 20 years teaching phys. ed. in eastern Ontario and still had a bit of the jock about him—the retired jock on a steady diet of fast food.

The Social Good team was wrapping up a videoconference with Ed, Joy Kobayashi, and two communications people from the union.

The idea of buying time on the ten o'clock news turned out to be the hit of the day. Beck wasn't sure they got the rest of the strategy, but the team could explain as they went.

Just as they were finishing up, Ed Scrimshaw turned to the camera. "So you're behind this, Beck? You think this will do the trick?" he said.

"Yep, totally on board, Ed. It's a good campaign; you have no worries on that front."

"It can't be cheap, though, Beck, with all that national air time?" Ed said. He looked to be enjoying himself.

"Nope. It's not cheap, Ed. But you gotta pay to play; you know that," said Beck.

"You got that right. You gotta pay to play in this game," he replied with a chuckle.

The screen went blank.

Beck turned to her team. "Just one more thing. See if we can buy 30 minutes of time on cable. If we can get that, then we'll shoot a documentary—a documentary that has real teachers, real parents, social workers, cops, everyone in the village who's helping to raise a child. We can make the 30-second spots from it and have content for YouTube. If the members love their TV spots, think of what they'll do with their own fucking show."

By the time Beck got back to her office, Tilda Grubbs was standing at the door with a sheaf of papers in her hand. Beck walked in and sat behind her desk.

"I've got these cheques for you to sign. Nick's already signed them," Tilda said as she sat down in the chair opposite Beck.

"Hey, Tilda," said Beck, taking the cheques from her and beginning to sign them. "How are you doing? How are things?"

Beck saw Tilda as a glass-half-empty kind of person. She seemed to find it hard to see the bright side of things, and it showed in the way she looked and dressed. Tilda had a smaller-than-average build for a woman. Her face had the texture and colour of onion skin, and her blonde hair was thin—baby fine, Tilda called it. She routinely complained of an array of vague illnesses, like restless leg syndrome and tinnitus—a ringing in the ear—and she laid a forceful claim of a virulent allergy to wheat. She'd been with the company for just over a year. At the time they'd hired her, Beck and Nick had felt she was "no nonsense," a suitable trait for a bookkeeper.

"How are *things*?" said Tilda, repeating Beck's question and raising her eyebrows. "*Things* seem to be okay for the moment, everything considered."

"And what are we considering?" asked Beck, with her arms folded on her desk.

"The billings are keeping up with how much we're spending," said Tilda.

"Well, that's got to be a good sign." Beck looked at Tilda and then the clock on the wall. It was 4:04 p.m.

"But we'll not be able to keep up with expenses," Tilda added, "if you keep spending so much. Here's your cellphone bill from last month. I've marked the questionable calls."

Beck laughed. "Questionable calls? I didn't realize I had any of those," she said as she took the August bill from Tilda's hand. Tilda had highlighted three calls to the same number. The number looked familiar, but Beck couldn't place it at first. Then it clicked. It was Henry's. *Holy shit.* One call was for two hours. She had been in Vancouver at a conference; she remembered opening a bottle of wine and calling him, but two hours? That was a lot. *I guess I finished the bottle,* Beck thought.

"I dunno, Tilda. Maybe I was having a conference call, or maybe I didn't hang up the phone when I thought I did," said Beck.

"Ten o'clock at night?" Tilda asked in disbelief.

Tilda stared at Beck. Beck stared at Tilda.

"Anything else, Tilda?" Beck asked as she looked up at the doorway. "Todd is here, and I need to meet with him before I leave for the day."

"That's all for now," said Tilda, grabbing her stuff and walking quickly from the office.

"Hey, Tilda," Beck called out. Tilda turned around, and Beck held up the pile of cheques. "Don't forget these," she said.

Tilda took the cheques out of Beck's hand and left without a word.

What the fuck? thought Beck as she waved in Todd. As she'd predicted, he'd arrived at her doorway at 4:15 on the dot.

To Beck, Todd looked like someone with military training. His movements were precise, and his shirt looked like it had just been ironed. The raw-silk maroon tie was narrow and tied in a perfect Windsor knot. And the shoes, black loafers, were clean and polished.

She got up from behind her desk, walked over to the couch, and sat down, tucking her legs up underneath her. Todd sat in an armchair.

"You missed lots of the action with the teacher thing today," Beck said, weariness creeping into her voice.

"Lots of work, hey? Now I hear you're planning to shoot a 30-minute doc," he said and laughed.

"*If* we can buy the time," replied Beck. "I've got my fingers crossed that we can. And, you know, we might as well be hung for a sheep as a lamb. You've been on the road today?" she asked him.

"I met with Sylvia Bumley, the vice president of development over at the National Breast Cancer Society," said Todd, "the NBCS. They're tendering their whole program—communications *and* fundraising."

"The whole thing? That's a lot. Why are they doing that?"

"New leadership," said Todd. "You remember T. J. Avery? He used to be at the Liver, Heart, and Lung Foundation?"

"Yep, I do indeed remember T. J. Avery."

"Well, he's the new CEO of NBCS."

"T. J. Avery? Head of breast cancer?" said Beck, raising her eyebrows. "That *is* a surprise. I didn't think his interest in the breast extended to the medical."

T. J. Avery was known as a bit of a player in the sector and had a reputation as a turnaround guy. As far as Beck understood, he never lasted much more than two years in any posting. He was touted as a "he came, he saw, he conquered" kind of guy. But Beck informed Todd she had also heard he was a "he came, he saw, and he fucked things up" sort of person.

Todd laughed. "The Board brought him in to shake things up. It's changing fast over there. Revenue is down. Four of the founding board have been replaced. Two pharma guys, a prof from U of T, and this woman who's a patient advocate or something from out west have come on in their place. The first change they made was bringing T. J. in. Now he wants to make his mark—changing agencies is only one thing."

"How much is the contract worth, would you say?" Beck asked.

"It could be as big, or bigger, than the teachers," said Todd. "It's huge."

"How many bids are they looking for?" asked Beck.

"They're taking all comers. It could be as many as 20," said Todd.

"How many could actually, physically, do the whole thing?"

"Fundraising and communications? With non-profit experience? Probably four, maybe five," he replied.

"So in reality," she said, "we are only competing against four or five firms?"

"That's how I see it," said Todd.

"And none of the usual suspects have dedicated media-relations departments?" asked Beck.

"That's right."

"Christ, I just can't stand all that pink shit," said Beck. "Would we have to do the pink shit?"

"That would be up to you, I guess," Todd said, shrugging his shoulders, "but breast cancer and pink, you know, it's kind of associated now."

"How long do we have before we submit?" she asked.

"Four weeks."

"All right," said Beck, nodding her head. "Most of the teachers' campaign will be up and running by then. Good one on you, Todd."

"How are *you* doing, Beck? How are the kids?" Todd asked, softening his voice and crossing his legs.

"They're pretty good, as far as I can tell, Todd," said Beck with a tight smile. "I'm okay, you know … keeping busy. Thanks for asking. How are things with you? How's Daniel?"

"He's good," said Todd. "He's been on tour with the opera company for the past four weeks, but he came back on Monday night. We're going away for the weekend, a little retreat in Niagara on the Lake."

Beck's phone chimed and she picked it up. "Speaking of the kids," she said.

"You go ahead and take that. We're finished up here, I think," said Todd. "Have a good weekend."

The text was from Mick.

> *Hey Mom, how are things in Toronto? i'm on my way to aunt maggie's for dinner and thought i'd say hi … HI!!!! … hope your day went well. Love ya.*

She texted back.

> *Hi, Micky. Great to get your text. My day was good, very busy. I had lunch with my friend Sam. This whole teacher strike thing is going to be a big deal. I think I'm going to shoot a video. How's the weather out there? How did that history paper go? Did you get it in? Love you. Miss you like crazy!!*

Her phone dinged again.

> *Paper is in; weather is foggy! Like always ☺ That's okay, gotta go. Shooting a video sounds like fun. Talk later XO*

Beck checked the time. It was five o'clock. She texted her daughter, Annie.

Hey, Annie. Happy Friday afternoon! Do you have any plans this evening? Thinking of you. Miss you. Love you!!!!!!! Let's chat on the weekend.

Annie dinged back.

Sure thing, Mom!!! Just heading out for dinner with Priya and Mel. We're going to have burritos and then to see the movie Maleficent. *Call me on Sunday afternoon xoxoxoxoxoxo*

Shoving her laptop in her bag and grabbing her coat, Beck got ready to leave the office. She stopped by to see Nick, Bain, Asmi, and Yvonne to ask if they needed her. They didn't. She could have kissed them for saying so.

She pulled open the office door and headed for the elevator to ask her cranky sailor if he'd give her a ride to the ground floor for the last time that day.

CHAPTER 15

When Beck started high school, she rode the yellow school bus on the 15 miles of paved road between Herring Neck and the bigger town of Twillingate. Every mile or so, Billy Dinney, the bus driver, swung the 72-seater onto the gravel shoulder to pick up the students that dotted the sides of the road looking like hooded seals on an ice pan. They clutched brown lunch bags in their freezing hands and tucked their schoolbooks into the crooks of their elbows as they'd seen high-school students do on American TV shows. As the bus door jerked open, they stomped up the steps and barked:

"Hiya, Billy."

"Hey, Bill."

"How are ya, Billy?"

Their hair pointed in every direction of the compass. The hats and mitts their mothers had knitted to shield them against the weather were stuffed deep into their pockets. Their white knuckles strained against red raw skin, dried out by the biting wind.

"Where's your hat to?" Billy asked as they tromped aboard the bus.

"I wouldn't be caught dead wearing that scratchy old thing Mom made," they'd say, laughing and rolling their eyes.

"Well, now, you won't have to worry 'bout your brains bustin' out of your skull, that's for damn sure," Billy would say.

On Beck's first day of high school, her cousin Jimmy Duggan stood in the school parking lot waiting for Beck to step off the bus. He was about to christen her with a nickname, something she'd been dying for as long as she could remember.

"Hiya, Becks! How's the Cove?" he said, hopping from one foot to the other, cupping his hand over his mouth and giggling as soon as he saw her, wanting everyone to know she wasn't from town.

Beck's Cove was one cove of several smaller coves that made up Herring Neck, a long narrow peninsula that was part of the Twillingate Isles. These formed an archipelago that lay in Notre Dame Bay, 300 miles northeast of St. John's, Newfoundland. It was 50 miles from Gander International Airport. Built as a transatlantic fuelling stop, Gander Airport was once the largest airport in the world. In modern times it is better known for receiving the more than 6,000 passengers and crews from 38 aircraft grounded by the terrorist attacks on September 11, 2001.

About 600 people lived in Herring Neck, 200 of them in Beck's Cove. It amounted to five or six families who'd fished in the cove for years. Twillingate was the closest town to Beck's Cove, had the biggest harbour, and was the location of the high school for all of Twillingate Isles. Twillingate had a population of 1,500. Jimmy had grown up there and felt he possessed a degree of sophistication his cousin did not.

The distinction was important to Jimmy, because while the historical class system in Newfoundland cleaved along the merchant/fisher fault line, the lingua franca of more contemporary socio-cultural divisions on the island was a townie/bayman paradigm, wherein the degree of superiority was in direct relation to how close you lived to town.

At its core, the system was a simple one. To townies, everyone outside the St. John's was a bayman and vice versa. But the townie/bayman framework became, as frameworks often do, somewhat more nuanced and could reflect a person's behaviour as well as geographic proximity. You could live in a bay, a cove, a neck, a bight, or an arm, and your upstanding behaviour might result in you being referred to as "from around the bay." No harm, no foul. "Have you met my cousin? He's from around the bay and teaches school."

In the middle of the spectrum, if you weren't as gracious as you could be, you might be called a *bayman, bay wop,* or just *wop* for short. It didn't matter where you lived. "Did you seeing him over there pickin' his nose? A fuckin' wop if I ever saw one."

At the complete other end of the spectrum, if you behaved as if you weren't around people that often, you might be called a *savage.* "That crowd over there on Blackhead, the youngsters has the same fathers as grandfathers, for Chrissakes. Sure, they're nothin' but a bunch of savages."

For Jimmy, in that moment of time, defining the geographic distance between him and his cousin was of primary concern. Every time he saw her he called her Becks, just so everyone would know she was from Beck's Cove and took the yellow bus to school. He and his friends looked tidy when they walked to the high school with their hair combed, not like the early rescues from the Shackleton expedition that piled off the yellow school bus.

"Hiya, Becks, the bus is here," he'd call out if he saw her in the hallway. "You better run catch it!"

"What home room are you in, Becks?" he'd yell. "Do they let you out early to get the bus?"

"Did you find anyone to take you to the dance, Becks," Jimmy would taunt, "or do you have to get the bus home early?"

"Don't mind him," said her best friend, Maggie Blackwood, whose father was a captain in the Coast Guard. "Jimmy's stunned."

"Maggie, I don't mind stupid Jimmy. He's doing me a favour," replied Beck.

Beck had come to her parents long after her mother thought she could have another child. Her brothers, Mikey and Alf, were 18 and 20 years old by the time she was born—old enough to be her father, they'd tease.

"We named you Gloria because you were my miracle baby," her mother told her. "You were glorious."

But Beck didn't like the name. Even Poppy, who Beck followed around like a puppy as soon as she could walk, and who used to call her Glory, couldn't change her mind about her name. Beck considered it old-fashioned and hard to pronounce.

So when Jimmy started to call her Becks, she was happy. By the time she graduated high school, even her teachers were calling her Becks. When she went to university, she dropped the *s* and became Beck. She was Beck Carnell from Notre Dame Bay, whose father was a fisherman and whose mother had been a teacher before she got married. And that was that.

CHAPTER 16

The phone in Beck's office was ringing. With her eyes focused on the spreadsheet in front of her, Beck reached to activate the speakerphone. "Beck Carnell," she announced.

"Beck?"

"Yup, it's Beck."

"Beck, it's Sam. Can I talk to you now—for a minute—please?"

"Sam!" Beck exclaimed, swinging away from the computer screen to pick up the handset on the phone. "Sam, what's up—what's goin' on? Are you okay? Did you get fired?"

"No, Beck, that's not it—not yet anyway. Beck, I need to talk to you. Can you come out? I'm in the parking lot across the street. Can you come down?"

"Of course, Sammy; I'm coming now. You're in the Mazda, the red Mazda?"

"Yes, parked in the third row, toward Spadina," said Sam.

"Okay, hang on. I'm coming down." Beck hung up the phone and grabbed her cell and her bag. She texted Asmi to tell her she had to go out, stopped by the kitchen and stuffed two bottles of water, a can of juice, and a handful of Kleenex into her bag.

As she strode out the front door, she could see Sam's car. Sam was sitting in the driver's seat with her hands folded over the steering wheel, head down. "Fuck," breathed Beck as she started to cross the street.

Sam didn't see Beck coming. She jumped when Beck tapped on the passenger side window. Then she unlocked the door and Beck got in. Sam's eyes were red, her face pale. She looked to be in shock.

"It's okay, Sam. I'm here, sweetie," said Beck, trying to gauge her friend's state of mind. "Let's just rest here a minute, and then you can tell me what's going on. I brought you something to drink. You want water?"

Beck cracked open a bottle of water and handed it to Sam. Sam took a few gulps and handed it back to Beck. "It's bad, Beck. It's not good. It's bad. I just came from the doctor."

"The doctor? What doctor?" asked Beck.

"You know, the family doctor, the one I saw about my sore shoulder? She called this morning. She wanted to give me the results of the ultrasound they took last week. I mean, *she* didn't call. The secretary called to say the doctor wanted to go over the results of my tests with me. She asked me if I could come in today. I said I didn't know, I was jammed at work. You know, I've got the board meeting tonight and all that shit. She said it would be a good idea to come in. I didn't want to go, but Carla and Letty told me I was being stupid, that if your doctor wants you to go in, you're supposed to go in. I said, 'Okay, okay, I'll go.'"

Beck and Sam were turned in their seats, facing each other.

"So I go to the office, over at Danforth and Greenwood," said Sam. "There's that new medical centre. I drove over, and the secretary brought me into the doctor's office. The doctor was sitting there, and she looked upset ... like *really* upset ... like she was going to cry or something. I asked her what was wrong.

"She put a box of Kleenex on the table in front of me," Sam continued, "and said, 'I don't know how to tell you this ...' I said, 'Tell me what?' She said, 'Samantha, we've received the results of the ultrasound that was taken last week ... and I'm afraid the news isn't good. It shows you have a mass on your pancreas.'"

"She said you have a mass on your pancreas?" said Beck in disbelief.

"Yes, a mass on my pancreas," said Sam, "*and* on my liver. She said it looked like cancer."

"Cancer?"

"You know my mother had cancer," said Sam. "So did my aunt—and my grandmother. We have a lot in the family."

"Well, a lot of people do," said Beck. "A lot of people have a lot of cancer in their family."

"After the appointment, I drove home," continued Sam as if she had to force herself to speak, "but I couldn't get out of the car to go into the house. I just drove back down here and parked. Then I called you … I didn't know who else to call, Beck, and I thought, *Who do you call when you're in a scrape? Call Carnell; she'll have an angle.* I figured you'd be here."

"I'm glad you called, Sam, but let's just hold on a minute here. Just hold it," said Beck, looking intently at Sam. "This whole diagnosis is based on one ultrasound? Pancreatic and liver cancer from one ultrasound? I think that's a bit of a leap, don't you? I mean, how much can they tell from that? You are going to have a lot more tests before they can say something like that, don't you think?"

"She said I needed a CT scan," said Sam.

Beck took hold of Sam's hands. "I know this is serious, Sam, very serious. I'm not saying it's not, but let's just think about this here a minute … let's figure out exactly what we're dealing with here."

Sam took a deep breath and bowed her head. "Christ, Beck. What am I doing to do?"

"The first thing we need to do is get you home," Beck said, fumbling with the water bottle and her bag. "Here, let's switch seats. I'll drive. And I'll come in the house with you if you want."

"Thanks, Beck; that would be okay, I think."

"Where is your place again?" Beck had never been to Sam's house.

"It's 44 Prescott—two blocks south of St. Clair, off Christie. It's one-way going west."

"Is Maria Luisa home?" Maria Luisa had lived with Sam for years, ever since Beck had known her. She was a housekeeper and nanny but could also have been a relative, maybe on Constanza's father's side. Beck had never asked. She'd never met her.

"She's there."

"She's going to need to know, right?" said Beck.

"Yeah, I know. I'm so sorry about all of this, Beck. Thanks for coming. Thanks for driving me." Sam leaned back in the seat and closed her eyes.

Maria Luisa saw Sam coming up the walk with Beck. Sam's hair, brown and blonde, long and wavy, blew every which way in the cold wind.

Beck's hair, brilliant red and too heavy for the wind, floated behind her like a headdress. Beck had her arm wrapped around Sam. Maria Luisa came to the door.

"*Qué pasa*, Sammy, *qué pasa, querida?* What's wrong?" Maria Luisa looked at Beck. "I know you are Beck. *Entra en, por favor.* Please come in. What's wrong, Sam?" asked Maria Luisa, looking alarmed.

"Come in, Beck, please do," said Sam, motioning to Beck and putting her hand on Maria's shoulder. "Maria, can you make some tea for all of us together, please? I've just got to freshen up a bit." Sam turned to go up the stairs.

Even on this grey day, Sam's house looked bright. There was a huge Mexican painting of a sun hanging over the fireplace. Pots of flowers and herbs stood in little groups all over the kitchen. The living room had a comfortable couch, chairs, and a red carpet with yellow diamond shapes in the middle of the room. Chunky pottery mugs stood on the counter. Stanzie's piano was in the dining room, sheet music spread across the top.

"Your home is beautiful," said Beck, "so bright and cheerful. And it's lovely to meet you. I've heard so much about you."

"Me too," said Maria Luisa. "Please come in. Something is wrong with Sam? She went to the doctor today?"

Beck nodded.

Sam came down the stairs. She had changed her clothes and was wearing an oversize shirt and a pair of leggings. They sat around the kitchen table. Sam told Maria Luisa about the appointment, and they all agreed that more testing was needed before they thought the worst.

"Do you want me to call the office for you, Sam? Tell them you'll be missing the board meeting tonight?" Beck asked.

"Could you, Beck? You can speak to Carla or Letty," said Sam.

Beck walked toward the back of the house to make the call. She knew Sam's staff from working with them and from what Sam had told her. Beck hoped they'd be discreet. As she was returning to the living room, she saw Maria Luisa and Sam sitting together on the couch.

"I'm going to head back downtown, unless you guys need me for anything else right now," Beck said as she came back into the room.

Sam held out her hand to Beck. "So many thanks to you for coming to help me, Beck. It means a lot."

"Call or email me later if you need anything. I'll call you in the morning if I don't hear from you. I told Carla that you'd call tomorrow, and I asked her to call your board president and tell him you're dealing with a personal emergency. I told her to keep it under wraps, but the news is probably halfway across town by now. I'm going to call a cab."

She hugged Sam and Maria Luisa and then went out to the front porch. She called a cab, took out her red-and-gold pack of duMaurier, pushed it open, and pulled out a cigarette. She lit it and had a long drag, pinched the corner of her eyes to relieve the tension in her forehead, and took another puff. Looking up at the sky, she could see no blue, only grey clouds strafed with silver. She shivered and looked down at her arms. She hadn't put on her coat before leaving the office.

PART
TWO

They sat together in the park
As the evening sky grew dark
She looked at him, and he felt a spark tingle to his bones.

—"Simple Twist of Fate"
Words and music by Bob Dylan

CHAPTER 1

Twenty-two-year-old Anthony Murray sat behind a large wooden desk that was covered in books and newsprint in the office of the student newspaper at Memorial University in St. John's. His thick, dark hair almost touched his shoulders, and he was wearing a red flannel shirt and jeans. He stared at a flickering green screen and was biting his nails when Beck walked into the office.

"Can anyone join the paper?" she asked.

"Ah, uh ..."

"I'm Beck Carnell, second year poli-sci," Beck said, "and I've been thinking that I'd like to volunteer. Can anyone join the paper?"

Beck's mother had suggested she consider teaching as a profession. Her father had said she should be a lawyer, since she argued about everything. But she said she wanted to be a writer, a journalist, maybe, and that the student newspaper could teach her a few of the ropes.

"Can anyone join the paper?" Beck repeated, her voice a bit louder this time. Her blue jeans were tucked into her tan leather boots, and she wore a thick cable-knit sweater that looked homemade. A couple of bracelets jangled on her left wrist, and she had a large brown leather bag slung over her shoulder. It looked heavy; a notebook stuck out of the top.

"Oh, ah—yeah, sure. What are you interested in?" Anthony said as he sat up straighter in his chair.

"Writing, longer pieces—feature writing, I think," she said. "Do you have a spot for that?"

"Have you ever done any writing?" he asked.

"Essays and stuff," she said. "I did well in English at school. I do a lot of reading; I'm a bit of a news junkie, I guess you could say. I'm interested in politics."

"What do you want to write about?" Anthony asked.

"Could be a number of things, couldn't it—depends on what's needed by the paper," she said, pulling over a heavy wooden chair and sitting down. "Stuff going on at the university, the fisheries, education funding, music … Are you an editor?"

"I'm one of the editors," he said, looking down at his fingernails and sliding his hands under the desk. "Most people start with shorter stories and then work up to features. There's only so much room in the paper, and people with more experience get the chance to work on the longer pieces. It all depends on how fast you can write and how good you are. Everybody's pieces get edited."

"What's your name?" Beck asked.

"Uh, oh—sorry," he said, extending his hand. "My name is Anthony. Anthony Murray, third-year history, getting ready for law school the year after next."

"Is there any kind of orientation?" she asked. "You know, where you go over stuff with new volunteers?"

"Yep. Every Monday night at seven o'clock, here in the office," he answered.

"I could bring some story ideas on Monday night. Will you be here?"

"Yeah, most likely," he said. "I'll have to check, but it's pretty likely I'll be here. I'm here a lot in the evening."

"Okay, we'll see you then," she said as she stood up. "Thanks for your help, Anthony."

Anthony stood up when Beck did. As she walked through the door, she turned her head and gave him a wave. He smiled and gave a little wave back.

After a couple of months of getting to know people, Beck plunged into work at the student newspaper. She learned the inverted-pyramid format for writing a news story, in which you put your most important facts up top and worked down from there. She started to listen to what people were actually saying to her, take good notes and to write fast. And she learned that when someone asked you for 500 words, you gave them 500 words—not 750 words or 250 words. She also discovered that if you were going to survive in the student newspaper office, references to obscure music, quick-witted responses to the mostly ironic repartee that stood in for conversation, and a willingness to cast the occasional look of disdain were necessary communications skills. All of these—happily, in her mind—came to her naturally.

She did five or six stories about what was happening on the student council, a women's conference being held at the university, and the smaller stories Anthony told her to write. When she wasn't in class, she hung around the newspaper offices jousting with other would-be writers and journalists. In that moment, they were all young, eager, and full of enough shit to think that what they did mattered. For Beck there was no more question of what she wanted to do with her life. She'd found her calling and started work on her first feature.

"She's Leaving Home" told the story of three young women from northern Newfoundland who had never been away from home before they came to Memorial. They made Beck swear she wouldn't tell anyone their real names. Anthony ran the story. Lots of first-years told Beck they liked it. There was even talk of setting up some kind of support group.

She managed to grab an interview with the world-renowned mentalist, The Amazing Kreskin, when he appeared at the St. John's Arts and Culture Centre and got a picture of the two of them together to send to her mother. Anthony ran that, too.

Her story about a campus security guard who was accused of raping a student caused a stir. During the trial it came out they had both gone to the same high school in St. John's. "If she put out then, why would she stop putting out now?" was the security guard's defence. Anthony ran that quote from the guard's testimony across the centre spread as a headline.

Soon, Beck was spending as much time at the student newspaper offices as she did in her classes. In her mind, working on the paper had become the point of going to school. One Saturday morning, Anthony called her up. "I feel like going for a drive," he said. "Do you want to go out and see your mother today?"

"What are you—cracked?" she exclaimed. "You want to drive four hours to Twillingate today?"

"Sure, why not?" he replied. "We can stop for lunch in Clarenville if you're hungry. And we can drive home after supper. We'll be home by eleven o'clock."

"Okay, it sounds a bit crazy," Beck said, "but let me call Mom. I can be ready in half an hour, and I'll make a sandwich for lunch. Clarenville will be crawling with people today."

She put down the phone and looked across the table at Maggie and Jimmy. They were gaping at her.

Beck, her friend Maggie Blackwood, and her cousin Jimmy Duggan had all come to Memorial together and stayed in residence the first year, not an experience any of them had wanted to repeat. For second year, they rented a house together on Elizabeth Avenue, within walking distance of campus. They were like a little dysfunctional family, Maggie said, but one that always had homemade bread and jam and a clean bathroom where they could wash up in the morning.

"You're going to get caught on a jig line if you keep your mouth open like that," Beck said, laughing at Jimmy.

"You're going to Twillingate today!" he exclaimed. "Can I come?"

"No, Jimmy, you can't come. We're only going for a drive there and back—that's all."

"How do you know he can drive?" asked Maggie.

"Well, he's got a car now, doesn't he?" replied Beck. "That must count for something."

* * *

Before long, Anthony was spending so much time at Beck's place that Maggie and Jimmy wanted to start charging him rent. But he occasionally brought dinner over, and he took them to the supermarket a couple of times a month so they could buy detergent, flour, paper towels, toilet paper—all the heavy or bulky stuff that was such a pain to cart home when you didn't have a car, so he made himself useful in that way.

The Murrays were an old Newfoundland fish-merchant family. Anthony's grandfather, Anthony Murray Sr., was a minister of finance in Joey Smallwood's government.

Beck had met Anthony's parents exactly one time. And it was Chester Murray, Anthony senior's son and a St. John's lawyer, who greeted Anthony and Beck at the door of their house on Circular Road, a tree-lined street full of large old homes occupied by merchants and the politically powerful.

"Hello, Beck! Come in. Come in. Good to see you," he said, with the same practiced joviality that Beck thought he probably used with his legal clients. He shook Beck's hand. "I can see why we're not seeing much of Anthony these days. That's quite the red hair you've got there, Beck—and maybe a fiery temper to match." Turning to Anthony, he admonished, "You better watch out, my son!"

Mr. Murray had a full head of dark hair and looked to be in his 40s, much younger than Beck's parents. He wore tan pants, a white striped shirt, and loafers. He his complexion was darker than Anthony's, and his eyes were brown. He was shorter and bit stockier than Anthony, but he looked very fit.

"Well, now. Is this the girl Anthony has been talking so much about?" Anthony's mother, Florence, asked as she walked into the hallway, pulling at the light blue sweater she had draped over her thin shoulders. Her light brown shoulder-length hair was cut in a bob and curled out slightly. Her face was long and thin, and her light blue eyes were partly hidden behind gold-rimmed glasses.

She pronounced each word distinctly and stretched out her son's name, An-THO-nee, taking great care to pronounce the *th*. She wore a short-sleeved pink shirtdress and had a gold watch on her left arm. Her wedding rings were prominent on her thin fingers. Anthony said she played tennis a couple of times a week and went sailing at the yacht club in the summer.

"Hi, Mrs. Murray. I'm Beck Carnell," Beck said, holding out her hand. "It's great to finally meet you."

"Hello, Beck," she said as she turned away to give her son a kiss on the cheek. "Nice to have you home for a change, An-THO-nee. Why don't we go into the living room for a drink before supper?"

Beck put her unshaken hand back by her side, took off her shoes, and followed Anthony into the large living room. A baby grand piano was nestled in the far corner. The couches and chairs were various shades of blue. Beck sat in a big armchair that was white with thin navy stripes. A bookcase, lining one wall, was filled with books; some of them, Beck could see, were very old and probably rare. Prowse's *History of Newfoundland* was there on a little side table of its own. She longed to pick it up and leaf through it.

"Now, what can I get you, Beck?" Anthony's father asked, holding ice tongs in one hand and a highball glass in the other.

"I'll have juice or water, something like that."

"Are you sure, dear?" asked Mrs. Murray. "We usually have a glass of wine before dinner."

"No, no. Water or juice is fine—thanks though," she said.

Anthony looked over at her. What was the big deal? she thought as she looked back at him. Not wanting to drink wine, which she didn't like the taste of anyway, on an empty stomach? She was already starting to feel uncomfortable. It was a feeling she wasn't used to. Was she acting like a bayman? Did her hair, which she hadn't tied back, look, as her mother would say, "like a birch broom in the fits"? Her leather bag seemed a lot more scratched up sitting in this room than it did in her living room at home. The knitted cotton vest she wore with her jeans looked a bit grubby in this light, her socks ratty against the silky blue carpet.

Mrs. Murray looked at her as if she were a codfish flapping around on the carpet. *I wonder if Florence Murray's got her own cat-o'-nine tails in the cupboard,* thought Beck grimly.

"So you're from Twillingate, Beck," Mrs. Murray said, opening and closing her mouth but keeping her head perfectly still.

"Yes, close to Twillingate. My family is from Beck's Cove. It's on Herring Neck, about 15 miles from Twillingate."

"So you're Beck from Beck's Cove," Mr. Murray said with a laugh. "That's something. They should make you the mayor!"

"My mother had a cousin out that way at one time," said Mrs. Murray. "Oldford was her married name. She was born in Twillingate. Of course, her father was a Peyton."

Anthony and his parents had two drinks in the living room before supper. When they went to the kitchen to eat, Mrs. Murray pulled out of the oven a dish of canned baked beans to which she'd added a chopped raw onion. They had that with pork chops baked in canned mushroom soup.

"Did your mother go all out on my account?" Beck asked Anthony when he was driving her home. She watched his face to see if there was a flicker of acknowledgement, a conspiratorial wink that said the evening had not gone well.

Anthony Murray had spent plenty of time in the kitchen in Herring Neck while Beck's mother brought him tea, homemade bread, jam tarts, and little cups of soup to taste. She'd fed him cod tongue, lobster, and fresh fish, and he'd sat there eating it all, like some kind of puss gut, thought Beck.

"You don't have to be like that," said Anthony, shaking his head as he pulled the car over in front of Beck's house to drop her off. "Sometimes we have roast chicken. Mom likes to keep it simple."

"Well, perhaps you should have yourself checked for scurvy, then," Beck said as she got out of the car and strode into her house.

CHAPTER 2

It was five-thirty, the day was done, the teachers' strategy was locked up, and a new client had appeared on the horizon. Beck's cranky elevator sailor deposited her on the ground floor with his usual creak and complaint. She'd been dreaming of going back to bed all day. Now, lying down and closing her eyes was the last thing she wanted to do. Her mind was racing, her body keyed up—adrenalin on bust. Pink, orange, and yellow clouds were forming in the western sky. The angle of the setting sun made the sandstone buildings twinkle. She dug out her sunglasses. The phone chimed again. It was Henry.

> *Meet you at the Blue Door? I'm heading over there now. Martin and Nell are going.*

It didn't take her long to text back.

> *Will head over now. Do we have any more pot? Did you buy wine?*

Her phone dinged again almost immediately.

> *Great. Yes. Yes.*

Letting out a deep breath, Beck relaxed her shoulders. She shifted her leather bag to the other shoulder, re-arranged her upper body, and walked with a steady pace to the Blue Door five blocks away.

The bar's name—suggested only by the flashing neon Labatt's Blue sign on which only the word *Blue* was lit up—was the only indication it was a drinking establishment at all. Plus the door itself, of course, was blue.

Yvonne was the one who had found it first—more urban juke joint than neighbourhood pub, she'd said, and she'd booked it for the media launch of a social justice client's new website. The original mahogany sheen of the bar, a long narrow servery that ran practically the length of the place, had long ago been scuffed off, leaving only a few telltale shiny spots that hinted at its once-possible greater glory. The padding on the bar stools was mostly worn away, but in their favour, the stools had backs to lean against that could feel kind of comfortable after a couple of glasses of wine. About a dozen round tables showed off their glass-sized stains, after-images of drinks long past. Dark brown wooden chairs with curved backs circled the tables like ponies around a hay bale.

At Yvonne's media launch, Beck had warmly shaken hands with the client's supporters, looked people in the eye, and marvelled at their client's accomplishments. Afterward, she had stayed for a drink and to watch cable news on one of the two TV screens mounted on the wall behind the bar. After her first half bottle, she'd looked down the bar and noticed a guy at the far end—*a real guy*, she'd thought when she saw him, *a guy who looks like he could actually drive a nail, hoist a sail, or change the oil in his car.* He wore a jean jacket that fit him, jeans, and a pair of work boots. His blond hair, longer than his collar, swooped off his face. After one more drink, she looked down the bar again. The guy was sitting in the stool beside her.

"Hiya," she'd said, holding out her hand, "I'm Beck Carnell."

"Hey, Beck Carnell. I'm Henry … Henry Hill," he had replied, taking her hand and smiling. "How are you doing?"

"Do you really want to know?" she'd said.

"Of course," he'd replied. "That's why I asked."

"Here comes the Queen!" Nell called out as soon as Beck walked through the front door of the pub; she raised a shaky hand in greeting and started to stand up. Nell was a regular at the Blue Door. Henry was a regular too—he went there every day. No one in Beck's world knew she had also become a regular at the Blue Door, although she wasn't sure about Nick. Not much got past Nick.

"Don't get up, Nell; I'll come to you," Beck said, walking over and giving her a hug. She threw her bag on an empty chair beside Nell. "Is Henry here?"

"Not yet, Beck. Soon, though," said Nell.

"I have to go to the bathroom," Beck said as she patted Nell's shoulder. Nell watched Beck walk away with her red hair bouncing. Nell's own hair was grey with a few strands of black. She kept it tied back with an elastic band. Her face was slightly bloated, a side effect of her medication. Her eyes were hazel, and she carried a cane in case of dizzy spells.

It hadn't always been so. Nell used to be the head of the computer department in a bank when computers programmers used punch cards, which had to be run through a mainframe computer. Sometimes they'd have to line up to wait for mainframe time. She'd managed the staff, talked to the programmers about coding, and kept them patient and organized.

She says now that she could feel herself losing the strength she needed to resist the anxiety she'd felt with varying degrees of intensity all her life—the panic when she woke up to go to school, and her stomach balled up in knots when she was about to leave school to go home. With any movement from one thing to another, every transition, she had to convince herself she would be okay. One day, her coaxing didn't work anymore. Her argument with herself was as articulate and as rational as ever, but the anxiety wouldn't listen. It couldn't be beaten back. The levy broke. Fear washed over her, wave over wave, causing her to choke on her words and paralyzing her.

Three days after she hadn't showed up at work with no phone call, a couple of programmers went to her door looking for her. They found her in her bed, unable to speak, and they called an ambulance.

Nell never worked again after that and went on long-term disability, with the bank's insurance company paying two thirds of her salary and medical bills. She'd recently told Beck she was about to turn 65 and would move from insurance payments to Canada Pension. She said her social worker told her it wouldn't make much difference, but Nell said she was worried all the same.

Beck had to slow down as she approached the hallway to the ladies' room. Cases of empty beer bottles were piled along one wall. The stack got bigger as the week wore on. By Friday, a boozy tapestry of blue Labatt, red and white Molson, yellow Corona, and bright-red Sleemans ran the whole length of the hallway. It was stacked higher than Beck's head, and she had to turn her body slightly to get through.

When she got to the bathroom, Beck stuck her face up close to the mirror and grimaced. Her eyes were red and bloodshot. She backed away, pulled some Visine out of her pocket, turned her head to the ceiling, and plopped two or three drops in each eye. Blinking quickly, she grabbed a tissue to mop up the overflow coming down her cheeks. So refreshing.

She swiped her lips with reddish-brown lipstick, took out the clip she had put in her hair that morning, and ran her fingers through her hair to rearrange it. The bathroom was warm. The sink was clean. The lights were low. If only they had better wine, it would be perfect here. She walked back out to the table and saw Nell's friend Martin come in the door.

Nell was taking a sip of her coffee and called out, "Hi, Martin!" as she raised her cup to greet him.

"Don't get up, Nell. I'm coming right over," said Martin. Since Martin was from London, England, it sounded like "I'm coming right o-vah."

"You ready for a little music trivia quiz tonight, Nell?" he asked, rubbing his hands together and bending down to give her a hug. Martin had been in Canada for 30 years, but his accent was as strong as if he'd just gotten off the boat. He had thinning grey hair and light brown eyes. He wore a Chelsea FC ball cap and scarf. He had been born into the house of Chelsea, a professional football club based in London, he liked to say, his father and older brother being fans.

He drove a cab all day, and every day at five-thirty or six o'clock he parked it in his driveway, one block away, and came to the Blue Door for a beer. He and Nell had been meeting here for years. It was like a family.

"'Ello, 'ello, 'ello—there she is," Martin called out to Beck as soon as he saw her. "You're looking lovely tonight, as usual." He stood up to give her a hug and then pulled out a chair for her to sit down. The bartender came over and slapped a couple of coasters down on the table.

"Hey, Beck. You want the usual?" he said.

"Sure, Bill; I'll start with half a bottle of Pinot with a glass of ice," she said.

"Okay. Martin, are you and Henry going to have a pitcher?" the waiter asked.

Martin looked at Beck. "Will Henry have a pitcher? Should I order one?"

"Yeah, that's a safe assumption," Beck said.

"All right—a pitcher of Rickards then, Bill," said Martin.

"Got it," the bartender said, looking toward the door. "Here comes Henry now."

Henry strode in, carrying an LCBO bag in his arm. He was wearing jeans, work boots, a blue shirt, and brown leather jacket. It looked as if he'd had his blond hair trimmed at the barber.

"Hey, hey, the gang's all here," said Martin while Nell looked on, smiling.

Henry clapped the bartender on the back. "Hey, Bill. We'll have a pitcher of Rickards and two glasses."

"Got it, Henry. Martin's already put the order in," Bill said.

Henry slipped into the chair next to Beck and kissed her on the cheek. "I stocked up," he said, nodding to the bag he was about to put on the floor.

Beck pulled her chair closer to Henry's and, heads together, they both looked inside the bag. There was a bottle of Crown Royal—the low light made the amber liquid shine—plus two bottles of Fevre Chablis and two of Mondavi Fumé Blanc. "Yum ... they'll be so good when they're chilled," Beck said. She took one hundred dollars from her purse and gave it to Henry.

"Thanks," he said, taking out his wallet and sliding the bills into it.

Before long, the first pitcher of beer was done, as was the second. The third one was half full. Beck was almost finished her second half bottle of wine.

"Your turn, Beck," said Nell, the colour high in her cheeks and her coffee cup held in hand. She was referring to the music trivia game. Nell knew more about '50s and early '60s music than anyone Beck had ever met, and she loved playing the game. Beck had yet to stump her.

"Okay, here goes," said Beck, trying to keep the tune of the song out of her head so she wouldn't give it away. The game was to answer the questions posed by the lyrics.

"'There once was a girl who came out of a locker. She was as nervous as she could be.' What was she wearing?'"

"An itsy-bitsy, teeny-weeny, yellow polka-dot bikini!" cried Martin almost immediately.

"Shit, Martin. I can't believe you got that. I've been working on that all week!" exclaimed Beck.

"Ha ha! That's an easy one," said Martin. "You know I'm going to know any song about girls!"

"Well, that covers a hell of a lot of tunes," said Henry, laughing.

"Okay, my turn. Here's one for you," says Martin.

"This lovely lady doesn't want to be told what to do, what to say, or to be put on display. Who is she?'"

"Hang on, hang on, I know this one," said Beck, closing her eyes to think. She loved trivia games of any kind and played them with intensity. After about a minute, she slapped the table. "It's Lesley Gore, 'You Don't Own Me'!" and she began to sing the song.

"Good girl, Beck," said Martin, "good one on you."

"Okay, Nellie," said Martin, taking a gulp of beer and rubbing his hands together with anticipation, "it's your turn. Hit us with your best shot."

Nell took a breath, and all eyes focused in her direction. "Okay. Here's one … what would this woman rather do than see you walking away from her?"

Martin looked down into his lap, up in the air, down into his lap, and then up in the air again. "Jeez, I dunno, Nell. I'm stumped. You know, Henry?"

"What would this woman rather do than see you walking away from her?" said Henry slowly, repeating the question, biting his lip and thinking. "I dunno either," he said finally. "I'm stumped."

Beck sat back in her chair. "She'd rather go blind," Beck said with satisfaction. She loved being able to answer the questions. "This woman would rather go blind—she'd rather go blind than to see you walking away from her."

"You've got it," Nell exclaimed, looking pleased. "Beck's got it. I knew she would."

Henry drained his glass, looked over at Beck, and raised his eyebrows. "Well now, I know when I've been beat. Do you want to go back to my place, Beck?" he said with a laugh. "I don't want you to go blind by seeing me walking away from you or anything."

"Oh yes, I'd love to," Beck replied with a giggle. "We can uncork one of those bottles of wine."

"I'm going to walk Nell home first," said Martin, "but I might join you lay-tah."

"Right on," said Henry. "Call first."

Beck waved to Bill, the bartender, and got out her wallet to pay. "Put Nell's coffee on my bill, uh … Bill," she said looking up at him and laughing, surprised at her own wit. "Put it on my bill—Bill."

"Never heard that one before," said Bill, taking Beck's card over to the cash register.

"Good night, Nell," said Beck, standing up to say goodbye. "It's always fun to see you. Are you going to be all right now, walking home with this mischief maker?" she asked, motioning to Martin.

"If he tries anything, I'll whack him with this." Nell laughed as she held up her cane.

"Don't worry, Beck. I'll take good care of her. Won't I, Nell?" said Martin.

"That you will, Martin. You always have done that," Nell said, beaming at her friend.

Beck grinned at the two of them—so sweet. Henry tapped her shoulder. He was holding up her coat. Beck put her arms into the sleeves and said thanks. Bill brought back her Visa receipt. She signed it and put the card away.

Picking up her bag and slinging it over her shoulder, she tipped slightly with the force of the movement.

"Here, hold my arm," Henry said. Henry had Beck on one arm and the LCBO bag in the other. Martin stood up straight, with Nell on his arm. They all left the bar at the same time, Beck waving at the bartender as they walked out the door.

* * *

Flushed from the walk to Henry's place, Henry and Beck sat down at the granite-topped island in the middle of Henry's large kitchen. There was a big stainless-steel fridge, stove, and matching dishwasher, and a 27-inch iMac monitor perched on a small desk attached to a Bang & Olufsen sound system. Martin called it Henry's Party Palace.

Beck liked being where Henry was. It was like walking away from her life and into someone else's. All she needed to do was to show up. He took care of everything once she arrived.

Henry had worked as a contractor until there had been some kind of accident on the job site. The scaffolding had collapsed, and he'd been pinned under a steel bar. Several vertebrae had been fractured; he was lucky not to have been paralyzed, but he was in pain a lot of the time and hadn't worked in two years.

"Hand me a couple of those duMaurier," Henry said to Beck. She took three cigarettes out of the package, gave Henry two, and lit one.

After a couple of minutes of mixing the cigarette tobacco with a film canister of pot that he'd emptied onto the counter, he looked up at Beck. "You wanna know how to roll a proper joint?"

"Sure," Beck said with a laugh. "Who wouldn't want to know that?"

"First thing is, your hands have to be clean," he said, showing her both his palms. "They can't be oily, because it'll make the papers stick." He got up to wash his hands at the sink and sat back down. "Pull out a few papers, depending on how many joints you want to roll," he added, taking a several papers out of a packet of ZigZags.

"Then hold the paper lightly ... very lightly ... in your hand," he said, holding one rolling paper in his left hand to show her.

Beck took a puff of her cigarette. She was paying rapt attention.

"Mix the tobacco and the pot together first, before you sit down to roll," he said, pointing to the little heap he'd already made. Now, watch this.

This is the most important part. Load up the paper at the ends," he said, sprinkling the pot and tobacco mixture at both ends of the paper. "Don't put any in the middle, or it will bunch up. That's important. The middle will fill in naturally."

He rolled the joint between his fingers and licked the paper to seal it. "If you want, you can put a little piece of cardboard in the end," he continued, tearing a piece off her package of cigarettes and fitting it into the end of the joint to make a filter.

"There's your joint," he said, holding up a perfect cylinder.

The glow from the Chablis softened his handsome face.

"Thanks. It's beautiful," she said, taking the joint from his outstretched hand and lighting it. "Does that mean I have to roll my own now?"

He smiled and topped up her wine.

CHAPTER 3

"Aren't your parents going to have a conniption fit if we get married?" Beck asked Anthony about six months after their dinner at the Murrays.

Beck never expected the Murrays to welcome her with open arms. They probably thought Anthony would go out with someone more like him, someone from St. John's, whose parents they might have known. It could also be her personality that had put them off, Beck thought. She had pretty well grown up as an only child. Poppy had spoiled her. Her mother had paid her a lot of attention. So had her father and her brothers, who were so much older than she was. Perhaps, as a result, she was a bit overconfident, and Mrs. Murray didn't like that.

Anthony was a good man. He was smart. He had ambitions for himself and for her. They dreamed about the life they'd have in Toronto—a life separate from the Murray name. He said that all the time. In Toronto, he'd be at school, and she'd work on her writing. Anthony always supported her work and *always* told her she had a great future. He believed in her. He wasn't going to be relying on Beck for money, either—that was one thing her mother had told her to avoid in a man. "Don't be in a position where you have to work to support him," she'd said. Anthony would be getting an allowance left to him by his grandfather, Anthony Murray Sr., which would pay for school, rent, a car—all his expenses.

"It will be okay as soon as we get out of Newfoundland," Anthony said. "We'll have our kids as soon as we can, and then we'll all grow up together." She put her arms around his neck, and he hugged her tightly.

"Let's do the reception in Herring Neck," Beck suggested. "It will be fun, and Mom will love it."

"I think it might be too much work for your mother," Anthony replied as he brushed a stray piece of hair out of her face. "You know, having all those people over at your place. It's a lot. And the plumbing in Herring Neck might not be able to take it. Let's do it in St. John's. I'll talk to Mom tomorrow."

Plumbing in Herring Neck wasn't as automatic as it was in St. John's, where water magically appeared when you turned on the tap. In Herring Neck they had a deep artesian well that was her father's pride and joy, but the pump that brought the water to the surface could only work so hard, which meant you could only flush the toilet so many times in a row before the pump couldn't keep up. It's not something you'd even notice when it was just the family, but if there was a lot of company, well, then the pump might slow things down.

When Beck's father had decided they were going to close off the dug well and switch to an artesian well, he'd gotten a diviner, an old man from Merritt's Harbour, who had come with his divining rod, a forked stick that was supposed to pull down over any spot where there was water.

The diviner walked foot by foot up and down the sloped meadow behind their house, with his forked stick in his hand. He bent over at the waist and never took his eye off the stick. Beck sat on a rock at the end of the meadow and watched him. She looked out at the harbour and back at the stick. Could the stick tell the difference between salt water and fresh water? she wondered. Then she saw the man look up and wave at her father. Dad strode over, chin out, arms bent and swinging at his sides. The man pointed to the ground. Then he walked away without saying a word.

The well digger arrived the next week. It was a red truck with a towering 100-foot drill on the back. Beck's heart was in her throat as she watched the truck inch back and forth, back and forth, until it was perched on top of the rocks, the drill centred over the spot chosen by the old man from Merritt's Harbour.

Day after day, the drill pounded the rocks. *Boom, boom, boom.*

"That's diamonds they got on the tip of that drill," her father told her. "Hardest thing ever made, harder than rock."

They dug for four days. By that time, Beck's mother had her apron wrung out with worry. The well diggers charged by the foot. "What if that old diviner was just foolish?" her mother said. But they couldn't stop now and end up with nothing.

When Beck got home from school on the fifth day, she found everybody smiling. They had found water at 110 feet. They were going to send it into St. John's to be tested before they put the casing down the hole. "Thanks be to Jesus!" said her mother.

Every day after, and with every glass of water her father ran out of the tap, he'd raise it up and pronounce that there was no water on this earth better than the glass of water he held in his hand.

* * *

When Anthony came back from seeing his mother about the wedding, his face was red and his hair matted to his head with sweat. He looked as if he had gone 10 rounds inside a boxing ring.

"Good Lord, Anthony," she said. "You look beaten up! What's the matter?"

"We can have 30," he said, letting out his breath in a whoosh.

"Thirty what?" asked Beck.

"We can have 30 guests in total," he said, "fifteen from each side. Mom and Dad will host the reception at their house on Circular Road."

"Okay," said Beck, "but I think it's only fair if Mom, Marlene, and Cory do the cooking."

"All right," said Anthony, "I'll tell Mom. And oh, we've gone ahead and picked a date. I thought it would be okay with you. We picked Saturday, July 6."

CHAPTER 4

Asmi sat on the living room floor, leaning up against the sofa, head thrown back on the cushion, eyes on the ceiling, and cell phone growing hot in her hand. She'd been on the phone for close to an hour.

"If it is a wedding here in India among your family you want, then you shall have it," Asmi heard her mother say finally. "It's as simple as that. You are not to worry anymore about this, Asmi. I am telling you. We will simply host the wedding in their city of Chandigarh. That way, Jai's family need only drive down the street from their home. There are beautiful halls for rent in Chandigarh, and we will rent one of those. They have people who will take care of everything. We only need pay them. Jai's father, mother, and brothers will be spared having to come to our home and eat a meal here. It will be neutral. This will make it easy for them."

"Okay, Ma, okay. I'll speak to Jaisalminder," Asmi said into the phone. Jai was lying down in the bedroom with a magazine in his hand. The TV was on with the sound turned low. Every couple of minutes he peered over the top of his magazine, eyes darting nervously toward Asmi.

"We will do something small," her mother was telling Asmi. "We don't need to do all the ceremonies, just the ones you want. If they want to see their son married, they'll come. And they *will* come, Asmi—don't worry."

"Okay, Ma. I will go talk to Jai now and call you tomorrow. Bye-bye …" Her voice trailed off, and her mother hung up. Asmi reached up to put the cellphone on the end table to cool off. She hoisted herself up from the floor, walked to the bedroom, and sat on the edge of the bed to explain the plan to Jai.

Though he said he felt sickness in his stomach, Jai agreed to call his mother. The call lasted 15 minutes.

"She has said yes," Jai said as he put down the phone and let out a long breath that sounded like a low whistle.

"Good job," Asmi told Jai.

"My heart is still beating fast though," he said breathlessly, hand on his chest. "I'm glad we've finally done it! But I had no idea what she'd say, of course." He laughed, giddy with relief.

CHAPTER 5

On July 2, 1992, four days before Beck and Anthony's wedding, the Canadian Government declared a moratorium on the North Atlantic cod fishery. After 500 years, the fishery had collapsed. There would be no more cod fished off the coast of Newfoundland. Between freezers ships, trawl nets, and quotas, the North Atlantic had been fished out. With the stroke of a pen, 35,000 Newfoundlanders lost their jobs. Emergency assistance payments of $225 a week would be made for the 10 weeks until fisherman and fish plant workers qualified for unemployment insurance. Signs went up in outport communities all over the island: House and Contents $5,000—it was enough to take your family to Fort McMurray, Alberta, were the oil economy would provide them with jobs.

The wedding turned out to be more like a wake than a celebration. Her mother and father; Mikey and his wife, Marlene; Alf and his wife, Cory; Maggie and her parents; and Jimmy and his parents made up the 15 Mrs. Murray had allotted them, and there were enough people from St. John's to fill out the room. The drinks flowed. It was noisy. Everyone was talking about the moratorium. How could they not? Not only was it the biggest single layoff in Canadian history, but it also took away the island's reason for being. What was Newfoundland with no cod fishery? No one knew the answer.

Mikey took Beck aside. He was a big man, tall, with broad shoulders, dark red hair, and a large, handsome face like her father's. He had always had a soft heart. Ever since he was a child, it had hurt him to see anybody else feeling bad.

"Good for you that you're gettin' outta this place, Becksie," Mikey said, peering into her face while his hands rested on her shoulders. "Sure, there's nothing here no more for nobody. Issa good thing yer leaving, my duck. Yer better off. Good for you." Mikey was choking up, his lips pursed and tears springing to his eyes.

"But sure, Mikey, you'll be okay, won't you? You got the shrimp and the crab licence," Beck said to him, taking his arm.

"Yes, girl, I'm okay, thanks to your mudder over there, who saw it all coming," he choked out. "She's the one who made me get the longliners rigged out for shrimp and crab. But sure, I'm the only one in the whole of Herring Neck, aside from yer brother Alf, who will be okay, Becksie, my duck. Tha's not right, my love, is it?" he asked, tears now streaming down his face.

Beck saw Mikey's wife, Marlene, looking over. She quickly turned her head away, so Beck would not see her tears. Beck hugged her brother till he could get hold of himself.

Beck's mother was sitting up as straight as an arrow in the comfy chair that Beck had sat on when she'd had her one and only visit at the Murray's. Her hands were folded in her lap, and she looked about the same as she did when she was reading—calm and quiet.

Beck's mother was good at numbers as well as words. She would be down on the wharf every day when Beck's father came in with the catch, making a note of the weight and number of the fish, which she copied into a ledger. She saw what was happening with the cod. They were getting scarcer and smaller. It was she who'd suggested they outfit their longliners to catch shrimp and crab. That had been five years before the moratorium. She'd saved the family. He'd be lost without her, Dad said time and time again. And had that ever turned out to be true.

"Hi, Mommy," said Beck, her cream-silk sheath dress allowing her to slip easily into the big chair. She put her arms around her mother and rested her head on her mother's shoulder.

"Everybody loves the food," Beck said as they watched her father standing with three of Mr. Murray's friends, his arms waving and his eyes bright. They were talking about the fishery, the same thing everyone was talking about.

To the side of them, the dining room table was filled with plates of fresh scallops, shrimp, and crab, all caught by her father and brothers. There was moose stew, potato salad with sweet mustard pickles, coleslaw, sliced tomatoes, lettuce, cold turkey, and ham, all cooked and brought in from Herring Neck. The wedding cake rested on the sideboard. It was a fruitcake her mother had made and Alf's wife, Cory, had iced and decorated. Cory was hovering around to make sure the icing survived. With her blonde hair tied up in a bun and her calf-length summer dress showing off her strong shoulders, Cory stood guard with a Tupperware container of extra icing and a few pink sugar rosebuds in a baggie.

"Remember to save that top layer for your first baby's christening," Beck's mother said. "With all the rum in it, it will keep, but you can put it in the freezer just to make sure."

"I will, Mom," Beck said, her head still resting on her mother's shoulder. She took her mother's hand and held it against her face. It was cool.

Beck and Anthony decided to put everyone out of their misery; they left the reception at ten o'clock to head over to the Battery Hotel on Signal Hill for the night. They made a little ritual of it, and Beck threw her bouquet to Maggie. Maggie made a few squeals, and Jimmy called out, "You got one for me, Becksie, my love?" Everyone laughed.

Mr. and Mrs. Murray were standing by the door, a mini receiving line to see the newlyweds on their way. Mr. Murray took Beck's hand. "Welcome to the family, Beck," he said as he kissed her on the cheek.

"Thank you, Mr. Murray," she said, smiling.

Mrs. Murray held her hand out to Beck. "Yes dear, welcome," she said as she took Beck's hand with a smile.

Then, without changing her expression, Mrs. Murray squeezed Beck's hand as hard as she could, as hard and as tight as a pair of Vise Grips. Tears of pain and shock sprang into Beck's eyes. She saw Cory look at the two of them and frown. Her mother's back was turned. Cory was helping her with her jacket. Beck pulled her hand back. Her mother hadn't seen.

PART
THREE

*In my Father's house are many mansions: if it
were not so, I would have told you.
I go to prepare a place for you.*

—John 14:2, Holy Bible, King James Version

CHAPTER 1

The elevator bumped to a nauseating stop at the third floor with Beck already regretting the decisions she'd made so far today. She cursed herself for not having left the Blue Door until MSNBC's *Rachel Maddow Show* was over at ten o'clock. That meant steady drinking with no dinner from about six to ten. *Who in their right fucking mind does that?* Did she have to make everything worse on herself by drinking on an empty stomach in the middle of the week? And the news about Sam wasn't good. It was, in fact, terrifying, but she had to put that out of her mind now. Instead, she added up the firm's monthly billings in her head like a child lumbering through her multiplication tables.

She had the cab drop her off at Starbucks, where she picked up a cup of tea and walked with hundreds of other people heading to work, most of them with their heads down, a lot of them on their phones, either texting or talking. When she saw a reflection of herself in a shop window, she stopped with a jerk and a sharp intake of breath.

November being the soul-destroying month it was, when Beck had opened her closet door in the morning, sick with a hangover, she'd decided she wanted a pick-me-up, something colourful to brighten her mood. She'd chosen a layered floral crepe skirt topped with a white long-sleeved tee, and a cable-knit sweater with toggle buttons. She'd accessorized with ankle-length Frye boots made from white distressed leather and pulled her hair back into a soft ponytail resting at the nape of her neck. Now she couldn't quite fathom what she saw—a briefcase-toting cheerleader wearing a set of Laura Ashley curtains looking out at her with a horrified expression on her face.

She put her head down and marched quickly to her office. The skirt that had felt light and playful when she put it on this morning was bunched up and stuck to her thighs with static electricity. Every little shock caused her neurons to fire pissed-off messages to her brain. Sitting down at her desk, she pulled open drawer after drawer, looking for the spray can of Static Guard she knew she had in there somewhere. She found it at the back of the bottom drawer, gave her skirt a couple of sprays, and watched it float back down to her knees. The pantyhose she didn't know why she had put on this morning made her feel like ants were crawling over her legs.

When she turned to check her email, her skirt started bunching up again. The bulky sweater rolled up around her middle, and her panty-hosed legs looked like two broomsticks shoved into white majorette boots, which, on their own, looked as if they belonged in the Santa Claus parade. She stood up, grabbed her bag, and marched out of the office.

With the sidewalks less packed, the street revealed itself to be a mess of construction, and Beck's senses felt the full assault of it. Backhoes picked at open scabs of pavement. Cranes pierced the foggy mist like hypodermic needles. The huge crater at the end of the street, destined to become an underground parking garage, was symbolic of a city whose very core, much like her own, was in the process of being hollowed out and excavated.

She made her way up to Queen Street and walked into a shoe store, where she tried on and bought a pair of black leather lace-up boots and thick socks. She wore them out of the store. In the next shop, she tried on a pair of black jeans, a thick leather belt with a heavy buckle, a slate grey silk-and-cashmere-blend pullover, grey silk scarf, and a tapered hip-length black leather jacket. She walked out of the dressing room with the clothes on, paid for the outfit, and asked the clerk to cut off the tags. She stuffed her old clothes into a shopping bag. As she walked out the door, a garbage truck pulled up to collect the hundreds of bags of recycling that had been piled up on the sidewalk the night before.

"Can I throw this bag up there?" Beck called out to the guy who was tossing the recycling in the back of the truck.

"What's in it?" he yelled so he could be heard over the screeching of the truck as it crushed its load.

"Clothes," she yelled back and walked toward him.

"Okay," he said, pointing to the gaping steel mouth on the back of the truck, "fire away."

Beck heaved the white plastic shopping bag containing her skirt, sweater, boots and panty hose into the back of the truck and watched with satisfaction as it was flattened to a pancake and rolled out of her sight. She had absolutely no time for clothes that did nothing for her.

On the way back to the office, she stopped by the bookstore and picked up an armful of magazines, including current issues of *The Walrus, The New Yorker, Wired, Mother Jones,* and *Vanity Fair.* Susan Delacourt's book about selling politics was out in paperback, so she picked that up too. When she got to her office, she sat on her couch and started to read.

Nick walked in. "You gonna get through all those this morning?" he said, smiling.

"Maybe, but that's not really the point, I guess," she said. "What's up?"

"There's news on the breast cancer society pitch," said Nick. "It looks like we've been shortlisted for the next phase of the tender. We're one of four. They want to meet to go over credentials, to assure themselves the firms who are bidding can do everything they need and to get a sense of our overall approach."

"When's it set for?" asked Beck.

"Two weeks from Thursday at two o'clock."

"Okay, can we talk about it more later? I'm feeling pissed and fried."

"Sure—just coming in to give the news, for now. Anything I can help with?" Nick asked, looking down at Beck with a frown. "Didn't I see you wearing something else when you came in this morning?"

Beck looked up. "Yeah, but I felt too much like a curtain, so I changed. I made the wrong wardrobe choice this morning."

"Ah yes, of course—good that you dealt with it decisively." He laughed as he turned to leave the office. "Love the jacket."

Beck looked down at her magazine. She felt weak. Energy was evaporating from her body and her mind, seeping out of every pore, directionless and scattered. She needed to replace it. She needed new information, new impressions, new experiences, and new data coming in, or when she reached for a thought, it wouldn't be there. For if she didn't have a thought, a position, or a reaction, well then … the whole thing came crumbling down, now didn't it?

Beck breathed a long breath in, counting one, two, three, four, five, six, seven, eight as she did. Her phone dinged. She breathed out slowly. It was an email from Sam.

> *Hey, Beck,*
>
> *Still hadn't heard about the time for my CT scan so called the clinic today—the request didn't go through!!!!!!!!!! When they tried to fax it (fax it!!!!!!!!!!), the line was busy, and no one got back to it. The fax had been sitting on someone's desk since last Friday.*
>
> *I'm dying here, and they forgot to send the fucking fax. I drove over and made them fax it while I was standing there in the room. Then I waited until my doctor followed up with a phone call. I'm booked for next Thursday at 3:00. Went to buy that book* Cancer Is a Word, Not a Sentence. *I haven't read that much about pancreatic cancer, but I figure it's not good.*
> *Nosotros venceremos, Sam*

Beck typed a reply email:

> *Sam,*
>
> *Jesus, Mary, and Joseph! What are they trying to do over there? Kill you? Can we call someone? Maybe the president at the cancer agency we're pitching? No, wait—they only do breast. Ridiculous! Good for you going over there—just imagine having to do that. Hang in there, partner.*
> *Beck*
> *PS: I went out for drinks last night. Now my tummy hurts!*

Another ding on Beck's phone.

Hiya, Beck,
  I'm okay for now. I'll email after the CT scan. Hope your
tummy feels better ;)
NV, Sam

Beck spent the rest of the day feeling as if she were walking through porridge. Even her staff seemed to be moving in slow motion. After work, and wearing her new black leather lace-up boots and jacket, she trudged along Queen Street to the Osgoode subway station. It was starting to rain, and the wind was picking up. As if she were a codfish, she followed the school of humanity into a subway car, rode the four stops north to St. George Station, and swam out again. On the escalator, she stood to the right as people streamed by on her left. Once out of the station, she tramped along the sidewalk on Bloor Street, making her way to Koerner Hall, part of the Royal Conservatory of Music.

Feeling anxious, she fished around in her bag to make sure she had the ticket for the Massey lecture. On the weekend, she had heard physicist Neil Turok, the director of the Perimeter Institute for Theoretical Physics, being interviewed on the radio. In an accent that, to Beck, sounded more British than South African, he'd described how the universe and dark energy were expanding to block out the light, ultimately (maybe) leading to another Big Bang.

To Beck, at that moment, it had sounded like the very thing she needed to know more about, and she'd opened her laptop to buy a ticket. She hoped it would make her feel better.

Now, as she walked into Koerner Hall, the sweat beaded up on her forehead. She was still nauseated from last night and hadn't eaten all day. But she was here now. She showed the usher her ticket and found her seat. Grateful for the hush, she put her bag down, took her jacket off, and sank into the soothing atmosphere of the magnificent room. Being in this space was almost enough to transform her state of mind. Swaddled in the perfection of its sound and the burnished glow of its wooden beribboned canopy, she looked straight ahead and unconsciously opened her mouth a fraction, ready to breath it all in.

CHAPTER 2

The alarm clock was beeping, and Beck reached over to turn it off. It was a quarter after seven. She put her hand to her throat. It was on fire. Throwing back the covers, she got out of bed to go to the bathroom, grabbed a thermometer out of the medicine cabinet, and stuck it in her mouth while she sat on the toilet—39.9. No wonder she had felt like crawling out of her skin yesterday.

She finished peeing, stood up, and peered into the mirror, triaging the seriousness of her illness. Her face was pale and her colour was high—two red circles had perched on her cheeks, lending her a feverish air. Her eyes were cloudy and bloodshot. She opened her mouth to say aahhhh and winced. Digging out the flashlight she kept in the vanity, she shone it down her throat and could see it was red-hot and swollen. Pushing her tongue down as far as she could, she searched for the little white spots that would indicate strep throat. If she had strep, she'd have to call the doctor, but she didn't see any white spots. She felt her lymph nodes—they were enlarged, all worked up to fight an enemy invader.

She ran the tap, splashed water over her face, and looked in the mirror again. Picking up the hairbrush, she pulled her hair back from her forehead into a thick ponytail and held in place at the base of her neck by a covered elastic band. It hurt too much to swallow.

She leaned against the bathroom sink and hung her head. She'd taken her temperature, checked for strep, pulled back her hair, and washed her face. What else could she do for herself? Drink tea and honey maybe? Take something for the fever?

She went downstairs to turn the kettle on and rummaged around in her purse to find the little bag of Percocet Henry had given her a couple of weeks ago for a headache. Her throat hurt so much she didn't think she could swallow the pills whole, so she crunched two up and put them in a spoonful of jam, the way her mother had used to give her aspirin when she was little. Taking it bit by bit from the spoon, she allowed the sugary jam to dissolve in her mouth along with the Percocet and then sucked on ice cube to calm her throat before she called Nick's cellphone.

"Nick Taylor," he answered.

"Nick ..."

"Yep, it's Nick."

"Nick, it's Beck."

"Beck! Is that you? You don't sound good, Beck. What's the matter?"

"I'm sick. I've got a really sore throat; I can hardly talk. I have a fever, too—39.9—can't come in ... for a couple of days, probably," said Beck, straining to get the words out.

"Holy shit, you sound bad," said Nick. "You did seem out of sorts yesterday. You need anything? Do you think you'll need antibiotics or something?"

"Don't think so ... don't think it's strep ... going back to bed ... hopefully sleep ... feel so bad."

"Okay. Have you taken something for the fever?" asked Nick.

"Two minutes ago."

"Okay, Beck, you go sleep it off. Don't worry about anything here. Talk later."

She took her tea, walked back upstairs, got a cold cloth for her head, and went back to her bedroom. She lay down, put her head on the pillow, and closed her eyes.

When she opened her eyes again, she was lying on her back. It was dark. She felt a heavy weight on her chest; she tried to take a deep breath, but it wouldn't go all the way down to her lungs. Thinking that if she rolled over on her side it might help clear her chest, she tried to move. She strained to turn her head but couldn't. Her left arm was bent with her hand close to her left ear; her right arm lay down by her side. Both legs were straight. But neither her arms nor her legs would move. She was paralyzed—stuck to the bed.

Dread spun around her like a swirling cloud. The fear was alive in her, crawling in her stomach, creeping up into her throat. The weight on her chest was getting heavier. It felt as if an animal was sitting on her. It was dead weight, holding her down. She tried to call out, but no sound came.

"Just pretend it's not there," she heard her mother say. "Just pretend it's not there, and it will go away, because it's got nothing to feed on."

She was back in Herring Neck. She had just walked in the kitchen door, her face as white as a sheet. She had met a dog coming home over the road. Beck was afraid of dogs, and she'd crossed the road so she wouldn't have to pass it. But the dog had also crossed the road and had followed her. Beck had been afraid to run home, because the dog would run after her, so she had forced herself to walk slowly. Her mother was talking to her.

"The worst thing you can do is let a dog know you feel fear," her mother said. "They can smell it, and the smell attracts them. You just have to walk by the dog and pretend you're not afraid. Whatever you do, don't let the dog know you feel fear."

Beck closed her eyes again.

Her mother put a cool hand on her forehead. Beck sighed with relief. "It's okay, my love," her mother said. "Here's a cold cloth. You just lie still there for a minute. Those little baby aspirin will bring your fever down, and they're chewable too. You don't mind those kind."

"Will you sit beside me, Mom? Will you sit beside me and hold my hand? Please, sit beside me, Mom," pleaded Beck, her green eyes fixed on her mother's face and her pink cheeks flushed with fever.

"Okay, my love. Just hold on now until I pull Poppy's stool over to sit on. I'll hold your hand, my darling. Just let me sit down here now," said her mother as she pulled over Beck's little stool, the one her grandfather had made for her, sat down on it, and picked up Beck's hand. Beck looked up into her mother's face until her eyes got heavy and she fell asleep again.

CHAPTER 3

Getting undressed for her CT scan, Sam pulled her sweater up over her head, catching her earring on a piece of unravelled wool. "Ow, ow, ow!" she exclaimed when she felt the earring start to rip her ear lobe. With the sweater still halfway over her head, she removed the tangled earring from her sweater and bent over awkwardly to lay it on a little bench.

The cubicle was not much bigger than a phone booth. Her elbows knocked the sides as she reached behind her back to undo her bra and slip it off her shoulders. Blue hospital gowns, two of them, lay on the bench. She picked one up, put it on, and did up the string at the back of her neck. She put the other one on and did the string up at the front.

Leveraging the toe of one boot against the heel of the other, she slid off her worn cowboy boots without bending down, unzipped her jeans, and slid them down. She put her earrings, watch, and bracelet in her jeans pocket and rolled everything up like a sleeping bag. The nurse said she could keep her stuff in the cubicle. Paper slippers lay on the bench. She'd have preferred to wear her own socks or bare feet but did as the nurse who'd put them there had asked and slipped them on.

Sam, meet cancer. Cancer, this is Sam.

She had dreaded making the call to her brother, David. Sam knew it would change his life the minute he picked up the phone. Of course he would immediately fly to Toronto. He would feel that he had to come. He would want to come. Right now, while she was in this box getting undressed, he was in the waiting room, fresh from guiding tourists around Squamish, British Columbia. He was a bright-eyed, sun-browned, windswept mountaineer staked out in the fluorescent-lit, linoleum-floored, plastic-chaired waiting room of a downtown Toronto hospital, keeping his big sister company.

Sam walked out of the change room. The nurse was waiting; she motioned with her arm, saying, "Right this way."

Sam sat down and then lay down on a narrow gurney. Strapped in place, she felt as if she were in a madman's laboratory. The nurse was plunging an IV line into her arm. When she finished, Beck had to stretch both arms over her head to fully expose her torso and abdomen to the radiation, 500 times greater than a regular X-ray. As she was sliding into the huge doughnut-shaped machine, she felt a burning sensation in her right hand and up her arm, where the iodine compound was seeping into her veins. "We want well-contrasted pictures," her doctor had said.

The taste in her mouth was metallic, and she felt flushed. The machine whirred and clicked around her, circling her body like a charmed set of knives being thrown by a crazed magician who wanted to take her apart slice by slice. She heard the technician sporadically say things like, "Hold your breath; okay, you can breathe now; hold your breath again; we're almost done," and she did as she was told.

When it was done and she was dressed, Sam walked back to the waiting room with a technician dressed in blue scrubs, who was talking to her about the results going back to her family doctor. She could see David sitting on his chair the way a bird sits on the branch of a tree, relaxed but alert, ready to spring up in an instant. He turned his head slightly when he saw Sam, and she saw his face darken as if a cloud had just passed over the sun.

He sprang from his seat. "Sammy, what happened to you? Are you all right?"

"I think I'm going to throw up, David. I feel sick. Please, I gotta go."

"Some people find the CT scan a little unnerving," the technician said to David, her eyes narrowing as she surveyed Sam, "especially when you're not used to it."

"Come on, let's go," said David, slipping his hand around Sam's waist. "Let's get you home."

David and Sam walked back to the car. David got in the driver's seat. "It's that fucking machine, Sam," said David, starting the car and looking at her with his bright eyes and a concerned expression.

"It sucks the life out of you, you know. It's alien—it's not human. That's why you feel weird. Here, take this," he said, pulling a joint out of his pocket and handing it to Sam. "Light this up. It'll help take the edge off, bring you back to earth. We'll go home; you can take a bath with some of that lavender shit you like. I'll make you lunch. You'll feel hungrier by then. And maybe we can make an appointment for you to get your hair done—you know—to help you feel—you know—a bit better."

CHAPTER 4

"Hey, Nick." Yvonne poked her head around Nick's office door. "Have you seen Beck? She's not in her office, and we were supposed to go over the page layouts for the teachers' website. She said she wanted to see it before it went to the developer."

Nick was sitting at his desk, shuffling through black-and-white photos. "Beck's got some kind of wicked virus or flu or something," he said to Yvonne's disembodied head as it appeared around the door frame. "She called this morning. I could hardly understand her. She had a sore throat and a temperature. She'll be out for the rest of the week, by the sound of it."

"Oh yeah?" said Yvonne, lifting her chin as she considered what Nick had just said. "Sick, hey? Bummer." She walked into Nick's office and sat down.

"Can you take a look at these for me?" she asked, pointing to what she'd just put on his desk while quickly texting on her phone. "It's the wireframe for the teachers' website. Bain is out, and we need to get it signed off today. Can you do it?"

"Yeah, okay," Nick said, picking up the outline and leafing through it, "but I'll need to read it first. If you can spare a moment away from your adoring public, why don't you get Bain in here, and you can both show me what you've got."

"You're sounding a bit testy, Nick, to be honest."

"Testy?'

"Yeah, you're coming across as irritable."

"I'm in a perfectly equitable mood, Yvonne. Just get off the fucking phone and go get Bain if you want me to sign off this wireframe."

"All right—point taken," Yvonne said, sipping her coffee and looking around at the baseball posters on Nick's wall. "I'll get Bain, but can we meet in Beck's office? There's more room in there."

Five minutes later Bain, Beck, and Yvonne pulled their armchairs around the glass coffee table in Beck's office to go through the website outline. It included a "town square" for up-to-date information on what was happening in individual schools, a members' section for teachers, a history section for everyone, a media section with downloadable photos and classroom footage, and a sign-up option for people who wanted to get alerts about school closings and other developments.

Nick spread the pages out over the glass coffee table and stared at them. Bain, Beck, and Yvonne stayed quiet. After about 10 minutes, Nick picked up a pen and made a few notes.

"Can we keep the sign-up option on the same place on every page—in the upper right-hand corner? It needs to stay stationary throughout the whole site."

"Yes," said Yvonne.

"The materials in the media section need to be downloadable in a high enough resolution for broadcast or print. Can we make sure everything in that section meets the requirement of both print and broadcast journalists—that's everything, without exception?"

"Yes," said Yvonne.

"And will all of this be downloadable in a version suitable for the user's device—phone, laptop, iPad, and so on?"

"Yes," said Yvonne.

"Are you just saying yes because you know that's what I want to hear, or are you saying yes because you are going to make sure it gets done?" asked Nick.

"I am saying yes because I'll ride the developers. If I have any problem, I'll come back to you," said Yvonne.

"Okay," he said as he initialled the top of every page and added the words "with the following changes."

"There's your sign-off," he said as he gathered up the pages and handed them back to Yvonne

"Now, have a look at these photos," he said, opening his laptop.

Nick had been working directly with the campaign photographer. The pictures were shot in a photojournalistic style. They were not staged or styled, and the authenticity showed. One picture had a teacher, with her arms folded, at the back of a classroom with about 30 students, some with their heads bowed as they wrote, some staring off into space, others reading. There was another one of a gym teacher walking down the hallway and talking to a group of kids wearing hoodies. Nick's favourite was a teacher and a female junior-high student caught in a close-up profile, clearly talking about something very serious or meaningful to both of them. It was a stunning collection of shots that supported the concept of teachers not only caring about the future but also understanding the reality of what the future looked like.

Bain clapped Nick on the back twice when he finished looking through the photos. "Well done, mate," he said. "Campaign or no campaign, they capture the imagination in a good way—for our side, anyway."

"They'll work hard for us," Nick agreed.

"Knock, knock."

All eyes turned to the doorway, where Todd was standing.

"Is Beck here?" he asked.

"No, she out sick—a bad flu, by the sounds of it. She might be out the rest of the week," said Nick.

"Bummer. I wanted to go over the plan for the breast cancer pitch with her."

"Well, let's go over it now," said Nick. "You've basically got the pitch team here, and we're just finishing the teachers' stuff."

"Great ... yeah ... why not?" he said as he came in and passed around a folder containing the credentials of the entire firm.

"Looks impressive," said Bain, chin down and leafing through the pages. "What else is going on?"

"Beck wants this to be treated like an issues-management pitch, not a fundraising pitch," said Todd.

"Bain," he continued, "she wants you to do some research into the cancer industry, the sector, or whatever you want to call it—who the players are and a review of the public opinion.

"Yvonne, she wants you to do a media scan along the same lines— looking at what's being said about cancer fundraising in both traditional and on social media."

"And Nick," said Todd with a smile, "she wants you to think of a way to break through the ambient noise."

Bain nodded his head. Yvonne made notes. Nick laughed. "That's more her area of specialty, I think."

"I don't know. You guys make a good team," said Todd. "But I'd also like to talk about bringing some creative with us. The art department would like to share a few treatments of tag lines they're brainstorming. It might be good to put on a bit of a dog-and-pony show at the pitch. What do you think?"

"Yes, get the art directors working on it," answered Nick. "At least we'll have the option of bringing it with us."

"I need that stuff from you guys by the end of the week," Todd said to Yvonne and Bain. "Is that okay?"

They all nodded.

"How's it going with the teachers?" Todd asked.

"Everything is on schedule," said Bain. "The website is coming together. The photos are excellent. We'll be out of the gate soon."

"Will they really do an illegal action in the new year if the legislation gets passed?" asked Todd.

"They will, almost definitely," said Bain.

"That kind of worries me, you know," said Todd. "Shouldn't we be advising them against that? Sounds like a lose/lose situation to me. Won't they be flushing all the credibility we're building up with this campaign right down the drain?"

"Well, when it comes right down to it, teachers will still get a lot of public support, no matter what," said Bain. "Everyone, or most people anyway, have a soft spot for at least one teacher, maybe a teacher of theirs or their child's. On the other hand, that can backfire too," he acknowledged, "because almost everyone has had a bad experience with a teacher. But it's not like the teachers listen to anyone anyway," he said, shrugging his shoulders, "so they're not going to let us make that call."

"So you figure the strike will go ahead, then?" asked Todd.

"Oh, they'll strike, laddie, no question," Bain continued. "But my read of it is that the Government will get an injunction immediately because of the new legislation, which they'll have just passed with this very purpose in mind, and they'll be back to work quickly. It'll be one day, two at the most, I'd say, if common sense prevails, which you can't necessarily count on, I suppose.

"I'm reading it as more symbolic than anything else. But when they *do* return to work, it will be work-to-rule. They will only do what they have to do, by the book. No extracurricular activities, class trips, or stuff like that. Work-to-rule will likely go on till the school year ends in June. People won't be happy, but if we're successful with our Teachers Care campaign, after all is said and done, the Government will bear the brunt of the blame, not the teachers."

"I hear what you're saying, Bain, but it sounds pretty risky to me," Todd said.

"It *is* somewhat risky," said Bain, "given the fickle nature of the court of public opinion. Our job is to mitigate that risk—not just among the so-called general public, but among their members, too."

Todd shook his head. "It doesn't sound like an easy job."

"Well now, I can tell you it's *not* an easy job. We only make it look easy." Bain laughed and Todd laughed too.

"Do you think Beck will be in tomorrow?" Todd asked.

"Not likely, Todd," said Nick. "From the sound of it, I'd say she's out for the rest of the week—hopefully back on Monday."

"Knock, knock," chimed a voice in the doorway. It was Asmi.

"I've just come to ask Nick if he knows where Beck is, and I am overhearing Beck is sick. I am not happy hearing this. How sick is she? And why, may I ask, have I not been told? I can go to her right now and drop something off, if necessary. Ginger ales or something?"

"Sorry, Asmi, I meant to tell you right after she called, but I got caught up with this," said Nick. "By the sounds of it, I think she'll be sleeping for a while. Why don't you text her in a few hours? She might need you to bring her something. That's nice of you to offer."

"Offer? Of course I would offer. It is Beck who is sick!" She turned, leaving the room and the distinct impression that if it were they who were sick she wouldn't be showing up with ginger ale.

Yvonne broke the silence. "Oh, oh, oh—I forgot to ask," she said, sitting upright in her chair. "Is she too sick to get started on that documentary?"

"Today, the answer is yes. She is too sick to get started on that documentary," Nick said with a sigh. "We'll have to pick it up again on Monday. And I wouldn't worry. Once she gets her mind around it, she'll put it together pretty fast."

CHAPTER 5

When Beck opened her eyes, the clock read 4:23 p.m., and she was lying on her stomach with her arm wrapped around a pillow. Where had she been? Who had been with her? She must have been delirious from the fever. Had she really had a visit from the old hag? She always thought the idea of an old witch sitting on your chest in the middle of the night was only a superstition. And had her mother really come to sit next to her on Poppy's stool? She'd felt awake the whole time.

Rolling over on her back, she looked out the window and saw the cherry tree in the backyard. It had been fully-grown when they'd moved into the house ten years ago. In the spring, it covered itself with pale pink blossoms, and Beck could drink in its ephemeral beauty without getting out of bed. After blossoming, the tree burst with big, juicy cherries—enough to feed all the raccoons on the block. In an attempt to minimize the invasion, Beck's neighbour had gotten out his stepladder to pick what cherries he could reach. Every night afterward, Beck had watched as the raccoons dined out on what was left of the fruit. For the rest of the summer, the trees' leafy branches provided shade. Now, in the gloomy days of November, it was cold and bare, almost frozen.

The sun was going down, and Beck's nightgown was soaked through. She picked up the corner of the sheet and wiped away a film of sweat from her face. The pain in her throat had changed from the feeling that she'd been sliced through with a sword to a dull throbbing ache. She took a sip of water. It hurt. She felt around her neck. Her lymph nodes were still swollen. The cold cloth she had for her forehead was sitting in a warm lump on her soggy pillow.

I have to get up out of bed, because I've got to go to the bathroom, she thought. *If I'm up out of bed, I can probably put clean sheets on the bed and change my nightie. I'm not going to get better in this mess of germs.*

It'll be dark soon. I'll rest here for a few minutes and get my bearings. Then I'll sit up and have a few sips of water. I'll get used to that for a few minutes and see how I feel. I can pull the sheets off the bed and throw them into the hamper—that's the easy part. Making the bed up again, that's harder, but I can take it slow, sit down between putting on the fitted sheet and top sheet if I have to. I should try to do that.

Depending on how it goes, I'll walk downstairs to the kitchen to get something to drink—and maybe have one of those Popsicles in the freezer. I can bring up some cold drinks to the bedroom in a plastic bag. That way I can grab hold of the rail if I feel dizzy.

After that, I'll turn on the shower and stand under it for a minute or two. Then I can get back into a clean bed in clean clothes and not have to go anywhere, except the bathroom, until morning.

Okay … here we go, she thought as she swung her feet out to touch the floor.

It was dark when Beck got back into bed. She brought her laptop with her so she could check on Sam. She was worried Sam might have the same flu.

> *Hiya Sam,*
>
>   *It turns out shit wine wasn't the reason I was feeling sick yesterday. I've come down with a bad bug and am home in bed with a burning throat and having delirious dreams. Are you okay? Are you sick?*
> *Beck*

Sam emailed her back right away.

> *Hi Beck,*
>
>   *That sounds terrible!! Glad to hear you're in bed. Stay there! I'm not sick, and I don't feel like I'm coming down with*

anything like that. CT scan was today—horrible! Will keep
you posted.
NV, Sam

Beck shut her laptop and reached for Henry's Percocet. She took two out of the baggie, put one on her tongue, and took a sip of water to see if she could swallow it without the jam. It went down like a piece of jagged rock. She put the other one in her mouth and swallowed it with a larger sip of water. Lying back on her pillows, she stared at the cherry tree. Its bare branches were darker than the night that surrounded it.

CHAPTER 6

"Beck, could you please put An-THO-nee on the line."

Beck had woken up with a start that morning—just over two years ago now—with the phone ringing beside her head. The clock had said 5:35 a.m. Half asleep, she'd picked it up. It was Florence Murray on the line, saying, "Beck, it's Florence. Could I please speak to An-THO-nee?"

"Is everything okay?" Beck asked.

"We've just lost Ches, Beck. He's gone. Could I speak to An-THO-nee, please?"

Beck shook her husband by the shoulder. "Anthony, Anthony … Anthony, wake up! Your mother is on the phone. You need to speak to her … come on now … wake up."

Anthony opened his eyes and focused them on Beck. "What is it? What's the matter?"

"Your mother is on the phone, Anthony. You need to speak to her now. Okay?" She handed the phone to him and watched him as his mother delivered the news.

"Dad is dead? Oh my God. Oh my God! I don't believe it," Anthony gasped into the phone. "When? Were you with him?"

"Oh Jesus, Mom—oh Jesus, Jesus, Jesus. Are you okay, Mom? You must be in shock. Are you all right? I can't believe it! … Okay, I'll call you in a couple of hours."

Anthony hung up the phone and looked at Beck.

"When did it happen," she asked.

"This morning. Mom said it was peaceful. She and Dahlia, the nurse who's been living at the house, were with him. The funeral home is on the way to pick him up," Anthony said, heaving a wracking sob. "Lord Jesus …

Christ Almighty, he's gone … how can he be gone? Lord dying Jesus, help me." As Anthony sobbed, Beck smoothed his hair.

"Shh, now, shh, Anthony … that's okay now … you'll be okay." When he quieted down, she settled him back on the pillows, went to the bathroom, and ran cold water over a clean facecloth.

"Here, Anthony," she said, carefully laying the facecloth on his forehead. "I'm going downstairs to make tea. I'll bring you some juice."

When she'd brought the orange juice back upstairs, she found him sitting up in bed. He took it from her hand, had a sip, and put it on the night table.

"What am I going to do, Beck? What am I going to do now?" he'd asked, his face pale. He laid back against his pillow. "What I am going to do? It's only me. At least you have your brothers."

"Well, the first thing you're going to have to do is get ready to go down there. You're going to have to get a flight to St. John's this morning or early afternoon if you can. Do you want me to book it? Call your office?"

"Yeah, that'd be good," he said, eyes staring out the window. The sun was coming up.

"Okay, we'll get you on your way, and then the kids and I will take a later flight. I'll have to see what's available."

"Oh my Christ, we'll have to tell the kids," Anthony said, looking miserable.

"Yes, we will, but they'll be asleep for another hour or two yet. I'll bring the tea up. You want toast and an egg with that? You'll have to have breakfast."

Anthony nodded.

Beck went back downstairs to get a tray ready. Annie's and Mick's rooms were still dark and silent. They'd wake up soon enough.

Anthony sat with the bed tray on his lap, drinking his tea and eating breakfast. Beck had her laptop open and was looking at flights.

"There's an Air Canada flight leaving Pearson at eleven," she said, staring at her laptop. "You'll have to be at the airport at ten o'clock at the latest. That means a car would need to be here at nine-fifteen, or nine o'clock to be on the safe side. It'll get you into St. John's four o'clock their time. That's the earliest that will work. Can you manage that?"

"What am I going to do when I get there?" he said, wretchedness written on his face.

"You're going to be your father's son, Anthony. You're going to comfort your mother, help make arrangements, and receive condolences from others. Your father was a well-liked man, and people knew him all over St. John's. Many people will be sad that he's passed. I'd say the funeral is going to be pretty big."

Anthony had his head down and his arms slack at this sides.

"And Anthony," Beck continued, "you know you did everything you could do over the last year while your father was sick. You went down there to be with him for his treatments. You took time off work and arranged it so you could be with him when he needed you. I know that wasn't easy for you, but you did it. You did the best any child could ever do."

Anthony hugged Beck. "Thanks for saying that, darling."

"It will be hard on everyone, but you have to play the cards you're dealt; there's no getting around that. Will there be anyone to pick you up at the airport?"

"I'll talk to Mom about it when I call her. I might as well get up and have a shower. Thanks for breakfast," he said, smiling and patting Beck's hand. Beck nodded and watched him go into the bathroom.

Anthony was already dressed in jeans, a blue shirt, and a linen sport coat; he was sitting at the kitchen table drinking coffee when Annie and Mick shuffled downstairs in their pyjamas. He told the kids he was leaving on the next flight to St. John's because Grandpa had passed away earlier in the morning. His voice broke when he told them Grandpa had been in a lot of pain at the end. He said Beck was booking a later flight that day so they could all come down. They'd all be in Newfoundland for a few days, he said, but he would be staying longer, most likely.

The kids walked Anthony to the door that day. Annie gave him a long hug. Anthony tousled her hair. Mick, who was taller than his father, put one hand on Anthony's shoulder. In that moment, Mick looked like the adult and Anthony the child. The driver had already come to the door to pick up

Anthony's bag and was standing by the car waiting to open the passenger door for Anthony. They all stood in the living window to watch the car drive off. Annie blew kisses. They kept waving until the car went down the street and turned the corner.

Beck walked back into the kitchen.

"What about school?" Mick asked.

"It's up to you," said Beck. "There's a flight at six o'clock that will get us into St. John's at one o'clock in the morning. I think that's better than having to get up early for a flight out tomorrow. But that means we'd have to leave here by three o'clock because of rush hour. It's up to you. Do you have any tests or anything?"

Michael shook his head. Annie said she didn't either.

"Okay, why don't we say to hell with school for the day?" said Beck, patting Michael on the shoulder. "I'll have to phone the school anyway to explain that you'll be away for a few days. Then we have to take stock of what you guys have to wear that's going to be appropriate for a wake and a funeral. We might have to go shopping—for shoes and a black tie for you, Michael, that's one thing I know for sure. Then we'll have lunch out somewhere, come home to pack, and then get going to the airport. Let's take a look at the clothing situation first."

Annie wrapped her arms around her mother's waist. Michael patted Beck's arm. "I got it, Mom. I'll go have a look at what's in my closet."

Annie sat down at the kitchen table and put her head in her hands.

"You okay, Annie, my duck?" asked Beck.

"Will Daddy be all right, do you think? Will he be able to manage?" she asked.

Beck sat down and took Annie's hands in hers. "Oh, I think so, Annie," she said. "It's tough, but he'll be okay. He's got all of us around him to help. And he's not made of sugar, my sweetie; he won't melt."

Annie hugged Beck.

"Okay, my dear," Beck said, patting Annie's back, "go up and see what clothes you've got in your cupboard. Besides your regular stuff, you'll need three dressy-type dresses, one in a dark colour for the funeral, and some decent shoes—and some kind of purse that isn't a bright blue canvas bag."

Annie stood up and blew her nose in a piece of paper towel she pulled off the rack. "Okay, Mom. I'll go do that now."

"All right, Annie." Beck bent down to put the dishes in the dishwasher. When she stood up, she felt light-headed and had to hold onto the counter.

Looking down at her hands, she felt the tears welling up out of nowhere and falling down her cheeks. Her mother had told her that whenever there was a funeral, you remembered all the people that you'd loved who had died, and that as you grew older, funerals became an accumulation of grief. So it was for Beck the day Chester Murray died.

She sat down at the kitchen table, buried her head in her folded arms, and was transported to the night 15 years ago when she'd gotten the news about her mother. The phone had rung out of the blue then too.

"I'm afraid I've got some bad news, Beck," her brother Mikey told her. "Mom's gone. She passed about suppertime. It was a heart attack. She was over at the hospital in Twillingate."

"Oh my God, Mikey, how can that be? I was talking to her on the phone on Sunday! Lord dyin' Jesus, Mikey, what happened? For the love of Christ, tell me what happened," she said, gasping for air and thinking her knees would give out right then and there.

"She was doing pretty good, Beck," Mikey told her. "She really was. The chemo was over, and she was getting better. You saw her yourself at Christmas. But she got up this morning and said she didn't feel well. Dad called me around lunchtime to come over. She was very weak when I got to the house; she was lying on the couch in the living room, and Becksie, my darling, she didn't have the strength to raise her head. I called the ambulance and me and Dad followed them in the car. She had a heart attack just after they wheeled her in. They couldn't save her, Beck. It wasn't the cancer that got her in the end, but it was all a lot of pressure on her heart."

"Oh my God, Mikey! How's Dad?"

"He's in pieces, Beck, in pieces. You should come home now. You can bring the youngsters. We can put them together with ours. Marlene's mother said she'll come to the house and look after them. But you can sleep down to Mom's. There's more room down there."

Beck put down the phone and stood frozen in that position, trying to decide what she needed to do next, until Anthony came into the room and asked what was wrong. Little Mick was 4, and Annie had just turned 2 1/2.

Now, sitting in her kitchen 15 years later, Beck still didn't know if she could believe it. Living so far away, it was easy to let herself think her mother was still at home in Herring Neck, alive and hoisting up the clothesline until it towered over her head, the clothes puffing up and billowing in the wind. Whenever Beck's mother turned away from the line, she never looked back. She was confident that the clothes wouldn't blow off, that her clothespins would hold it fast.

With her head high, her shoulders back, her long legs taking generous steps, and her arms as fluid as a dancer's—moving in the same way Beck did—Beck felt that her mother could be, right this minute, walking back toward the house with her eyes on the boats in the distance. Or maybe she was making bread in the kitchen and just couldn't get to the phone.

PART
FOUR

No one knows what it's like
To be the bad man,
To be the sad man,
Behind blue eyes.

No one knows what it's like
To be hated,
To be fated,
To telling only lies.

—"Behind Blue Eyes"
Words and music by Peter Townshend

CHAPTER 1

Beck had been back in Toronto with Annie and Michael for about a week after Chester Murray's funeral. Anthony was still in St. John's, helping his mother straighten everything out. *It's handy to have a lawyer in the family,* thought Beck, although Chester Murray had left his affairs in good order, as far as she could tell. She was clearing up the dinner dishes when the phone rang. She looked at the caller ID.

"Hi, Anthony!" she said without waiting for him to say hello.

"Hey, Beck, how are you doing? How are the kids?"

"They're good, but they aren't here," she said, walking toward the living room at front of the house with a dishcloth in her hand, "Annie is at the final rehearsal for the school show, and Mick, he's out with a friend for coffee. They're catching up, now that everyone's back from university for the summer. How are things in St. John's? You sound a bit stressed."

"I am a bit stressed, Beck ... and there's something I've got to tell you—something important."

"What is it Anthony? What's wrong?" she asked, stopping in mid-stride, dishcloth hanging limply in her hand.

His voice sounded strained. "Beck ... I've got to tell you this ... I'm not coming home."

"Don't worry about that Anthony, for God's sake," said Beck, waving the dishcloth in the air as if to remove a pesky fly. "Stay as long as you like. We're here for you. Don't hurry back before you're ready."

"No, that's not it, Beck," he said. "The thing is ... I'm not coming back to Toronto. I'm staying in St. John's. Dad left the company to me, and I'm going to stay here in St. John's to run it, and ... you know ... and look after Mom."

"Well, I don't really *know,* Anthony. What are you talking about? I've got the business here, and the kids have their home here. I don't think we can move to St. John's. That's not really in the cards, is it?"

"I don't expect you to move down here, Beck," he replied, his voice losing its strain and becoming more assured. *That's his courtroom voice,* thought Beck, the dishtowel now balled up in her hand.

"The kids will both be away at school next year," he continued, "so it won't make that much difference to them where I'm living. I'm staying here in St. John's, and you can stay in Toronto."

"What the hell are you saying, Anthony Murray—*exactly?*"

"I want a divorce, Beck. I'm not coming back to Toronto."

The line went silent.

"Am I dreaming here?" said Beck, her voice rising. "Is this for real? Are you, my husband, calling me up from St. John's and telling me you're not coming home—that you're going to leave your wife and children to stay at home with your *mother?*"

"I've met someone," said Anthony.

"*Met someone?* You've met someone? Who in the hell have you met? You've only been there a week!"

"I met her last year when Dad got sick. It's Dahlia."

"Dahlia! Your father's nurse? You have to be kidding me—you've got to be fucking kidding."

"Beck, there's no need to start swearing."

"Swearing? *Swearing?*" she said, her voice getting higher. "What the fuck are you talking about, Anthony? Swearing? You've been going back and forth to St. John's all this year and last, using your father's *cancer* so you could fuck around with his nurse! Oh Anthony, I gotta tell you, that is some pretty cheesy shit."

"It's not like I did it on purpose, Beck."

"Not on purpose? What are you talking about? Not on purpose? You're *married.* You have two children—" Beck stopped talking. She had to consider the words she was saying. What was happening here? A minute ago she'd been loading up the dishwasher.

"You're just walking away from all of us?" she asked, her voice quieting down. "I would never have thought this was even possible, that we'd ever be having this conversation—that you would ever *do* such a thing, Anthony. I truly am at a loss …"

"I'm not walking away from the kids, Beck. They're practically grown up. They'll both be away at school next year. Michael is already here at Memorial," he said, his voice getting impatient. "I'll be physically closer to him than you are when he comes back down here in September."

"Well, if that's what you think," she said, her voice sliding from hurt to anger, "you really are an idiot, Anthony, and a lying piece of shit. Though I'd warrant you've made your mother a very happy woman today, Anthony, you little prick-face."

"What's my mother got to do with it, Beck? You've always had something against her."

"What are you going to tell Annie and Mick, Anthony?" asked Beck, loosening her grip on the dishtowel again. "Have you considered how you're going to explain it to them?"

"Well, after a couple of months, when they are used to me being gone and Anthony comes down for school, we'll talk about it," he said. "I don't see the big hurry."

"Wait for a couple of months? Are you dreaming, Anthony? On drugs?" Beck said in disbelief. "I'll tell you what. You do whatever the hell you like with the rest of your life, but you are going to get on a plane, come back here to Toronto, and tell me and the children what exactly your plans are—in person—tomorrow."

"Beck, you always do this—"

"Do what? Do what, Anthony?" She flung the dishtowel onto the couch cushion. "Let me tell *you* something, you lying son of a bitch. After I hang up this phone, I'm going to make one call to 1-800-GOT-JUNK, and every single thing you own in this house—every suit, every record, every toy, every CD, every sock, every shoe—will be scheduled to go to the dump at 5:00 p.m. tomorrow. If I don't see you before that time, it's all going to be gone."

"You can't do that, Beck."

"You are a disgrace, Anthony, a disgrace. I'll see you tomorrow. I'll keep

Annie home from school and make sure Michael is here, so you can tell them to their faces."

Beck hung up the phone. Her body shook as she stood in the middle of the living room, wondering what to do next. She wasn't going to be able to hide it. Mick and Annie would notice something wrong right away. She walked back through the house and down to the basement to see if she could find some wine to help her calm down.

Two hours after Beck got off the phone with Anthony, she was sitting in her living room in Toronto, a glass of wine in one hand and her chin in the other. The front window looked out onto a glassed-in porch. The fireplace worked, and the mantel held pictures of the kids and the family. There was no TV in the room. It was lined with bookshelves.

She ran her hand over the couch. It was the colour of oatmeal and textured. Four armchairs, in shades of brown and grey that matched the couch, were placed around a rectangular cherrywood coffee table—the conversation pit, Anthony called it. End tables were scattered, meant to be within easy reach of all the chairs. The coffee table was the only surface in the house that didn't have newspapers, books, or magazines piled on it. Instead, a solitary piece of driftwood decorated the top. It was from Lake Ontario—Anthony had found it when they were walking with the kids along the Scarborough Bluffs and had wanted to bring it home.

She stared at her orchid plants. They were the only other living things in the room. Her heartbeat quickened when she saw an orchid. She visited nurseries looking for different colours and varieties and bought books on orchids that were able to hold her attention for hours. Once a week, usually on a Saturday, she gathered them all and brought them to the kitchen sink, where she ran them under the tap until the roots were soaked, but not soggy. *Orchids don't like wet feet,* the woman at the nursery had told her.

Orchids were opportunistic plants that grew wild on tree bark in the rainforest. Japanese writings dating back to 2500 BC reflected on their beauty. Samurai warriors reportedly took *Neofinetia falcata,* a white slender-petal orchid plant, with them into battle so they could enjoy a moment of serenity in between skirmishes. They became popular in Europe when plant collectors travelled to South America seeking ever more unique plants to sell to British horticulturalists. They used dormant orchids as packing material for shipments of exotic plants harvested from the mountains of Brazil.

In 1818 one of those horticulture enthusiasts was astonished when the packing material, which looked to him like twigs and bark, burst forth with the most spectacular blooms he'd ever seen. Demand for orchids grew. Intrepid orchid adventurers and commercial collectors tramped through the swampy, bug-ridden rainforests of South America looking for undiscovered plants. Being no more discerning than their colonial brothers who extracted resources from the ground, the plant collectors decimated entire orchid habitats. Whole trees and forest areas were chopped down to make the process of collecting more efficient. Orchid plants were shipped to Europe by the crate and by the ton. It didn't matter if the habitat was destroyed. It would prevent competitors from getting hold of them.

Beck was startled when she heard the familiar sound of Mick tromping up the front steps and the clicking of his key in the lock. The spell her orchids had cast was broken and she was dropped back into real time.

Had Anthony just called her to say he wanted a divorce? Had that just actually happened? Beck turned on the end-table lamp and checked the last incoming call. The area code was 709 and the caller ID said C Murray. It hadn't been a dream.

"Hey, Mom—I'm home," Mick called out as he opened the door, peering toward the kitchen and the family room at the back of the house. He turned his head and saw Beck sitting on the living room couch.

"Hey, Mom. What's going on? Are you all right?" He sat down next to her. "Have you been crying?" he asked with growing alarm. "What's the matter?"

Her son's eyes were green like her own, his hair and complexion dark like his father's. He was wearing jeans and a white T-shirt with a long-sleeve dress shirt over it. He wore a bracelet on each wrist. The left one was made of braided leather. A girlfriend had brought it back to him from Ecuador. The other one was silver, with an engraving of a humpback whale; he'd bought it for himself in Newfoundland.

Before Beck could answer, Annie burst through the front door next, throwing her blue canvas bag on the couch. "Hey, guys. What's going on?" she asked.

Annie's eyes were also green like Beck's. She had Beck's frizzy red hair, and although she was slighter in build, she was almost an exact replica of her mother, so much so that some people found it comical. She hauled an armchair over to sit next to them.

"What's happening?" Annie said, her voice anxious as she looked at her mother's pale face.

"Jesus, guys, I hardly know what to say," Beck managed to get out in a voice that was hardly above a whisper. "I got the strangest call from your father just now. He says he's not coming home."

"*He says he's not coming home?* What do you mean, he's not coming home?" Mick asked, leaning forward with his hands on his knees as Beck told him what she knew.

Annie looked incredulous. "Are you sure, Mom? Are you sure that's what he said? Maybe he just has to stay down there a while longer—you know, to look after Grandma."

"That's what he said, Annie," said Beck, as she took a sip of wine. "I didn't know if I believed it myself at first. But yes, that's what he said. I'm sure of it. Grandpa left him the business, the law firm. He said he's staying in St. John's and that he's found someone else … Grandpa's nurse, Dahlia."

"Oh my God, Mom! What does it mean? What will happen to us?" Annie said, pulling on Beck's arm.

"Oh, Annie, for heaven's sake, calm down," said Beck, taking her hand into hers. "Nothing is going to happen to us. We'll still live here and everything. You will finish high school and go to university, just like you planned to do. Your brother will go back to Memorial in September, just like he planned to do. Your home will be here. Your room will be here. We'll just be short one person, I guess."

Beck shook her head. "It's an unbelievable shock, I know—for me too," she said, patting Annie's hand.

Mick and Annie hung their heads.

"He might come home tomorrow to tell us in person," said Beck.

Both their heads snapped up. "He is? Really?" said Annie.

"Well, I can't be sure," said Beck, "but I told him that if he didn't fly up here tomorrow and tell us his plans face to face, I would send all his stuff to the dump by the end of day."

"You said that?" said Mick, leaning back and looking at his mother with admiration.

"I did, but he didn't say for sure he'd come," said Beck.

Annie started to cry.

A couple of hours later, Beck got a text from Anthony.

Getting a morning flight. Will be in TO at about 11:30. Probably fly back tomorrow night.

She went downstairs to tell Mick and Annie. They were at the kitchen table. Annie had already changed into her pyjamas.

"Come and sit down, Mom," she said. "Have a chocolate-chip muffin. I just made a batch."

"Perfect. Thanks, Annie. I will have one." She sat down in the chair, picked a muffin from the plate, and took a bite. "Ummm ... really good, darling, a nice batch," she said as she broke off a piece and put it in her mouth.

"I just got a text from your father," Beck said, taking out her iPhone and bringing up Anthony's text message "He says he'll be here about eleven-thirty tomorrow morning. You guys should be here."

"Do you think I should stay home from school?" Annie asked, eyes getting wide.

"Yes, I do, Annie. It's important that we all be here."

Mick nodded. "I'll be here, Mom," he said with grim determination. "Don't you worry about that."

"What's he going to say, Mom?" asked Annie.

"I don't know; I really don't," said Beck, putting her muffin down and looking across the table at Annie. "He might repeat what I've already told you; he might want to talk to you guys alone—I'm really not sure. He says he's flying back down to St. John's tomorrow night." Annie started to cry again.

"I'll punch him in the fucking face," said Mick.

"Hey, hey, hey," said Beck with alarm, "what kind of language is that coming out of you at the kitchen table?"

"Sorry, Mom, but I might," he said, clenching both his fists and resting them on the table.

"Nah," said Beck, putting her hand over Michael's fist. "I get it, but you don't need to do that, Mick." She smiled at him. "You just leave that up to me."

✳ ✳ ✳

As soon as the sun rose the next morning, Beck got up out of bed and pulled on her jeans and a long-sleeve T-shirt. She didn't bother to put up her hair. She texted Nick to tell him she'd be away from work for a few days, stuff to do with the family. She figured that, what with Anthony's father's dying, it wouldn't seem too weird to be dealing with family business. She went downstairs to make tea and clicked on the radio. It was going to be sunny and warm, a beautiful June day, the announcer said. Anthony would be arriving at about noon. Annie would be staying home from school.

Five hours later, when Beck heard Anthony's key in the lock, she was surprised. She'd thought he would knock at the door or ring the doorbell. She stood up and walked toward the front door. He walked in with his keys in his hand.

"Come in," she said. "Where would you like to sit?"

"I dunno," he said, walking past her through the living room and dining room and into the kitchen. "Does it matter?" He opened the fridge and poured himself a glass of cold water from the Brita jug Annie insisted they use for tap water. He looked at her as she stood in the kitchen. "The plane made me dehydrated."

He drank the full glass in one go and looked up. "I gotta go to the bathroom," he said, turning to go up the stairs. "I'll be back in a minute."

"Stop right there, Anthony Murray. Don't you dare walk up over those stairs. If you want to go to the bathroom, use that one," Beck said forcefully, pointing to the powder room off the kitchen. "You don't live here anymore."

He said nothing, but he walked into the powder room and closed the door. Beck went up to get the kids. Mick was in his room on the computer. Annie had her headphones on and was lying on her bed, red hair spread out like a circular pillow under her head. They were both dressed.

"Your father's downstairs," Beck said. "You'll want to go down and see him now, I think."

As they left their rooms, she went into the bathroom to look at herself in the mirror. Her hair partly hid her face. On the outside, she thought she looked pretty much the same as she had yesterday morning. Her colour was good, and she'd recently had her eyebrows done, so her face looked tidy. But, on the inside, she felt as if she'd been hollowed out like a cave, dark with jagged edges, an empty, dangerous hole. She put on some lipstick and went downstairs.

She could hear Anthony's voice. "This is between your mother and me," he was saying. "It's nothing you guys did … you can come visit me any time you want … we can take trips together. It'll take some getting used to, but you'll be okay. I think once you're away at school, you won't notice much difference," he added, sounding like he was trying to strike an optimistic note.

"Are you going to marry that nurse?" asked Annie.

"Well, it's a little early for all that, Annie. Let's just take it one step at a time."

"You're a shit," said Mick, "a chicken shit."

"Now, Michael, I know this is a shock, but there's no need to talk like that."

"Go on, Dad, just have a fling—whatever you need to do—there's no need to go away *completely*," Annie said. They were sitting down at the kitchen table. Annie had her face turned toward him, arms outstretched, palms up. She was starting to cry.

"Annie, it's not like that. Come on, now, don't be like that," Anthony pleaded.

Beck walked into the room. Anthony looked relieved. "Ah, Beck, there you are," he said. "Since I'm here, I'd like to get some copies of papers from upstairs."

"Okay," said Beck, hands in her pockets, "I'll go up with you."

She turned to the kids. The colour was gone from Mick's face. Annie's lip was quivering. Beck smiled a grim smile and cocked her head toward her son. "Put the kettle on, Mick, and make some tea for your sister, would you?" she said and turned to follow Anthony up the stairs.

They walked into the bedroom, where Anthony opened the bottom drawer of his dresser, pulling out the box where he kept copies of his will, birth certificate, and banking information. "The lawyer will be in touch with you about a separation agreement," he said, crouched on his knees and looking up at Beck, who was standing still with her hands in the front pockets of her jeans.

"Well, Anthony, if there is one thing I do not want from you, that is one fucking red penny of your fucking family fortune," she said, her voice hushed, barely above a whisper. "Not one red cent. I want no ties to you, financial or otherwise. And—"

Anthony stood up with surprise.

Beck heard what she had just said. It wasn't smart, what she'd just said. It was, in fact, stupid, she thought. "You'd cut off your own nose to spite your face," her father would have told her.

"Except," she said, catching herself on her words, "except every single dollar, every cent, every stick of chewing gum that goes into the mouths of those children while they are in school, you will pay for. You will pay for everything: fees, tuition, living expenses while they're in school, their flights from school to home—*this* home," she said, gesturing to encompass the room—"for their bachelors' degrees, masters, their PhDs, plumbing school, basket weaving, whatever the hell they decide it is they want to do. It's your dime. I'll have my accountant prepare an invoice for you on a quarterly basis.

"And," she continued, "I want this house paid for and your half signed over to me. Then I don't ever want to see your face or the faces of your family again. *Ever*," she said, pointing her finger at him, "as in *never*. You get your lawyer to write *that* up, and I'll sign it.

"Now go," she said, pointing toward the bedroom door. "Get out of here. Make some arrangement to get your stuff packed up. If it's not gone in three days, I'm pitching it."

She watched him leave the room to go downstairs and heard him try to hug the children.

"Come on, Mick, don't be that way."

"Fuck you," said Mick. "I want nothing to do with you."

"Daddy will email you later," Anthony said to Annie. She couldn't make out what Annie said back to him.

When Beck had heard him go out the front door, she walked downstairs.

Mick was sitting down, slouched back in his chair, his arm stretched out on the kitchen table, staring across the room. Annie was leaning against the counter, biting her nails and looking at the floor.

"Come on now, my darlings," Beck said as she walked into the kitchen. "Come here, come here." They stood up and she gathered them into an embrace. The three of them stood together in the kitchen, arms wrapped around each other.

"It's not good. I know it's not good," Beck said. "It's going to be hard for all of us. But we are more than up to the task of managing this. I know we are."

CHAPTER 2

It was mid-morning on Monday, and Beck was back at work after spending five days at home with the flu, five days of feverish dreams and being chased by ghosts, dead *and* alive. But now her fever had dissipated, her throat was no longer sore, and her lymph nodes were almost back to their normal size. She had just finished going over the outline of the teachers' documentary with Nick and was settling in behind her desk.

She'd done a draft of the outline on Sunday. She was feeling much better but was still tired and didn't want to get out of bed, so resting on a sea of pillows, she took a pad of yellow lined paper from her night table and wrote Teachers Care about the Future across the top. Drawing three vertical lines, she divided the page into columns, giving each column a heading: Says Who? Care about Who? Do What? She filled the columns in with the answers to the questions, lay back, closed her eyes, and imagined the pacing of the show. Then she listed, in longhand, the people they needed to interview: classroom teachers, parents, maybe the police or social workers who could talk about the issues facing students.

On the next page she wrote Shot List at the top and thought about visuals that would help tell the story. Shots from the back of a police car might be good, she thought. Let it be about the issues teachers are facing in the classroom, she reflected, instead of at the bargaining table. When she went through it with Nick, he liked it and suggested they hire a well-known (and sympathetic) musician to write a soundtrack. They had enough to take to Joy Kobayashi. She could give it to Asmi to format.

"Knock, knock."

Beck looked up. Asmi was in the doorway, holding a tea tray.

"May I come in, Beck?" said Asmi. "I've brought you tea and some fruit. I figured you could use a snack about now, since you are just getting better from your flu. You will have to take it easy for a few days, you know. We don't want any relapses," she said, laying the tray on the coffee table and stopping to smile at Beck. "It's nice to see you back in your chair."

"Sure, Asmi. Thanks. I was just about to come by your office to give you the outline of the teachers' documentary to format for me. Can you take it now?" Beck asked as she held up the folder.

"Yes, by all means, Beck," said Asmi, taking the folder from Beck's hand and flipping it open to take a look. "I see they kept you busy while you were at home sick," she said, shaking her head with gentle disapproval. "At the same time, I know Bain and Yvonne will be happy to see this. I will have it ready in a couple of hours. Is that okay?"

Beck nodded.

Asmi stood still. "But ... ah ... do you have a minute, Beck? May I talk to you for a minute?"

"Of course," replied Beck, motioning for Asmi to sit down.

"Beck, I need to ask you a huge favour ... and I know this is a terrible time to be asking for favour," she said, "what with the teachers' campaign, the big pitch for breast cancer and, of course, your being sick and everything."

"What is the favour you're thinking about?" Beck asked.

She looked at Asmi, who now had a little smile forming on the corners of her lips. "Aha!" exclaimed Beck, clapping her hands together. "I know! Jai finally spoke to his mother. That's it, isn't it?"

Asmi nodded and allowed the smile to break open on her face. "In a manner of speaking," she explained, telling the story of her calling her mother and her mother saying she would take care of everything, then Jai getting up the nerve to call his own mother.

"Thank goodness! Finally," Beck said. "This is good news, don't you think? This is what you want, right?"

Asmi nodded.

"I'm very happy for you, Asmi. I am. I can say now I was beginning to worry a bit."

"Me too!" Asmi said. She laughed and then got serious.

"But I will need some time off work, Beck—most likely a month, and this is the favour I am requesting. I can use up my holidays, of course, but I do understand that being gone for a month is a long time. I will train someone here to fill in for some of the things I do, but I know, Beck, that you rely on me for many things."

"It's okay, Asmi," said Beck. "I do rely on you, it's true, but we'll manage—*I'll* manage—for a month. Have you set the date?"

"My mother is getting suggestions for an auspicious date from the people who know about such things," Asmi said, as she took out her iPhone to look at the calendar, "but we are thinking it will be the month of May, next year."

"Okay. Wow. Well, we have a little time to plan, then. At least May is usually a bit slower around here, what with everyone getting ready for summer."

Beck looked at the clock. "I'm sorry, Asmi, but I've got that meeting here in five minutes.

"Right, you do," said Asmi, "and you don't need me, right?"

"Right," Beck said and nodded.

"Thanks for being so understanding, Beck," said Asmi as she stood up with Beck's file in her hand. "To you, I owe everything. My whole life here in Canada, I owe to you. You took a chance on me. This I will always remember."

"Thanks for the tea, Asmi. You're doing a great job," said Beck. "Let me know when you get the auspicious date finalized."

As Asmi was walking out the door, Todd was walking in with his Moleskine notebook and a file in his hand.

"Hiya, Beck," he said, sitting down in an armchair. "How are you feeling now? Is everything okay? You're doing all right?"

"Yeah, yeah, I'm good."

Bain and Yvonne came in with their heads down and carrying their notebooks. Nick ambled in empty-handed, trailed by art directors Sebastian Bøllt and Desi Lu. Sebastian was very tall and blond, and he wore his hair long. Desi Lu may have been five feet tall at the most; she was of Asian descent. Her dark, straight hair hung down to her waist, and she carried a portfolio in her hand.

They were both wearing black from head to toe.

"The purpose of the meeting," began Todd, "is to convince the National Breast Cancer Society that we can execute all aspects of the fundraising and the communications program they're tendering on.

"Beck, while you were out sick," Todd continued, "we asked Sebastian and Desi to prepare a couple of boards for us—so we can have something creative to take to the pitch meeting."

"Sebastian, why don't you start?" said Todd, looking over at the art director.

"We all know *creative* is the key that will unlock a whole strategy," Sebastian began, "so we've put together tag lines for three potential campaigns. And remember, they're just ideas, right? It's not based on anything." He drew a square in the air and pointed to the middle of it. "Okay, think donors as audience."

Desi pulled out a board that gushed soft pink with undertones of yellow and blue, giving it a retro surfer look; it reminded Beck of John Van Hamersveld's *Endless Summer* movie poster. A young man and women stood in the foreground, with looks of surprise on their faces and their hands in their pockets as if they were looking for their keys.

Desi announced the tag line. "A cure for breast cancer could be hiding in *your* pocket!" she exclaimed, underlining *your* in the air for emphasis. She stopped and saw a few nods.

Sebastian brought the next board.

"This one is more subdued," said Desi. "A *gentler* approach."

It was a grainy black-and-white picture of a woman sitting on a park bench gazing off into the distance. There was no colour in the picture except a pink bandana on the woman's head. "We're asking the question 'What if it was *your* mother?'" said Desi, once again underlining *your* in the air.

Desi paused—she didn't seeing anyone nodding.

"Okay, this one is a bit more fun, a bit more uplifting," she said, raising her hands as Sebastian held the board.

It featured a crowded city sidewalk. The pedestrians were facing the camera and smiling; a stylized cityscape towered in the background. The footwear on each pedestrian was pink and looked as though it had been coloured in by crayon. All the boots, shoes, sandals, sneakers, and slippers had been filled in with pink crayon. "The tag line?" said Desi. "All for one and one for all!"

No one said anything.

"Well, guys—what do you think?" asked Desi. "I mean, they are just preliminary ideas, but what do you think so far?"

"We're not bringing creative into the meeting," Beck said.

"What do you mean?" said Sebastian. "You have to bring creative to a credentials meeting, or else you're going in there with one hand tied behind your back. Creative is *key*. We have to show them we can make their ideas look good."

"We're not interested in their ideas," said Beck. "They are interested in ours. Creative is not key. It will distract them, and they'll start talking about type size and the use of the colour pink," said Beck.

"As much as there are good elements in each of these boards, creative is not a strategy," she added. "Creative is a *commodity*. The NBCS is looking for a *strategy* that will solve a problem. And what's the NBCS problem? That they don't have the right tag line? That they need another shade of pink? No, that's not their problem. Their problem is that their supporters are lost in the Barbie aisle. And the people who *are* seeing them are getting pissed off because they perceive them as a pink monster with its hand out looking for money or sympathy or both. But they've got this huge infrastructure to maintain, and revenue is down. *That's* their problem. And a tag line is not going to solve it."

"What are you going to say to them if you don't bring creative?" asked Desi. "Everyone else will be bringing creative."

"I'd say to them exactly what I just said to you," responded Beck.

Beck made a sketch on a yellow pad. "But here is something we *can* bring to the meeting."

She tore the yellow page off the pad and handed it to Desi. Todd and Nick leaned in to look.

"Let me see that in a variety of type treatments," Beck told the art directors. "Upper case, lower case, block type, reverse type. I'll look at however many you want to do."

"Okay," Desi said with a nod. "I think we get it."

"All right, good. I'll choose one, and we'll make it a PowerPoint slide," said Beck, "and we'll take that to the meeting instead of you guys."

Sebastian and Desi stood up. "Thanks, Beck. Sorry you didn't like the work," said Desi.

"Nah, it's not that I didn't like it," she said, standing up to shake their hands. "It's just that creative is not what we need right now. Do a strong type treatment with what I just gave you," she said, pointing at the yellow paper. "That's what I need right now." They nodded and left the room.

"It's risky," said Todd.

"No kidding," said Beck.

* * *

At the end of the day, Nick stopped by Beck's office. She was standing in front of her desk, just about to put her coat on. Nick took the coat from her and held it up so she could slip her arms into it.

With her coat on, she turned around to face Nick, and he put his hands on her shoulders. "How are you doing—how are things?" he asked, looking into her eyes. "Are you okay?"

Beck slid her arms around Nick's waist and pulled herself close to him, her head resting just under his chin. She was able to hear a faint heartbeat through his shirt. "I'm okay, I think, Nick. I was pretty sick last week," she said. "It was kind of scary. I was scared."

"You want to grab a drink or something?" Nick asked, putting his hand on the back of her head and smoothing her hair.

"That's okay, Nick. I've got someone to go drink with tonight, thanks," she said, smiling and raising her head to look at him.

He laughed and kissed the top of her head. "All right. Just let me know if you need anything."

"I will," said Beck as she let go of his waist.

"Okay," he said, squeezing her shoulders before he turned to walk out of the office, graceful and paced.

CHAPTER 3

"Where is Tilda Grubbs?" Beck asked. She was sitting at her desk, talking on the phone with Nick. "Have you seen her around?"

"Hmmm ... let me think for a second," Nick answered. "Let's see ... she called in sick last week, and I don't believe she's been in since. Let me check."

"Could you?" asked Beck, "I just got a call from Bill Barnacke over at Tedesco Data and Letter telling me they are holding on to 350,000 pieces of the Seniors' Organization of Canada membership mailing because they haven't received a cheque from us to buy the postage."

SOC's mailings were worth tens of millions of dollars a year, and they received the vast majority of their revenue from them. The most lucrative mailing of the year was their November membership mailing—it was the first of the renewal notices sent for the next calendar year and the one to which most members responded.

All expenses for producing a mailing like this could be billed after they were incurred, all expenses except postage. Canada Post didn't give anyone postage unless they paid for it up front. Social Good fronted the postage to the vendor and invoiced the client. Most times, Social Good received the postage money from the client well before the mailing.

Now a trusted vendor was saying they hadn't received the postage cheque.

Beck explained the situation to Nick. "Bill said *our* project manager told *his* production coordinator that she was about to call Dmitri Wattage to tell him the mailing might be late because she didn't have the postage cheque to send to Tedesco. The production coordinator at Tedesco's end told Bill. Bill told her to leave it with him and Bill called me to see if there was a problem. Is there a problem, Nick? Can you see if a cheque was cut and where it is?"

"Yep, I'll look," said Nick, "and I'll be over in minute."

"Thanks." Beck put down the phone—*Tilda fucking Grubbs.*

Nick gave a little knock on the open door of Beck's office and strode in carrying a file in his hands.

"There's no postage cheque in here, Beck," he said, flipping through the pages, "and I don't see one in QuickBooks that's ready to print. The invoice is here, but no cheque."

"You're sure you don't see one already cut?" asked Beck.

"Nope, I double-checked," said Nick. "There's nothing here for Tedesco and nothing for that amount, which would be just over one hundred thousand dollars, made out to anyone else."

Beck watched Nick as he sat down.

"Beck," he said with a grim face, "I called Tilda a minute ago. I wanted to see if she could remember doing the cheque. Her number was no longer in service."

"When's the last time you heard directly from her?" asked Beck, the blood draining from her face.

"I got a text from her a week ago to say she was feeling sick," said Nick; he had his iPhone in his hand and was scrolling through his messages.

"When was the last time she was in the office? That we actually saw her?"

"Let me figure it out exactly," said Nick, sitting back in his chair to think. "Today is Thursday. She hasn't been in this week at all. And the text she sent telling me she was sick was from last Wednesday. But she was in last Monday." He sat forward. "It was last Monday, Beck, a week ago Monday—10 days ago; that's the last time I actually saw her in person."

"Knock, knock." Todd poked his head around the door and looked at the two of them. "What's the matter?" he said. "What's going on?"

"Come in. Sit down, Todd," said Beck, waving her hand.

"We haven't seen Tilda Grubbs in 10 days—have you?" Nick asked. "I just called her, and the number is no longer in service."

"Haven't seen hide nor hair of her," said Todd. He stood still and looked down at the alarm spreading across both of their faces. "Uh … could that spell trouble?"

"Let's not go too far down the road until we know for sure," said Beck. "Since she's not answering her phone and we haven't heard a word from her for more than a week, we should go over to her house to see if she's okay. Maybe she's got a new phone. Maybe she's sick or something's happened to her." Beck thought of Nell from the Blue Door and how her computer programmer friends had come to rescue her. "It's weird we haven't heard anything. You'd think if something very bad had happened, someone would call us."

Beck looked at Nick and Todd. "Can you guys go over to her place and check it out?"

Nick nodded. "She lives in Cabbagetown; I think. I have her address," he said, scrolling through the contact list on his phone.

"I don't know if I'm the best one for this, Beck," said Todd, looking uncomfortable. "Honest to God—they see Nick and me, a longhair and a black guy, knocking on some white lady's door and peeking in her windows, someone is going to call the police, and believe me, they'll ask questions later."

Beck looked at Todd. He was serious. "You think they might—"

"Oh yeah, no question," said Todd emphatically.

"Okay, yeah, I get it. Fuck, okay, fuck, shit," said Beck, calling up several injustices at the same time. She looked at Nick.

"You'd best wear your suit jacket, Nick," she said, "and take Yvonne with you. If there's no answer when you knock a few times, don't go poking around, just call the police. Tell them you are worried about her because you work with her and haven't seen or heard from her in more than a week and you're coming to check it out. Todd and I will deal with Tedesco."

Beck sat up straight as she remembered that it was *her* production manager who might have raised a false alarm with Dmitri Wattage.

"And if that friggin' project manager breathed one word of this to Dmitri Wattage—which as sure as I'm sitting here, she did—he'll be calling any minute, reading me some kind of goddamn riot act about his mailing not dropping on time. And Todd is going to have to stop me from telling him he can wipe his friggin' arse with his goddamn mailing.

"Shit!" she said as she slapped the top of her desk.

* * *

Nick and Yvonne took a cab to Tilda's address. It was a three-storey building, with what looked like four large studio apartments on each floor. It was set back from the road, with a small lawn and trees in front. When all the trees were in full bloom you would barely be able to see the entrance. Earthenware pots containing ornamental cabbages decorated either side of the front door. Nick and Yvonne looked at the brass plates indicating the apartment numbers and mailboxes. Nick had his iPhone in his hand and said, "It says apartment 204."

Yvonne scanned the brass plates, found 204, and pressed it. They waited. Nothing. She pressed it again. No answer.

"What do we do now?" she said to Nick.

"Press the button that says superintendent," said Nick, biting his lip.

"Can I help you?" a male voice came through the intercom. He sounded as if he was chewing something.

"We're looking for Tilda Grubbs," said Yvonne loudly, a bit more loudly than was entirely necessary, thought Nick. "We are her work colleagues, and she's been missing for over a week. We. Are. Coming. To. Check. On. Her," she said, enunciating each word to feel sure she would be understood.

"Okay, I got it. I'm coming right up," he said.

Beck's cellphone vibrated. It was Yvonne.

"Beck, the police are here now. Nick is talking to them. There was no answer at the door, so we buzzed the super and called the cops. They came pretty quick. Tilda lives in a nice little building—a bit old-fashioned, but with a lot of character—pretty cute. I should probably get something like it for myself, at some point—"

"Yvonne, stop it," Beck interrupted. "Just tell me what's going on."

"The super told the cops she left 10 days ago. She moved out. She didn't say where she was going. She's gone. Everything's gone. The super took the cops upstairs, and there's nothing left in the place. It's empty. She's pulled a vamoose. We're heading back to the office as soon as Nick finishes talking to the police. We're gonna grab a cab."

Nick and Yvonne headed straight for Beck's office as soon as they returned. Beck called Todd and closed the door when he got there. Beck sat behind her desk and the three of them pulled their chairs around it. No one said anything.

"What did the police say, Nick?" asked Beck.

"They said it looked like it *could* be suspicious," Nick said, "that it *might* have been planned. But we have to figure out what funds, *if any*, are missing. They asked about the amount of money that went through her hands, how long she'd been with the firm, and when she was last seen at the office. The super said she moved out of her apartment a week ago Tuesday and was probably already out of town when she texted me on Wednesday saying she was sick. Once she got my response, the phone was likely thrown away. That was eight days ago. The cops said she could be anywhere by now, and they don't have any reason to look for her—although they did say they'd run her name for priors."

Yvonne chimed in, reading from her notebook. "They told us that if we find anything amiss, a detective will come to see you," she said, "but they suggested that you not use your staff to investigate it."

"I'll call the accountants," said Beck. "Any issues would have to have been this fiscal year, I think, since everything balanced out last year—unless she had a shell company going. We'll need some kind of an emergency audit."

"We'll give them the presentation room to work in," said Nick, "like we do for a regular audit. No need to spread this any further. We might have to say something to the rest of the staff if there's an investigation, but we'll wait."

Todd and Yvonne left, and Beck looked at Nick. "This could be so bad, Nick. What if she's been giving postage money to herself? That would be millions of dollars."

"It's probably not postage money, Beck, or we'd have heard," he said, "just like Bill Barnacke called you. Mailings would have been held up, and we would have had unexplained mailing results, so I don't think there's bags of mail sitting in a warehouse somewhere with no postage. She might have set up some kind of shell company to pay herself for services, like you said earlier."

"But if she did that, why would she stop, I wonder?" said Beck. She sat with her arms folded on her desk, and she looked baffled. "There were no suspicions at our end. We were oblivious."

"It's gotta be something that she figured nobody would notice right away," said Nick. "If it was a shell company, that's all well and good; we look stupid, but it's money under the bridge, if you know what I mean. We've already incurred the losses. We're stupid and have lost money being stupid. But if she's done something that makes us liable for the funds she may have embezzled, that's another story."

Beck nodded. "It's the legacy she could be leaving us with that would explain why she hauled up stakes and left town. Or maybe she just hauled up and left town for a reason that's got nothing to do with us."

"I hope you can get those accountants here soon," Nick said, slumping further in his chair, "and I never thought I'd be saying *that* in a million years."

CHAPTER 4

The firm's accountants, Helen Breach-Üpsay and Cassandra Lowender, did their work. It took them five days. Tilda's computer, her desk, her files, everything she touched had been wheeled into the presentation room. They went through every cheque, every invoice, every email, and every note—everything that Tilda had ever come into contact with.

They provided their report in the way a funeral home director might approach a grieving client.

Helen offered as good news the fact that Tilda hadn't emptied their bank account, so there was money to pay bills, salaries, and so on, and a "small amount" of profit from the first three quarters.

The bad news was that she hadn't paid, and maybe hadn't filed, the Harmonized Sales Tax for the past three quarters.

She'd actually prepared the paperwork for each quarter's filing, signed it, and prepared a cheque to cover it, which both Nick and Beck, blissfully unaware, had signed. Maybe she'd filled in the Payable To section on the cheque *after* she'd gotten the signatures, or maybe the cheque had just been in a pile that had needed to be signed, they suggested.

"You may have been distracted," Cassandra suggested by way of an explanation, "and just looked to see that the amount on the return matched the amount on the cheque and then signed it, without looking at who the cheque was actually payable to."

Beck looked at both of them without saying a word. *That's exactly what I did,* she thought, *except I didn't bother to do the part about matching the amount on the cheque and the amount on the return.* She shifted in her chair.

Cassandra handed one of the cancelled cheques to Beck. There was her signature—big and bold. The payee was written in as C. R. Argentum.

Beck handed the cancelled cheque back to Cassandra. "Well, fuck *her*," she said. "How much do we owe for three quarters of HST remittances?"

"It's just over $300,000. It's $327,000 to be exact," said Cassandra, checking her file. "That's a preliminary estimate, plus interest and penalties."

"Will CRA give us a break with this, since we seem to be the victims of a crime here?" Beck asked.

"No chance," said Cassandra. "As far as they're concerned, you have their money in your pocket, and they want it. They don't see the fact that someone robbed you as their problem. Any day now, you are probably going to be red-flagged on someone's computer, either for not filing or not paying."

"You'll probably need to get a lawyer," said Helen, taking off her glasses and looking at Beck with sympathy, "and do what they call a voluntary disclosure. They might give you some leeway because of a police investigation, but only in terms of payment schedule and potential interest, not about the amount owing."

"And just so you can plan your financial position," said Cassandra, handing Beck an invoice, "the professional service cost you've incurred for our work to date is just shy of $15 thousand. And we'll need to bill another $10 thousand or so to get this stuff ready for the forensic auditors and continue to liaise with them."

Beck nodded. Her comparison to funeral home directors was holding.

"What are we looking at in terms of interest and penalties?" Beck asked.

"On $300,000," asked Cassandra, "for the better part of a year? You're probably looking at $70,000, maybe $100,000."

"So altogether, for the HST money Tilda stole, the potential penalty and interest from CRA, your fees, and the lawyer's fees, we're looking at about $450 thousand dollars?"

"Yes, that's about right, Beck, and you might want to call that police detective now," said Helen. "We can come tomorrow and brief him, if you want. You can talk to your lawyer about that too. And Beck," added Helen, "I know we've given you a lot to think about, but we can place one of our juniors here for the time being, so your current financials are being looked after."

Beck turned pale at the thought of having someone new coming in to deal with the books.

Cassandra saw Beck's expression. "If he screws up, we're liable," she said, closing the file on her lap.

"Okay, let me sit with all this a minute," said Beck. She felt as if the wind had truly been knocked out of her sails.

"Sure thing," said Helen. "It's a lot to process."

Beck stood up, walked to the terrace, and lit a cigarette.

Jesus H. Fucking Christ, she thought as she sat down on the café chair. *That fucking bitch. That Tilda Grubbs going on and on about cellphone bills. The little Miss Priss, pretending her nose was out of joint over a telephone bill, making herself so unbearable that Jesus Christ Almighty couldn't wait to see the back of her. She did that on purpose. She knew I was hiding* something. *She* played *me. And now she's gone—with my money. Worse yet, with CRA's money! What a sack of shit she turned out to be.*

"Well, now, Beck," said Milton Cary, a partner of the firm of Cary, Bratty, Drew, and Lively, "that's quite a story. I gotta say I'm sorry to hear that."

Beck had known Milton from the time she'd started her company. They knew a lot of the same people and often bumped into each other at social functions. He knew that when you were calling him for advice, it wasn't the best day of your life.

"You've been bamboozled, that's for sure," Milton said with gruff jocularity. "Don't worry, Beck; I'll hook you up with our tax people. It's pretty specialized stuff. I got a couple of good guys back there. And they'll be cheaper than me—ha ha ha. I expect you'll want to be getting that started pretty soon. Today or tomorrow? I'll get one of them to call you. The CRA are pricks to deal with."

"Milt, I'm juggling a lot of balls here. It sounds like a lot of legal and accounting stuff—your guys working directly with the accountants. Am I mistaken about that? Do I have to be sitting in on all this?"

"Good God—no, Beck," he replied, "not at all. Quite the opposite, in fact. You should have a briefing meeting with all the professionals in the room and leave them to it. Ask them to give you a report every week, or every couple of days for the next little while, since things are still fluid. Your job is to come up with the money to pay them—*and* the CRA, of course. You'll have to concentrate on that."

"What about the criminal charges against Tilda Grubbs?"

"At this stage, I don't think you need representation on that matter," said Milton. "Just give the police what they ask for. It could be a part of a bigger swindle, you know. It seems very surgical to me. Maybe some kind of embezzlement ring? The police and their forensic auditors will be wanting to look at it closely, I'd say."

"I feel pretty stupid, Milton, I gotta say—like I was asleep at the wheel," said Beck with a sigh.

"Ah, don't be too hard on yourself, Beck," he said, his voice softening. "People who get duped always feel dumb. But the bad guys, it's their profession. They practise being bad guys. That's why they're good at it. You're a good guy, Beck. Don't worry. You'll get through it. And come on—she didn't clean out your bank account, right?"

"Okay, Milt, you should have quit while you were ahead. I'll call you later."

"Bye, Beck. Don't worry; you'll be fine."

Beck was slumped in a chair on the terrace with her coat on and having another cigarette when Nick came out.

"Do you mind," he asked, picking up her package of cigarettes. "Can I have one?"

"Sure. Have a seat," she said, not moving her head but shifting her eyes in his direction.

Nick sat on the other café chair. His hair was blowing in the wind. His expressive face, usually alert, present, and quick with a smile, was tense, as if he were trying to focus but his mind was continuing to move in a million different directions. He ran his hand through his long hair and leaned forward in his chair to look intently at Beck. He was squinting like a pitcher trying to read the catcher's signs. She was sure that if he had been wearing a baseball cap, he would have taken it off, smoothed his hair, and put it back on again. But instead of winding up to pitch, he took the lighter off the café table and lit his cigarette.

"I let you down, Beck," he said, taking a puff of his cigarette. "I should have picked up on what she was doing. I can't believe I missed it. Signing off on those cheques—huge cheques. I feel really stupid—really, really, stupid—and now you're paying the price."

She looked across at him without changing her expression.

"I get that. I do, Nick, especially the feeling stupid part. I feel stupid too," Beck said. She wanted to kick her own shins black and blue.

She continued, "We're supposed to be so smart, right? We make our living at supposedly being so smart. Milton Cary said people who get swindled always feel dumb. But it's not your fault. I don't see it like that at all. It's that fuck-ass Tilda Grubbs's fault. That's whose fault it is."

Beck put her cigarette out in the ashtray. "But we're going to have to bring in more money," she said. "That's the only way out of this. It's the only way that I can see, right now, anyway. We're going to have to rock the breast cancer pitch and get *that* job for starters. And make the most money we can from the teachers' campaign *and* start leaning hard on that dickhead Dmitri Wattage, billing him for every fucking minute you or I spend even thinking about his problems. Because from what I understand, once CRA gets the scent of blood, they'll scratch out our eyes and come back for the sockets."

PART
FIVE

Gonna get a little bit high today,
Yes, I think I will.
Cause I got some pain to medicate,
And I'm all out of pills.
Whaddaya say, honey?
Want to go for a ride?

—"High"
Words and music by Lindi Ortega and Bruce Wallace

CHAPTER 1

Just as she was headed out to the Blue Door to meet Henry, a police detective called Beck to say they wanted to interview her about the possible embezzlement case the next morning.

The idea of being interviewed by the police made her stomach ache. Just as Tilda had sensed, they would know she was hiding something. They were pros at that. And they had lots of secrets to choose from. How about the fact that instead of being so smart, she'd come around full circle to stupid? That her best friend was staring death in the face and *she* was the one who couldn't cope? That her social life consisted of hanging out in a shabby bar with other people whose lives were also broken? *What has happened to me?* she asked herself, imploring the gods to answer as she walked quickly toward the bar. She sure as hell was hiding the car crash her life had become—how could she answer the detective's questions without spilling *those* beans?

Henry wasn't there when she arrived. She sat on a bar stool, wriggled out of her coat, and hung her bag on the back of the chair. Bill, the bartender, brought over half a carafe of wine and a glass of ice. The supper-hour news was on TV, and the Rob Ford debacle led the newscast again. The media coverage was unprecedented. There were new revelations every day. Unsealed court documents contained accusations of him driving drunk, buying drugs, sexually harassing staff, being violent with staff, consorting with criminals, making threats, and being stoned at public events. He had been deli meat on all the late-night shows for weeks. Stewart, Kimmel, Fallon, Letterman, Colbert, O'Brien, and Leno had pieces about him every night. Yvonne had kept her supplied with the YouTube clips.

A Florida county sheriff delivered the coup de grâce when he arrested Mayor Barry Layne Moore of Hampton, Florida, for possession and selling of drugs. "This is not Toronto," County Sheriff Gordon Smith said emphatically. "We will not tolerate illegal drug activity in my jurisdiction, by anyone, including our elected officials."

Rob Ford needs to stuff his bullshit right back down his throat, thought Beck as she put more ice in her wine—*just like the rest of us do.*

Henry arrived and ordered a pitcher of Rickard's Red. Beck ordered another half bottle of wine.

When they left to go back to his house, Beck didn't know what time it was or how long they'd been at the bar, but she was pretty tipsy. Henry had to put his arm around her. She felt as if she might start to cry.

When they got to his place, he poured a couple of drinks. She lit a joint and looked at him. *Wiry* was the word that came to her. He was strong, but it was all long, lean muscle and tendons, the way a long distance runner looks, not bulky like a bodybuilder. But because Henry's back was sore all the time, his movements were slow and methodical. He wore jeans and leather jackets mostly; tonight his blond hair was combed back off his face and his eyes were mostly bloodshot.

They were sitting in his kitchen, in the party palace. The music was reaching the part of her head that had been teary-eyed half an hour earlier. As she smoked the joint, she could feel the tears evaporate. They were replaced by the sensuous and liberating sounds of a saxophone being joined by a full horn section. She closed her eyes to ride the wave of harmony, an expression of feelings she couldn't even begin to name.

She opened her eyes and saw Henry holding out his hand with a big smile. A new song had just come on. She recognized it right away. It was an old one by the Drifters: *This magic moment / so different and so new / was like any other / until I kissed you.* She took his hand with a laugh, and they held each other closely as they slow-danced in his kitchen: *Sweeter than wine / softer than a summer night / Everything I want I have / whenever I hold you tight.*

She'd always found the song unbearably beautiful. Tonight it felt rapturous. Henry lifted her chin up and kissed her lips, gently at first, and then more urgently. He kissed the side of her neck and her shoulder. She closed her eyes to absorb the tenderness, the warmth, and softness of his lips on her skin.

He put his arm around her shoulder and led her upstairs to the bedroom. They both lay down on the bed, and she looked deeply into his eyes, feeling as if she could dive in and float around in their shimmering glow.

When Beck woke up, the clock on Henry's night table said 2:14 a.m. She was fully clothed, lying crossways on the bed, and she still had her shoes on. She looked at Henry. He was fast asleep, still wearing his down vest and boots. *Nothing to see here,* she thought, with some relief.

As she lay her head back down on the bed and looked up at the ceiling, she still felt kind of drunk. Had she already screwed up her interview with the cops? Before she even got there? Would she smell like a booze can? She'd be going in there feeling sick, for sure. That was a definite disadvantage. As soon as all the alcohol left her system, it would be replaced by a nauseated stomach, aching head, stiff neck, and an even more powerful sense of self-loathing than she possessed at this very minute.

How much actual time did she have to get ready? The cops were coming at ten in the morning. It was now two-thirty in the morning.

From where she was lying, a soon-to-be-hungover puddle on Henry's bed, she calculated that she'd have seven and a half hours until her appointment with the cops. Figuring on an hour to get home from here and an hour to get to the office, that meant five and a half hours. How to best spend five and a half hours? Not sleeping—resting maybe, but not sleeping.

Beck thought she should take care of how she looked on the outside first; that's what people saw. She'd wash and condition her hair so it would smell good and look soft. She could do that before a bath, so it would be conditioning at the same time she'd be relaxing. She thought she'd wear a suit, a nice suit, with pants and a jacket—the dark green one with the jacket that came down to the knee. It had a good cut and would work with a black turtleneck and small earrings. She'd rinse her mouth out a gazillion times, so as not to breathe boozy breath on everyone, and wear a little bit of makeup—not a lot, but some. And since her hair would be freshly washed, she'd leave it down.

She figured she might not feel like eating but vowed to make something light—salad, lean meat—to eat, put on some tunes, and pretend she was getting ready to go somewhere she wanted to go. And she'd think through the questions the cops would probably ask. Hopefully they'd be done by noon, so she wouldn't have to hold it together with them for too long.

But first, she decided as she sat up on the bed, she was going downstairs to smoke a joint and have a cup of tea. That would make the sobering up a lot easier. She looked at Henry's night table. *Hmmm … and maybe I'll borrow a few of Henry's Percocet, in case I feel really bad. He won't mind. He'll understand. It is a painkiller, after all.*

CHAPTER 2

Todd was on his way to see Nick about the teachers' documentary when he saw the two cops sitting in Beck's office. He froze in his tracks.

The guy in uniform was young, with neatly trimmed black hair and medium brown skin; he looked Asian. He was sitting on the couch, his bulletproof vest riding up around his ears. The other guy was white, in plain clothes, brown pants and a beige shirt, and was sitting in an armchair. He was middle-aged, a bit paunchy and balding, and he wore glasses. He looked more like an accountant than a cop.

They both had their notebooks open and looked to be writing stuff down. But, then again, maybe they were writing nothing down, or writing down something entirely different from what Beck was saying, Todd thought.

His felt his notebook get damp in his hand as his palms started to sweat. He could hear his heart beating loudly, and his breath became shallow. He thought he might throw up right there on the spot, just at the sight of them.

He turned around, walked straight back to his office, and closed the door. He figured that if they saw him he'd be under suspicion right away.

He sat in the chair behind his desk feeling as if he might faint. Having cops around was bad news. Todd could remember his nightmare with the cops as if it were yesterday.

CHAPTER 3

After her meeting with the police, Beck went straight home and changed into jeans and a T-shirt. She hadn't texted Henry because she didn't have the energy to meet him. She didn't dwell on him kissing her. She could barely remember what had happened and doubted very much that he would remember it at all.

The meeting with the cops went as well as it could have. She'd kept up her end, she thought. She had answered their questions and was happy enough with her performance. She'd noticed Todd passing by the office looking as if he'd seen a ghost. That was strange.

Now she was home, curled up with a blanket in the bright yellow family room off the kitchen and looking out on the backyard. The overstuffed couch was good for sitting up or lying down. She'd made herself something to eat, uncorked a bottle of wine, and flipped open her laptop open to read an email from Sam.

> *To: Beck Carnell*
> *From: Samantha Reed*
> *Re: Good news?*
> *Sent: Wednesday at 4:12 p.m.*
>
> *Hi, Beck,*
> *I guess the news is good. The doctor burst into her office with a piece of paper in her hand and a big smile on her face … admittedly that beats the Kleenex and sad face from last time, but I seriously could have used a bit less drama. I'm still upset about them messing up on the request for my CT scan and am*

trying not to show it because I might be making a mountain out of a molehill. I asked the doctor if I was the first cancer patient she's ever treated. She said no-o-o-o-o *in the way a teenager responds if you ask them if they've been playing video games when they should be doing their homework.* No-o-o-o-o, *like,* duh?

But the worst part was when I saw her face, and I saw her smiling and so happy—you know what went through my mind? And this is the sick part. She seemed so happy, and they've been so disorganized, I thought she was going to tell me it was all a big mistake. Honest to God, Beck, I thought that's what she was going to say.

But she didn't say it was a mistake. It turns out she was happy because the CT scan didn't detect anything on the pancreas (the opposite of what she told me in the first place) and that's good, right? I mean it is good. She said I only have a tumor on my liver and that it was the size of a grapefruit. There was laughing, carrying on, and general celebration. Maria Luisa, David, and Stanzie, my beautiful, now burdened daughter were there. Only on my liver! Only the size of a grapefruit! Huzzah! I'm the only one not celebrating. I want to cry. They're laughing. I want to cry.

I kind of freaked out a bit at the CT scan. It didn't hurt per se. It was more nightmarish than physically painful. First, there was a tiny little phone booth I had to change my clothes in. I couldn't help but think it was like a coffin. Then I had to lie on this very thin gurney and they gave me an IV with iodine for "contrast." The gurney was like a conveyor belt and slid me through a machine—like a huge mechanical doughnut—that made clicking, swishing noises. To tell you the truth, I haven't been the same since. When I'm home, in my regular clothes, I can kind of ignore it, but when I'm in the hospital or doctor's office, I'm cornered. If it weren't for Stanzie, I wouldn't go back to the doctor. I'd stay home, plan the garden for spring, and go to bed when I'm tired. David is here from BC for the next little while. He is coming to my appointments with me and was there for the CT scan. I was such a mess, I actually needed my little brother to help me walk out of the hospital.

I'm not up to going out or seeing anybody. It's not that I feel sick. I just can't bear it. It's pretty messed up, and I'm not sure when I might feel differently. I'll let you know.

But I do need to sort through what's in my mind. I feel I must do this in order to get some kind of equilibrium back. I've never been able to write in a journal. We've talked about that before, right? Writing when no one is going to read what you're saying has always seemed kind of sad to me, so I'm asking you to be my witness, Beck, to be my reader, to be the face I think of when I'm writing all this down—to be the face I can't face (ha ha). I also know you can handle whatever I have to say. I know you can. It's not going to scare you. And don't be thinking, "If only people knew how soft I am on the inside." I know that about you too and still think you're tougher than the rest.

Will you do this for me, Beck? Will you be my pen pal? (I'll do most of the writing at my end ☺). You can just grunt in response if you want.

Nosotros venceremos,

Sam

A tumour the size of a grapefruit? Beck could feel a sob welling up in her throat. And what the hell was it with the fruit thing? Tumours were always being compared to fruits and vegetables. Beck wondered if there was a laminated chart that featured tumour size samples and their associated fruit—a plum, a pear, or an apple. And following that, was there an international version featuring tropical fruits—guava, mango, papaya? Beck closed her fist. It looked about the same size of as a grapefruit. That was pretty big. The thought of it all made her feel sick. She threw the blanket to the side, got up to retrieve her purse from the kitchen table, and pulled out the little tin of joints Henry had rolled for her.

How long had the tumour been growing there, inside Sam, while she was going about her life, getting pissed off at her board, watching Stanzie practise piano, having lunch with Beck? Sam had just been living her life— and all the while this thing had been growing inside her, like a demonic embryo.

Beck lit the joint and sat back to smoke it, feeling the sob that was stuck in her throat dissolve with each drag. She closed her eyes as tightly as she could, scrunching up her face and holding it for a couple of seconds, then letting it fall into a relaxed position. She did the same with her shoulders, squeezing them up around her ears and letting them fall back down. She finished the joint, took a sip of wine, pulled the blanket around her knees, and reached for her laptop again.

To: Samantha Reed
From: Beck Carnell
Re: Good news?
Sent: Wednesday at 4:53 p.m.

Sammie, Sam, Samantha, dude, darlin':

I read your email twice. The short answer (visualize a grunt) is YES, I want to know what's going on in your head. I've always been interested in your thoughts, and I'm sure I will find them increasingly fascinating. Consider this as the forum for letting your freak flag fly.

Having a tumour the size of a grapefruit on your liver (I made a fist, and my fist is about the size of a grapefruit) is devastating—devastating. It's traumatic and devastating. It's not a cause for celebration. It's horrible. And you know as well as I do, because we've talked about this, that the cure could be worse that the disease. You feel like you're in a nightmare because you are in a nightmare. Let's call on Thomas Hobbes here to capture the moment. He said (more or less), "Life is nasty, brutish, and short." You're in for the nasty and brutish part, but it's <u>because</u> we don't want your life to be short.

Sometimes you hear talk about cancer like it's a path to zen, a cause for greater understanding, a road to self-actualization. How is that possible? It seems more like a book from the Old Testament, where God rains down punishment, doubt, and plague on the guilty and the innocent alike. He's punishing a species he finds irritating and offensive. And, you know, I don't blame God. I don't. I'd be pissed off if I were him too. I just wish he'd differentiate a bit more.

You said if it were just you, you wouldn't go back to the doctor or the hospital. I think I'd do the same if it were just me. Ties to other people hold us back like a leash on a dog. But what are you going to do? They are as real as anything else.

I look forward to hearing from you whenever you feel like you have something you want to say. Instead of doing lunch, we'll do email.

Beck

CHAPTER 4

E yes on her iPhone as she opened the heavy translucent door to the office, Beck read Yvonne's morning tweet and smiled.

"I am not a criminal," says Rob Ford, #provenCRACKrecord.

Once inside, she looked up, startled. A young man sat in the waiting room, wearing a black suit and shoes, stiffly ironed white shirt, and plain navy tie. There was a black briefcase lying in his lap. He sat with intention, looking like a Mormon on his missionary year.

"Hi," said Beck as she walked in, "can I help you with something?"

"Ah yes, Ms. Carnell. You're just the person I'm looking for," he replied, laying his briefcase to one side and jumping up to greet her. "I'm with the accounting firm Builder & Boss. I'm the junior accountant Helen Breach-Üpsay told you about. I've come to fill in as finance manager—until everything with the books gets sorted out."

"You've got some kind of ID?" asked Beck, eyeing him with suspicion.

"Yes, ma'am," he said, taking out his driver's licence and giving it to Beck with a business card. "You *are* Beck Carnell, aren't you, ma'am?

Beck looked at the picture on his driver's licence, up at him, and nodded. "Helen didn't say who, *specifically*, would be coming," she said, handing back the driver's licence and putting the business card in her pocket.

"I totally understand and appreciate your care regarding the admittance of someone who claims to want to help you with what is, of course, a very sensitive portfolio," he said.

"A-hem," he coughed, lowering his voice and leaning closer to Beck. "I am very sorry, ma'am ... *very* sorry ... about what happened. It sounds like

you've been left with a bit of a mess, if I may say." Then he straightened up and backed away from Beck.

"I'm Trevor Price," he said, extending his hand. "Very pleased to meet you, Ms. Carnell."

Trevor was a good head taller than Beck, and his legs seemed to fold and unfold like those of a German shepherd puppy. He had lots of black hair that matched his eyebrows. Both were neatly trimmed and framed his brown eyes. His oval face didn't look as if it had seen much sun, but his lips had colour.

"Please call me Beck," she said.

"I wouldn't dream of it, Ms. Carnell. But you can call me Trevor," he responded, smiling and shaking her hand enthusiastically.

Just then, Yvonne came through the reception area, her coffee and cellphone in one hand and a sheaf of papers in the other.

"Ah, Beck! You're just the person I'm looking for," she exclaimed. "Nick is out this morning, and I need someone to sign off on this media buy. It'll give you one last chance to look it over before we commit."

She looked at Trevor Price, then back at Beck. "Who's that?" she asked, pointing at Trevor.

"Yvonne, he's standing right there; he can hear you," said Beck.

Trevor smiled at Yvonne.

"Trevor Price, Yvonne Precipa. Yvonne Precipa, Trevor Price," said Beck. "Trevor, Yvonne is our media-relations manager. Yvonne, Trevor is a junior accountant with Builder & Boss, coming in to help us since … since … well, since—"

"Since Tilda left?" said Yvonne.

"Yes, that's it," said Beck finally.

Yvonne extended her hand, and Trevor shook it.

"I'm very pleased to meet you," he said to Yvonne, bowing slightly.

"Oh, the pleasure is all mine, I'm sure," said Yvonne, smiling up at Trevor and giving what looked to Beck like a shallow curtsy.

"Yvonne," said Beck, "since Nick's not here, could you get Trevor sorted out at a desk? For now, put him where … um … where—"

"Where Tilda sat?"

"Yes, put him there for now, but can we get that smaller office emptied of junk and put him in there as soon as possible?"

"Sure. I'll get Asmi to give me a hand. But," she said, holding out the paper she held in her hand, "how about while I'm getting Trevor here sorted out, you take a look at this media buy and sign it off for me?"

"Okay. It's a deal," said Beck, taking the paper from Yvonne.

"All right, Trevor Price. After you," said Yvonne, gesturing with her arm to indicate that he should precede her.

When Trevor's back was to her, Yvonne turned around to look at Beck, jabbed her finger toward him, mouthed the word *hot-tie!* and pretended she was touching the stove.

Beck shook her head and watched them walk into the production room together.

CHAPTER 5

To: Beck Carnell
From: Samantha Reed
Re: The surgeon visit
Sent: Thursday at 3:00 p.m.

Hi, Beck,

David and I got to the surgeon's appointment today (finally!). David made me get my hair done beforehand. He said it would make me feel better. He said it's better to look good when you're going to the doctor. (Does everybody think this, or is it just David?)

When we sat down in his office, the doctor started complaining about his sore finger. See that? he said, holding his hand up and pointing at the ring finger on the left one. I hurt it last night playing hockey, he says. A surgeon with a sore finger? Not impressed.

He says he's 99 percent sure it's liver cancer. He wants another ultrasound, but whatever it is, he says it has to come out.

I was trying to behave like a serious consumer of health care. They encourage that in the book I'm reading—if you're not satisfied, ask questions, get a second opinion.

I told him that I thought since he was a surgeon he would naturally lean toward a surgical solution, but since what I appear to have is so serious, maybe we should get a second opinion. He said, you know, you can do that if you want, you can get a second opinion, but you can also ask around here, and *they'll tell you I'm "the guy" (quotation marks his). I'm the guy they send the toughest cases to. Google me, he said, and you'll see. You are welcome to get a second opinion, he said, but I'm telling you honestly, in your position, I am the guy you want.*

I googled him when I got home. He's a big hombre all right—does all kinds of things other doctors won't touch—and has good results. His patient testimonials are off the charts. He wants to schedule surgery. They'll be doing a right hepatectomy. That means they're taking the right lobe of the liver. I'm scheduled for December 2.

How are things with you? The teachers' thing is hitting the fan now, for sure. I hope it's not keeping you awake at night.
Nosotros venceremos,
Sam

CHAPTER 6

A pair of pink sequined running shoes twirled inside a glass case, giving the impression they were suspended in mid-air. Round and round they went, twinkling in the sunlight that flooded the reception area of the National Breast Cancer Society, and generating a bobbing, weaving light show on the pale grey walls.

Across the room, 20 women with linked arms burst out of a wall-sized poster. They were jogging through the finish line of a race, shoulders thrust back in pride and heads topped off with curly pink fright wigs.

Pink tinfoil stars were taped to another wall, looking as if they'd been hung to impress parents at a school open house. Pieces of construction paper, some with scalloped edges, others cut with pinking shears, were glued to the stars and contained handwritten messages. "Mom, I ran for you today. RIP," said one. "I miss my darling bride. Love, Faizal," said another. "Fuck breast cancer!" shouted another. A Post-it note half-covered the word *fuck*.

A row of chairs ran around two of the four walls. Beck, Todd, and Nick sat on one side, Yvonne and Bain on the other. They were about to pitch their biggest job ever to T. J. Avery and Sylvia Bumley of the National Breast Cancer Society. Beck wore a black turtleneck, short skirt, and calf-length jacket. Her hair was half up, half down.

A stack of brochures lay on the end table next to a big glass bowl of what looked like jumbo pink marshmallows. Beck picked up one of the balls and squeezed it in her hand. It felt like a mushy version of one of those stress balls, but it had a little nub. She held it up to read the writing on the side. "Feel your boobies," it said.

She picked another one out of the bowl. "Don't forget your mammy!" it admonished.

"Ah, fuck, it's a bowl of titties, for Christ's sake," she said, holding it up so the others could see.

Sitting in the chair next to her, Todd started to laugh. Nick looked up and smiled. Beck frowned, staring at the bowl.

"Are we babies now? Is that it? They can't talk to us like adults? They have to talk to us like we're babies?" she said, gathering steam for what was beginning to sound like a rant.

Maybe it was because they were nervous about the pitch or tense about everything happening at the office, but the three of them started to giggle and couldn't stop. Yvonne and Bain, who were in a deep, serious conversation on the other side of the room, looked up.

Beck had her breath drawn and mouth open, ready to direct another round of admonishment to the bowl, but she collapsed with laughter instead.

There was no receptionist in the room, but the young woman in the first of a long line of offices, who'd poked her head out when they'd arrived, poked her head out again.

"Everything okay here?" she asked.

"It's okay. We're good," said Bain, ignoring the giggling trio and smiling at the young woman. "Thanks very much for asking."

"Let me check on T. J. and Sylvia," she said. "They said they'd be about 10 minutes—that was 20 minutes ago. I'll go see."

Bain glared at the three of them. "What are you guys doing—trying to get us kicked out of here? Get a bloody grip on yourselves."

Just as Bain spoke, the conference room door opened, and a large group of people streamed out, one after another, after another. The line seemed endless. *I've seen big pitch teams,* thought Beck, *but this?*

Finally, when Roger Rhodes and Rick Range walked out at the end of the line, Beck and Nick realized that the big group was from Rhodes Range Associates, Canada's "direct and digital marketing masters." It looked as if they'd brought the whole company. There were at least 30 of them milling around in the reception area, talking and laughing, and they all wore pink scarves. The scarves were draped around their necks, tucked into their jackets, or tied into bows at the front; one woman wore a pink hijab.

Having regained control after Bain's scolding, Beck and Nick stood up to shake hands with Roger Rhodes and Rick Range.

"Looks like the gang's all here," said Nick as he smiled and shook Roger's hand. "Nice scarf," he added when he saw the fuchsia material peeking out from under Roger's jacket.

"You bet, Nick. It's a big piece of work," Roger said, out of breath from all the excitement.

"No kidding. Well, good luck with it, Roger," Nick said, clapping him on the shoulder.

"You too, Nick. To the victor go the spoils! Ha ha!" he said as he turned to leave.

Beck shook hands with Rick and Roger but didn't make conversation. She was, despite the tittie-ball and pink-scarf distractions, trying to focus as she walked over to speak with T. J. Avery. He was wearing a beautifully cut medium blue suit, light blue shirt, and deep red tie. He was busy shaking hands with more people than Beck had had at her wedding and was looking impatient.

Sylvia Bumley stood next to him, looking awkward. T. J. had insisted on doing all the pitch briefings in one day, and she'd booked them 40 minutes apart, figuring there would be ample time for bidders to get in and out without having to run into each other. Now look at the mess her planning had become!

"It looks like you'll need a few minutes to say your goodbyes here, T. J. Maybe we can just head into the conference room?" suggested Beck.

"Of course," said Sylvia. T. J. nodded.

Beck motioned to her group, and they all walked into the conference room with Sylvia.

When they got there, Sylvia closed the door behind her, and all went quiet. Todd approached Sylvia. "Wow, that was quite something," he said, shaking her hand and patting her on the shoulder.

"Hey, Todd. No kidding. It sure was a lot of people. How are things going with you guys? Do you have a PowerPoint? Do you need the projector?"

Yvonne smiled. "We have one slide. Should I just connect to this?" A projector was set up on the middle of the boardroom table, which was now littered with half-empty bottles of water.

"Yes, please do," she said to Yvonne. Turning to the group, she added, "Would anyone like some water?"

"That'd be great," answered Todd. "Here, let me help get rid of these for you," he added, quickly picking up the water bottles on the table and taking them to the blue recycling bin at the end of the room. Yvonne helped, and the table was cleared in a minute.

Sylvia looked at Todd gratefully. "Thanks," she said. "I'll be right back."

When Sylvia returned, T. J. was with her, buttoning the middle button of his suit jacket as he entered the room. "Sorry about the delay, you guys," T. J. said as he scanned the room, his eyes landing on Beck. "Aha, Beck Carnell. It's been a very long time since I've seen you. I keep hearing good things."

"Nice of you to say, T. J., and congratulations on the new job. They've clearly brought in the cavalry to shake things up."

"Well, that's nice of *you* to say, Beck," he said, smiling widely and motioning to Sylvia Bumley. "We *are* trying to dust the cobwebs off, aren't we, Sylvia?"

T. J. was tall and fit, with just a touch of greying hair, a spirited and polished guy in a well-made suit who probably had regular manicures. He had an infectious smile and animated blue eyes.

"Great," said Beck with a laugh. "Let's get dusting."

"Okay," said T. J. as he sat down. "Pitch away."

"I'm going to ask Jack Bain to start us off with an assessment of how we think your organization is currently positioned," said Beck. T. J. nodded.

Bain let his Scottish accent fly. "Well," he started, "it's gr-r-r-eat to be with you today! I'm here to situate us in the facts. Firstly," he said, holding up one finger, "there exists a growing backlash against what is perceived as the 'breast cancer industry.' People trying to raise money for other serious cancers, like lung cancer or pancreatic cancer, are becoming frustrated by what they see as the breast cancer contingent's cornering of the fundraising market. There was an ad campaign in the UK recently telling people they were 'lucky' if they had breast cancer. By *lucky* they meant that at least money was being raised for a possible cure. Some people felt it was a bit off colour, but even *they* said they understood where the frustration was coming from.

"Secondly," said Bain, making what looked like a peace sign with two of his fingers, "there's a growing concern about the number of pink-ribbon products on the market. That concern has a name; it's called 'pink-washing,' and people are suggesting the companies are using breast cancer to sell products. Some see fundraising organizations as complicit in this.

"Thirdly," said Bain, holding up three fingers, "there are organizations springing up in the USA and Canada to counter what they see as 'mainstream' breast cancer charities. There's way too much money going into the wrong pockets, they say, like Big Pharma and expensive research projects. These groups are garnering thousands of new supporters every day. Right now, in North America, there are dozens of legally constituted groups who are specifically dedicated to critiquing whatever it is the so-called mainstream breast cancer organizations are doing.

"Four," he said, holding up four fingers, "some—specifically, well-respected and articulate feminists—see the pink as the infantilization of both a serious disease and the women's movement."

"Finally," he said, holding up his whole hand, "there's rising concern about where all this money is going. In the last few years, there have been four bestselling books by well-known authors that talk about what they see as problems in breast cancer fundraising and treatment. Despite messaging to the contrary, breast cancer is not being beaten. Some studies actually show it is *increasing*. So naysayers are asking, 'What's going on?' and 'What's happening to all that money?'

"In short," said Bain, "breast cancer fundraising and breast cancer organizations generally are beginning to have a serious credibility problem. The pink bubble of breast cancer fundraising is set to burst. Maybe not this year, possibly not next year, but in three to five years, this is all going to go up in smoke," Bain said, making a *poof* with his hands like a magician.

"If it's money you're looking for, pink is not sustainable. In three years, it will look about as healthy as red Jell-O."

Yvonne picked up the narrative from there. "In our media scan of breast cancer stories," she told them, "for every three positive stories—stories promoting fundraising events, personal victories, or promising research—you'll find one complaining about breast cancer fundraising itself, where the money is going, or the efficacy of treatment and screening options. This number has been steadily climbing over the past three years, and we believe it will continue to climb as more organizations and high-profile individuals critique breast cancer fundraising and research. As the organizations Bain referred to gain strength—and that is absolutely guaranteed to happen—it will become harder for your message to resonate.

"Perhaps," Yvonne said, looking directly at Sylvia, "you've noticed it has become much harder to get press out for your events: the walks and runs, funding announcements, and so on."

Sylvia nodded.

"Not your fault," asserted Yvonne. "The fact is, there is a tremendous amount of media fatigue and growing skepticism about breast cancer funding and fundraising. Reporters are increasingly reluctant to quote breast cancer-related press releases and much more inclined to offer critique.

"Right now, if you are a reporter," continued Yvonne, "the much bigger story is what's wrong with breast cancer treatment, funding, and fundraising. That's what they are interested in. And, as Bain said earlier, as the groups who are critiquing breast cancer funding and research get stronger, the more of that type of coverage you are going to see. Guaranteed. There's no getting around it."

"How come you are the only guys saying this?" T. J. asked. "You are the only firm we're talking to who is saying this stuff."

"I can't speak for the other guys," said Beck, "but we don't design communications or fundraising campaigns based on perceived altruism, optimism, and guesswork. We manage issues, and sometimes we manage crises. On any given day, we are doing as much research and communications as we are marketing and fundraising. We develop our campaigns with a thorough understanding of what's actually happening in the market, as far as that can be understood by anyone. We study regular media, social media, blogs, journals, and reports. We talk to people all day, every day, and not just to the people who agree with us. It's our business to know what's trending and in which direction."

"This change is happening already, T. J." said Todd. "All the signs are there. People are challenging what's going on, not only in breast cancer fundraising but *all* cancer fundraising."

"But what can be done? We're only one organization," said T. J., throwing up his hands.

"Here's what you can start to do," said Nick, reaching over to click on the only slide they'd prepared for the meeting. It came up on the screen as a square black block.

"It's a black block," said T. J. "I don't get it."

Nick pressed the space bar, and words appeared: block letters in Helvetica Bold Condensed.

THE UN-PINKING
OF BREAST CANCER

"The un-pinking of breast cancer," Sylvia Bumley read aloud.

"Yep, that's it," said Beck. "That's the strategy."

"Wow," said T. J., sitting up straight in his chair, "that's huge!"

He shook his head, and then he looked at Sylvia.

"If I *un-pink* breast cancer," he said, "what am I going to do with all the money coming in from those corporate deals that are based on the pink-ribbon marketing? How many of them do we have now, Sylvia?" he asked.

"There's 43 deals in the pink-ribbon partnership category—from luggage to razor blades," she answered.

"And how much are we making from that?" asked T. J.

"Hmmm—let me take a guess," Beck interrupted. "We know 80 percent of consumers are more likely to buy a product tied to a charitable brand than a comparable product which is not. So there is motivation for any company to get on board some kind of cause in order to be the product with the charitable angle in its category. You almost have to do it, don't you? The pink-ribbon razor blade company might give you ten cents for every three coupons a consumer sends in. That's three packages of razor blades that have to be purchased *and* sent in before you see a dime—literally. And how long does it take to go through one package of razor blades—a month, maybe?"

"What do you think, Sylvia?" asked T. J.

"It's not a lot of money per partnership, T. J. It's more about awareness than actual money at this point. And because we have so many pink-ribbon partners, it adds up," she said. "And we do have a minimum of $25,000 for each pink-ribbon partner."

"A $25,000 minimum? How many pink-ribbon partners raise more than $25,000 for us?" T. J. asked.

"Well, none of them," said Sylvia. "That's why we had to institute the minimum. It would take 250,000 people to send in their razor blade coupons to make $25,000, and the buy-in is nowhere near that amount. It is more about awareness."

"How much more awareness do you need, T. J.?" asked Beck. "Unless you've been living under a rock, you know what a pink ribbon means. It's ubiquitous."

Yvonne chipped in.

"The amount of earned media you will get over this un-pinking strategy—internationally—will be like nothing you've ever experienced. And we'll set up a concurrent fundraising plan that makes sure the increased exposure turns into dollars for you. Companies who want to get behind the brave new world will come on board with more actual money than they're giving now. The un-pinking of breast cancer will make news, front-page news, and the people who want to be a part of that will come along for the ride."

"How sure can we be that it will make more money?" asked T. J.

"Well, T. J., there's no guarantees in this business," said Nick, "but the change is going to come, and you can either be leading it or following it. It's already happening."

"This is a big thing, T. J.," said Beck, "and a decision of this magnitude would have to be discussed at the highest levels of the organization; we understand that. Take your time. If you're interested in this kind of approach, we are here to help you. If you're not interested right now, we totally understand. You can just let me know when you're ready. It's a big change, but if you want to dust off the cobwebs, we're here to help you do it."

"Would you guys work with us if we kept the pink?" asked T. J.

"Well, we liking working on *successful* campaigns, T. J., campaigns that break new ground. That's why we're suggesting this," said Beck.

"Here's a credentials package for you," Todd said, handing T. J. and Sylvia a crafted book bound in soft leather. "It summarizes the services we offer and the experience of our people—from strategic to production, mail to digital, media to account management—along with documentation of our presentation."

"It's a one-stop shop, T. J., and for something like this, we'd need a lot of hands on deck," said Beck, smiling and folding her hands.

"How much would you charge to execute?" asked T. J. Avery.

"Sixty to seventy-five thousand dollars," answered Beck.

"That's it?" said T. J., raising his eyebrows.

"A month," said Beck, "in fees only."

"Okay then," said T. J., opening his palms, "what can I say, Beck? It's a big idea, but we'll definitely consider it. As it happens, the board is meeting in two weeks." He surveyed them all. "Thanks for coming over and for giving this your best thinking. You've given *us* a lot to think about."

"You're welcome, T. J.—and you too, Sylvia," said Beck, looking at them both with the sympathy that big decisions warranted.

Beck and her team shook hands with T. J. and Sylvia. They remained seated in their chairs; they were looking shell-shocked.

CHAPTER 7

Trevor Price walked into Beck's office at exactly the appointed time, wearing a dark grey suit and grey tie. He had an open laptop in his hand.

"May I sit down, Ms. Carnell?" he asked.

"You can, Trevor. But I have to tell you, I've got no time to talk to you about cellphone bills and taxi chits. If that's what you want to talk about, I'm not playing."

"With all due respect, Ms. Carnell, why would I want to talk to you about that? Your cellphone bill is not going break the company, I presume? Not as far as I can see, anyway. No, I think we have bigger fish to fry." He was looking at her with a serious expression.

"Bigger fish?" she said, her heart sinking.

"Yes, ma'am. I'd like to talk to you about margins. I've been working on some scenarios, and I'd like to talk about your current profit margins. The company is profitable, yes, but it's slim … your margins are slim. Slim," he repeated, showing a small gap between his index finger and thumb.

"And I think there's a couple of ways we can make them wider. Wider," he said again, showing a bigger gap between his index finger and thumb.

"Okay, Trevor, I've got the slim and the wide thing down," Beck responded with a slight smile.

"Good," he said, "because, in reality, that's the only thing *you* ever have to worry about.

"Now," he continued in a more serious tone, "I've looked at your staffing scenarios for the last five years and compared it to your overall billings for each of those years. The amount of resources you are spending per dollar of revenue earned has increased quite substantially.

"For example, five years ago, you were spending 83 cents for every dollar you made. That means you made a profit of 17 cents on every dollar. Last year, you spent 95 cents for every dollar you made; that's a profit of 5 cents on every dollar. You've made incrementally more gross revenue, which gives the appearance of making more money, but you are not making more money. You are, in fact, making less money, a lot less."

"Spending 12 cents more for every dollar we earned? That seems like a lot," said Beck, surprised at the difference.

"It *is* a lot," emphasized Trevor. "Do you want to know how much that was for your last complete year of billings?"

"Sure."

"Three hundred and ninety-six thousand dollars."

"Three hundred and ninety-six thousand dollars? You're kidding me!" said Beck. "That's what we're essentially leaving on the table? That's a lot of money—especially given our current situation."

"Yes, indeed, Ms. Carnell. The answer to your predicament may not *all* be on the revenue side of the equation."

"Well, now, that would be news," she said.

"The makeup of your business has also changed in the past five years—quite significantly, in fact," said Trevor.

"How do you mean?" asked Beck.

"Five years ago, 50 percent of the revenue came in direct marketing—direct mail, in particular, including production and fees. Last year, it was 37 percent. But your spending in that area grew—you added four new positions and bought a very expensive piece of software for production management. Spending more, making less," he reiterated, hands showing a wide gap, then a narrow gap.

"Can you show me your spreadsheets?" Beck asked.

Trevor nodded with enthusiasm. "May I lay my computer on your desk?" he asked.

Trevor took Beck through revenue versus expenditures, year by year, for the past five years, showing how expenses had incrementally increased at a much faster pace than billings. If you just looked at year over year, it didn't look like such a large amount. But, by looking at five years, it became apparent they were getting a bit bloated.

"Well, maybe Little Miss Muck Fuck did us a favour in the long run," she said to Trevor when he'd finished.

"Well, Ms. Carnell," he replied, "it's always admirable to try to look on the bright side of things."

CHAPTER 8

Dmitri Wattage was already seated at a table by the window when Beck walked into Canoe, a table Asmi had had to book three weeks in advance. Canoe was on the 54th floor of the TD Tower on Wellington Street, in the centre of Toronto's bustling financial district. It was one of the most highly rated restaurants in the city, and the view was truly breathtaking. Beck would have loved to have been there by herself with a bottle of chilled Chablis and a tasting menu.

She could have spent the afternoon watching Porter flights taking off and landing at the Billy Bishop Airport, sailboats zigzagging on cold Lake Ontario, and the ferry boats churning up water as they filed back and forth from the Toronto Islands to the mainland. From her perch, she would see eye to eye with the crane operators and watch them lift 16-thousand-pound slabs of concrete, floors for the new condo buildings, as if they were toys in a playroom. But there would be no fun for Beck today. She was here to schmooze Dmitri Wattage, the executive vice president of the Seniors' Organization of Canada, her second-largest client—and that was all work and no play. She arrived 10 minutes early for their twelve-thirty reservation, and he was already there.

When she saw him gazing out the window, Beck assumed that he was thinking he was ahead in some little game: *Oh, this is a win for me. I'm here first; I'm lying in wait. Beck is at a disadvantage.* That was the kind of game Dmitri always played, thought Beck. Every encounter was a battle over a hilltop, and his getting to the restaurant first was winning the hilltop. But any advantage Dmitri thought he had just won by being there first was non-existent. He held no advantage, because she didn't consider his being there first a disadvantage. She squared her shoulders, walked over to the table, and prepared to greet a man who, in her consideration, had already started to play himself out.

Dmitri stood up and held his arms out to greet Beck. He had a barrel chest that extended to a barrel belly. She thought that the two of them were about the same age. His hair was black and full, parted on the left and combed over to one side. His complexion was dark and his eyes brown. The padding underneath his cheeks stretched the skin so his face was shiny. His suit was black and well fitted; several yards of material had gone into its construction. His shirt was white. The yellow and red poof sticking out of his breast pocket matched his tie and looked like a miniature version of the puppet Finnegan, from the old children's TV show *Mr. Dressup*.

"How are you doing, Beck Carnell," he said jovially, taking her by the shoulders and giving her a kiss on each check. "That's kissing the European way, ho, ho," he said, laughing. "Long time no see." He pulled out her chair.

"Thanks, Dmitri," she said, surreptitiously wiping her cheeks as she watched him sit down.

The waiter came over and lay down two menus. "Can I get you something to drink before lunch?" he queried.

"Sure, I'll have sparkling water," said Beck. "Maybe a bottle for the table. Is that okay with you, Dmitri?"

Dmitri nodded, smiling. "I'll have whatever the lady is having," he said exuberantly to the waiter. "She's the boss!" The waiter walked away to get the drinks.

"Nice to see you," Beck said as Dmitri settled back in his chair. "Have you been enjoying the view?"

"Oh yeah, it's a great view, all right," he said, looking out the window. "Those crane operators especially," he said. "You have to know your stuff to sit up in a crane all day. My daddy was a crane operator. He worked on cranes for years."

Dmitri looked away from the window and faced Beck. "He went up in the crane in the morning with a full lunch bucket and an empty pickle bottle, and he came down at the end of the day with an empty lunch bucket and a full pickle bottle!"

"Ha ha," Beck laughed, "that's funny. Are you on Twitter, by any chance?"

"A bit, not much," he replied.

"Well, there's a crane operator, the one in that crane right over there at the L Tower," she said, pointing to the new condominium tower designed by Daniel Libeskind, the famed architect who was also part of a team that had designed the new World Trade Centre. "He tweets pictures from his crane all day long—fabulous pictures of the city, the clouds, the weather— sometimes hawks and eagles. I follow him on my Twitter. I'll bet your dad would like something like that."

Dmitri's smile disappeared, and he looked almost ready to cry.

"Oh, I'm sorry, Dmitri! Have I upset you? Is your father okay?"

"Never mind, Beck. It's all right," he said, looking out the window again. "Cancer took Dad from us last year."

"My sympathies to you, Dmitri. I'm very sorry, I am," said Beck with a look of concern.

"You sound like you know what you're talking about, kiddo. Is your father still alive?"

"No, I'm afraid my father's been gone for quite a few years now," Beck said.

"What happened to your father?" said Dmitri, "if you don't mind me asking. It's okay if you don't want to talk about it. I know you're a private person. I understand."

There he goes again, thought Beck, *always trying to blur the lines. If I don't answer, the Beck-Carnell-as-bitch-with-no-feelings narrative goes unchallenged. If I do answer, I'm bringing up a life-changing event I don't want discuss—especially with him.* She wondered if his line about his father having died was even true. He may have heard something vague about her father and made up a story about his father, just to trick her into giving personal information—information that he would no doubt use to try and manipulate her at a later date.

Beck returned his gaze. "He drowned, Dmitri," she said. "My father drowned off the coast of Newfoundland. There were two other men on the boat. They were all drowned—lost at sea." The words felt strange coming from her mouth. She didn't think she had uttered them in more than a decade.

"Jeez, Beck, that must have been a helluva shock for all of you," said Dmitri, lowering his head.

"Like I said, Dmitri, it was a long time ago now."

The waiter returned with a chilled bottle of sparkling water. "Have you had a chance to look at the menu?" the waiter asked as he put down the glasses and poured the drinks.

"Have you had a look, Dmitri? I think I know what I want."

"Yep, I'm ready," said Dmitri. "I'll have the foie gras to start and then the flat-iron steak—rare and bloody—just walking out of that kitchen, ha ha ha!"

"I'll have the lobster club, and the iceberg lettuce salad to start," said Beck, closing her menu. The waiter nodded, collected the menus, and walked away.

When the salad and foie gras arrived, Dmitri leaned in. "Everything with that postage cheque work out okay, Beck?" he asked. "You had your account manager a little worried for a while. She said she didn't know when it was coming. To tell you the truth, I was surprised she called me."

"Well, Dmitri," replied Beck, "as Todd and I told you on the phone, the bookkeeper went off sick, and a couple of things fell through the cracks. When Bill Barnacke called me, we sent a cheque right away. There was never any danger of that mailing dropping late."

"Still … it had us worried," Dmitri said, raising his eyebrows.

"You were worried about that, Dmitri?" said Beck. "Clearly we are making things a bit too easy for you, if you're worried about nothing to worry about." She laughed to take the edge off what she'd just said, and Dmitri laughed too.

The waiter arrived with his flat-iron steak and her lobster club. "What do you think of the little challenge put to us by this vendor I emailed you about?" asked Dmitri, after taking a bite of his steak. "Social Good does a mail campaign, and these other guys do a mail campaign," he said, looking at her with his fork in his hand. "A test package—head to head—of 100,000 pieces each. See which one does better.

"Don't get me wrong, Beck," he said. "They're not going to hold a candle to you. No one could. But I know you don't mind a challenge either … or a little bit of fun," he added, putting his hand over hers.

Beck looked down at Dmitri's hand. He didn't move it. She looked up at him, and he still didn't move it. She slid her hand out from underneath his.

"Hands off the merchandise, Wattage," she said.

"No harm, no foul," he said, smiling and shrugging.

"That depends on who's doing the harming and the fouling," said Beck, looking at him with no smile on her face. She gave a little shudder as if to shake the whole thing out of her mind.

"Anyway, Dmitri," she carried on, "you're a smart guy. I get that, and I know your job may not offer you all the challenges you're up for. Holding mailing contests between vendors may be amusing to you, but it's not going to give you the kind of results, the kind of profile, you're looking for. You've got a huge organization there—350,000 people over the age of 55—that's one of the biggest associations in the country, probably second only to CAA. But I don't hear that much about you in the media. I don't see you having much visibility on Twitter, and believe me, Dmitri, seniors are the biggest new users of social media. Even the Prime Minister is using Twitter for policy announcements. What does your communications department do?"

"It's a small department. They send out newsletters, pull together the annual report. They've done a membership survey. They're talking about doing a special newsletter on health issues, since many of our members say they have concerns about their health," he said.

"Do they have a media-relations strategy?" asked Beck.

"No, they definitely don't," replied Dmitri. "Their strategy is to keep us *out* of the media. They don't see media as a good thing."

"Well, Dmitri, I have to tell you, as I'm sure you know: media *is* a good thing—especially when you are an organization trying to advocate for a potentially vulnerable demographic, and especially when you have 350,000 signed-up members. There's a whole range of issues you can be commenting on. Is there a spokesperson? The CEO?"

"No, she definitely doesn't want to be a media spokesperson. She wants to retire," he said.

"Maybe you, then? Maybe you can be the spokesperson?"

"Maybe," Dmitri said, eyeing Beck suspiciously, "that might be fun, but what are you getting at, Beck, exactly?"

"I'm saying that you have to stop messing around with mailing challenges," said Beck, "and start spending your time doing something that will give your association a higher profile and significantly higher mailing results."

"I've never done media before." He paused. "Though I have been told I have a good voice for radio."

"Well, a bit of media training will help," said Beck, encouragingly. "I can have our media-relations people draw up a plan for you. It'll make sense when you see it all on paper."

"Okay, have them do that," said Dmitri, "and we'll set up a meeting to go over it."

"Okay," said Beck, "we can come to your offices."

"No, I'll come down to you," he said.

"Okay. I'll talk to Yvonne Precipa, our media-relations manager," said Beck, "and get back to you about when we can have a proposal ready—roughly two weeks, I'd say, but I'll confirm."

"Okay," he said, smiling at her.

"Now," said Beck, "I have to go back to the office, so I'm going up there to pay the bill and to have the waiter bring you a cup of coffee and a glass of Taylor Fladgate 20-year-old Tawny Port. You can enjoy the view and think about your media profile. Okay?"

"Okay, thanks, Beck," he said as he got up from his chair to say goodbye, kissing her on both cheeks the way he had when she'd arrived. Just as she was about to turn away, he kissed her a third time, on the lips. Then he stood back, watched the expression on her face, and laughed. "Gotcha!" he exclaimed.

"You knock that off, right now!" she said, jabbing her finger toward his chest. "Knock it off, Dmitri. Or you'll get no media-relations plan and certainly no more lunches at Canoe. And forget the port. There is no 20-year-old port in your immediate future."

"I'm just joking," he said, holding his hands out in protest.

"I'm not laughing." She walked up to the bar, paid the bill, and left.

When she got out on the sidewalk, Beck lit a cigarette and considered what Dmitri was playing at. In the months after Anthony had left and her divorce had become public knowledge, a few men she'd worked with had taken her out for lunch to let her know they had "open" marriages. "Wow, good for you," had been her only reply.

But she didn't think Dmitri Wattage was actually interested in her sexually. In Beck's mind, it wasn't about that. It was a power play, pure and simple. He was the one who didn't want to be vulnerable to anyone else's game. He probably thought unwanted sexual advances disguised as schoolboy antics would be humiliating enough to put her at a disadvantage. He wanted to hold all the cards in his hand. That's how bullies operated in the playground, and as they got older they just got more nuanced.

Well, she thought, if all went according to *her* plan, he'd soon be falling in love with his own publicity.

CHAPTER 9

B eck decided to walk back to her office after her lunch with Dmitri. It was a beautiful day, and she wanted to be one of the thousand little sidewalk specks she had just seen from the tower. It surprised her when she realized it had been 10 years since she'd talked about her father, 10 years ago this month, in fact.

Why was that? Why did she never talk about it? Anthony had never brought it up after the first year, and her brothers weren't going to. So who was there to talk about it *to*?

Some people equated fishermen to farmers. They saw a similarity between the harvesters of the land and harvesters of the sea. Beck saw no comparison in it at all. To Beck, farmers stood as tall, stiff, and silent as the stalks of corn so many of them grew by the acre. Fishermen, by comparison, were windswept and agile, and they lived to tell their tall tales. A farmer didn't surrender his fate to a merciless mistress every morning when he went to work. Fishermen were more of the sea than they were of the land, and they embraced it, more out of need than out of love.

If you were a fisherman, you were grateful because the sea put food in your mouth and in the mouths of your babies. You sang songs about her, cherished her, and gazed longingly at her when she was too icy to mount. Your wife and children were afraid of her, until the boys reached a certain age and came over to your side, *her* side.

Beck had been around fishing boats and fishermen all her life, but the boat she'd felt most comfortable in was the one in which she and Poppy used to drink tea, the one that had been hauled safely up on the beach rocks.

Her mother and father, and her brothers Mikey and Alf had always insisted she wear a life jacket when they were out on the water. "Just in case," they'd said.

"What about you, just in case?" she'd asked. "Why aren't you wearing a life jacket, just in case?"

"Don't be talking back, Miss Mucky Muck," they'd said. "You just do as you're told."

Beck had been scared out on the water, even with her father at the helm. It was wild, dark, and deep, the sea foam like monstrous soap bubbles, and she knew it could swallow them up without a trace. When her father taught her how to spot whales, she'd had something else to worry about; she was afraid a whale would come up under the boat and lift them right out of the ocean on its back.

Her father had said not to worry about being afraid. It was right to be afraid, he'd explained. It was people who *didn't* feel afraid of the sea that got into trouble. If you were afraid, it meant you'd be all right.

* * *

She must have been about 8 or 9 years old the evening her father turned off the *Fisheries Broadcast*, a Newfoundland radio program of fishing news, and announced they should all go to St. John's.

"The Portuguese White Fleet is going to be in St. John's on the weekend," he said to her mother. "Why don't we take the youngster in to have a look? They're not going to be coming around much anymore. The White Fleet is starting to die out now. And it would be a sight for her to see."

Beck thought he might as well suggest they fly to the moon. No one took trips to St. John's unless they had to go to the hospital.

"Well, now … I don't know, Baxter," said her mother. "That seems a long way to go, doesn't it?"

"Maybe you're right, girl, maybe you're right. It *is* a long way," he said, about to turn his attention to something else.

"But I suppose we could, though, Baxter," her mother chimed back in. "I could visit Aunt May when we're in there. She's up in the Grace Hospital with a broken hip. Maybe Mikey could do a bit of the driving. You know, Mikey's more used to the traffic in St. John's."

"Well, missus, I don't suppose I need Mikey to do my driving—" he started to say, but then he thought better of it, because it was hard enough to get Beck's mother to leave Herring Neck, and he realized he'd better not do anything to stand in her way.

"Okay, my duck, why don't you give Marlene a call to see if she can spare Mike from the house on the weekend? We'll have to stay in St. John's for one night. Do you figure we'd stay up to your aunt May's?"

"For God's sake, no, Baxter! I don't want to stay at anybody's *house*," she said. "Maybe we can get some kind of rooms at a hotel or something. Not the Hotel Newfoundland, mind you. That's a bit expensive. Maybe up at the Battery on Signal Hill?"

"Do we have the money for that, Rachel?" Beck's father asked, thinking his practicality might be encouraging.

"Yes," said her mother thoughtfully, "I believe we do. And I've always loved the Portuguese White Fleet, those white boats. How beautiful they look in full sail—one of the most beautiful things I have ever seen, with all the wooden dories piled up on the decks. We'd get a good view of them coming into the Narrows from the Battery Hotel."

"We could get two rooms—one for you and the little missy sittin' there," her father said, nodding in Beck's direction, "and one for me and Mike—if Marlene can spare him, that is," he said, careful not to take too much for granted.

The Battery Hotel sat halfway up Signal Hill, a lookout that had been used as a military and merchant communication hub between land and sea. Flags had been raised and lowered on Signal Hill for hundreds of years. Then Marconi had transmitted the first transatlantic wireless signal from there in 1901. The hill overlooked an expanse of the Atlantic Ocean as well as the Narrows, a thin passage into St. John's Harbour. The Narrows was invisible from the sea. Sailing along the coast, you couldn't see it until you were almost on top of it. It would, indeed, be a great vantage point to see the White Fleet coming into the harbour.

"What's the Portuguese White Fleet?" Beck asked.

"Why don't you get that picture book down from on top of the bookcase and show her, Baxter?" her mother said as she dried her hands with a dishtowel.

Beck's father hopped off his chair to get the book and thumbed through it until he came to the picture of St. John's Harbour he was looking for.

"See there, my duck," her father said, pointing at five white ships that stood out among the rest. "This is an old-fashioned picture, but these are sailboats that sailed—they *sailed,* mind you, using the power of the wind to cross the Atlantic Ocean to fish off the Grand Banks of Newfoundland, for centuries.

"You see those little wooden boats piled up on the side of her decks, the way your mudder stacks the bowls in the cupboard?" he asked Beck.

She nodded. She could see the stacks of tiny boats.

"When they come to the fishing grounds, they'd lower a man down into each one of those little boats, and he'd jig cod all day, either with a short line or a long trawl line, a line with little bait hooks that ran a quarter mile behind his boat. They weren't nets, mind you," he said to Beck. "He had the long line or the short line, that's it, and he fished all day."

"Are there motors on those little boats?" Beck asked.

Beck's father laughed. "The only motor on them dories was the muscle a man has in his arms, my duck, and a little sail they used, if the wind was right. In the morning they'd get dropped over the side, and they rowed to where they wanted to fish. 'Not too far,' the captain would say. He didn't want them a long ways away from the boat. Then they rowed back to the ship when their dory was full. Every boat had three oars, two to row and an extra, just in case one got lost."

Her father continued, "At the end of the day, the fisherman heaved his catch aboard the big boat, and they hoisted him and his dory back on board. After dinner, they cleaned and salted the fish they caught that day. They worked like the devil, those men did. They're good honest men, those Portuguese fishermen, always have been.

"But," he said as he tapped the page of the book, "those boats are not going to be around much longer. There's faster ways to fish now. Everything now is on big ships. They've got mechanical nets. Those trawl nets will pick up a season's worth of fish in one week. Plus anything else that can be dragged up with it," he added.

It turned out that Marlene could spare Mikey, and they got up on

Saturday morning for the drive to St. John's. When they got to their rooms at the Battery Hotel—Mikey took care of getting them checked in—they looked out their windows and could see the White Fleet in the distance, coming toward the Narrows in full sail. The boats were bright white against the dark sea. The closer they sailed, the better they could see the fisherman and crew out on the deck, getting ready to come through the Narrows.

"If we watches them here for another few minutes and then gets into the car to drive down to the waterfront, we'll see them come in that way," Mikey said.

Beck's mother called out, "Baxter, look. Take a look out there. Is that the *Gil Eannes*?"

Beck's father took a couple of quick steps to the window where her mother was pointing. Beck looked too. It was another white ship. This one didn't have sails; it was big and white with a huge red cross painted on its smokestack.

"Yes, Rachel, I believe you're right—that *is* the *Gil Eannes*. Mikey, look, see," said Beck's father, "there's the *Gil Eannes*."

"I can see it, Dad," he said. "She's a beauty."

"What's a gillyannus?" asked Beck.

"What are you saying, child?" said her father, eyes still on the window.

"What's a gillyannus?"

"Oh, right," said Mikey. "First, it's not one word. It's two words, and it's a person's name. The first name is Gil, like short for Gilbert. Second name sounds like ee-AN-us. His name is Gil Ee-AN-us and he was a Portuguese explorer, like Gaspar Corte-Real who's got his statue up by Confederation Building, only Gil Eannes didn't come to Newfoundland, and that ship is a Portuguese hospital ship named after him. They've got everything on that ship—operating rooms, X-ray machines, a dentist chair, and they've got nurse and doctors, too. We saw a film about it in school. It looks after all the men in the Portuguese White Fleet. If they gets sick or injured, they can get aboard that ship and be looked after. They can do everything a hospital can do. You'd be better off getting sick in the White Fleet than you would in Herring Neck, for that matter.

"Hey, Mudder," Mikey called out, "Per'aps we should go get yer aunt May and put her aboard the *Gil Eannes* to get her hip done?"

"Oh, Mikey, you're foolish," said Beck's mother, but she laughed.

By the time they got the car down to the harbour and found a place to park it, other people were congregating on the waterfront to welcome the White Fleet. People waved at the boats, and the fisherman waved back.

The ships were docked four deep into one berth at the wharf. The men in the ship tied up furthest from the dock had to jump over three ships to get onto the wharf. The boats wouldn't be here for long—24 hours, maybe 36 hours, to get supplies.

Her mother bought Beck some fish and chips from a stand, and they milled around with the others who'd come to see the fleet. The Portuguese fishermen were dark and exotic looking. Beck watched them jump from ship to ship. Some of them started to play a game with a black-and-white ball they kicked around, sometimes using their heads to pass off to each other.

Beck's father and Mikey were talking to a group of three fishermen, all of them with their hands and arms going full speed. She saw her father clap them on the back and heard him laugh.

Beck was delighted. Her father and Mikey were having fun. So was her mother. She'd rarely seen her mother enjoying something so much. She pointed out lots of little things to Beck, the way the men wore berets on their heads or how the captain stood outside the bridge of the ship, looking down on his men with a smile. They walked by the *Gil Eannes* and saw the crew, men *and* women, all dressed in white, looking out at the people on the waterfront. They smiled and waved.

"Now, look at that, my love," her mother said, crouching down beside Beck and pointing up at the pure white boat. "Have you ever seen a ship so white and clean? Imagine," she said, "a hospital ship. See up there? There's women on board. They're the nurses."

Beck had never seen a boat so beautiful as the *Gil Eannes*. The women were waving and laughing.

"Don't you think that's a gorgeous sight?" her mother asked. "Imagine if you were sick at sea and you saw that boat coming toward you with all those people on board wanting to make you well. Wouldn't you think you were going to heaven?" she asked, laughing.

* * *

It was 10 years ago that month, the month of November, that Mikey had called Beck with the news of her father.

Her dad had never recovered from losing her mom, Beck thought. He was lonely and at loose ends all the time, hanging around over at Mikey and Marlene's or Alf and Cory's, looking for something to do, someone to talk to.

Then he, Uncle Sceevie, and this fellow from Merritt's Harbour had the idea they were going to fix up one of Dad's old longliners. They were going to do some hobby fishing, they said. They couldn't go fishing for cod because of the moratorium, which never got lifted, but they wanted to do something to fill the time. Alf said it was more likely they wanted to go hobby *drinking*, not hobby *fishing*. "But what can you do?" he'd said. "They're grown men."

"They were out in that old longliner they fixed up," Mickey to Beck, his voice cracking over the telephone. "The weather was getting bad, Beck. It's middle of November, for Chrissakes, but they're paying no heed, getting on board that boat at one o'clock in the afternoon, steaming out, for what purpose, I can't say. Maybe they just wanted to set anchor and have a bit of peace and quiet?

"A storm came up quick, as they do this time of year, and must have caught them off guard. They were gone for 28 hours before the Coast Guard found the capsized boat. She was lying on her side, the lifeboat still aboard her and the life jackets still in the locker," he said. "We didn't want to call you before we knew for sure, but Dad is missing and presumed drowned. Come home, Becksie, because we'd love to see you, but there's not going to be a funeral. We don't have a body to bury."

Beck didn't take the kids to Newfoundland that time. They were both in school, and Anthony wasn't able to come, so she thought it might be easier if she just went by herself. She stayed with Alf and Cory. Their three kids were grown up and married by then. The day after she arrived in Herring

Neck, the captain of the coast guard ship that had found the capsized boat came to see them. It was her friend Maggie's father, Captain Nate Blackwood. He came to the house in his uniform.

"Come in and sit down, Captain Nate; please come in," said Alf.

Cory came in from kitchen, drying her hands on her apron. "Can I get you anything, sir? A cup of tea? Would you like a drop of rum?"

"No, thank you, Cory; I can't stay long." When Captain Blackwood saw Beck, he took both her hands in his and held on to them. "I'm sorry, Beck, my dear. I know you loved your father, and God knows, he thought the world of you. Are you all right? Maggie sends out her love, as does Mrs. Blackwood."

"I'm okay, I think. I'm still in a bit of shock," Beck replied, tears coming to her eyes as she looked into the captain's face and realized, at that moment, that her father could actually be gone.

"That's only natural, my dear," said the captain. "You're going to feel out of sorts for a while, but time will make the pain easier to bear."

"Captain Blackwood, I'm so grateful for you to come see us like this," said Beck as they sat down in the living room, "and I'm sorry to ask you this, because I know it doesn't make any sense. I know it doesn't, and I feel foolish, but how do you know Dad and those other men are gone for sure—I mean, no bodies and everything. Is there even a small chance?"

Mikey bit his lip. Alf gazed down at his shoes. Captain Blackwood put his hand over Beck's.

"I know you know this, my love; you've grown up with this all your life. I understand why you have to ask, so don't feel foolish for that, but you know how the ocean can be. Let me tell you the rules of rescue that we go by at the Coast Guard, okay?"

Beck nodded.

"They call it the one-ten-one rule. If you fall into the ocean off the coast of Newfoundland *with* a flotation device, you have *one* minute to recover from the gasping reflex that happens when you hit the water—that's one minute to cough up the water that's already in your lungs. Then you have *ten* minutes before you fall unconscious from hypothermia, because the water is so cold. Then you've got *one* hour to be unconscious before you are unable to be brought back alive from the hypothermia. That's one minute, ten minutes, one hour. Your father was missing for 28 hours before we found the boat, my love, and there was no other craft in the vicinity that could have picked them up. If there had been, we would have seen it on the radar, and we didn't see anything else in radar range. I am very sorry for your loss, my dear."

"I know," Beck said, bowing her head and sighing. She looked up again. "Do you have the coordinates of where you found the boat?"

"Yes, I do; I have them right here," he said, reaching into his pocket. "Would you like to have some kind of commemoration out there?"

"If the weather is okay," she said, turning to her brother. "Mikey, what do you think?"

Mikey sniffed and wiped his eyes. "I'll clear the weather with the Coast Guard here, and maybe we can steam out tomorrow. We can take the shrimp boat."

"I'll have them check the wind and precipitation for you, Mike," said Captain Blackwood. "It shouldn't take you long to get out there from where you're tied up. Not more than two hours, I'd say. Two hours there and two hours back and one hour at the site. You want a five-hour window. Chart your course Mike, would you, and drop it off down at the ship in Twillingate? If I'm not on board when you come by, you can leave it with the purser. We want to know where you are if we have to come after you. We're going to be docked in Twillingate for the next few days. We've towed the longliner back to Twillingate, by the way, but there's plenty of time to deal with that," he added.

"Thank you, Captain," said Mike and Alf, and both stood up.

"Thank you, Captain Blackwood, for coming down," said Beck.

"You'll be all right, my love," he said, resting his hand on Beck's shoulder. "Your father was a good man, and you be a good girl, now." Beck nodded.

It took them about an hour and a half to steam out to the coordinates Captain Blackwood had given them. It was overcast and misty, but the sea was calm. There were six of them: Beck, Mike and Marlene, Alf and Cory, and Cory's friend Anita, who had come to sing "Amazing Grace." Cory had brought a few hothouse roses to throw overboard.

As the shrimp boat rose up and down with the swell, Beck looked around her and saw nothing but grey sky, grey water, and the salty mist. It stretched out as far as she could see. There was nothing else around them, not even a seagull. Squinting her eyes through the mist, she imagined the *Gil Eannes* appearing over the swell, a beautiful white ship with a red cross painted on the smokestack. She thought of her father being scooped out of the cold ocean by men and women dressed in white. They were bent over, carrying him to warmth and safety. Her mother was on board the *Gil Eannes* too—smiling and happy and waving, just as she had been that day on the waterfront when the Portuguese White Fleet had sailed through the Narrows.

CHAPTER 10

To: Beck Carnell
From: Samantha Reed
Re: Under the knife
Sent: Sunday, December 1 at 8:23 p.m.

Beck,

I've just had my last cup of tea for a few days—mint—and I'm more or less ready for surgery tomorrow. I want it done now. Thankfully, I've got Dr. Hombre Grande heading up the team. David, Stanzie, and Maria Luisa are all coming to the hospital with me and will wait at the hospital for it to be over. All of my thoughts are on hold until then. I'll get David to text you when we're done.
NV, Sam

CHAPTER 11

The edit suite was dimly lit and had dark green walls. Three 27-inch monitors were clustered at one end of a long desk displaying flickering images of children in a schoolyard, a teacher in the classroom, and a man and woman being interviewed in what looked like their living room.

Beck sat in one of the two black high-back office chairs that were drawn up to the desk. Her head was down. She was looking at a page with numbers in one column and words in the other.

The editor, Oliver Dvorak, was sitting in the other chair. He was in his mid-thirties and wore black jeans and a black Smashing Pumpkins T-shirt with a stylized heart containing the lowercase letters *s* and *p*. He and Beck had worked together on video projects for more than a decade.

"The in-point on this next cut is 01:23:13," Beck said to him without looking up, "and the out-point is 01:24:05."

"In-point 01:23:13 and out-point 01:24:05," Oliver repeated as his hands flew over the keyboard. On the screen, the couple sitting in their living room, mantelpiece full of family photos, flowers on the dining table behind them, and a dog resting at their feet, were talking about how it takes a village to raise a child.

"I just have to clean up that in-point," said Oliver as he reached for his mouse. "He's kind of tripping over his words there off the top."

Beck heard a *ta ta ta* and finally the full word, as Oliver went back and forth on the keyboard until he got the husband saying "it" cleanly.

Beck nodded. She and Oliver were editing the 30-minute teachers' campaign video.

The full 30-minute show would be aired, commercial free, on cable TV. Clips from the video would be put up on YouTube and the 30-second ads would be taken from its footage. The 30-minute broadcast was like the messaging mother ship, from which messaging in all other channels would derive.

After talking to parents, a few high-school students, social workers, and cops about the role of teachers in the lives of young people, Beck had had the interviews transcribed with the time code, so she could identify the location of the quotes she wanted. Beck knew the answers she needed would be there, because she had asked the questions she wanted the answers to. And because the campaign had already started, she knew the specific points on which the union was most often being criticized, and she had a chance to counter that criticism, not necessarily in an overt way but with something that could weaken its premise.

The receptionist came into the room. "Have you guys thought about what you want for lunch? I'm putting the orders in now. Here's the choice today," she said, laying out menus for a Thai restaurant, a pizza place, and Swiss Chalet.

"You want Swiss Chalet, Beck?" asked Oliver.

"Chicken sandwich on a kaiser with fries, I think—extra sauce," said Beck as she filled in her order form and handed it back to the receptionist. "Can I have a quick cig break?" she asked Oliver.

"Sure," he said. "You're the boss. Will 10 minutes be long enough?"

"Yep. Meet you back here in 10," Beck said as she grabbed her phone and her cigarettes.

When she got outside, she lit a cigarette and checked her phone to see whether Sam's brother, David, had texted anything about her operation. Nothing. It was probably way too early to hear anything. She scrolled through her emails. There were three from Dmitri Wattage, one giving his available dates for media training, one asking what he should wear to the training, and the third asking when the strategy would be ready. He didn't mention anything about his behaviour at Canoe, and she hadn't expected it. She emailed him back.

> Hi Dmitri,
>   Yvonne will have the media strategy ready in a few days. Why don't we take one of your available media-training

dates and turn that into the day you're coming down to hear the strategy? Don't worry, we'll get to the media training soon enough, probably in three or four weeks—maybe first thing after Christmas. I'll pass these availability dates on to Yvonne, and she'll confirm with you. How are the results on the membership mailing?
Beck

She pressed Send and then forwarded the email to Yvonne, asking her to pick a date to meet with Dmitri.

When Beck got back to the edit room, Oliver was looking at her paper edit and starting to pull cuts on his own. Beck slid in beside him. He passed the pages over to her, and they picked up where they'd left off.

The Swiss Chalet food arrived, and they sat back in their chairs and watched the 11 minutes they'd put together so far. Oliver turned to Beck. "How does that float your boat?" he asked. Beck smiled. That was how Oliver asked if you liked something.

"It's looking pretty good so far," she said, eyes on the screen as she dipped her chicken sandwich into a cardboard container of sauce. "We're getting the content nailed. There might be a couple of things I'd like to re-order once we get the whole thing laid down. I'm happy for now."

They both heard a loud hum and thought for a moment it was coming from the speakers, but it was Beck's phone vibrating on the desk. She picked it up and looked. It was a text from David.

Hi, Beck,
It's David. I'm here with Maria Luisa and Stanzie. The doctor just came to see us. Sammie is out of surgery. He said it went well and that she'd be in recovery for three or four hours before she gets down to a room where we can see her. He said we should go home, have a bit of a rest, and come back around 6:00. Full diagnosis will take a few days. He said she's okay for now. Hope you are well!

Beck texted back.

Thanks, David. Love to you all.

She put the phone down with a heavy sigh.

"Everything okay?" Oliver asked, eyes still on the monitor. "Something back at the office?"

"No," said Beck, looking at what Oliver was doing on the screen, "a good friend of mine is having cancer surgery today. Her brother just texted me to say she was out of surgery and that it went well."

"Sorry to hear that, Beck," he said, continuing to fiddle with his keyboard. "Cancer is one nasty piece of work. What kind of cancer does she have? Breast cancer?"

"Nope. They're saying it's liver cancer," said Beck, grateful for the dim light, "but the full diagnosis will come after the operation and the pathology report."

"Oh," replied Oliver, turning his head away from the screen to look at Beck, "that's pretty serious."

"Yeah, it is serious, isn't it?" she said.

"It's not good," he said, shaking his head and patting Beck on the back. "Come on, let's dive back into the show. We've got a good pace going. If we can keep this up, I might let you go home early."

"Yes, boss," she said, looking down at her sheet. She was warmly insulated in the edit suite with all the noise of the outside world blocked out.

Beck and Oliver were lost in the rhythm of their work when Beck's phone pulled them out of their groove again. She looked at the caller ID and answered the phone: "Beck Carnell."

"Hi, Beck. It's T. J. Avery from National Breast Cancer. How are you?"

"Hey, T. J., I'm good," she said but her stomach clenched at the sound of his voice. Whatever he said would be news. "How are things over there?"

"Well, things are a bit crazy, as you might expect. Listen, Beck, I've only got a few minutes, but I've just come straight from the board meeting and I wanted to let you know the Board has signed off on the campaign you're proposing, and we want to engage your firm on the full execution."

"Wow, T. J., this is an amazing—what amazing news! I thought it might take a bit longer at your end."

"It's a huge commitment for us," said T. J., "and a monumental change in direction, but we think you are a strong leader with bold new ideas and that you have a very skilled team. None of the other bidders came close in their vision or execution. You were in a league of your own, and you are right, we have to do something. We're ready to break a few eggs, Beck!"

"Breaking a few eggs to make the omelet," replied Beck. "It's an amazing opportunity to turn things around, T. J., and I'm grateful for your confidence. This is really big!"

"I'm excited too, Beck, I really am. I think we can do good work together. The sky's the limit. So, Beck, I've gotta go. I only had a minute, but I wanted to let you know. It's not public yet, but I'm sure you can confide in your pitch team. We'll have to consult on the announcement, see how much we want to give away out of the gate. You can be thinking about that and getting your troops together. I'm taking a few days off. Let's get a kick-off meeting together next week. You can arrange it through Sylvia Bumley."

"Okay, T. J., will do. Thanks for calling."

"Righto. Bye, Beck."

"See you soon, T. J." She pressed End on her phone. "Holy shit!" she said.

CHAPTER 12

To: Beck Carnell
From: Samantha Reed
Re: The surgeon visit
Sent: Thursday at 4:03 p.m.

Hey, Beck,

Last couple of days have been a haze—just beginning to come out if it now. The hombre grande just left my hospital room. The operation went smoothly. He said it looked like the tumour had been growing there for about five months. The surgery took care of it, and the margins of the tumour were very clear, he said. That's good news, in terms of the liver, anyway, but they've done the testing and the word is that I have aggressive B cell non-Hodgkin lymphoma, stage 3 or 4. They called it NHL. Hilarious, right? In a hockey-mad country, the disease I have is called NHL? (Who plays Gary Bettman? Ha ha.)

It's cancer of the lymphatic system, which could cause cancer anywhere else, just like it caused cancer in my liver. I wish I could keep the hombre. He's grown on me and handles it pretty straight. But he's handing me off to an oncologist for treatment—they're the ones that dispatch the chemical weapons. It'll take about a month for that appointment. Hombre says chemo can work with this kind of cancer, though, and I'll believe him for now. Will be in the hospital for a few more days, and I'm resting here

pretty comfortably, I have to say. We're all going up to Blue Mountain to spend Christmas—David is staying. We can all use the break. What are your plans? When are the kids getting home?
NV, Sam

CHAPTER 13

Trevor Price had his PowerPoint projected on the wall of the presentation room. The featured chart was about eight feet high and sixteen feet wide. As Beck, Nick, and Todd walked through the shaft of light, they cast giant shadows on the wall, and when they sat down, they had to lean back in their chairs to take the whole thing in. Trevor sat erect in his chair, back straight, chin up, eyes front as though he were preparing to give a military briefing to the joint chiefs of staff. His hand rested on the mouse he had set to the right of the laptop open in from of him.

Trevor turned to Beck. "May I start?" he asked.

"Please do," said Beck with a nod.

"I understand," Trevor began, "that you've all been through a very difficult time because of the shenanigans of your bookkeeper. I have been lent to the firm by my employer, Builder & Boss, to help you through this difficult time and to potentially make recommendations on how to make the firm more productive—" He paused. "Insofar as profit margins are concerned, that is. I'm sure you all are, generally speaking, very productive in your work, at least that's the way it seems to me.

"Ah, um … thank you for giving me the opportunity to present my ideas to you," he said, giving Beck a quick nod.

Beck nodded back, and then, as she glanced toward the door, she saw Yvonne walk past the room slowly and then double back and stop. She had her hands cupped around her eyes and was peering through the glass door.

Pointing to her own eyes, Beck tried to motion to her that she could see her, but Yvonne, seemingly oblivious, continued to stare until she eventually walked away of her own accord. Trevor hadn't noticed and was ploughing ahead.

"The six columns on the wall representing the six streams of revenue for the firm," he intoned. Trevor pressed the space bar on his laptop. Six more columns appeared. They were lighter shades of the same colours and paired up with the revenue columns.

"These are the expenses related to each revenue stream," Trevor pointed out, "and you'll note that, on the top of each column, the percentage of the firm's expenses is represented."

None of them even remotely matched. While direct-marketing production earned 17 percent of revenue, it drew 28 percent of expenses. Digital marketing brought in 18 percent of revenue and used 5 percent of expenses.

"The idea is not to make these numbers match exactly, because the potential margins are different in each division. They don't have to be in lockstep," he said, straightening up in his chair. "You'll make more on digital than mail, for example, because production costs are so much lower, but then again, you're making money on markup, so that evens it out. But, overall, it gives you a sense of areas you might look at to increase your efficiencies."

Another column appeared on the wall. "The seventh column—the one you now see at the right of your screen, the violet column, has no revenue specifically attached to it. It is an expense column and reflects the salaries of the firm's top management, including you three. It could be pro-rated over all aspects of the firm, but I've left it separate for now."

Trevor looked at Beck. "Now, I'd like to take a more granular look."

She nodded, and he took them through 12 more charts that ended up with the number of staff hours going into each client's work, the fees paid by each client, and the margin on each one. The firm's three smallest clients—a shelter, a youth drop-in group, and the seniors' daycare group—the ones they knew they weren't making any money on, came in dead last in terms of margin on revenue and expense.

"The numbers don't look too good on these last ones," Beck said.

"No, not good at all," replied Trevor, "on the face of it. You are spending money to serve these clients. But you wouldn't be doing it unless you got something out of it, I presume, whether personal satisfaction or grassroots credibility. We can quantify what that 'something' is. We can weigh these numbers to see what we're getting out of it besides money and then make a model to reflect that."

"What do you do in the off season, Trevor?" asked Nick. "Are you in any baseball pools?"

"Heh heh," Trevor said with a slight smile, "not at the moment. I find my work keeps me pretty busy.

"Important side note, though," Trevor added, raising his index figure and cocking his head. "These models are to help map a way forward, to help get out of your current … ah … predicament." Trevor folded his hands together and continued, "If you make a decision to improve your margins on an ongoing basis—and, in my initial assessment, I believe there is room to increase margins without too much pain—then permanent changes would have to be made."

"What kind of changes?" asked Beck.

"Changes that would reduce the expenses the firm incurs when meeting the obligations of its contracts," explained Trevor. "If there is the possibility of less people doing the same amount of work of equal quality, that could be an option, but there are other options."

"Layoffs?" asked Nick.

"Possibly. If it made sense."

"What other options?"

"Well, you can work better volume deals with suppliers, negotiate a larger percentage of agency fees on media buying, or bring in profit sharing to motivate employees and give them a bigger stake in the results of the firm's performance."

"What do *you* think?" asked Todd, closing his notebook and looking up at Beck. Nick was looking at her too.

"We are being told that we are billing more and our margins are getting smaller. Who needs more work and less money? Clearly, something is not breaking our way. Let's see if our Trevor can figure out why that is." She turned to Trevor. "What more do you need?"

"I have to look inside every contract and see how it's being resourced. In other words, how much are we paying to get the client's work done?" he answered.

"Can you get him all that, Todd?" Beck asked.

"Whatever I can help with," Todd answered.

"Okay," said Beck, backing up in her chair and looking around the table. "Can I go now and leave this with you guys?"

"Sure thing, Beck," said Nick. "We got this." They smiled at her as she walked out of the room.

It had been a good month, she thought. They had landed the breast cancer account, she had a plan to get Dmitri Wattage to increase his spend, she had finished the documentary, and Sam was out of surgery. But before Beck headed out for a drink, she had one stop to make. She poked her head around Yvonne's office door.

"Hey, come in, Beck. Come right on in and sit down," Yvonne said jovially, standing up and pointing to the chair. "Right this way. To what do I owe the pleasure?"

"I could see you peering into the presentation room when we were in there meeting with Trevor," Beck said. "You do know that if you're in the light looking into the dark, people can see you, right? It has to be the other way around to work. You have to be in the dark looking into the light in order to be hidden from view."

"Oh, Trevor! How's he doing? He seems to be settling in well," she said, sitting down again. "How was the presentation?"

"Enlightening ..."

"Glad to hear that. He's got a very interesting ... uh ... *mind*, Trevor Price," said Yvonne, arms folded on her desk, head tilted slightly to one side.

"You're not going to start consorting with our junior accountant, are you?" asked Beck with a slight pleading in her voice.

"Ha ha ha. Beck, you're so funny! Don't worry, I am an utmost professional in matters of the heart." She laughed, arms still folded on her desk, head still tilted slightly to the side, with what Beck was sure was a gleam in her eye.

Ah fuck, thought Beck. *We're doomed.*

Todd remained seated in the boardroom after the meeting with Trevor. It looked as if the issue of equity could come on the table without him having to bring it up—profit sharing was a step toward equity. But they'd have to know, wouldn't they? They'd have to know about the arrest. Maybe he should just come out and say it. But how could he? He'd spent all these years trying not to think of it. But now, every time he looked around, he felt as if he were being stalked. In that moment, he knew enough to know that he was getting paranoid, but he was afraid that he'd soon lose his equilibrium completely.

When she got back to her office, Beck put on her coat, walked out to the terrace, sat down, and pulled her cigarettes out of her pocket. Lighting one, she looked at the traffic beginning to snarl on Spadina Avenue and stared at the backs of the old factories on Richmond Street. Fire escapes zigzagged across the brick buildings like diagonal roadways. Once-thriving workshops manufacturing tin, fabric, and even socks, were now a tenement of ad firms, designers, and publicists, the soft, so-called creative industries that mostly existed to mess with people's minds.

It's pretty ephemeral really, the creative industry, she thought as she puffed on her cigarette and blew the smoke out to let the wind take it. It didn't produce anything. On the other hand, it did provide employment; you could say that much for it. It was a source of livelihood for many, many thousands of people in the city.

She had 35 employees in her company alone—35 people, 35 families, and 35 incomes. Even if what Trevor Price was saying were half right, some of them would have to go. Some of them *should* have to go and possibly be replaced with other kinds of talent. It was always a mistake to hire people when it wasn't sustainable, thought Beck. But who knew? *I guess I should have known,* she thought, biting her lower lip and taking another puff of her cigarette. *There's a lot I don't know, mistakes I've made. I've screwed things up, for sure. I'm distracted, just not paying enough attention and, truth be told, hungover a lot of the time.*

But then again, she thought as she stood up and stubbed her cigarette out in the ashtray, if anyone was getting laid off around here, that fucking bitch who told Dmitri Wattage about the postage cheque was going to be the first one on the list.

PART
SIX

Once there was an elephant, who tried to use the telephant—
No! No! I mean an elephone who tried to use the telephone—
(Dear me! I am not certain quite, that even now I've got it right.)
Howe'er it was, he got his trunk entangled in the telephunk;
The more he tried to get it free, the longer buzzed the telephee—
(I fear I'd better drop the song of elephop and the telephong!)

—"Eletelephony"
Laura Elizabeth Howe Richards

CHAPTER 1

B eck was about to step up to the lectern at the funeral chapel to recite a poem she had chosen to read for Nell's eulogy.

Two days ago, when Henry had called her and asked if she could say something at the service, she'd said no at first. As far as Beck knew, Nell was a fragile older woman who'd come to her fully formed, alongside her best friend, Martin, in a chair at the Blue Door, ready to play Music Trivia. She didn't *know* her. Henry had said he understood, but an hour later, he called her back to say that no one in the family thought they could speak in public, and that if Beck would do it, they'd be grateful. She said she'd do it, but she had to call Henry back to ask him if he knew Nell's last name. He told her it was Fisher. Her full name was Nellie Fisher. She didn't have a middle name.

The previous evening, Beck had sat on her living room floor, put her ashtray next to her wineglass and unscrewed a bottle of Villa Maria Private Bin. She was beginning to know her way around the liquor store, and when she'd stopped by on the way home, she'd headed straight for the refrigerated section. The Villa Maria was good—a sauvignon blanc from New Zealand that was easy to drink, fruity, and light. She put two bottles of that into her basket. She saw they had Oyster Bay Sauvignon Blanc, also from New Zealand. She reached way in the back to pick out two of the coldest bottles and nestled them carefully beside the others.

Beck had been unsettled since before the Christmas holidays. She'd been looking forward to having the kids at home, thinking that maybe a break with her children would help get her balance—loosening the increasingly tight knot in her stomach and easing the pain in her head. She'd bought a tree, dragged it into the house, and decorated it herself so they'd have something festive to come home to. She was even thinking of talking to them about how she was feeling, or maybe part of it.

Mick and Annie arrived the day before a huge ice storm pushed through the northeastern United States and ground eastern Canada to a halt. Toronto was hard hit. Accumulated ice felled thousands of trees and utility poles, taking power lines down in the process. From darkened neighbourhoods you could hear the creaking sounds of falling trees and the tinkling of ice-coated branches breaking apart when the trees hit the ground. Hundreds of streets were impassable. The streetcars and subways stood still. More than 300,000 homes, many of them apartment towers, were without power. Whole neighbourhoods, including Beck's, went completely black when the sun went down. Altogether, about a million people were affected. It was two days before Christmas, and the temperature was below zero.

Beck, Annie, and Mick stayed in the house until Christmas Eve, when it got so cold they decided to check into a hotel. Beck tried to get a suite with a kitchen, but they ended up in adjacent rooms, and they were lucky to have that. She and Annie took one room and Mick was in the other. The kids tried to make the best of it, but they wanted to see their friends, and since they couldn't invite them over, they were out a lot. Beck had to be back and forth to the house to make sure the pipes didn't freeze, and that interrupted everything they tried to do, so it didn't feel as if they were together. Henry had gone to Cuba on an all-inclusive, so even he wasn't around to have a drink with. Beck ended up taking a few walks on her own, smoking what pot she had left, and spending one full day at the Blue Door by herself.

Altogether it was four days before they could move back into the house. All the food in the fridge and freezer had gone rotten, a disgusting mess that took Beck three days to clean up and replace with new food. They hauled down the dried-out Christmas tree and put it in the backyard, where it would stay until spring. Hydro workers were busy getting the trees cleared off downed wires. The head of the hydro company stated, "It truly is a catastrophic ice storm that we have had here, probably one of the worst we've ever had."

City Hall couldn't agree on what was happening. Despite all evidence to the contrary, Mayor Rob Ford—the only person empowered to do so—saw no reason to call it an emergency; he said he didn't want to cause panic. *Panic,* thought Beck. *Are we on an airplane now?* He was the panicky one, knowing full well that if he declared an emergency he would become irrelevant and his power would cede to people who actually knew what they were doing.

"My house is freezing cold," he whined. "I have little kids. We might have to go to a hotel tonight; I'm not quite sure what we're going to do. It's not good to wake up and have a freezing-cold shower."

The citizens of Toronto expressed outrage on social media: #darkTO, #freezing, #frozen, #outage, #outrage. Letters to the editor lit newspapers on fire. "How is this not an emergency?"; "We desperately need help as this nightmare drags on."; "This is unforgiveable." *We get the message,* thought Beck. *It's coming in loud and clear: people of Toronto, you are on your own. Keep your pets inside, and check on your neighbours.*

That's pretty well how things had unfolded for Nell, thought Beck. Four weeks after Christmas, and she had still been on her own. It was Martin who'd found her. He was dropping off her weekly supply of smuggled cigarettes, $20 for a bag of 200. She hadn't answered the door, but Martin had a key and had let himself in. The door had hit against something when he'd tried to open it. Martin had looked around the door frame to see what was blocking it. It was Nell. She was dead and had been lying stiff in her own piss and shit for two days.

As she'd sat on her living room floor the day before the funeral, smoking duMauriers and drinking wine, Beck had flipped through book after book, stopping to read a verse or a passage. She'd implored the pages to cough up something that might bestow a shred of dignity on what was a wretched way for Nell to perish—alone in a city with no one except your bar buddies to look out for you.

Beck had stopped to gaze at her orchids, about half of which were in bloom. Their beauty never failed, *never* failed to take her breath away. The buttery white ones with blossoms the size of side plates were creamy and soft, enough to make her mouth water. The palest pink ones looked as if Cupid had gently exhaled over them, turning the cascade of blooms into a breathy, rouge-tinted ball gown. Three of the plants were yellow and looked for all the world like canaries dipping their beaks as they extended their wings;

another one, deep purple, almost black, with a jagged slash of yellow at the centre, smoldered on the stem, dark and seductive, slightly dangerous. Those without blooms looked like barren twigs stuck in pots of tree bark. "Don't ever think your orchid is dead," the lady at the nursery had told Beck.

Beck returned her attention to the books she had stacked on the living room floor. Most of them had belonged to her mother. After her father had died and there was no one left in the house, she'd packed up all her mother's books and had them shipped to Toronto. A lot of them were from the time her mother was in teachers' college, and she had used the books to teach Beck English Literature, as she referred to it.

Against a backdrop of ragged rocks and winds that often howled, they had spent hours reading together. Her mother had declared that learning poetry by heart was good training for her mind. Every Sunday she had given Beck a poem and asked her to practise it until she was able to recite it from memory for her the following Saturday.

When she was a young girl, she'd memorized little nonsense verses like "Eletelephony," ("Once there was an elephant, who tried to use the telephant ..."), her favourite poem as a child. Lately she'd found herself reciting it again and again, this time as a kind of mantra to calm her mind.

As she grew older, the content of her recitations varied: Walt Whitman (Oh captain! My captain! Our fearful trip is done / The ship has weather'd every rack / the prize we sought is won); Emily Brontë (In summer's mellow midnight / a cloudless moon shone through / An open parlour window / and rose trees wet with dew); Shakespeare's *Henry V* (We few, we happy few, we band of brothers; For he today that sheds his blood with me / Shall be my brother).

Beck would stand in the kitchen and recite the piece she'd been asked to learn that week. As her mother made bread and pudding, cut up meat, and split fish, she listened to Beck's performance. Every so often, when her mother was reaching for something from the cupboard, Beck would sneak a peek at the book she had hidden behind her back.

"Great literature will give you solace," her mother had said. "Whatever feeling you have, whatever thought that goes through your mind, whether it's a good thought or a bad thought, it is very likely a poet or a writer that has put it into words. Don't think you're the first one on the earth to ever feel pain," she'd told Beck, "or joy, for that matter.

"Use the English language, my love," she'd said. "Use it to know yourself and to express yourself. There are many who will have already trod the path you are on right now. It's all there for you, if you bother to look."

Now, as she got up to stand in front of a couple of dozen mourners at the Alternative Funeral Home, Beck felt light-headed and thought she might throw up. She was hungover and emotional. She had forgotten to put her lipstick on and figured she must look pale. Her eyes watered, and her throat tightened up. What was she even doing here? This wasn't her family. She didn't belong here. She looked out at the people scattered in the pews. Henry and Martin were on the front bench, both wearing suits. Next to them sat Nell's brother and his wife. They looked stricken.

They'd told her that, over the past year, Nell's condition had worsened. They'd gotten her a cellphone that she wouldn't answer, set up meetings for assisted housing that she didn't attend, bought her clothes she didn't wear, and come down from Northern Ontario as often as they could. But still Nell had died alone. That was the final, indisputable, unchangeable fact they were left with, and their faces were sunken with grief and guilt. There was nothing that could be fixed here.

Beck didn't know any of the other mourners, but they looked to be from the neighbourhood, similar to the lost souls who wandered around Sam's community centre. As they gazed up at her with placid, medicated faces, Beck realized it didn't matter who *she* was. They didn't care if she was fucked up or un-fucked up. She could be anybody. She was there because the occasion called for someone to say a few words, and she had been asked to say a few words, something her father would have said she didn't need any help managing whatsoever.

Her mother's full maiden name, Rachael Ann Wareham, was handwritten on the inside cover of the book she held in her hands. They'd read it together and taken turns saying each verse out loud. The pages were faded; the cover felt warm and familiar in her hands.

Beck took a sip of the water the attendant had left on the lectern and licked her lips. When she opened her mouth, she was back in the kitchen reciting verses while her mother shaped the bread dough to fit in the pans, the smell of yeast and salt in the air. She took a deep breath.

"In memory of the beautiful Nellie Fisher," she began, "I'm going to read a poem by the beautiful Elizabeth Barrett Browning, who also passed well before her time."

> *If God compel thee to this destiny,*
> *To die alone, with none beside thy bed*
> *To ruffle round with sobs thy last word said*
> *And mark with tears the pulses ebb from thee.*
>
> *Pray then alone, "O Christ, come tenderly!*
> *By thy forsaken Sonship in the red*
> *Drear wine-press, by the wilderness out-spread,*
> *And the lone garden where thine agony*
> *Fell bloody from thy brow—by all of those*
> *Permitted desolations, comfort mine!*
>
> *No earthly friend being near me, interpose*
> *No deathly angel 'twixt my face aud thine,*
> *But stoop Thyself to gather my life's rose,*
> *And smile away my mortal to Divine!"*

CHAPTER 2

Sitting on the examination table, Sam looked down at her torso. The scars from the liver operation were fading from red to pink. She marvelled at the incisions—thin curved lines that divided her torso into three more or less equal parts, similar to a Mercedes Benz logo. The cuts were flawless, and the stitches invisible. *Das beste oder nichts.* The best or nothing.

It looked like upscale body embroidery. Hockey injury or no hockey injury, her *hombre grande* surgeon was a master at his craft.

She laid her shirt on the exam table and picked up the hospital gown; this one was white with little flowers. It had been five weeks since she'd been discharged from the hospital, and she'd been feeling pretty good. But the days of clear margins, definite lines, and fine needlework were over. She hadn't brought anyone with her to this appointment with the oncologist. The place she was headed now was down a fucking rabbit hole, where the cure, she pretty nearly felt sure, was worse than the disease. People had things to do, for Chrissake, she thought, lives to live, and she had a few things to say for herself, as well. She wasn't going to be dying with her head in the fucking toilet, no matter how many sad faces she had looking at her around the dinner table, that's for sure. But then again, unless this was all *complete* bullshit, she might be cured. There was always the outside chance of it. Wasn't that worth some discomfort?

Shifting on the examination table, she felt the site of the bone marrow biopsy in her hip. It was still sore. The first thing the oncologist had wanted to do when she saw Sam was learn if the cancer had spread to her bones. Not having considered the possibility of it spreading to her bones, Sam had asked if a biopsy was necessary.

"Of course it's necessary, Samantha," said the officious, white-coated, dark-skinned Dr. Judy Seevaratnam. "Don't you want to know the full extent of what we're dealing with here, so we can make sure we get it all under control?" she asked, looking at Sam with a frown.

When, on their last visit, Dr. Seevaratnam had jammed the hollow-point needle into Sam's hipbone to aspirate some of the tissue, it had seemed to Sam as big as a knife plunging into her muscle and she'd felt the deep, dull pain of the needle hitting her hipbone. She had a mind to report it to Amnesty International, because surely, it must, at some level, constitute torture. When the doctor informed her that she hadn't gotten what she needed the first time and would have to do what she called a re-dip, and jammed the needle in again, Sam wished she could pass out.

Sam wondered what was in store this time. She didn't have to wait long after the door opened. "It's not spread to your bones, yet," the doctor said as she walked into the examining room with her eyes on Sam's chart, presumably looking at the result of her bone-marrow biopsy. The doctor raised her eyes over her reading glasses and nodded toward Sam. "That's a good enough start."

After performing a quick examination and commenting that Sam's scar was healing well, Dr. Seevaratnam declared Sam healthy enough to receive a course of chemotherapy called R-CHOP, which she referred to as the standard treatment for NHL—non-Hodgkin lymphoma. They'd start with a 21-day cycle for four months. We'll get you scheduled into the infusion centre," she said, handing Sam a pamphlet and looking at her watch. "This will tell you what you need to know, and they will call you directly for your appointment."

R-CHOP was chemotherapy cocktail. The acronym stood for five different drugs: *rituximab, cyclophosphamide, hydroxydaunomycin, Oncovin,* and *prednisone.* Dr. Seevaratnam recommended that Sam attend a chemotherapy orientation session, which ran in one of the hospital's classrooms three times a day, Monday to Friday. "You should be able to make the two o'clock slot if you hurry."

"Okay," said Sam, wanting to leave the examination room as badly as Dr. Seevaratnam appeared to want her to leave. She was surprised to discover that having a deadly illness didn't necessarily mean the people responsible for your care were going to be nice to you. She had thought that would be a no-brainer, but then, lots of things had surprised her, including getting sick in the first place. She slid off the examination table and reached for her shirt. She'd give this fucking toxic torture treatment one chance to work, but then she was going to be fucking calling her own fucking shots.

She didn't look up as she left the office. Her eyes were focused on her hospital map. She made it down to the classroom and quietly opened the door just as the facilitator was handing out folders. He smiled warmly at Sam, saying, "Hey there, come on in, you're not late. Take one of these." He handed Sam a folder.

"Thanks." She smiled at him, sat down, and looked around, counting 29 other people in the room, of all shapes and sizes and every colour of the rainbow. Sam wondered if every session had about the same number of people as this one. That would mean 30 people, three times a day, five days a week—that was 450 *new* cancer patients a week, at this hospital alone. Maybe the two o'clock session was the popular one. Even so, that told you something about cancer right there or, at least, cancer treatment.

Everyone had opened their folders already and was rifling through the pages, searching for something revelatory in the contents. There was information about the cancer care team and what to expect from treatment; little schedules to help keep track of appointments; a map of the hospital and location of the cancer centre; a fridge magnet with the phone number of the centre and a combination pen/highlighter with the hospital's donation line emblazoned on the side. There was a pamphlet to let you know what you should bring to chemotherapy sessions (a book, a music player, food, drink, and a significant other, if desired) and a $2 coupon for a case of Ensure, apparently the cancer patient's drink of choice. Sam frowned.

The fellow at the front of the room, the one who had given Sam her folder, was white and bald with a few wispy bits of hair on the top of his head. His cheeks were pink and healthy. He wore a white shirt with buttons straining around the middle and tucked into tan pants held up by a black belt. He had a lanyard with a photo ID security pass hanging around his neck that said in block letters VOLUNTEER. He was relaxed and confident; he told them he was a retired businessman and prostate-cancer survivor.

Most of the questions at the session were about side effects of chemotherapy. Everyone wanted to know what to expect. Would there be hair loss, tingling fingers, nausea, constipation, mouth sores, skin changes, eye changes, bedwetting, flulike symptoms, weight gain, fluid retention, pain at the injection site, or fatigue? These were some of the things they'd heard friends or family had experienced. The volunteer answered each question with patience and warmth. Sam had to hand it to everyone in the room. They were gamely trying to get out in front of this, to get a leg up on what was coming. There was no room for the larger questions. Will I make it? Will it be cured? How bad will it hurt? Is there a god? Those were up to each individual to answer on his or her own and, Sam ventured, would be revealed in the natural course of time.

CHAPTER 3

Jack Bain sat across the desk from Beck and sipped a cup of Tim Horton's coffee, double cream, no sugar. It was the second-last Friday in January. "The day of reckoning has arrived, Ms. Carnell," he said dramatically. "It's official. I've just gotten off the phone with Ed Scrimshaw at the Ontario Teachers' Union. They are ready to let the world know their opposition to the suspension of their bargaining rights and are rolling out with their illegal strike on Monday."

"Well, well, well. Here we go, and here's to you," replied Beck, raising in a toast the cup of tea she had picked up at Starbucks. "The witching hour has finally arrived. Do you think we've laid down enough padding for a soft landing?"

"You couldn't ask for much more padding, Beck, to tell you the honest-to-God truth," Bain said. "It was—it *is*—an excellent effort. The whole campaign has given Ontario teachers a credibility that will take them well beyond these actions. Ditto for the leadership credibility among the membership. It has worked like a charm. Everyone's feeling loved. It was the perfect balance of channels for them. You know that they'll be wanting to continue the TV till the end of May?"

"Really?"

"Yep," said Bain, "and we have enough in the can so we don't have to shoot anything extra. We can use the ones we have or simply edit a few new ones to keep things fresh."

Out of habit, Beck immediately translated the work into its monetary value and went through the revised potential billings in her head. On retainer, they were invoicing one client $50,000 and one client $30,000; that was $80,000. Then, four clients were being billed $20,000 each; that was another $80,000. As well, they had three clients at $10,000 each; that was $30,000. Altogether that was $190,000. She had about $150,000 in project billings and another $160,000 or so in production markup. That was roughly $500,000 in all. But expenses were going to be higher because of the additional costs they'd incurred.

Giving her head a little shake to let the numbers topple back down, she asked, "How long do you think it will take for the Government to legislate them back?"

"It doesn't even look like it's going to come to that, Beck. They've decided they want to define it more as a 'day of protest' as opposed to a strike—they'll be in and out in a day. But it is a strike, of course, an illegal one at that, and the Government has the ability to fine each of them $2,000 a day for their trouble. Will they do that? I'd be surprised if they did. They don't want the bad blood. Nah, the teachers will make their point and will then switch over to work-to-rule. The cloud of a province-wide teacher walkout will have lifted."

"When are they announcing it publicly?"

Bain looked at his watch. "In 20 minutes, at ten o'clock."

"We're prepared on our side?" asked Beck.

"Yep, website updates and social media is all ready to go. Yvonne's got that all organized. The union is handling the media at their end. They don't need us lurking around for that. Everyone on both sides knows what needs to be done," Bain said, taking another sip of coffee. "All we can do now is wait."

"Wow!" Beck sighed as she sat back in her chair. "Man, oh man, this feels good, doesn't it Bain? This one feels good to me right now."

"It's one for the books, I'd say," said Bain.

"What do you say we grab Nick and go out for lunch to celebrate?"

"I'll drink to that," Bain said, laughing and holding up his coffee cup to toast to the idea. "It'll be good to have lunch with just the grown-ups. Are you going to take us to Canoe?" he asked, stifling a smile. Beck had told Bain and Nick about the lunch with Dmitri Wattage.

"I'm not sure I can get us a window table at Canoe today, but we'll go somewhere nice," said Beck with a smile and a shake of her head.

"Somewhere with a TV, so we can watch the response to the teachers' press conference?"

"How about somewhere *without* a TV for a couple of hours, dearie? We're not likely to miss anything. They'll be repeating whatever is happening on the eleven o'clock news."

"Okay, how about we get reservations for the Senses Café at the Soho Hotel? We can walk down from here." Beck picked up her iPhone to text Asmi.

Beck laid the phone back on her desk. "Did I tell you that the Seniors Organization of Canada has signed off on the media-relations plan?" she asked Bain, realizing as she said it that she hadn't added it into her revenue calculation. Maybe it was time to start turning the whole thing over to Trevor Price, she thought, and have him tell *her.*

Her iPhone dinged. It was Asmi texting.

Reservation confirmed.

"Yvonne's been keeping me apprised of the SOC job. Don't know much about these direct-marketing people and their dynamics, but it sounds like this guy, Dmitri, is a bit of a handful. Maybe a bit of a loose cannon, do you think?" said Bain.

"Well, the hope is that he feels we are useful to him for his *personal* career development so that he won't fuck around with us too much," said Beck. "That's kinda the whole plan. They hire us to improve SOC's media relations, which you know is currently a travesty. In the process, we teach him media skills that increase his personal value in the market. Ideally, he realizes that he needs us and so stops messing around with us on the direct-marketing program—which is where the big money is—and we get some money to fill up the hole Tilda Grubbs left for us."

"Well, lassie, he may have met his match in you," Bain said, "*maybe.*" He gave his finger a little wag at Beck. "But you know, some people are just plain trouble, trouble dressed up in a suit."

"Asmi says she doesn't trust him either," said Beck, "but at the end of the day, we are a vendor supplying a client with a service. We just have to manage the boundaries with him more carefully than with most."

"Aye, but this guy seems to lack boundaries," replied Bain. "Maybe because of some childhood problem? Or maybe he's one of those smart alecks who wants to muddy the boundaries he *can* recognize.

"And Beck," added Bain as he raised his eyebrows, "just because you are willing—and able—to go head to head with Dmitri Wattage, that doesn't automatically mean you *have* to."

"He's got the devil in him, I know," said Beck, "and I will keep an eye out."

She was feeling a bit more rested today. A couple of weeks after the kids had gone back to school, she'd had the idea that she would go to her family doctor and tell him how she was feeling and how it was beginning to affect her work.

He'd written prescriptions for an anti-anxiety pill during the day and a sleeping pill for the evening. Beck thanked him and left the office, putting the prescriptions in her wallet, which is where they stayed until the day of Nell's funeral, after which she went directly to the drugstore to fill them both.

When she got home, she retrieved the pills from her purse, tore the white paper bag open, and took both bottles out.

What would it be? The sleeping pill? Or the anti-anxiety pill? At that moment, feeling exhausted more than anything else, she decided on the sleeping pill. She looked at the clock on the kitchen stove; it was 5:03 p.m. She walked upstairs, changed out of the skirt and blouse she'd worn to the funeral, brushed her teeth, and got into a pair of leggings and a T-shirt. After swallowing the tiny white sleeping pill with water from the glass on her nightstand, she lay down and slept for 14 hours, waking up at 7:00 a.m.

"I was sorry to hear about your friend, by the way, Beck," said Bain, narrowing his eyes slightly as he looked at her. Beck still had her tea in her hand and was leaning back in her chair. "Nick told me you went to the funeral yesterday and that you had to say a few words. How did it all go?"

Beck had no idea what Nick and Bain knew about how she spent her time away from the office. Before Anthony left, they would have assumed she went home to her husband and kids. They didn't say much. But guys ... guys didn't make a big deal out stuff, did they? It was part of their charm. She had told Nick she was going to a funeral and the circumstances of Nell's death. He was horrified and had put his hand on her shoulder. "Oh my God, Beck," he'd said. "Are you okay?"

"Oh yeah, I'm fine," she'd replied. "I'll be out of the office for the whole day, though."

With his hand still on her shoulder, he'd said, "I'm so sorry."

"Jesus, Bain," Beck said to him now, putting her cup down on her desk and leaning forward. "It was bad, not good at all. It was bad, to tell you the truth. Her brother and his wife were down from Northern Ontario—devastated, they were, just slaughtered. There are no words for it, are there? Did Nick tell you how she died?"

"Yes, he did, lass. It's a tragedy of incredible proportions, I'm afraid. She's likely not the only one to have passed on in those circumstances in our beloved city, the poor dear. God rest her soul."

Beck nodded sadly, recalling the faces at the funeral. "It's neglect, Bain, pure and simple."

"Aye, it is ... it's a *callous* neglect is what it is, my dear. People like your friend are victims of a *callous* neglect."

CHAPTER 4

"What have we got so far?" asked Nick Taylor, pinching the corners of his eyes in an attempt to release the tension in his forehead and neck. He was sitting at the board table in the presentation room leading a breast-cancer strategy session with Bain, Yvonne, Todd, Asmi, Kumail, and art directors Sebastian Bøllt and Desi Lu. Beck had had to go out for a lunch meeting, and she'd texted him to say she'd be back late. *Go ahead with the meeting,* she'd written. *I'll be back,* but she still hadn't come. He was getting a headache and getting worried.

They had already been there for an hour and a half and were grappling with the vastness of the "un-pinking" campaign. The full impact of winning the pitch to un-pink breast cancer was sinking in. Nick felt like a salmon swimming upstream in a marketing environment full of thick pink sludge. They had developed a suite of peripheral materials, but they needed the underlying theme, the one freestanding factoid, as Beck called it, to tie it all together, and they were nowhere near anything that could be called a resonant message. He looked at his watch.

Beck was sitting on the front steps of St. James Cathedral, wearing jeans, knee-high boots, and a long black winter coat; she was surveying the February traffic on King Street and smoking a cigarette. The streetcar lumbered along its tracks. Cars followed it in herky-jerky motions, trying to move around the streetcar at the first opportunity but having to stop when the streetcar doors opened to allow passengers to get on and off. The cars that did manage to pass sped forward like horses from the starting gate only to have to apply the brakes when the light turned red 100 metres up the road.

The weather was mild and the sun strained to appear behind the clouds, but the wind was picking up. She pulled her collar up around her neck and dug her gloves out of her pocket. After her lunch meeting, she'd texted Nick telling him to start the breast-cancer strategy meeting without her.

The un-pinking pitch had thrown down the gauntlet to the National Breast Cancer Society. The arguments were compelling. All the evidence pointed to change. She and her team were right to approach it the way they were. *She* was right, but they were all struggling to wrap their arms around it, and she felt she had nothing to give them. The pink bow on the breast cancer industry was tied so tightly that it cut off the blood to everything else. It was going to take a hard, clean slice to get that ribbon off. For days and weeks she'd been walking around thinking about what the scalpel might look—still nothing. A gust of wind rode up the sleeves of her coat, and she put her gloved hands on the concrete step of the cathedral and pushed herself up. It was too cold to sit here, she thought. She turned left to walk through St. James Gardens and back to the office.

* * *

"Okay, let's get a handle on where we are," said Bain, noticing Nick's pained expression. Rubbing his hands together in faux anticipation, he looked around the room and said, "Let's enlist the whiteboard. Kumail, would you do the job of being our scribe?"

"I'd be honoured," said Kumail. He stood up and offered a deep bow to Bain, his dark hair covering his face as he bent over.

Bristling in his chair, Bain narrowed his eyes into a squint. He stared at Yvonne and pointed at Kumail. "Is he giving me the high hat?"

"Absolutely not," Yvonne said, indignantly, "Why would you think that? You're not giving Bain the high hat, are you Kumail?"

"Me? No way. I'd never do that. I'm just trying to keep it light here," said Kumail, picking up the marker and standing in front of the whiteboard. The track lighting above the whiteboard and the dimly lit room made it look as if he were on a stage, about to break out in a song and dance.

"All right, all right, sorry, lad. I'm just a bit tense, that's all," said Bain, standing up to take his jacket off. He threw it down on a chair. "The pieces of this just aren't coming together for me yet. We're missing the underlying framework that brings it all together."

"Okay, let's just get what we've got down on the board," said Nick, running his fingers through his hair, which was hanging loose around his shoulders and now resembled a thicket.

Walking toward her office, Beck leaned into the wind with her hands in her pockets. St. James Park, one of the oldest parks in the city, was usually filled with people and flowers. But now, in February, the trees were bare, still weeks away from anything resembling life. The bandstand was empty, and the arches usually covered in roses were devoid of any growth. In 2011, Occupy Toronto had taken over this park. Tents had covered the grass. There had been cooking areas and even a makeshift library. Protest signs and bedsheets had hung everywhere, singing out their messages: "What about the 99 percent?"; "People, not Profit"; "For Sale: Democracy"; "Eat the Rich"; and "The Revolution Will Not Be Privatized."

While some saw the occupy movement as unfocused and a bit of a joke, Beck had felt it was capturing the zeitgeist of the time. Money was winning, and people could feel it.

In the movie *All the President's Men*, about the *Washington Post* investigation of Watergate, Bob Woodward's anonymous informant, Deep Throat, had told him to "follow the money." Just keep looking at where the money goes, he was advised, and you'll find out what's going on. Beck believed this—and its reciprocal—to be true. And the 99 percent the Occupy people talked about was where the money *wasn't* going; they knew that also told a lot. She threw her cigarette on the ground, ground it out with her boot, and walked quickly out of the park. When she got to the street, she hailed a cab to her office ten blocks away.

"All right," said Todd, "let's start at the beginning. What are we up against?"

"Pink-washing," said Yvonne, Asmi, Sebastian, and Desi in unison.

"Who benefits from pink-washing?" asked Bain.

"Corporations who attach their name to it," said Yvonne. "They make more money because people are more likely to buy their product if it has a pink ribbon on it. Like we said when we pitched the NBCS, 80 percent of people are more likely to buy a product linked to a pink ribbon. Consumers believe they are helping women with cancer. It may also relieve any guilt they feel about their patterns of consumption."

"Charities benefit," said Desi Lu. "Charities raise more money by using pink to sell stuff. They use it everywhere—from the colour of their website, to the actual pink ribbons they distribute, to the products they license. What was it with the NBCS? They had licensed 43 products, or something like that? It's like sugar. It easily melts in your mouth.

"Did you know," continued Desi Lu, tapping her index finger on the table, "that the actual pink breast-cancer ribbon started out as a *peach* ribbon? The original breast-cancer ribbon was peach, but the group who'd originated it refused to let a cosmetic company make it part of a cross-promotion. The company's lawyers suggested they just change the colour—and so today we have the pink ribbon."

"Is there no end to it?" muttered Yvonne.

"Pharmaceutical companies benefit," said Bain. "They benefit because they get money to do research, and of course, they sell breast-cancer drugs. Did you know that a pharmaceutical company is actually co-founder of Breast Cancer Awareness Month in October?"

"You are kidding me!" said Todd, as Kumail wrote "Big Pharma" on the board underneath corporations, consumers, and charities. "They started breast-cancer awareness month?"

"That's what I mean, Toddy, this runs deep—very deep," said Bain, shaking his head.

"Do women benefit?" came Beck's voice. "Do women benefit from all the pink?"

Bain jumped in his chair. Beck was sitting right next to him. "Holy Mary, Mother of God, Beck—you scared the bejesus out of me. When did you get here?"

"Sorry, Bain. I just got here a minute ago. I snuck in. I'm sorry I'm late." Her hair looked windblown, her cheeks were red, and she smelled like cigarette smoke. "Do you think women are benefiting from the pink?"

"No," said Yvonne definitively. "They are not. There are huge numbers of women with breast cancer in this country who can't even afford child care to get to their treatments, who lose their jobs because they are sick. This pink shit *completely* ignores the reality of women's lives."

"That's the whole thing about pink-washing, isn't it? It doesn't help women," said Beck. "I should say it doesn't help women *necessarily*. Occasionally, in the process of helping corporations, charities, and Big Pharma, the outcomes *might* help individual women, but the whole thing is not set up to help women, is it? It's set up to help sell stuff. That's what it is, right? It's not health policy. It's a marketing campaign. But we know that, right? We don't need to be pitching ourselves on that premise, right?"

"It's feeling like a maze right now," said Nick with a sigh, resting his head on his chin.

"So what does un-pinking really mean?" asked Beck. "I mean, *really* mean. If not pink, then what? After corporations, charities, and Big Pharma get their cut of all this pinkness, what's left, and where does it go? I can tell you where it's *not* going."

Beck's arms were extended onto the table, and she was leaning in so far it looked as if she were going to put her head down. "It's not going to help women. Breast cancer is about women, about women's health and women's lives. We have to change the entire focus.

"That's what un-pinking means. It's a signal that we're working for women. The National Breast Cancer Society is going to be working for women. *That's* the unifying framework. Un-pinking breast cancer is a message *and* a promise: 'We are working for women. We are working for *you.*'"

The room went silent. Kumail wrote the words "We're working for women. We're working for you" on the whiteboard.

Bain slapped his hand down on the table, and everybody jumped. "That's it!" he cried. "That is absolutely it!"

"Of course, it can't be just what the NBCS is *saying* they are going to do. It has to be what they are actually *doing*," said Nick.

"We'll propose an entirely new structure of communication and fundraising that enables them to be responsive to the needs at the community level," answered Beck, "similar to the way a political party operates from central messaging but delivers the vote on a riding-by-riding basis. The thing will have to evolve."

"But wouldn't that mean a marketing campaign is determining the actual *programming* of an organization?" asked Kumail, still standing at the whiteboard and holding the marker in his hand, "like the tail wagging the dog?"

"You're kidding, right?" said Yvonne as she laughed until tears came to her eyes.

Kumail laughed and nodded.

"Because if you *are* kidding, that's *hilarious*," said Yvonne, wiping her eyes with a Kleenex.

"As if," said Bain, and everyone in the room laughed.

"When do you see us launching this?" asked Yvonne. "Kumail and I will have to seriously consider the earned-media strategy on this one—like, very seriously. This needs to be front-page news."

"I think we should aim for a late March or early April launch," said Beck.

Bain got up from his chair to pick up his jacket and clapped Kumail on his shoulder. "Good job, lad, nicely done."

"You doing okay, Yvonne?" asked Beck, as she saw Yvonne's laughing face turn into one that looked ready to cry. She walked around the table to sit down beside her.

"Oh yeah, sure, sure. Don't worry about me, Beck. I'm okay. Been a bit emotional lately—working a lot sometimes does that to me. But Trevor and I are going to a show tonight and then chillax back at my place.

"Trevor Price?" asked Beck.

"What other Trevor would it be?" asked Yvonne, looking up at Beck and then making a face. "Aw, shit. I meant to tell you earlier, Beck, but I've been putting it off because I know you're not thrilled. I guess Trevor and I are a bit of an item."

"It's all right, Yvonne," Beck said with a sigh. "I figured that might be coming. But here's something I need you to know. Trevor is very helpful to me and could be a big part of this firm's future, right?"

Yvonne nodded.

"So, that means, if things go south between you two, I'm not going to dump him. But he's a pretty by-the-book kind of guy, and I don't want circumstances to become difficult for him so he feels *he* must leave—and you, I don't want *you* going anywhere, either. So, could you please have *that* talk with him?"

"I will, Beck; I swear, I will," said Yvonne, "and thanks for your blessing."

"Hey, hey, now, Yvonne," said Beck, holding up her hands and shaking her head, "that's not a blessing, it's the ground rules."

When everyone else had filed out of the room, Beck walked over to Nick and put her hand on his shoulder. "Do you wanna go for a cigarette?"

"Sure," he said and smiled. "I could use some fresh air."

"What's the matter? Do you have a headache?" she asked.

"Yeah, a bit."

"You want an Advil?" She dug into her purse, found a small bottle of tablets, and handed it to him.

"Thanks," he said taking the bottle out of her hand. He took two pills and a swallow from the water bottle he had on the table and then handed the pill bottle back to Beck.

They walked together back toward their offices. Nick grabbed his jacket, and they went out to the terrace. Beck handed him one of her cigarettes, holding her lighter up to light it. He took a drag and sat down, pulling his jacket around him.

"Tell me you didn't leave us sweating it out in there so you could make a dramatic entrance and save the day?" Nick said with chagrin.

"Is that what you think?" Beck shook her head at Nick and tapped the ashes off her cigarette into the ashtray. "Nope. I wish. I was sitting on the steps of St. James Cathedral when I texted you. It was getting cold, and I decided I'd walk back here through St. James Park to grab a cab. I got a visit from the ghosts of Occupy Toronto, who told me to follow the money, or to at least look at where it's *not* going.

"And Nick, I gotta tell you, I'm hurt by what you just said. I would never want to leave the team sweating. The grand entrance, maybe. I see a bit of me in that. But leaving the team sweating. I don't think that's me, do you?"

"No, it's not you, and I apologize. I meant it as a joke, which wasn't funny."

Nick picked up Beck's hand off the little table. "Is everything all right with you, Beck? I'm asking you because I want to know. I'm worried about you all the time. Can you tell me what is happening with you? So much is going on here—so much of everything. But I'm not seeing it in your face, I'm not sure it's even registering with you. Some days your eyes seem empty. Are you shutting down on us, Beck? What's happening? Tell me."

Beck lowered her head. "Holy fuck, Nick. What can I say to that?" She squeezed his hand and took a deep breath.

"Okay, Nick, listen to me now," she replied, raising her head to look at him. "I am not sure how this looks on the outside, because I'm truly trying to make sure what is going on the inside is *not* showing on the outside. But I'm totally fucked up right now—totally fucking fucked. If I let one piece out, I will not be able to stop the rest, and believe me, *that* is not going to be any good for anyone. But I went to the doctor and got some sleeping pills, and I have slept well two nights this week. That's an improvement. That's it. I don't know if that helps explain, but that's all there is to say. I'll update you when there's a change. I have to work this through somehow."

"Okay, I guess I'll have to accept that for now," he said, leaning back in his chair with a sigh, "but you listen to *me* now, Beck. If you get in a jam—and I don't care what kind of a jam it is, or where you are—you call *me*, okay? I'm the one you call. It's me, right? It's not anyone else. You understand that?"

"Yes, I do, Nick," she said. "Thank you, and I will."

"'We're working for women,' by the way, is a simple and brilliant concept for breast cancer," he said.

"Well, my politics-loving, baseball-playing, hunky-looking dearest darling, coming from you, that is a huge compliment," she said as she picked up his hand and kissed it.

CHAPTER 5

After having her weight, temperature, and blood pressure taken, Sam was escorted to a chemotherapy-infusion chair, a large brown recliner that would be her home while she was being injected with cancer-fighting drugs. There was a little table hooked onto the arm of the chair that could be moved from side to side depending upon whether the patient was right- or left-handed. Sam was right-handed, so the nurse would adjust the table so her left arm was the IV one, leaving her right hand free for movement.

"Have a seat, Samantha. My name is Kelly," a nurse said as she approached the chair with Sam's chart in her hand. "I am your oncology nurse." Kelly had cropped blondish hair and a round, open face with brown eyes. She wore green hospital scrubs and had a stethoscope hanging around her neck. Three stud earrings pierced the top part of her left ear. "I coordinate your overall care while you are at the centre. Lean back and get comfortable. You'll be here for about three and a half hours, I'd say, maybe four. Do you want to take your shoes off? The infusion nurse will be over shortly to set up the IV that will deliver the chemotherapy drugs to your system. Do you have any questions for me?"

Sam sat back in the recliner and looked around the large room. There were about 50 chairs like hers, and four nursing stations skirted the perimeter. One whole side of the room was windows, ostensibly to provide cheerful natural light, but the blinds were drawn because the February morning sun was too bright for comfort.

"Are all these people in here having chemotherapy?" Sam asked Kelly.

"Yeah, they are … for all different kinds of cancer, so it's not exactly the same drugs," said Kelly.

Still Sam continued to stare, finding the sheer number of people overwhelming.

"It does look a bit like an assembly line, I know," Kelly said as she followed Sam's gaze, "but the drugs do work. It's tough medicine, but it can work, especially for your kind of cancer."

Sam looked past the nurse. There was a person walking toward her wearing thick blue gloves, a heavy gown, and goggles. She was wheeling a stainless-steel trolley. It looked like a woman to Sam, but she couldn't tell behind the suit she was wearing.

"Here comes your infusion nurse now," said Kelly. "Her name is Daphne. She's dressed in her dancing clothes. That's protective clothing she's wearing. There's a whole set of rules about what you have to wear if you are administering chemotherapy. If the drugs get on her skin, they'll damage it."

They missed this in the orientation session, Sam thought.

Daphne gave a little wave from behind her suit.

"And that's what's going in my veins?" Sam asked Kelly, pointing to the bag of fluid on Daphne's tray.

"It's harsh stuff, all right, but it attacks fast-growing cells like cancer," said Kelly.

"Maybe," said Sam, "but what does it do to me, Kelly? That's what's freaking me out."

"Well, there's side effects, for sure, but just relax. You'll be fine. Here … let me cover you up with a blanket." Kelly unfolded a flannel blanket and draped it over Sam.

* * *

Sam felt someone push her from behind. Her face was in the dirt. The light was dimming because of all the dust being kicked up. It was blocking out the sun. She heard people chanting as if they were at a soccer game. *Vaaaaa-mos! Vaaaaa-mos! Vaaaa-mos!* She could see people with wooden sticks in their hands, raising them up and down, up and down, in unison, but Sam couldn't see the soccer pitch. The dust was too thick. There was a man walking through the crowd. He was taller than the others. The chanting got louder *VAAAAA-mos! VAAAAA-mos! VAAAAA-mos!* Why were they doing that? Why didn't they just shut up? Couldn't they see they were going to make this guy mad? If they didn't stop, bad things would happen. She knew it. Now the tall guy was bending over at the waist, sweeping his head side to side like a wild horse trying to get out of its bridle. His eyesight pierced the dust. He could see everything. It was her he was after. She knew that. She tried to get up, but she couldn't move because the crowd had hemmed her in.

Then the crowd started to melt away, as if they'd received some sort of signal to turn into a synchronized band. They shifted shape as they headed to the field. Their sticks became flags, flags that were unfurling with precision movement, creating waves of white, red, and green. Now they were morphing into the shape of an arrowhead and marching off to her right, raising their flags in unison. The chanting got fainter, but the wavy motion was making her stomach turn, and she was losing her cover. When the crowd moved away, she'd be lying out in the open. She'd be caught. But maybe she could get up and join them, falling in at the end. She had to get up.

She tried to raise herself with her hands just as she heard a high-pitched whistle and saw an arrow coming her way. It was aimed with such force and accuracy that, before she could move, it pierced the muscle in her forearm, shattering her bone, going all the way through and pinning her arm to the ground. She strained to move her head and struggled to open her eyes. Her arm was on fire.

Sam looked up. Kelly, the oncology nurse, was standing over her chair, "Hey, kiddo, what's going on over here? You okay?"

"My ... my arm is on fire," Sam stuttered.

"Okay, let's have a look," said Kelly, pulling up the significant-other chair and cradling Sam's left arm in her lap. "Looks like we've got some redness going on here. That would make it hurt, for sure. I'm going to bring Daphne, your infusion nurse, over to take this line out. You might need a portacath, a little rubber tube that stays under your skin throughout your treatment time. We can just hook the IV up to the portacath, and Daphne won't have to break open a new vein every time. Sounds gross, I know, but it makes all this easier. Inserting the portacath requires a bit of minor surgery—local anaesthetic—no big deal. I'll talk to your doctor—Dr. Seevaratnam, is it? I'll try to get that booked ASAP, okay? In the meantime, let's get this line outta here."

CHAPTER 6

To: Beck Carnell
From: Samantha Reed
Subject: A big favour
Sent: Monday at 10:00 AM

Hi Beck,

Congratulations again on the breast cancer account! Sounds huge, necessary, and brilliantly strategized. The un-pinking thing is brilliant too. I can't wait to see what that looks like. Breast is certainly the top-rung cancer over here. There's a separate quick-turnaround clinic where you can get a breast cancer diagnosis in a day! You know why? (I saw a pamphlet on it.) It's because of all the heartache and anxiety people who might have breast cancer go through while waiting for a diagnosis. Ah, well. It's a good thing those of us with Stage 3 to 4 B cell non-Hodgkin lymphoma don't have those pesky worry and anxiety symptoms!

Anyway, anyway, anyway, never mind that. Let the cynics have their day, and let it be said I take no joy from the misfortunes of others, or whatever that German word is that begins with the letter s that I can never pronounce, much less spell. I started chemo yesterday (it was awful, I had a daymare—nightmare during the day—and I have to get a piece of rubber tubing inserted under my skin).

There's nothing that's a sure thing about what's going on here, Beck, you know that, don't you? It's cancer, after all—I have to make some plans, pray for the best, plan for the worst, or whatever that saying is, right? Here's the situation. David is the only family I have. Maria Luisa is like family, but she's not related by blood, plus she's not a Canadian citizen yet, although that should all happen within the year, we're hoping. And David is amazing. You met him—the coolest fucking dude in the world. I know he loves me and Stanzie—no question. If anything happens to me, he will become one of Stanzie's guardians, you know, her uncle. But, Beck, I need a second legal guardian for her, someone here in Toronto who will look out for her but also someone who will break the fucking neck of anyone that tries to mess with her. You know what I mean, right? She'd still live in the house with Maria (who is like her grandmother), and there's no need to worry about money. I have a trust for that. So I'm not asking you to take her in. Maria will take care of her. But I've got to have someone watching over them, Beck, here in Toronto. If something happens to me, Jesus, I just don't know. Not that anyone is going to come claiming her (as in e.g. her father) but you never know, right? I know this is big and I've tried thinking of anyone else, but you do seem uniquely suited for the job. You're a great mom, your family seems used to picking up strays, and you are fierce, Beck, when necessary. Can you think about this for me, please?

Now I have to go get that piece of rubber installed in my arm, so they can have unhindered access to my bloodstream— "no biggie" says my oncology nurse, Kelly.

Nosotros venceremos,
Sam

Aha! Beck sat in her chair at work and reread Sam's email. Stanzie's father must be someone with resources, maybe someone powerful. When Sam had said Stanzie's father was "honourably" Spanish, Beck had figured he must have been somebody important, not just a regular joe. She never asked Sam specifically about it; she'd figured Sam would tell her if she wanted her to know. But Sam just wasn't the type to hang with regular joes, and why would she keep it a secret if he were a nobody? There would be no reason to, would there? The question was, if Stanzie's father was an *hombre grande*, where did he ply his trade? In the world of politics, commerce, or drugs? She would have to know, and so she typed an email back to Sam.

To: Samantha Reed
From: Beck Carnell
Subject: A big favour
Sent: Monday at 10:00 AM

Dear Sam,

Okay, okay, okay, sweet lady. You've got to tell me something about him now, just the basics. I'll make it easy for you. Here's a couple of multiple-choice questions.

Is he a
>A. *Politician*
>B. *Drug dealer*
>C. *None of the above*

Does he
>A. *Know about Stanzie*
>B. *Not know about Stanzie*

Does Stanzie
>A. *Know about him*
>B. *Not know about him*

Whatever the answers, rest assured I will, in the case it is ever needed, for whatever reason, before your baby turns 21, be one of her legal guardians and do my best impersonation of a lioness should the need arise. We can work out the wording with your lawyer.

Hmmm … Politician or drug dealer? Drug dealer or politician? Which one is it, Sammie? Inquiring minds need to know!
xox Beck

To: Beck Carnell
From: Samantha Reed
Subject: A big favour
Sent: Monday at 10:00 AM

Dear Beck,
   I can't believe you are gaming me when I've asked you such a serious question! That's a bit rude, don't you think?
   Answers: A, A, and A
   Thanks SO much. It does give me comfort. My lawyer will be in touch, and I'll fill you in some more. ☺
NV, Sam

The first time she met Stanzie's father, Sam wanted to bury her face in his neck. As the minister of the interior of the government, he was lending his support to the first lady, who had set up a charitable foundation to help the country's poorest children. He was touring the Para Niños centre, where Sam worked in Mexico City with the agency's international program director, and she was introduced to him.

At the time, the President was pursuing the economic integration of Mexico with the United States and Canada. Structural adjustments and free trade were creating massive unemployment. The President's wife wanted the people to know she and her husband cared, and she'd set up the Foundation as an expression of that caring. The two of them were significant donors to the Para Niños centre.

When they were introduced, the Minister asked Sam where she was from. When she told him she was from Canada, he told her he'd gone to school in Princeton, New Jersey. Had she ever been to New Jersey? he asked. She said yes and that she'd seen Bruce Springsteen play at the Meadowlands

Stadium in East Rutherford, New Jersey. "Ah," he said, "the Boss. *Muy bueno.*"

He told her she had a very beautiful name—*very* beautiful, he said, shaking his head slightly as he said it, as though forced to speak a truth he was trying to resist saying out loud. He put both his hands around her hand as he shook it. "People call me Sam," she'd said, laughing.

"A travesty," he said, looking directly at her and smiling. Sam lost herself in his face. There was a little crease in his forehead. His complexion was light brown, and his stubble beard matched his longish brown hair, streaked with a little grey. He wore a casual suit, with a checked shirt open at the neck. She could see the relaxed rhythm of his heart pulse at the centre of his *clavicula*. He smelled fantastic ... really good—a bit like dirt, maybe grass, maybe sweat—nothing she could put her finger on, but amazing.

"Do you have a card?" he asked. She pulled one from her pocket and gave it to him. He looked at it. "Samantha Reed," he said, *"Muy hermosa,* very beautiful. May I call you, Samantha?"

"Si, por favor," she'd said. "Yes, please do."

About a week later, the Minister of the Interior called Sam to ask if she would give him the pleasure of joining him for dinner at his house, just the two of them. His wife was in Europe with the children, he explained, and he'd love some company. They could catch up on their experiences of Bruce Springsteen, he said with a laugh. "May I send a car for you?"

Sam quickly showered, brushed out her hair, and put on a long white sundress with short sleeves. The Minister's chauffeur came at the appointed time. They ate dinner at a small table beside a large swimming pool, and he showed her around the first floor of his house. They swept across polished wood floors and under splendid archways made of white stone as he showed her his collection of art and sculpture. They sat in his study while he smoked a cigarette. He offered Sam one and she took it. "I don't smoke often, but I do enjoy it occasionally," she said. She saw the Princeton diploma on the wall and laughed.

Around ten-thirty, he asked if she was getting tired and would she like his driver to take her home. She said yes, that would be lovely, as she had to work the next day. He kissed her good night on the cheek and slowly brushed his hand down her arm before he opened the door of the limousine. It was the same driver that had brought her, so she didn't have to tell him her address. As they were heading home, she realized the Minister of the Interior had not asked for her address before he'd sent the car for her. Her business card, of course, had her work address. She imagined he had his ways of finding out things.

After the dinner at his home, he invited her out often—to shows or restaurants, some fancy and some rustic. He sent flowers, had his driver pick her up so they could go for walks together, and gave her little gifts. When they were together, she felt as if he could gobble her up. He asked about her work. They talked for hours about political issues around the world, systemic poverty, and the need to invest in women. He asked her about her life in Canada and freely offered details of his own life, as a child growing up in Mexico and as a politician. She'd even had him over to her place for dinner once, at the tiny table in her little courtyard, surrounded by bougainvillea, hibiscus, and dahlias. She'd made paella, and he declared it to be the best he'd ever eaten. He held her hand as they were drinking coffee. She so wanted to walk with him into her bedroom, but she wanted him to make the first move if, in fact, there was going to be a move. She picked up his hand, kissed one of the fingertips, and placed it back on the table. He smiled at her.

The next week, he called her to see if she would be so kind as to spend a weekend with him on the family yacht—to get away from all the world's problems, just the two of them, he said. That's when they made love for the first time, on a soft mattress right on the deck. Bathing in the light of the moon, the stars shimmering in the sky, they rode up and down on the gentle swell of the ocean. He gazed at her as he kissed her, looking at her as though she was the most beautiful thing he had ever seen. She could taste a trace of salt on his lips. They slept on the soft mattress under a cotton blanket and watched the sun come up in the morning, when they made love again.

When she thought about it later, Sam was convinced that power actually had a scent, a smell of its own. When you breathed it into your own lungs, you brought power into yourself, making it feel as though the sun were shining on you, like reflected glory or whatever they might call it. But when power coaxed you, wooed you, and courted you, well now, that was

242

something else entirely—to Sam, it was simply impossible to resist. So it was with her Minister of the Interior. He was glorious, and she felt glorious under his spell. For four years they were lovers, and she couldn't have asked for anyone more wonderful. He still had his relationship with his wife, of course. They had been separated for two years and lived in separate houses, but *"Of course* we are still in a relationship," he said, laughing. "She's my *wife*." Sam had no illusions, and she imagined that he also saw other women. It didn't matter to her in the least. A mistress gets treated a lot better than a wife, she wagered. There was nothing she wanted from him that he wasn't giving her.

In the fourth year of the relationship, Sam became pregnant with Stanzie. She couldn't actually figure out how it had happened and was almost three months pregnant before she realized anything was amiss. The doctor suggested her IUD might have slipped out. Much to her surprise, her minister was thrilled. "A child is a blessing always," he said, smiling and hugging her. "To be a mother is equally blessed," he added, kissing her forehead. In that same month, he had finally decided he was going to run in the primaries for the leadership of his political party. "My life is changing," he told her. "Campaigning is a different life, a life one leads on the road and a life that's obliged to the needs of the moment. But you must know that I carry you in my heart at all times," he said.

Sam understood. If her minister won that primary, he could very well be the next president, and despite the power of his allure—and the allure of that power—Sam wanted no part of it, especially now that she had a child to consider.

The day after they'd talked about the pregnancy and his run for president, he sent her a huge basket stuffed with plush toys, baby outfits, and a little engraved box containing gift cards to every posh children's store in the city. The note read, "I had such fun picking all this out for baby— and for you!" The note was taped to a red jewel box containing a heavy gold locket engraved, "To Samantha, with love." A woman named Maria Luisa delivered the basket. Maria Luisa also brought Sam a letter from the Minister. "My darling," he wrote, "I do not want you to be without help and comfort while I am unable to be with you. Maria Luisa is a wonderfully kind and pleasant woman. I think you two will be very happy in each other's company. Here are the funds to pay Maria Luisa's salary for five years. When the baby is born, I will be in touch with details of a trust fund for him (or her!). You will be a wonderful mother. I know this for sure. Yours always …"

He was truly the best lover, friend, and partner she'd ever had. She'd never met or been with another man who came remotely close to him.

When Stanzie was 4 and ready to start school, Sam decided it was time to return to Canada. Just as her Minister had predicted, Maria Luisa and Sam had by that time become inseparable, and so Maria Luisa came to Canada too. The Minister was able to set them up with all the necessary papers. They settled into the house on Prescott Street and began to lead a beautiful life. Stanzie grew up to be very like her father—smart and driven. It *was* a wonderful life, and Sam had everything she had always wanted: a child and a little family, and work that kept her engaged. But still she lived with a nagging fear. Her Minister had, as Sam saw it, given her two of the three people she most loved in the world: her baby, Constanza, and Maria Luisa. Especially now that she was sick, was it possible he could, with all his power and charm, take them away from her?

PART
SEVEN

All hands on deck, we've run afloat
I heard the captain cry.
Explore the ship, replace the cook,
Let no one leave alive.
Across the straits, around the horn,
How far can sailors fly?

—"A Salty Dog"
Words by Keith Reid, music by Gary Brooker

CHAPTER 1

"Good evening, ladies and gentlemen, and welcome to CNN's *Prime Time Live with Candy Simkins*. I'm Candy Simkins. In a move that stunned marketing observers across North America today, Canada's largest breast-cancer charity announced it was "un-pinking" breast cancer. After 20 years of handing out pink ribbons and colouring everything from razor blades to cement trucks pink, Canada's National Breast Cancer Society will reinvent itself by dropping Cupid's colour. I have with me now, from Toronto, the Society's CEO, Mr. T. J. Avery."

Candy Simkins: Good evening, Mr. Avery.

T. J. Avery: Hi, Candy. Great to be with you.

Candy Simkins: Mr. Avery, doesn't what you're doing fly in the face of the old marketing adage, If it ain't broke, don't fix it? Why are you making this move now, when there is so much support for the pink ribbon?

T. J. Avery: Well, that's just it, Candy; the pink effect has become so ubiquitous, it's begun to lose its meaning. What is it really saying anymore? We are challenging the pink-washing effect, which is essentially a company slapping a pink ribbon on something and calling it a day. We have been listening to people, to critics, to women, and to health professionals across the country, and we believe the day of pink is truly done.

Candy Simkins: Won't you lose donors? Aren't they used to giving to the "pink" cause?

T. J. Avery: The NBCS is not alone in its desire to put the pink to bed. This is a new day for breast cancer fundraising, where we will, in addition to our continued fight for a cure, be responding to the needs of the women in the community—women who can't schedule their chemotherapy because they have no child care, who have to quit their jobs in order to undergo treatment. This is not just a marketing campaign. We are making a proclamation and a promise to every woman from coast to coast to coast, any woman who can hear my voice now, and that proclamation is "We are working for you." That is what we are here for. We are not here to make corporations look good; we aren't here to finance Big Pharma. We are here to work for women. We are here to work for you, and we are taking that message to communities across the Canada in the most forceful way we can. For us, it means dropping the pink.

Candy Simkins: That's pretty strong language you're using, Mr. Avery. Are you alienating your corporate support?

T. J. Avery: Actually, you know, Candy, this pink-washing effect has become so pervasive, there are many corporations in our country—and most likely yours too—that have been staying away from the pink, because they know there's criticism that comes with that territory. So overall, no, we'll likely come out of this with *more* support.

Candy Simkins: What are you current supporters saying though, T. J.? The people who have raced in the pink races, donned the pink wigs, and worn the pink sneakers? Do they feel abandoned?

T. J. Avery: We are here to work for women, Candy. We will have a laser focus on prevention. We will help women when they are sick. We will be putting money into answering the question of why women are getting sick. We will be focused on the needs of women in their community—for women of all shapes and sizes, all colours and creeds, and in every walk of life. Next week, starting on April 7, we are declaring the "Week to Un-pink Breast Cancer" challenge to raise $100 million in seven days." That will demonstrate, beyond a shadow of a doubt, that the days of pink are done. We are moving to a strategy where women and their needs are at the centre of everything we do.

Candy Simkins: Phew! $100 million in seven days is a lot. How will you do that?

T. J. Avery: It's a huge amount, Candy. You're right. It's never been done before here in Canada. We'll be operating in every channel: social media, TV, print—everything. You can check it all out on www.unpink.com. It's all there. Anyone can contribute.

248

Candy Simkins: Thanks, T. J. I'm running out of time, but before I let you go, I have to ask you, because my viewers will kick me if I don't, how did a man end up as the CEO of Canada's largest breast-cancer charity?

T. J. Avery: Ha ha ha. That's okay, Candy. I get asked that all the time. You know, I applied for the job … and they gave it to me. Ha ha ha ha ha.

Candy Simkins: There we have it—breaking new ground in Canada with the *un-pinking* of breast cancer. Now I'd like to bring in Helmut Pastiche, Editor-in-Chief of superbrand.com, an award-winning and globally recognized authority on branding. Helmut, thanks for being with us this evening. What do you think of the goings-on in Canada?

Helmut Pastiche: Good to be with you again, Candy. It's very daring what's happening up there in Canada—a *very* daring marketing move, I have to say. The critique for breast cancer marketing has become nuanced lately and, quite frankly, a lot louder in the past few years—that is, for anyone that's been listening. At some point it simply had to break. Someone had to be the first, and it looks like our friends in Canada have dived in.

Candy Simkins: Do you think this un-pinking of breast cancer will spread? Will other organizations "dive in," as you say?

Helmut Pastiche: Right now, it's a watch-and-wait situation, Candy, watch-and-wait. Don't get me wrong. There is a *ton* of interest in this, whether people in the breast cancer industry want to admit it or not, but they'll want to see some sign of success before they jump on the bandwagon. At the same time, I'll bet the ad agencies with breast cancer accounts have their smart phones vibrating in their pockets right now!

Candy Simkins: Do our friends in Canada know something we don't, Helmut?

Helmut Pastiche: Well, now, there's the gazillion-dollar question, Candy, and you've hit the nail on the head, as you so often do. What is their research telling them? What do their surveys say? How deep is their marketing intelligence, and who are they talking to? But you can bet your bottom dollar they are not doing this without their top sponsors already on board—whether they are old sponsors or new ones. One thing I can tell you though, Candy. This is my absolutely favourite story of the week, and we have lots more to learn in the coming days!

Candy Simkins: And we'll be staying on it. Thanks, Helmut!

Helmut Pastiche: You're welcome, Candy. Good night!

Candy Simkins: You're watching CNN's *Prime Time Live with Candy Simkins*. We'll be right back with breaking news on that California earthquake. Stay with us.

CHAPTER 2

To: Beck Carnell
From: Samantha Reed
Subject: Prednisone crash
Sent: Sunday at 2:00 AM

Beck, my friend,

   *I just saw your picture on the news tonight, about the breast
cancer coverage. I'm losing my mind. It's 2:00 a.m. and I can't
sleep … can't even close my eyes … teeth are clenched, and I'm
trying to stop from pulling my hair out (a joke, right?) and
banging my head against the wall. I'm in withdrawal, they
told me—steroid withdrawal. Remember I told you about
the R-CHOP, the combination of drugs they're giving me for
chemo? The* p *stands for prednisone. It's a steroid they tell
you to take for five days after the chemo. It makes you feel
stronger and helps with nausea. Then, after five days, you stop
taking it, until you get the chemo again. For five days I felt like
Superwoman, and I mean Superwoman. It felt great. Then,
on day six, you stop taking it. Now my body is in withdrawal.
There's a name for it. They call it the prednisone crash. Ever
heard of that? A prednisone crash? It affects some people more
than others. They're going to "taper it off" next time, they said.
Meantime, it's* Nurse Jackie *over here.*
Nosotros venceremos? S

CHAPTER 3

B eck was in the office early on Monday morning. The un-pinking launch had been Thursday, and everything was unfolding exactly as planned. The media was relentless. Yvonne and Kumail were turning in virtuoso performances. It was all about un-pinking, all the time.

Other breast cancer charities, the ones caught with their pink pants down, were keeping un-pinking in the news by taking huge whacks at the NBCS. Their top brass were out there telling anyone who would listen that un-pinking couldn't possibly work. You just couldn't do it, they said. Not only was the NBCS "dreaming in Technicolor," they claimed, it was "playing with fire."

Game on, thought Beck. *Fuck you.* The timing of the un-pinking launch and the subsequent Week to Un-pink challenge, to raise $100 million in seven days, was working out. The Society had already locked up $63 million of the $100 million un-pinking in sponsorship before they even launched. That meant they'd have to raise $37 million nationally. That shouldn't be too hard, given it was being supported by a shitload, an absolute shitload, of earned media, national and international.

It turned out that, when you scratched the surface, all kinds of people were frustrated and resentful of cancer fundraising. It seemed Social Good's analysis was just the tip of the iceberg.

Yvonne poked her head around the door of Beck's office. "Have you seen this?" she said, throwing the *Globe and Mail's* Report on Business section down in front of Beck. It was the profile of Beck that Yvonne had been working on with the *Globe* for two weeks. The photographer had been in three days ago to do the pictures.

Yvonne was smiling as she threw the newspaper down, but she

beseechingly said to Beck, "Puh-leease, Beck, I'm begging you—begging you here—not to ask me to call her to correct anything."

"Okay," said Beck, raising her eyebrows as she opened the paper to the two-page spread. "Maybe ..."

"Can I watch you read it?" asked Yvonne.

"Have at it," replied Beck.

There were two big pictures of Beck in her brown Comrags suit and patterned short-sleeved tee. She was making motions with her hands in one and laughing uproariously in the other. *It must have been a real knee slapper,* thought Beck. There was also a picture from the campaign, a black-and-white photo of a woman with the tag line "We're working for you." The website, www.unpinking.com, was in the caption. *Very nice,* thought Beck.

Yvonne sat quietly in her chair on the other side of the desk as Beck's focus shifted to the article.

No pink, please (b'y)—Marketing's latest It girl

By Judith Polgar, Staff Writer

Although there's not much trace of a Newfoundland accent when marketing guru Beck Carnell speaks, it's easy to see how her "gift of the gab" has helped her firm become one of Toronto's most successful marketing agencies.

Her clients include some of the country's largest and best-known charities and associations. Her "Teachers Care" campaign for the Ontario Teachers' Union is credited with a stunning turnaround in public opinion at the prospect of a provide-wide teachers' strike. The agency's recent, and some say "daring," campaign for the National Breast Cancer Society (NBCS) to "un-pink" breast cancer is reverberating in Canada and around the world. It very well may be her biggest risk, and her biggest challenge, to date.

NBCS CEO T. J. Avery heaped praise on Ms. Carnell. "Beck Carnell is out of the box—w-a-a-a-a-ay out of the box. She's not just thinking marketing. She's thinking everything. She's a genius."

Ms. Carnell was standing next to Mr. Avery when the announcement to "un-pink" breast cancer was made at the NBCS's newly decorated offices, on Thursday morning at eleven o'clock. The workmen had barely finished removing all the pink paraphernalia and putting up large and dramatic pictures of women, bearing the logos "We are working for women" and "We are working for you," by the time the camera crews had arrived.

"This is more than a marketing campaign," said Mr. Avery at the launch. "It is an entire change of focus onto the women we are here to serve. Our "Week to Un-pink" challenge to raise $100 million in seven days is only the beginning."

When asked how someone who grew up so far outside the hurly-burly whirlwind of life can now advise the top charities in Canada, Ms. Carnell paused before she answered. After thoughtful consideration, she spoke.

"I believe when one grows up away from the world, far from other people, away from"—Ms. Carnell waved her hand in the air as she searched for the right word—"you know, away from … things … with only the wind and ocean waves to consider, one focuses on what's in the heart.

"For isn't it truly in the heart that the resonant primary messaging lies?" she asked.

Ms. Carnell's two brothers continue to live in the tiny hamlet of Herring Neck and eke out a living catching shrimp and crab in season, a far cry from their sister's high-flying marketing world in downtown Toronto.

Beck put down the newspaper and looked at Yvonne. "Ha ha ha ha, ha ha ha ha!" she roared, "Ha ha ha, ha ha ha!"

Yvonne joined Beck in her laughter, stopping only long enough to tilt her head beatifically and repeat, "For isn't it truly in the heart that the resonant primary messaging lies?"

"Mikey and Alf are going to piss their pants when they see this," said Beck, wiping the tears from her face.

CHAPTER 4

To: Beck Carnell
From: Samantha Reed
Re: Drive all night
Sent: Saturday at 9:41 p.m.

Beck, Beck, Beck, Beck,
   "I swear I'd drive all night just to buy you some sh-o-o-o-o-o-o-o-o-o-oes."
   I've spent the evening watching Springsteen do a 10-minute VIRTUOSO performance of "Drive All Night" in a stadium in Gothenburg. I don't know how many times I've watched. Ten maybe? Twenty? Have you ever heard of that place? Gothenburg? I hadn't till tonight. It's in Sweden. The song starts ve-r-r-r-r-ry quietly with Roy Bittan on the piano—duh da duh duh da / duh da duh duh da / duh da duh duh da—and Max Weinberg on percussion. Not sure if it's a wood block or the side of his drum kit—and it's duh da duh duh da / clunk / duh da duh duh da / clunk/ duh da duh duh da / clunk. I love that clunk. *It's like the sweetest little period after a sentence. By now, I'm holding my breath … waiting … every single time; doesn't matter how many times I watch it, I'm still holding my breath until I hear that* clunk. *The camera switches to Bruce in a close-up, moving his head back slightly from the mike.*
   Then he opens his mouth and sings the first line with a little growl. When he says the word guts, *it's really GUTS—and I feel like it's here in my gut. He raises his right arm as he*

sings "prisoners all our l-i-i-i-ives" and his arm is covered in sweat—covered in SWEAT—covered. Can you believe that? The camera switches to a crowd shot, the Gothenburg crowd. They're so totally into it, swaying back and forth, making little lanterns with their cellphones. The camera switches back on Bruce; this time it's a profile, and you kind of go, "Hey, what's that he's got between his index and middle finger on his right hand? "IS THAT WHAT I THINK IT IS?" And when he raises both his arms up from his sides in time with the music, you can see it plain as day. There's his GUITAR PICK, and it's been there the WHOLE time. UNREAL.

David left to go back to BC today, but he bought me an ounce of pot and rolled some joints before he left. I think it's pretty good ... really helping with the nausea.
NV
S
PS: Watch this video!!!!!!!!!!!

CHAPTER 5

Asmi dragged a chair toward the second floor balcony of her parents' large home, situated in a small town of 20,000 people in the state of Uttar Pradesh in northern India. She hoped things were okay at the firm in Toronto. As things turned out, it had not been a good time for her to leave work at all. The un-pinking campaign had been like nothing they'd ever experienced. The earned media was unprecedented. It was hard to keep up. Yet Asmi couldn't postpone the wedding and had to leave for India right in the thick of things. She made Beck promise to call if there was anything she could help with, and she'd brought her laptop with her, just in case. She planned to check on things every couple of days.

As she made her way through the bedroom, the upstairs living room, the hallway, and finally out the terrace door, the chair's plastic legs bumped and scraped against the marble floor. She looked up at the blue sky and then down at the terrace, repeating the gesture, up and down again, to see where the shadows fell. Having figured the best position for maximum exposure to the sun, she set the chair down, sank into it, turned her face to the sky, and slowly felt the warmth fill every pore on her face, neck, arms, and legs—pores that had felt permanently chilled by the Canadian winter wind. Finally, back in the home of her parents—her home—she was thawing.

When she'd arrived the previous evening, Vishal, her excitable 18-year-old brother, had run around the car yelping like a puppy. He excitedly crammed three of the four large suitcases into the car and tied the last one on the roof. She would not have been able to tell their four black suitcases apart from the rest of the baggage unloaded from the Air France flight had she not insisted that Jaisalminder tie a red kerchief to the handle of each bag. As the suitcases rolled down the ramp, each waving their little red flag, she looked up at Jai with a flirty cobra-like shake of her head and smiled. Jai stood, hands in his pockets, eyes on the conveyor belt, happy to be organized in such a fashion.

The terrace at her parents' home was empty now. Over the next couple of days, the men with the rentals would appear, and the space would be decorated with marigolds, swaths of red chiffon, and hundreds of tiny twinkling lights. Cooking stations would be set up, and speakers would pound out dance music.

Asmi walked to the railing and looked down on the lane below. It was paved with concrete and had gutters on either side where rivulets were kept flowing by the raw sewage emptying from every house within 100 metres. She could smell it now, putrid and musky.

People on bicycles and scooters criss-crossed the alley. Men selling potatoes, carrots, nuts, and herbs pushed their vegetable carts. Students in white-and-burgundy school uniforms headed home, a few of them breaking from the main group to enter the Internet cafe with its dusty windows. The occasional car parted the wave of foot traffic.

There were wooden stalls, some with tables and chairs, in front of the shops. Shopkeepers roasted peanuts. Brightly coloured bags of chips were pinned to a taut string with small plastic clothes pegs, looking like tails on a kite. The glossy aluminum bags shone through the brown haze of dirt, dust, mud, and excrement.

A new house had been built across the way, and it was even bigger than Asmi's parents' house—four storeys, with green-stained windows from top to bottom and a balcony that nearly wrapped around the entire second floor. It looked clean and modern against the pockmarked pink, green, and blue bunkers left over from the years of British rule. The symbol for *om* was painted on a carved archway.

Asmi looked down into another neighbour's courtyard. One of their servants was hanging up rugs to air out. Their dog, a smallish St. Bernard, was chained up close to the house. The chain was short, one metre at most. The dog barked incessantly and had for years.

Asmi had spent the last three years away from her home, navigating a world foreign to her, one she meant to learn more about. But right now the world she was sitting in felt a bit foreign too. She missed Beck and all her friends from the office. They'd be interested in everything here, she thought, and would be full of questions.

She felt separate in Canada, as if no knew her. They would have to come here to know her. Yet she worried that the more time she spent away from this place, the less it became hers. There was so much about her everyday life that her family wasn't part of now. Ambition was the commanding hand on her back, insistent on forward momentum. Starting a new life and raising a family in Canada was a dream she and Jai shared. She loved her home, but she wanted more than her little town could offer her.

The sun was beginning to cast shadows on the balcony. Asmi left the chair where it was and walked back into the house and down the wide staircase. She trailed her hand along the polished teak railing. It was peaceful. Each room of the house was freshly painted in gentle colours: lilac, light blue, pale green, and yellow. Her mother had bought new furniture for the living room: three navy sofas, two settees, and a large, low glass table with a marble base. Silver and gold throw cushions added sparkle. Asmi sat in the living room, beginning to feel the excitement of her wedding—there would be three days of uninterrupted ceremony.

"Aha! There you are," exclaimed her mother, Raji, and Asmi jumped. Raji walked into the living room with a notebook and said, "Let me show you how far we've gotten with the gifts, *moytu*."

"Did you get the blankets and the *sarees* that I asked you to?" Asmi asked.

Her mother nodded and led her to the room where she'd been keeping the gifts for the wedding guests. Asmi and her sister had slept in this room when the entire house underwent renovation ten years ago. Today, half the room was stacked with a mountain of blankets that was taller than Asmi, each in its own carrying case. A smaller pile of gift-boxed designer wedding *sarees* stood next to the blankets.

"I want to show you the *sarees* to see who is for what, or … I mean … what is for who," Asmi's mother said, and she threw up her head to laugh.

"Yes, mama. Let's do that—"

They were interrupted by a loud voice and heels clinking on the marble.

"Are they in here? Are they in here?" the voice called out. The door burst open. In strode Asmi's older sister.

"Hello, hello, hello! Hello, *moytu*, my little love!" Missy exclaimed and hugged Asmi. "I've just this minute arrived from Pune. And the traffic from Gandhi Airport was awful, awful, awful—so uncivilized. But now we are here; we are together again." She gathered her mother and her sister in an ecstatic embrace.

"Ah, Mama; ah, Asmi—we are here together, and we are so blessed," she said as she surveyed the tower of gifts. "More gifts to be bought, I see. Give me one moment while I freshen up. Then we'll see what's what. Now that I am here, everything will go well. No worries," she said to Asmi and Raji, heading back out the door toward her room.

Asmi and her mother smiled. Help was on the way.

Missy was an organizer by nature and had a lot of a natural flair. She had danced at talent contests when she was a child, and it had boosted her confidence to a degree that confidence ended up being her most marked characteristic. She worked in the development office of the University of Pune. Her current project, raising money for a world-class eye institute, regularly took her to Singapore and Malaysia. She danced in the nightclubs with her work friends and enjoyed shopping in the duty-free shops. Describing herself as single, she told her mother on many occasions that she would like to try a relationship with a man who was not Indian, to see what it was like to be with someone who didn't have the same cultural values.

"I want a relationship where I can keep my career, to keep things up at my end," she said, raising her palms as if to make an offering to the gods. "How this will happen, I do not know."

In short order, Missy returned to the storeroom with a pen and paper in hand. "The blankets don't need any sorting. The *sarees* do," she pronounced and started to open the boxes one by one.

After running the fabric through her fingers, she would reflect for a second and then announce the appropriate recipient. "Cousin, cousin, daughter-in-law, auntie, cousin, sister, auntie, auntie, daughter-in-law," she proclaimed, one after the other, the quality of the saree being in direct proportion to the closeness of the relation.

"I don't see anything here for *sasuma,*" she said when she was done.

Asmi and Raji nodded. A special trip would be needed to find a suitable saree for Jai's mother. Missy made notes and counted off the list on her fingers—a *saree* for *sasuma*, 10 *sarees* for Asmi, jewellery for Asmi, cloth for the men's suits, 40 boxes of sweets for gifts, envelopes for gifts of money, plus *chudas*, *kalira*, an urn, a platter, and a pair of scissors.

"How many do we have coming?" Missy asked Raji.

"Four hundred," said Raji.

"When do they start arriving?" asked Missy.

"Thursday," said Raji. This was Saturday.

CHAPTER 6

Yvonne laid her iPhone down on the table and slowly pushed it away from her as though it were a stinky piece of cheese. She'd just finished talking to a producer on one of the country's most popular news shows, *ConsumerWatch*. He'd told her that the show's host, marketplace maven Joanna Coltrane, had been researching a story on breast cancer CEO T. J. Avery for months and that the resulting piece was going to be aired that evening, in about an hour. "Thanks, bud," Yvonne told him, "for the advance notice, I mean." The producer advised her that he shouldn't even be speaking to her until after the show aired and that he was already going out on a limb. "Okay, okay," Yvonne said impatiently, "what's the show about?"

T. J. Avery had apparently been caught with his hands in the cookie jar at the Liver, Heart, and Lung Foundation, the producer said, the place he'd worked prior to the breast-cancer society. He'd paid cheques to the tune of $700,000 or $800,000 to a bogus company he owned. When the board had found out, they'd told him they wouldn't press charges if he resigned. The show's source said the board hadn't wanted to "draw negative publicity to the organization," so they'd just absorbed the loss and cut him loose. They'd been about ready to air the piece on the Liver, Heart, and Lung Foundation when they'd received an anonymous tip about a payoff from someone at the breast-cancer society. "There seem to be a lot of people out there who don't like this guy," the producer said.

Now *ConsumerWatch* had footage of T. J. Avery in a downtown restaurant handing large padded envelopes of cash to two men, senior executives of HiLo Pharma, who also happened to be members of the National Breast Cancer Society Board of Directors. "He may have been paying these guys off for agreeing to hire him," the producer said, "—maybe. Maybe the money came from the un-pinking campaign.

"What do you think?" he had asked Yvonne. "Kinda makes sense, right?" Yvonne couldn't utter a word; she made some kind of noise that sounded like a grunt. "I know, right," said the producer, "but that's not all," he continued.

"We have a source inside the breast-cancer society," the producer went on, "who showed us an agreement signed by T. J. Avery and the President of the Board of Directors of NBCS agreeing to give HiLo Pharma LLC $60 million—$12 million a year for five years—for experimental breast-cancer drug research. We're not airing that piece tonight; it's coming next week, but you have to admit that kinda goes against the promise of 'we're working for women,' right? Makes it all look like a bit of a hoax, doesn't it? More like we're working for Big Pharma, right? I'm assuming you guys aren't part of this, are you? That you don't have any control over how they spend the money?"

"Call me after the show airs," Yvonne told the producer, and then she put her head in her hands.

Beck was sitting on her knees on the deck in her backyard. There were terra cotta pots, bags of potting mix, and trays of small flowers in front of her. She filled each pot with the soil mix, planted a *Coleus* for her centerpiece flower, some dusty miller for foliage, and an asparagus fern to tumble over the side—a thriller, a filler, and a spiller. She smiled and sat back to admire her work. It would be a breathtaking arrangement when the plants grew in. The June sun was setting, and she thought she felt a twinge of contentment. She took a sip from the mug of wine beside her and sat back to smoke a joint. She was almost finished the joint when she felt her phone vibrate in her pocket. It was Yvonne.

After the call, Beck put her phone back into her pocket and slowly walked into the family room, the mug of wine in her hand. She turned on the TV as Yvonne had instructed and hit the record button on her remote control. She couldn't quite believe what she was seeing. Was that T. J. Avery being chased across a parking lot in the rain by Joanna Coltrane and her *ConsumerWatch* camera crew? It looked exactly like him, at least from the back.

"Why won't you speak to us, Mr. Avery? We've called and emailed you, sir. Will you comment?" Joanna called out, speaking into her microphone and, as she trotted after T. J., holding it out in the off chance he would turn around and talk to her.

"Turn the fuck around, T. J. Turn around," Beck said out loud. "What the fuck is the matter with you? Turn the fuck around and speak to her."

"Mr. Avery, do you have anything to say about the videotape of you handing envelopes of cash to senior executives of HiLo Pharma?" Joanna Coltrane continued breathlessly. She finally caught up with T. J as he reached the door of the building that housed the breast-cancer society offices.

"Mr. Avery, why won't you speak to me?" Joanna Coltrane beseeched as T. J. fumbled with his passkey. "Why were you giving your board members cash, Mr. Avery? Can you just tell us that?"

Beck had to give it to Joanna. She was relentless, but T. J. disappeared through the back door of the office building without saying a word.

Still in the parking lot, and with the rain coming down harder, Joanna Coltrane addressed the viewer directly. "Clearly, Mr. T. J. Avery of the National Breast Cancer Society doesn't want to speak with *ConsumerWatch*. Stay tuned for tonight's feature story, 'When Good Works Go Bad: A Charity Executive on the Take.' We'll be back after this quick break."

Beck picked up her pack of cigarettes and lit one with a shaking hand. She still had her phone in her hand. She texted Yvonne.

> *This looks bad. I think I might need you. Can you get Nick, Bain, and Todd? Meet here? After the show?*

Yvonne texted back.

> *Affirmative.*

Beck started to write a text to Asmi to ask her to come over before realizing Asmi had left for India to get married three days ago. *Shit.*

After the commercial break, Joanna Coltrane was in the studio, propped against a red-topped stool, wearing black pants and a fitted peach shirt with an aqua-coloured chunky necklace that set off her dark brown shoulder-length bob.

"Good evening, and welcome to *ConsumerWatch*, where we make sure *the dollars you spend are dollars well spent*. I'm Joanna Coltrane. Tonight's exposé is the result of months of research and uncovers an unreported million-dollar theft from a well-known charity, a charity you, yourself, may have supported.

"When people give to charity, they are usually hoping to ease suffering, provide opportunity, or contribute to medical advancement. People often give with their hearts and not their heads," Joanna began, setting her story up for maximum outrage effect. "They trust their money will be well spent. But charity is a big business, and there are millions of dollars at stake. Tonight, I'm telling you a story of two charities and one CEO, a CEO who was, apparently, on the take.

"Let's begin at the beginning with Mr. Thomas Jonathon Avery, known in professional circles as T. J., the former CEO of the Liver, Heart, and Lung Foundation. He grew up in Stratford, Ontario, the only son of two doctors, and graduated magna cum laude from the University of Western Ontario in 1998 with a degree in business administration. His curriculum vitae, obtained from the website LinkedIn, where he was endorsed for his experience in fundraising and non-profits, includes stints working overseas for an international NGO and holding a variety of senior positions in Canadian charities. Three years ago, Mr. Avery was hired as the Chief Executive Officer at the Liver, Heart, and Lung Foundation, which has annual revenue of $173 million.

"Our confidential information comes to us via a courageous whistle-blower who is no longer with the Foundation," said Joanna Coltrane. "We have altered his voice and are not showing his face in order to protect his identity."

The whistle-blower went on to tell the story of how T. J. Avery had been dismissed from the Liver, Heart, and Lung Foundation when it was discovered that he'd written cheques worth hundreds of thousands of dollars to a company he owned but which had provided no services to the charity. Two former board members of the Foundation, who had resigned when the information came to light but did not go to the police, corroborated the story, saying Mr. Avery had been asked to resign because of what they termed "financial irregularities." The events were never reported to police because the Foundation "didn't want the bad press that would accompany the revelations."

"But T. J. Avery didn't stop there," Joanna Coltrane interjected as the visuals on the screen changed from close-ups of the Liver, Heart, and Lung Foundation corporate offices to the newly decorated reception area of the National Breast Cancer Society.

"Mr. Avery is currently the CEO of the National Breast Cancer Society, and based on an anonymous tip, we sent a *ConsumerWatch* producer equipped with a hidden camera to follow Mr. Avery as he dined at a tony downtown Toronto restaurant with NBCS board members who are also senior executives of HiLo Pharma LLP. If they are indeed what they seem, the two videos I'm about to show you are truly shocking and appear to show secret cash payouts to board members of the breast cancer charity."

Beck watched as clear and well-lit footage showed T. J. Avery sitting at a table facing two men wearing business suits. They each had a glass of red wine in front of them. It all looked innocent enough, until T. J. retrieved two large padded envelopes from his briefcase, which was on the empty chair next to him, and handed one to each man. The guy on the right actually reached into the envelope and pulled out what clearly looked like a wad of $50 bills. The guy on the left looked into his envelope and simply nodded. There was a date stamp on the hidden camera video. It had been taken four weeks ago.

Then, exactly one week later, the same scenario unfolded—with the same two guys, the same restaurant, at what looked like the same table— and T. J. Avery handed over two more envelopes. The guy on the right looked inside the envelope again and smiled.

"How can you be so friggin' brazen?" Beck said to the television.

Joanna Coltrane's voice-over continued. "Why is T. J. Avery, CEO of the National Breast Cancer Society, handing envelopes of cash to two board members of the NBCS who are also senior executives at HiLo Pharma?" she asked.

"Why are the men accepting envelopes of cash, and what are they doing with it? The breast-cancer society has just completed an unprecedented $100 million 'un-pinking' campaign, designed by marketing guru Beck Carnell, to switch the focus of the organization from the so-called corporate pink-washing effect to helping women at a community level. The campaign has received unparalleled attention from the international press and resulted in more donations than ever in the Society's history. Ms. Carnell can be seen here at the side of T. J. Avery at the media launch of the un-pinking campaign."

There Beck was, as large as life in the breast-cancer offices on the day of the launch, in her black suit with a white blouse, red hair down, leaning over and creating what looked to Beck like the perfect six-second Vine meme of her, Rasputin-like, dropping black pearls of wisdom into T. J.'s ear.

Joanna Coltrane went on. "The un-pinking campaign has received several marketing awards, including the coveted Effie award for best Good Works Campaign in North America, for which Ms. Carnell and her team were feted at a posh New York City hotel."

Videotape of Beck linked arm in arm with Nick and looking a bit pie-eyed—they had all had quite a bit to drink that evening—as they walked along a red carpet outside the Hotel Pierre. Yvonne, Todd, and Bain also had their arms linked together as if they'd walked off the set of *The Wizard of Oz*. Beck thought they looked smug and confident in their mastery of the universe.

Joanna Coltrane continued in her prosecutorial style.

"The National Breast Cancer Society may have other questions to answer. In his press tour touting the un-pinking campaign, T. J. Avery spoke compellingly about how the multi-million dollar Society was going to have what he referred to as a 'laser-like focus' on the needs of women in the community."

A piece of the CNN interview with Candy Simkins came up on the screen, the part where T. J. said, "We are making a proclamation and a promise to every woman from coast to coast to coast, any woman who can hear my voice now, and that is 'We are working for you.' That is what we're here for. We are not here to make corporations looks good; we aren't here to finance Big Pharma. We are here to work for women."

Joanne went on: "How might T. J. Avery explain the existence of a contract—a contract supplied to us by a confidential source—that he and the president of his board signed just two weeks ago with HiLo Pharma, guaranteeing $60 million to the pharmaceutical company's experimental breast cancer drug research project. If he has one, he's not talking.

"Next week, we are going to further explore T. J. Avery's involvement in the National Breast Cancer Society with our program, 'Un-pinking Breast Cancer: A Fundraising Hoax?' Until then, good night, and good spending from me, Joanna Coltrane, and our team at *ConsumerWatch*. Remember, if you are a consumer and you smell something fishy, let me know at the email or phone number on your screen."

Beck rose from the couch and slowly walked into the same bathroom she'd told Anthony to use the day he came to say he was leaving. She stuck her fingers down her throat and threw up the wine she'd been drinking. She opened the medicine cabinet, tore a new toothbrush out of its cardboard case, and brushed her teeth. The image of her leaning over to whisper in T. J.'s ear was looping in her brain.

As she walked out of the bathroom and closed the door behind her, her hands were trembling. T. J. Avery and his wolf-of-Wall Street friends, those cynical, hard-hearted sons of bitches, were prepared to prosper over the corpses of dying women, was that it? How in hell was it this Antichrist was allowed to live and get away with it? Surely to God the devil himself would come drag his arse back down to where it belonged.

Tears sprang to her eyes. She could hear her phone vibrating on the coffee table in the family room. *Vrrrrr. Vrrrrr. Vrrrrr.* The landline was ringing. *Bringgggggg. Bringgggggg. Bringgggggg.* She looked at the caller ID on the landline—C Murray, with the Newfoundland area code. *Holy fuck,* she thought, *something's happened in St. John's!*

She picked up the landline, "What is it now?"

It was Anthony's voice on the other end. She hadn't heard him speak in two years. "Everything's fine down here, Beck. We've just finished watching *ConsumerWatch* and are hoping everything's okay up there."

"I'm a little busy here right now, Anthony, and you're tying up the line, so if you don't mind—"

Her cellphone was still vibrating, and now the front doorbell was ringing.

"If you don't mind, I have to run." She laid the phone down in its cradle, grabbed her cellphone, and walked out to the front door. It was Yvonne.

Beck opened the door. "Thank Christ you're here. My fucking phone is ringing off the fucking hook. Come on in."

Beck turned around and headed back to the family room. Yvonne walked in behind her. They sat down at either end of the couch, intent on their phones. Beck wiped away a tear that was rolling down her cheek. Yvonne's head was down, and she was texting. They both looked up at the same time.

"Sylvia Bumley, the development director, has called me three times," said Beck.

"Joanna Coltrane's producer is texting," said Yvonne. "He wants to know if we have anything to say. Bain, Nick, and Todd are on their way over."

"Fuck. Fuck. Fuck. Fuck. Fuck," said Beck. "This is a fucking disaster."

"That cocksucker, T. J.," said Yvonne as she texted. "Did you see that twit-bag handing over envelopes of cash to those two pharma goons? Jesus, the thought of it makes me want to throw up in my mouth. I wonder what they've got on him. Or is it that he's paying them for giving him a fucking job."

"That idiot," said Beck, "and the idiot board for hiring him. And the other idiot board for setting him loose on unsuspecting people trying to do an honest day's work."

"And that fucking sixty-million dollar contract," said Yvonne, "did you see that? You know that's what made me feel the sickest. He's eaten us—and every other person who believed in something worthwhile—for breakfast and shit us out before dinner." She squinted at Beck. "Are you crying?"

Beck put her hands to her face and felt the tears on her cheeks. "I think so."

"No bloody wonder," said Yvonne as her phone vibrated again.

The doorbell rang. It was Nick and Todd. They'd driven over together.

"Come in," Beck called back as she got up from the couch and headed out to meet them, "the door is open."

"Do you want us to take our shoes off?"

"Don't worry about it; just come in." They stood in the front hall, Nick with his leather bag slung over his shoulder and Todd with his Moleskine notebook in his hand. "Thanks for coming," Beck said. "Let's sit here in the living room."

She pulled one of the armchairs around and turned on the table lamps, unable to stop and admire her orchids. Nick took his bag off and put it down on the coffee table next to the piece of driftwood. Todd sat at one end of the oatmeal-coloured couch, a crease of worry across his forehead and slight perspiration on his upper lip. Yvonne flopped down in a chair with her phone still in her hand. Nick pulled around another chair to sit down next to Todd.

"Can I get you anything?" offered Beck. "You want something to drink? Water or a Diet Coke or something?"

"Sure, some water would be good," said Nick, standing up. "I'll get it. In the downstairs fridge?"

"Yes," said Beck. "Could you bring up a couple of Diet Cokes too?"

Nick nodded, and Beck watched him walk across the room and head toward the kitchen. Her phoned dinged; this time it was Henry.

> *Just saw you on the news; that woman was insinuating some stuff. Want to come over?*

Beck texted back.

> *Thanks, Henry. Can't do now. Am meeting with my team. Am all right. Will call in a couple of days.*

Beck's heart hit the pit of her stomach when she looked up and remembered why her staff was at her house. She felt dizzy and grabbed the side of her chair. Yvonne put her hand on Beck's arm. "Easy does it there, boss. You okay?"

"I don't know. I'm not sure," she said.

Yvonne glanced up and saw Nick coming back into the room. She motioned toward Beck, who had her head in her hands. Nick pulled over his chair and put his hand on Beck's knee. "Here, Beck, here's a Diet Coke. Have some. It's cold," he said. She took the can from his hands and opened it. His voice sounded tinny, and her arms felt too heavy to move.

Maybe she should have a news conference first thing in the morning and then just dump the whole breast cancer society overboard, create distance, say they are shocked, renounce the whole lot of them and be done with it. They were fucked in so many ways. What would their other clients do? How would they be implicated? Un-pinking as a fundraising hoax? It couldn't get much worse than that, could it?

Her phone was vibrating again. It was Sylvia Bumley once more. Beck was about to press Ignore but hit Answer instead.

"Beck Carnell," she said crisply into the phone.

"Oh my God, Beck, thank God I have you," Sylvia said, sounding as if she'd been crying. "Did you see the television? Did you see that show about T. J.?"

"I just finished watching it and am sitting here with the team," said Beck. "We're having an emergency meeting."

"What I am I going to do, Beck? What can I do? I have no idea what to do!" said Sylvia, sounding panicked.

"Did you have any idea of what T. J. was doing?" asked Beck. "Any suspicion, any idea at all? Did anyone ever come to you with a question about his behaviour?"

"No, Beck, honest to God, if something was going on, no one came to me about it," Sylvia answered. "No one."

"Where would he have gotten that amount of cash?"

"People were giving tons of cash to the campaign," said Sylvia. "We had hundreds of thousands of dollars in cash coming in the door. People were holding events, taking up pledges from their friends. We were handling a lot of cash. That's where it would have come from, I'm sure."

"He would have needed help, though, wouldn't he?" asked Beck.

"Probably, but not necessarily," replied Sylvia. "Sometimes cash would be held in the safe before it was counted. There was just so much cash around. Beck, what am I going to do?"

"Did you ever have a personal relationship with T. J., Sylvia?" asked Beck, her voice clipped with tension.

"Why? We went out a few times. What has that got to do with anything?"

"Well, it could have a lot. He's screwed a lot of people. He's betrayed the trust of people who are dying, Sylvia. Betrayed our trust, your trust. He's fucked it up."

Beck was listening to Sylvia's voice in her ear, but she was looking around her living room. Todd was on the couch, hanging his head, and Yvonne and Nick had their eyes on Beck.

"We are not the people who can help you with this, Sylvia. You're going to have to call a board member you trust, call security at the office to make sure T. J. can't get back in there, and then you'll have to call the police."

"What? The police?" asked Sylvia, astonished.

"Oh yes—or they're going to be calling you." Beck hung up.

The doorbell rang and the front door opened. Bain walked through the front hall and stopped at the entrance to the living room. "Well now, what a cursed day this turned out to be! That miserable lump, T. J. Avery, has pretty well screwed us totally over," he said.

Yvonne sat up straight on the couch. "Thank God you're here, Bain. Joanna Coltrane's producer is hammering my phone asking if we have anything to say. They can still put something into next week's show."

Bain looked at Beck. "Can I keep my shoes on?" he said. She nodded.

He strode in, his rubber soles squeaking, and put a bag of oranges on the table. "Leslie sent these over. She said the vitamin C would help."

Beck took an orange and started to peel it. She realized she probably felt weak because she needed sugar or something. Bain's wife, Leslie, had been down this road before.

Beck heard a strained voice say, "I'm freaking out here." It was Todd, who hadn't spoken a word since he'd asked if he could keep his shoes on. He was sweating hard and his voice was shaking.

"What do you mean, freak?" said Yvonne.

"Do you know how many times Joanna Coltrane said the word *unpinking?*" said Todd, jabbing his finger into his own knee. "She said it 14 times. That's our word. Everyone knows that. We are totally associated with that word. The cops are going to be all over us with this. You guys have to know that, don't you?"

Todd sounded as if he were about to hyperventilate.

"Todd," Nick said, as he put his hand on Todd's back, "take a deep breath, mate ... you're breathing too fast ... you gotta slow it down. You're about to hyperventilate. The cops aren't coming for us. Seriously. Are they, Bain?"

"No, Todd, they're not," said Bain, "of course they're not. Where did you ever get that idea?"

"I have to tell you guys something," Todd said, holding his lips in a thin line, like he was trying not to cry.

Beck's living room went silent, with only the sounds from the mobile phones vibrating on the coffee table.

"With all this shit raining down you've got to know something about me before you hear it from somebody else," said Todd. "I was arrested once ... when I was 18. They took me away in the middle of a church service on a Sunday morning, while I was singing in the choir ... in front of everyone. I can still hear the howl from my mother.

"At the cop station, I was booked for armed robbery. They said I was dangerous, a gangbanger, and they transferred me to jail. I was put in a cell with 20 other guys. Scared shitless, I asked a guard if they'd move me. She said the only way I'd get transferred was if they thought I was at risk of harming others or myself. 'Do you feel that way?' she asked. I said I felt unsafe. She said, 'Well, I just gave you the magic words. It's up to you to say them.' She went to get another guard.

"He came over and asked what was wrong. I said I felt very overwhelmed and had dark thoughts. 'Suicide?' he asked. I just nodded, thinking that was what I needed to say. He opened the door, pulled me out, and called to get a seg cell ready for a suicidal inmate."

The firm's crisis faded from Beck's mind as the full picture of what Todd was describing became clearer.

"They took my orange jumpsuit, gave me a thin gown that looked like a hospital gown, and threw me in a segregation cell made of concrete, with a steel toilet and one grey blanket. God, it was cold. I heard two guards outside the door complaining about all the paperwork they now had to do.

"I freaked out and banged on the door, which only made things worse. The guard, the woman who told me to say the 'magic words,' knew exactly what would happen. It was like a piece of entertainment for her. I was in there for three days."

Todd took a handkerchief out of his pocket and blew his nose. "It ended up getting thrown out because the guy who did it was like 35 years old and had done another robbery on the very day I was arrested. But ever since I saw those cops in the office talking to Beck about Tilda, things started going haywire for me. I had to tell you in case someone starts taking whacks at us now and it came to light that way."

Beck sat back in her chair, unable to speak. She, apparently, wasn't the only person who wanted to keep some things hidden. She could empathize with Todd. Why tell people what they don't need to know?

In order to keep the body blow of Anthony's betrayal from entirely wrecking her life, Beck needed a strategy to deal with it. She used the principles of community organizing, with which she was so familiar, to help guide her way, in particular, the words of Saul Alinksy, the Chicago-based community organizer who'd regained a measure of fame when his methods were emulated in Barak Obama's 2008 run for president.

"Always remember the first rule of power tactics," Alinsky had advised activists. "Power is not only what you have but what the enemy thinks you have."

Beck reached out her hand to Todd, which he took hold of and squeezed. Thankfully, Todd was among friends, Beck thought, not enemies. He didn't have to hide his pain. He was safe. No one here would think any less of him. On the contrary, the stinging injustice of his experience put all this T. J. Avery horseshit into some kind of perspective. She looked at the strained faces around the room. Were these people her friends? They were paid to be here. Were they her enemies? Of course not. Did it matter how they perceived her? A crew doesn't rally around a fucked-up captain. They *gossip* about a fucked-up captain with one eye on the end of their shift. Before you know it, you're limping along like a dickhead, your ability to persuade anyone of anything turned to rat shit. Not a good quality in her line of work.

And, besides, not for one minute would she give *anyone* the satisfaction of knowing how much that stuck-up, conceited townie arsehole prick, Anthony Murray, had shagged her up.

CHAPTER 7

Friday was the day to visit the jewellery store to pick out Asmi's parents' wedding gift of jewellery to Asmi. Asmi, her sister, Missy Kalra, and her mother, Raji Kalra, hustled into a white Volkswagen Polk, with Asmi's father, Mr. Nitish Kalra, behind the wheel to drive to the larger town of Ambala.

Short and stocky, with a broad smile, Nitish Kalra surveyed his cargo and considered himself to be one very lucky man. When Asmi had come home, he'd hugged her tightly and cried like a baby. What children he had—two beautiful daughters and a son! Tears of happiness came to his eyes once again as he settled himself in to drive his lovely ladies into town.

Asmi sat in the back and looked out the window, as the car turned right, then left, then right again, fighting for space with scooters, motorcycles, bicycles, people on foot, and carts, and past the Punjab National Bank, a one-storey cinder-block building with a sagging chain-link fence. They drove past Asmi's former elementary school, a faded pink concrete fort, the largest building in town. The paint had peeled off, and the high black gates were shut. They drove past shops, stands, and stalls; people sat on steps, while children stared at the car. Half the town knew Asmi was home; some of them waved. Asmi waved back with a big smile.

That morning Jai had emailed her pictures of the jewellery his mother had picked out for her. A flood of relief had filled his heart when his mother had suggested he send pictures to Asmi so her mother could shop for the gaps in her collection. What more proof could he have than this? His mother was going along with it!

Asmi scrolled through the photos on her iPhone. Red velvet boxes opened their mouths wide, one displaying a heavy gold chain with a gold filigreed equilateral-triangle pendant, each point tipped with a pearl. The earrings matched; each consisted of two equilateral triangles joined together by a pearl; they were about four inches long. The next box held a pair of earrings that were also about four inches long and made up of alternating pieces of yellow and pink sapphires set in gold. The third box revealed six gold bangles about 1/8 inch wide, three plain and three engraved with curlicues.

Did she pick them out herself? Asmi texted.

Of course! She's coming around, Asmi. I wouldn't have believed it, but perhaps they want to continue to have a relationship with their son! Jai responded.

Asmi thought of Jai with great fondness. They'd met at business school. Unlike other female students, she hadn't batted her eyes, looked at him to tease, and then looked away to giggle when he eventually turned his head. She was cheerful, practical, level-headed, and knew exactly what she wanted. She wanted to create her own life and live it in a way that suited who she was—something she felt was not going to happen in her town, or in India, for that matter. As they got to know each other better, they talked about it over coffee, the many meals they shared, and walks they took together. They talked about where to settle. The US was not an option—too complicated and scary; Australia was too isolated. Canada, they felt, suited them best. Two of her cousins had already made the move there so could be counted on for some kind of support.

It had been October when Jai and Asmi had met in their first year at school, and by the time they graduated four years later, they had become an inseparable unit, making plans for themselves—plans that were separate from their families and their life in India.

But the religious wedding in India was necessary. To Asmi, it was like pressing Save on her computer. Until she did that, she felt everything was in danger of being lost. Being married here with the proper Hindu ceremonies preserved everything in her life up to now. She wanted a wedding—not a big one—nothing near the weeklong festival some girls still went for. Most of all, she wanted her parents' and, importantly, *his* parents' blessings.

"Okay, let's get this done," she said now from the backseat of her father's car, to no one in particular.

"I've been thinking about it," said Missy, "and we most definitely want a modern look, something *stylish*. It has to be diamonds—yes, diamonds for sure. They are always so sparkly and cheerful, don't you think? Lots of little ones. And 18-karat gold. It *has* to be 18-karat."

Missy called out to her father, "Papa, Raj Ramesh is the best jewellery shop. Yes, let's go there. Don't worry, *moytu*, I will help you," she said as she reached across the back seat to pat her sister's hand. Papa nodded. Asmi smiled.

Asmi's father dropped them off in front of Raj Ramesh Jewellers and drove off in the dust to find somewhere to put the car. The street was crowded with carts, dogs, scooters, and a white cow having a nap. Missy led them into the store single file. On the right a glass display case ran the length of the long narrow shop. Seats that looked like bar stools were positioned along the case so customers could sit and be comfortably served. The owner sat at the front of the shop by the cash register. He smiled broadly, bidding them welcome.

"Hello, hello, hello," he said, "come in, come in. A seat for the beautiful bride and her mother. Which one is the bride?"

Asmi gave a little wave of her hand.

"Excellent! Rajeesh, my most senior associate, will take care of you."

Missy was already taking her seat and bidding them to sit down on the three seats furthest away from the door. Missy explained to Rajeesh that they were looking for a nice gift that Asmi's parents would give Asmi for her wedding day.

"Would you like something to drink?" Rajeesh asked with a smile. He was wearing a white striped shirt, brown dress pants, and Oxford shoes. His face was open and friendly. He had a small gold bracelet on his right wrist.

"Chai, water, Coca-Cola?" Rajeesh offered.

Missy looked at her mother and sister to see what they'd like. "We'll have Coca-Cola," she decided.

A man standing behind them, wearing somewhat tattered loose grey pants and a long shirt, climbed the stairs to get the drinks, his plastic sandals slapping against his feet as he stepped. He returned with three glasses on a small tray. They took their drinks off the tray, drank the soda, and put them back. He disappeared up the stairs again with their empty glasses.

Rajeesh came out of the large walk-in safe with a dozen red velvet boxes in his arms. He opened each one and set the necklaces and matching earring sets on the glass case in front of Asmi. Gleaming gold, glittering ruby, emerald, diamond, and sapphire stones winked up at her, dancing pieces of light, captivating her and attempting to cast a spell. Determined not to fall into the trap of gazing at every one, Asmi scanned each box quickly and, without a word, closed it.

As she shut the boxes, Rajeesh would appear with a dozen more. Scan and shut. Scan and shut. Missy was silent. Rajeesh made six or seven trips to the safe. Scan and shut. Scan and shut. But Asmi was closing in. The three finalists lay open in front of her. Her mother had left her post at the counter and moved up to the man behind the cash register to begin the negotiations.

"This one, I think," Missy said as she picked up the most contemporary of the three and put it on her own neck. "See how it sparkles once it's on."

The attendant who had brought them their Coca-Cola shuffled slightly behind Missy to keep the necklace in full view.

"I believe it to be the most *stylish*, the one you will be able to wear well in Canada," Missy added.

Asmi tried on the earrings that belonged to the ruby set. They were long, almost touching her shoulders, one large ruby on a teardrop of gold. They framed her face in a way that made her look like royalty, even to her own eyes. Missy looked too. "They are splendid, *moytu*, of that there is no doubt, but think, my love, where would you wear them?"

"Now, these diamonds can practically go with jeans," Missy said, as she held up the gold pendant with dozens of sparkling diamonds in a stylized oval shape.

Asmi looked at her face in the mirror again and took off the rubies. She felt she had done her job. She had narrowed it down. She liked them all. Missy could take it from there.

"Okay, done. Diamonds it is," said Asmi. "Is it okay, Mama?"

Raji smiled at her daughter and nodded.

"Please weigh them," Raji Kalpa told Rajeesh as she went back up to the cash register to pay. At that moment, Asmi's father came in the door and smiled at them all, tears coming to his eyes once more.

CHAPTER 8

The sound of Beck's heels echoed loudly through the hallway as she strode toward Sam's hospital room. It was late afternoon, and two women wearing pale yellow scrubs and hairnets were pulling trays filled with jiggling containers of Jell-O, small cartons of 2% milk, and plates hidden under plastic covers from a supper trolley. They squinted at a little piece of paper on the corner of each tray, presumably containing the name of the patient, and strode off to deliver it to his or her room.

Beck had come to the hospital directly from the TV studio, where she'd just finished the Joanna Coltrane interview. The interview had taken an hour and a half, and they would probably use 10 minutes at the most.

How was that ever going to work out in her favour? Beck asked herself. No one could be interviewed for 90 minutes and not say something stupid. It was up to Joanna to pick what storyline suited her and what angle she'd want to take. As far as Beck's team saw it, Joanna had three choices: she could stop with the T. J. Avery as disgraced charity executive angle, use the (totally unjustified) un-pinking as hoax angle, or keep the show going as part of a wider story on the activities of charities.

They wanted to distance the un-pinking campaign as much as they conceivably could from the maleficence of T. J. Avery, and they knew that during the interview Beck could promote the idea that his behaviour was indicative of wider problems in the sector. The actions of the Lung, Heart, and Liver Society's board of directors, when it had turned a blind eye to criminal behaviour, was clear evidence of that.

The decision they made in Beck's living room that night was for Beck to do an interview with Joanna Coltrane and basically answer any question she might have—about T. J., about charities, about anything she needed to know. No holds barred. Bain and Yvonne drilled Beck on Joanna's possible questions for two days.

She and her firm were as shocked and appalled as Canadians in general, Beck told Joanna, and they "felt sick" about how much T. J. Avery's behaviour had hurt the cause of women's health. She hoped the organization could muster the leadership to recover. Until that time, they were suspending their relationship with the National Breast Cancer Society and would not be providing any advice or services to them until they got their problems sorted out. And what about un-pinking breast cancer? Joanna had asked. Was it done? "That un-pinking train has left the station," Beck had replied confidently. "There's no turning back the clock on that now."

Before Beck had gone to the interview, she'd imagined how she would write the piece if she were Joanna Coltrane. Anyone could rail against a crook like T. J. Avery and make great television. But if Joanna went with the lone-corrupt-individual angle, she'd have a big exposé and then nothing. The wider-malaise angle would give her stories from here to kingdom come. And the answer to the question she'd posed to her viewers on the last episode of her show—"Was *un-pinking* a fundraising hoax?"—would have to be answered with a resounding no. It was the opposite, in fact. It was an attempt at transparency.

When Joanna called a wrap, Yvonne bounded over from where she'd been sitting on the sidelines. "You were great!" she told Beck.

How often had Beck said that to her clients? "You were great!" she'd say. "That was amazing." At the same time, she'd be thinking about how to undo the damage that had just been done.

"I mean it!" Yvonne said, looking at Beck's frown. "Sheesh. Can't take a compliment now? Is that it?"

"It *was* good, Beck," said Joanne Coltrane, who had overheard the conversation as she came to shake Beck's hand. "I have a lot I can use, and I appreciate your being so forthright *and* coming in on such short notice."

Beck stood up to shake Joanna's hand. The sound guy walked over to her and motioned to the mike clipped onto the neckline of her dress. Bain had picked out the light grey silk dress with the tight boat-neck bodice and flowing calf-length skirt because he'd wanted Beck to look a little softer around the edges for the interview. She could be more hard-edged in her comments if she looked a bit more feminine, he'd thought, and Beck had agreed. But Bain had neglected to consider how the microphone would attach to the dress. There was no lapel and nothing to hang the battery on for a remote mike. So when the sound guy had initially handed the microphone to Beck, they'd both looked at it and at her dress.

"It'll have to go under the skirt, I think," Beck had offered.

"I'd say so," he said surveying her dress on the front and the back. "Looks like it. Do you want me to turn around while you do it?"

"Sure," Beck said and bent over so she could thread the mike and wire up inside the skirt of the dress. She then had to stand up and reach down into the top of her dress to pull the mike up so the sound guy could clip it, as inconspicuously as possible, to her neckline. After that, she had to manoeuvre the hanging wire around to the back of her dress so it wouldn't hike her dress up in the front.

Now that the interview was over, she unhooked the mike, gave the wire a gentle tug, and it fell neatly to the ground, where she picked it up and handed it back to the sound guy with a sigh. "Sorry about that," she said to him.

"Don't worry about it," he said, holding a rolled-up cable in his hand. "You were great!"

She thanked him and decided she could leave now and walk over to the Blue Door for a drink with Henry.

Then Yvonne handed Beck her phone. "I think this person really needs to speak to you," she said in her most serious tone. "He called a couple of times during the interview." Beck looked at the screen. It was Sam's brother, David, calling from Vancouver. Beck pressed Call on her phone, and he picked up right away. Sam had been admitted to hospital the night before with a very high fever, he told her. Apparently she had some kind of infection. David himself had been in Toronto until a week ago and said he knew Maria Luisa was there, but could Beck check on her, please?

"Okay," Beck said, "I'll go over right now."

When she told Yvonne where she had to go, Yvonne shook her head and wished Beck good luck.

Beck still had on her TV makeup and the grey dress, and her hair was bouncing behind her as she clacked down the hallway of the hospital. The heels she was wearing, which gave her the height to pull off the dress, according to her new fashion consultant, Jack McBain, were higher than she usually wore. Standing at six feet two inches, Beck felt like a red-headed version of the tall and willowy fashion designer, L'Wren Scott, who had recently committed suicide in her Manhattan apartment by hanging herself with a scarf. Beck had obsessed over that piece of celebrity news for a month. It had been a shock for everyone who knew her. She had been beautiful, had a great career, and had been Mick Jagger's partner for 10 years.

Beck looked down at the beaten-up leather bag she'd slung over her shoulder. L'Wren Scott, God rest her soul, wouldn't have dreamed of carrying that on the runway.

Then Beck realized she didn't know exactly where she was going. "Samantha Reed?" she asked a nurse who was standing in the hall looking at a chart.

"Third door on the right," the nurse replied. "The one where that guy in the dark suit is standing."

Beck nodded. Her heart was beginning to rise in her throat. She hadn't seen Sam in six months. In the meantime, Sam had been deathly ill and had undertaken six courses of chemotherapy. As far as she could tell from Sam's emails, it had been a hellish ride, but she was starting on the upswing again. Beck knew she wouldn't look like the beautiful lady provocateur she'd last had seen at her house on Prescott Street. She was likely to be thinner, of course, and her hair would be gone. She didn't even know if Sam would want to see her. This visit was David's idea. And who the hell was the guy standing outside her room?

As Beck approached the door, he smiled. "Senora Carnell?" he enquired.

"Yes, I'm Beck Carnell. Who are you?"

"A friend of the family," he replied, opening the door for her.

When Beck entered the room, she saw Sam's daughter, Stanzie, who she had only known from pictures, sitting next to the bed, holding Sam's hand. On the other side of the bed, a man who looked to be about 60 was sitting in a chair. There was no mistaking his identity. He was the spitting image of Stanzie. He stood up when Beck came into the room.

Beck bent down to hug her friend, who looked exactly the same as she had the last time she'd seen her, only a bit thinner and with slightly shorter hair; it was still streaked with sunny highlights.

"Oh my my," Beck said softly, "you've been through the wringer and now you are going to be able to start getting better again."

Beck stood up and held her hand out to Sam's daughter. "Hi, Stanzie. I'm Beck. I feel like I know you, and we've never met! How is your piano going?"

"I feel like I know you too, Beck," Stanzie said with a laugh. "My mother talks about you a lot, and I know you are a good friend. Piano is great. I just finished my grade eight exam—first-class honours," she said, blowing on her knuckles and polishing them on her chest. "Pretty tidy."

"I'm sorry, Sam," said Beck, looking around the room. "I've interrupted your quiet time," she said. "I'm sorry. David called me."

"Nonsense," said Sam and, pointing to the man who had stood up as Beck had entered the room, informed her, "This is Stanzie's father."

"Well, I can certainly see the family resemblance," Beck said, holding out her hand. "I'm Beck Carnell."

He shook her hand softly, "I am very happy to meet you, Ms. Carnell." Motioning toward Sam and Stanzie, he added, "Please let me presume to reassure you that I am not here to interfere with Samantha or Constanza in anyway. I am simply here for a few days to offer my help and my love.

"Please sit down," he continued, indicating the chair he'd just risen from. "I will go find us another chair. Would you like to help me, Constanza? Perhaps we can get your mother and Ms. Carnell something from that Starbucks I think I saw in the lobby of the hospital? Maybe a chai latte or a mocha mocha double double," he said with a laugh. Then he looked at Beck. "Or perhaps a simple cup of tea is what's needed." He held out his hand to Stanzie, and they quietly left the room. Beck sat down.

"Your hair?" Beck said, pointing at Sam's head. "It's extraordinary. It looks exactly as it used to, only shorter. I was totally expecting you to be bald or something."

"Oh yeah. That's the trick, see. Didn't I email you about this? When I was diagnosed, I went right to hairdresser and had her cut my hair very short so I could have it made into a wig. Then, as soon as I started chemo, she shaved my head, and I started wearing my own hair. So it's my hair, only a bit shorter because, you know, making the wig takes up a bit of hair length. Call me vain, and you'd be right, but I truly couldn't bear the thought."

"Well, it looks fabulous," said Beck.

Sam grabbed Beck's hand. "My minister of the interior is here," she whispered.

"Is that what he is—a minister of the interior?" Beck asked, also whispering.

"Well, he was; that's what he was when we were together. He's something else now, but clearly it's still something that requires security," Sam said.

"So I see. And that's okay with you?"

"Well, he needs some kind of security, I guess," said Sam. "Mexico can be quite dangerous now."

"No, I mean, is his being here okay with you?" asked Beck.

"Maria Luisa called him," said Sam, still whispering. "She was getting so worried. She made him promise he wouldn't meddle. He did promise, but you know, how can you ever know for sure, right?" She shrugged. "But it's amazing that he came, and I have to say, it's great seeing him after all this time. He's staying for a couple of days."

"Are you out of the woods?" Beck asked, biting the lipstick off her lip.

"I'm done the chemo, thank God," continued Sam, "and I should be okay after being here for a couple of days, getting rehydrated. Now that the temperature is down, I'm starting to feel better. I'll be monitored for five years, but I'm planning on getting back to work and carrying on with things as soon as I can. I don't want this shit to define my life—that is one thing I know for sure."

"Well, it's good to have you on the mend," said Beck.

"That's a great dress, by the way, but have you lost weight or something? You looked pretty wired. This un-pinking shit has hit the fan, hey?" Sam asked. "We've been following it."

They heard a quiet knock on the door. Stanzie and her father came in

WHAT THE ENEMY THINKS

with a cardboard tray of tea from Starbucks. The Minister's security man had an extra chair in his hand, which he placed at the foot of the bed.

They all sat down with their steaming cardboard cups in hand, blowing them to cool the hot liquid down.

"So, Ms. Carnell, I understand you've been kept very busy by circumstances in the past weeks," said the Minister. "Tell me, what's been your strategy so far? I'd be fascinated to know."

"Me too," said Sam, and Stanzie nodded.

Politics runs in the family, I guess, thought Beck as she regarded Sam's minister of the interior. His suit, although casual and made of crumpled linen, was immaculately tailored. His shoes were tan leather loafers, and he wore no socks with them. He looked unshaven, but he was beautifully groomed, not one consciously casual hair out of place. He smelled like something nice: dirt or grass, maybe; Beck couldn't make it out. Whatever it was, it smelled pretty good.

"Go on, tell us where you're at," said Sam. "We'd love to hear. Start at the part where the CEO got caught."

Beck told them how they'd found out about the whole fiasco, the gathering at her house to figure out what to do, and how her team had defined the main problems of the scandal and what they needed to do to mitigate it. She told them how her children had insisted she get back on TV to stand up for herself, about her strategy for the interview, of widening the focus to include the whole sector, and how they were working to preserve the un-pinking concept. She told them what Joanna Coltrane was like in person, and the story of the microphone and the dress.

Sam beamed, coming alive upon hearing the gossip.

"And then, after the interview, I got the call from Uncle David," Beck finished, looking at Stanzie, "so I came to see you guys. And now, I'm here!"

"*Muchas gracias,*" said Sam's Minister, laughing. "You are a good *cuentacuentos;* your storytelling is entertaining—and informative," he added.

Sam's Minister looked thoughtful. "I have seen many trying times in my political life and have sat in many sessions, just as you have described with you and your team." He laughed. "Even if you had asked me for such advice, which you haven't, but may I say, if it is at all helpful, that you have been artful in your response to this, Ms. Carnell. I can make no suggestion to improve upon what you are doing—even if you had asked!

"My only advice—unasked advice, I know—" he said, smiling, "and I beg your forgiveness for my presumption, but it is my experience that one needs periods to calm the soul. I have certainly found this throughout my political career."

Despite knowing Sam's Minister of the Interior was probably to the right of Genghis Khan—he would have had to be if he was active in Mexican politics at the time Sam lived in Mexico—she would consider what Sam's former lover had said. Political strategy favoured no party or ideology. He who does it best wins.

Beck nodded. "I will think very hard about how that might be done."

"Good," said the Minister, looking at Beck with a smile.

"Now," he said, turning to Sam and Stanzie, "let's toast to the beautiful Samantha, a sweet mother and a dearest love. We are happy you are well again."

Beck watched Sam, who was smiling. Her Minister had just pronounced her well again.

PART
EIGHT

If life is a river and your heart is a boat
And just like a water baby, baby, born to float
And if life is a wild wind that blows way on high
And your heart is Amelia dying to fly
Heaven knows no frontiers, and I've seen heaven in your eyes.

—"Heaven Knows"
Words and music by Andrea Corr, Caroline
Corr, James Corr, and Sharon Corr

CONCLUSION

Beck kneeled on the grass with her arm wrapped around a white marble gravestone. Her head also rested on the stone, so she looked as if she were cuddling up to her boyfriend in a movie theatre. The area of the marble that had been left rough sparkled with good humour and contentment in the July sunshine. And it was no wonder. If a millionaire lived in the town of Twillingate, Notre Dame Bay, Newfoundland, this is where he'd want to build his house.

The tombstones in St. Peter's Anglican Cemetery rested on a grassy slope that tapered off onto a pebbly beach. Rocky cliffs rose to a reasonable height on either side. Today the water made a *schloop* sound as it lapped up the beach, sounding a very distant cousin to the raging surf on a stormy day. World-renowned opera singer Georgina Ann Sterling, or Marie Toulinquet, as she was known professionally, was laid to rest not far from where Beck was sitting. Her headstone was in the shape of roughly hewn cross, the largest one in the graveyard. She was called the Nightingale of the North and had died nearly penniless. But such was her acclaim that 30 years after her death, her "adoring public" collected money to erect a memorial stone in her honour.

The inhabitants of St. Peter's Anglican Cemetery had a spectacular view. As they rested, they could watch the sun split the rocks on a fine day like this or see the sea wage its fury when the wind blew. The icebergs from western Greenland glaciers obligingly sailed by St. Peter's like slow-motion floats in a Henry Moore-inspired parade. They came in all shapes and sizes and had scientific names. "Tabular" icebergs were flat, like a table; the ones with rounded tops were "domed"; the "wedges" looked like pieces of cheese. "Blocky" icebergs had a flat top with steep sides. The one they called a "dry-docked" iceberg was U-shaped, close to the water in the middle with a column on either side. "Pinnacle" icebergs, the ones that looked like church spires, were the most magnificent, thought Beck. She could see one just coming into view about 100 yards from the beach. Twillingate was in Iceberg Alley.

Beck's spirit felt it could gaze out to sea forever, but her physical self felt the marble on the headstone digging into her cheek, so she raised her head and brought her arm back around to relax on her lap. She read the inscription on the stone: Rachel Anne Carnell (neé Wareham), 1927–1997. Beloved Mother and Wife.

Mikey and Alf had put a square block of marble in the ground next to their mother, and it read Baxter William Carnell, 1927–2004. Lost at Sea. Beloved Father and Husband. Mikey and Alf must have organized all of that, Beck thought. Or maybe it was their wives, Marlene and Cory, who had done the work. She hadn't seen the memorial stones until today. The last time she'd been here was the day of her mother's funeral, and the ground had been freshly dug. She took out her iPhone, snapped a picture of the headstones, and then crouched down to snap a picture of the view from her mother's grave.

After the second episode of *ConsumerWatch* aired, the one where Beck did the extended interview with Joanna Coltrane, Mikey called her on the telephone.

"I don't mean anything by it, Becksie," he said, "but you look like you're wasting away to nothing. Your eyes look like saucers, and you're pale as a ghost. Are you sick? Is there something wrong with you?"

"No, Mikey," she'd answered, "I'm just stressed out. This whole un-pinking debacle has been awful. Everything is going to hell in a shit-cart here."

"Maybe you need to come home for a while, come down to spend a couple of weeks with us in Herring Neck—or Foggy Neck, you might want to call it today, to tell you the truth, *he he he*. Think it over, and you can call Marlene to let her know the day," Mike said. "Bring the youngsters too, if you can find them."

At first Beck thought the last thing she could do was go home to Herring

Neck. But Sam's infection was better, and she was recalling the Minister of the Interior's advice to periodically "calm the soul." Todd and Nick could hold the fort. Asmi had returned early from India, having decided to forego the planned two weeks of holiday with her in-laws. "In this case, your pain is my gain," she'd told Beck. They had virtually no pushback from their clients from the un-pinking fiasco—quite the opposite. Everyone loved a celebrity, and apparently Beck was now a minor one. Joy Kobayashi from the Ontario Teachers' Union called with concern and excellent advice. Donald Pearson from the Canadian Peace Agency wrote her an encouraging email. It was all they wanted to talk about.

Even Dmitri Wattage got his two cents in. "Remember, no publicity is bad publicity. That's what you told me!" It wasn't quite what she'd told him, but she'd take it. And God bless Trevor Price. He'd already saved or made them more money than Tilda Grubbs had stolen, so on balance they were better off than before the embezzlement.

For his part, Henry suggested she not bring pot on the plane because sometimes they had sniffer dogs, even on domestic flights.

The breast cancer society was reeling from the shock of the misdeeds of their CEO, board president, and the two board members from HiLo Pharma. But the new board member, the patient advocate from out west who had come on at the same time as the two pharma guys had taken the bull by the horns. Tearing into the "black-hearted lawbreakers," she'd insisted the Society would overcome the crisis and emerge stronger. She also appointed Sylvia Bumley as interim CEO.

Before she'd come to the cemetery, Beck had been sitting at Mike and Marlene's kitchen table. She had arrived in Herring Neck late the previous evening and was still in her pyjamas. Marlene had made a pot of tea and put it down in front of her. Beck gratefully poured a cup and looked around at her brother's kitchen, which was the size of the house they'd grown up in. "You sure this house is big enough for you?" Beck asked Mike. "You don't want to add an east wing, do you?"

"It's plenty big, hey?" Mike said with a chuckle. "I've got my entertainment room downstairs and a poolroom. Best thing I ever did was get that crab licence," he said. "Your mudder's doing, need I remind you."

Beck asked Mike if he'd take her to the graveyard that morning. The kids were going to be arriving for the weekend, and there were a few things she wanted to do before they came. They both had summer jobs, so they couldn't stay long.

"You got a good day for it," he said as he opened up the kitchen door to see what the weather was doing. "It's sunny and warm. Not much wind. How long do you want to stay up there?"

"A couple of hours, I guess," Beck replied.

"All right, my duck. Go get some jeans on, and I'll drop you off. Then me and Marlene will pick you up at lunchtime. We'll go see Alf and Cory and have a mug-up down on the wharf. Would that suit Miss Madam?"

"Let me check my iPhone to see if the timing works," said Beck, reaching for the phone in her pocket. She saw a cloud come over Mike's face and said, "Ha ha ha, Mikey. Joke's on you."

"Never mind, you," he said. "Now go get dressed, and I'll drive you to Twillingate."

Mike drove her over in the pickup, which had a load of crab pots in the back that had to be taken in to Twillingate to be welded. He dropped her at the gate of the cemetery, which was a flimsy bit of wire joining up the white rail fence surrounding the graveyard. "Mom's in the middle there; you can't miss it," he called out before he drove away.

Two hours later, when she was crouched down to take a picture of the view from her mother's headstone, Beck heard the car horn. Turning around, she saw an arm coming out of each side of the pickup. Mike and Marlene were waving and yelling at her to come aboard. Beck put her iPhone back in her pocket and ran to meet them, climbing into the back door of the cab.

"You hungry, Beck?" said Marlene. "I hope so. We got a nice lunch cooked up."

"We got a little something to show you, Beck. Something you might be interested in. Alf and Cory are going to meet us over there. All right?" said Mikey.

"Okay, Mike, you're the boss."

"That's the ticket, then," he replied.

As they drove, Beck recognized every curve in the road: the parts where the shoulder was washed away, the bump when they drove over the causeway, the bend after the rock cut, and the spot where the school bus driver, Billy Dinney, had picked up her friend Maggie Blackwood. She knew the part of the road where you could rely on the moose coming out. As they drove the 15 miles from Twillingate to Herring Neck, she felt she could dissolve into the rock, the moss, the dirt, and the trees, could go back to where she felt she had sprung.

Mike stopped the truck after turning right and headed down toward the water. He and Marlene got out. Alf and Cory were waving. Beck got out, ran over, and huddled in their embrace. And if Mike was looking evermore like her father, Alf had all the features of her mother.

"Who lives here?" Beck asked, looking around at where they'd parked. There were two houses and a couple of small outbuildings. "Are we going to go down to the wharf?"

"Here, take a look at this now, Beck. Take a look at this place here. It's for sale. Old man Randell just died, and his son, Peter, who's been living in Alberta for this past 20 years, wants to sell the whole lot. There's two houses; this one here is the main one, the other a bit smaller."

Both were saltbox-style houses with peaked roofs, one storey in the back, and two stories in the front, similar to the one they'd grown up in. There was a back porch, big kitchen, a nice-sized living room, a bathroom, and three bedrooms upstairs in the bigger house. It was furnished and the beds were made. Beck could have laid down on one of them and gone to sleep.

"The kids might like to shack up in this one here, Marlene was thinking," said Mike as they walked over the rocks to the smaller house.

Marlene gave him a look and said, "Now, Beck, that's not as bad as it sounds. I was only sayin', you know, if you did want to come home, there'd be space enough for the kids. They can come have a look at it when they get here tomorrow."

"Now, here's the best part, Becksie," said Mikey as he pointed to a small outbuilding close to the water. "Look here. The old fish house is not much now, but me and Alf were thinking we'd fix this up right nice … make it into a studio for you. A studio, isn't that right, Marlene—a studio?"

"Yes," said Marlene, "a place where you could do your work. You know—a nice place for you to think up your strategy and so forth … where you could look over the water. Mike and Alf would do it up good for you. Put insulation in there, nice big windows. Oh, they'd do a really good job on it. I know they would."

"And we'd hook you up with the satellite Internet, whatever you need," said Alf. "What do you think? Perhaps Mikey will pull the two-way out of the crab boat," he said with a chuckle.

"Give her a minute, Alf; she just got here," said Cory. "Let's go down to the wharf and unpack our lunch."

Marlene and Cory each had a basket in their arms, and five chairs had already been hauled out. There was tea, sandwiches on homemade bread— cold roast meat and ham—cheese slices, fruit cocktail, macaroni salad, cherry cake, pecan bars, and snowball cookies. Beck's stomach grumbled, and she reached for a ham sandwich.

When Cory had cut up the cherry cake and passed it around, Mike spoke up again. "Now, Miss Glory," he said, using the nickname her grandfather had had for her, "I don't think it's doing you any good to be up there in Toronto by yourself all the time. It's too much worry for anybody, for that matter. The youngsters are getting bigger and need to be on their own way. You can't be depending on them. It's probably time for you to come home, at least for part of the year. We can get this property, everything you see here, for a very good price. I don't know how much money you're makin' up there in Toronto, but you can't be doing too bad, judging by the number of pairs of shoes you're after bringing with you."

Marlene laughed and slapped Mikey on the hand at the same time, saying, "Now, none of your tormenting, Michael Carnell."

"Okay, never mind that, but if you can't manage the financing, me and Alf, we can help you out. We've done all right with the crab fishery, and we can fix this place up for you too—this little compound, if you'd like to call it that. We can make it whatever way you want it. See that little garage-looking structure over there? We can turn that into a shed for you too, you know, in case you ever wants to be havin' a shed party wit' the b'ys—" Mike winked at Alf, who smiled and winked back.

"They don't have anything else to do, Beck," said Cory, half exasperated and half plaintive, twisting a paper napkin in her hand. "Honest to God, you'd be doing us all a favour. It'd be great to see more of you."

"Let us look out for ye for a while, my love," said Mikey as he reached out and took her hand into the two of his. He was almost 65 years old. His hands, twice the size of Beck's, were bent, hardened, and cracked by years of fishing. They looked like Poppy's hands, the same hands that had done up her clips and drawn her pictures of the cat-o'-nine-tails, a fisherman's hands.

"You're not alone in the world, little Glory; you got us to look out for you, don't forget," said Alf with such sincerity in his voice that she was shocked out of herself and felt the tears come hot and stinging to her eyes. Before she knew what was happening, she was sobbing so hard she couldn't breathe through her nose. She had to stop to get her breath, but she continued to cry without any sound coming out.

Marlene and Cory pulled over their chairs to sit on either side of her. "Oh, my love, sure that's okay, my duck, get it out now. Cry it all out now, that's a girl; you'll be all right."

Beck felt Cory rubbing her back. "Look at that poor little thing sitting there now," Beck heard Cory say. "Just look at her, will you? She's had all that bottled up inside of her since God knows how long. And that, God forgive me for saying it, but that—that—that *big shot* Anthony Murray and his relations, he didn't help either. I *knows* what went on there."

Mikey held Beck's hand in his as Marlene answered Cory. "See you just don't know the way they are up there in Toronto," said Marlene. "They walk all over people up there—I know they do. Sure, look at that show, where people get hauled up in front of those sharks or dragons or whatever they are. They're just *mean* on that show. Imagine working with the likes of that all day long. Not to say that Beck Carnell can't hold her own, God love her; she can do more than that. But sure, how much can one person take?"

"We probably don't know the half of it," said Cory, shaking her head, "not a *quarter* of it. That poor child! No wonder she's crying herself sick."

Mike put his hand on Beck's shoulders as they continued to heave. He ignored her crying as he began to talk. "Look at it this way, Becksie," he said. "You can come down here for a month or so in the summer, whenever you can get away, and you can come at Christmas, Easter maybe, and Thanksgiving. You don't even have to go through St. John's. Fly into Gander, and we'll pick you up there. That way, you're not gone for that long, right? And me and Alf, we'll look after the place for you. You don't have to worry *one second* on that count," he said emphatically.

"We could pick you up a little shitbox, too, if you'd like to have a car when you're here," Alf said in an encouraging way.

Still unable to speak, Beck nodded her head to let them know she heard what they were saying. She was feeling stunned that she'd somehow never factored the possibility of coming home into her calculations. The idea of having what was hers for the taking—a home and family—felt overwhelming to her, and it had been here all along. She shook her head, and the tears flowed again.

Alf dug into his jacket pocket and brought out a flask. "Here, Becksie, take a drop of this to help you calm down a bit. You probably don't want to be crying too much longer. You'll upset yourself."

Beck had a big sniff and blew her nose in the handkerchief Marlene had put in her hand. She took the flask from Alf and took a big gulp. It was dark rum, strong and sweet. She licked her lips and took another big gulp. Alf and Mikey raised their eyebrows and looked at each other with surprise.

Marlene and Cory each had an arm around Beck's shoulders. "Atta girl," Marlene said, "that'll help give you your strength back. You're coming around now."

AUTHOR'S NOTE

When I came to Toronto from Newfoundland more than 25 years ago, my first real job was as a counsellor at Interval House, one of North America's first shelters for abused women. I met hundreds of women during my eight years there, and I can picture their faces as I'm writing this now.

I can *exactly* recall the shy smile of one woman who'd come to Toronto from New Brunswick in order to get away from her husband. We were talking in the office late one night, sitting side-by-side on the couch, when she pulled a drawing out of her pocket. She had sketched an 18-wheeler transport truck in perfect perspective with the words Phantom 309 in block letters on the side. I knew the song *Phantom 309*. It was a country song, written by Tommy Faile and made popular by Red Sovine, about a hitchhiker stranded at a crossroads who gets picked up by "Big Joe" in an 18-wheel truck he's named Phantom 309 because: *There ain't a driver, or a rig, a-runnin' any line/Ain't seen nothin' but taillights from Phantom 309.*

After driving through the night, "Big Joe" drops the hitchhiker at a truck stop, gives him a dime for a coffee, and drives off: *Well, he tossed me a dime as he pulled her in low/And said: Have yourself a cup on old Big Joe.*

Upon hearing the hitchhiker's story, the waiter at the truck stop informs him that, over the years, "Big Joe" has picked up other hitchhikers at that same crossroads and dropped them at the truck stop, but saying that "Big Joe" had, in fact, died 10 years earlier at that very crossroads while swerving to avoid a busload of school children. The song finishes when the waiter tells the hitchhiker that the coffee is on him: *Here, have another cup and forget about the dime/Keep it as a souvenir, from Big Joe and Phantom 309!"*

What was the woman trying to tell me with her drawing? Were we like "Big Joe" to her? Picking her up at the crossroads, giving her a ride and dropping her off somewhere warm and safe with a dime in her pocket. Or maybe she was just showing me her latest sketch? At the time, it didn't seem right to have to ask her what she meant, but man, oh man, I'll never forget her or the other women at the shelter. And there was me, just in from Newfoundland, honoured that this woman felt like she could pour her guts out to me and just itching to do whatever had to be done to make her safe—to be "Big Joe" in the driver's seat of that 18-wheeler.

Most of the women at the shelter ended up okay. Not necessarily great, but okay. A few died violent deaths at the hands of their husbands or themselves. Occasionally, I'll run into someone I know from those days and we say hi.

But it was the women I met at Interval House, a long time ago now, who were and are the gale-force winds beneath these wings, that is for damn sure. They made me want to be the best fundraiser, best communications strategist, and most relentless advocate on the face of the earth. And they are the reason *I* feel I have a story to tell now, beginning with the introduction of Beck Carnell to the universe.

Screw your courage to the sticking place and we will not fail, says Lady McBeth. The same can be said for the women I met at Interval House. A frigging chorus of angels is what they are.

ACKNOWLEDGEMENTS

No matter how much you feel like you are being carried on the wings of angels, writing a book is an earthly task that requires much sitting down and not much going out, which in turn requires indulgence from one's family and friends. I am grateful.

I want to thank all the people who didn't advise me against writing the book. Even one naysayer could have tipped the balance. (While strategists are necessarily thick-skinned, fiction writers—this fiction writer, at least—tend toward the delicacy of a hothouse flower.)

Much appreciation is in order.

My initial thoughts for a book ended up being different from how it turned out. The first epiphany came when I was having lunch with the brilliant communicator and author, Jon Duschinsky, at the Spoke Club in Toronto. During the course of a lovely meal and conversation, he opened a door that Beck could eventually walk through. I appreciate that a lot, Jon. Thank you.

I also owe my brother Larry Picco a huge debt of gratitude. Larry is a recently retired air-traffic controller who worked for many years at Gander Area Control Centre, the busiest air traffic control centre in the world, which provides oceanic air traffic control for up to 1,000 flights a day. He's also an avid and knowledgeable reader, primarily of speculative fiction. My sister and I deemed him eminently qualified in both temperament and skill to give feedback on the manuscript, and pressed our advantage to encourage him to say yes. Thankfully, he took on the task with enthusiasm, read the earliest manuscripts and offered considerable advice—not the least of which was to point out that the word *Vise* in Vise Grip was actually spelled with the letter *s*, not *c*. "Don't mind that," he said when he called with the news.

He had recently read an article referring to something being situated "north of the boarder."

To my other siblings, Eileen Picco and Bob Picco, I am grateful for your continued support and excitement about the book and feel lucky to be in a family of which you are members.

To Jill Cunningham—you are a dear friend and muse. You *made* Sam, and that's all there is to it. And not only did you say to go for it when I first talked about writing a book, you read the first draft. Many thanks.

To Peter Byrne, who also read drafts of the manuscript, I am indebted for your feedback and blessed with your friendship.

To my children Katie and Evan, just the dearest darlings, your support is treasured.

And to you, Gentle Reader, I think you are great.

ABOUT THE AUTHOR

Gail Picco is an award-winning fundraising and communications consultant who ran Gail Picco Associates for 16 years, sold that company to industry-leader Stephen Thomas Limited, spent four years there as a principal strategist, and now works independently, directing campaigns and offering strategic advice on a range of fundraising and communications predicaments. She has designed and executed advocacy and fundraising campaigns for some of Canada's largest charities, international NGOs, as well as grassroots organizations. Prior to establishing Gail Picco Associates, she spent eight years as a counsellor at Interval House, Canada's oldest shelter for abused women and children. Her popular blog, yourworkinggirl.com, offers commentary on media, marketing, and the nonprofit sector. She also writes about baseball, F1 racing, and music. She was born and raised in Newfoundland, Canada.

Visit www.meetbeckcarnell.com for new scoops on the author, Gail Picco; Social Good's CEO, Beck Carnell, her team, and their clients; and for material not included in the book.

Printed in the United States
By Bookmasters